NIGHT TRAIN TO JAMALPUR

Night Train to Jamalpur

ANDREW MARTIN

faber and faber

First published in this edition in 2013
by Faber and Faber Limited
Bloomsbury House
74–77 Great Russell Street
London WC1B 3DA

Typeset by Faber and Faber Ltd
Printed and bound by CPI Group (UK) Ltd, Croydon, CR0 4YY

A CIP record for this book
is available from the British Library

ISBN 978–0–571–28409–2

2 4 6 8 10 9 7 5 3 1

Acknowledgements

I am grateful to Mr Phillip Shervington of J. J. Fox Limited (tobacconists); to Mr Paul Whittle of the Darjeeling Himalayan Railway Society; to Dr Ian Stephen, curator of Herpetology at Zoological Society of London; to Rahul Aggarwal of Travel the Unknown; to the staff of the Fairlawn and Lytton Hotels, Kolkata; to Bob Gwynne of the National Railway Museum; and to the staffs of the Gurkha Museum, the British Library and the London Library; and to my wife, Lisa, who having read the first draft of this work, or at least the last page of the first draft, asked, 'Why aren't I acknowledged?'

Author's Note

This is a work of pure fiction. No allusion is intended to any person who might actually have worked on the East Indian Railway in the 1920s, or lived in Calcutta or Darjeeling at that time.

Chapter One

I

'What *now*?' said the man at the far end of the dark carriage corridor.

The night train to Jamalpur, an express in theory, had come to a stand a minute before – the third time it had done so in half an hour. I had been trying to work out whether the man was English or Indian, but as he turned a little way towards me, I saw that he was both: a Eurasian, although it was politer to say 'Anglo-Indian'.

'Where are we?' I asked him.

'God knows,' he said.

Even though this fellow was probably born and raised in Calcutta, not more than sixty miles back, he was proud to know as little about our present location as I did.

The Indian trains gave the appearance of being armoured against the sun. They had overhanging roofs, and the windows were small, and fitted with venetian slats that could be controlled by a lever. A second lever allowed the raising or closing of the window glass. The Anglo-Indian was at one of the windows in that hot, dark corridor, I stood at another. I worked my levers, so as to try and see between the slats. In the smoky gloom, I made out paddy fields, the silhouette of a parked bullock cart, a block house.

The carriage lurched, and we were off again. A dark palm tree slid past the window; then a signal post.

The Anglo-Indian had abandoned his own window; he was eyeing me.

'Signals,' he said. 'Junction with . . . somewhere or other.'

He was minded to talk. In a minute he would ask me what I was doing in India, and I would have to tell him a lie. The compartment from which he had emerged was behind him: the one at the far end of the corridor, the rearmost one. I could tell because its sliding door was open. My own compartment was the next one along, and I too had left my door open. It occurred to me that I might have left my loaded revolver in plain view on the seat. Some yellow light spilled from those two open doors, but it was too weak and sickly to progress very far, and all the light bulbs in the ornamental, serpentine light fittings of the corridor itself were busted.

'They're replacing the opposite track up towards Jamalpur,' the Anglo said, 'so that'll be single-line working – expect a bad delay there.' He was approaching me, and holding out his hand. 'I'm John Young,' he said.

'Jim Stringer,' I said, since I didn't have to start lying quite yet. We shook hands.

'You look tired, Jim Stringer,' he said, smiling. 'Perhaps a drink is called for.'

I had been thinking much the same myself.

'I have a dozen of soda in my compartment,' he continued, rather disappointingly.

He turned and walked along the corridor towards his compartment. He did not look into mine on the way there, but I did and, yes, the Webley was there for all to see on the red leather seat. Alongside the piece was the Calcutta daily paper that I'd been reading: that day's *Statesman*, the date on the paper Monday 23 April. I slipped into the compartment and pulled the newspaper over the gun. I then glanced quickly under both seats. I stepped back into the corridor, dragging the compartment door shut behind me. John Young was standing by his own door, waiting to usher me in.

His of course was a repeat of mine: two red leather couches facing each other, three photographs of Calcutta scenes behind each; in between the photographs fancy electric lamps on curving stalks, giving a low, yellow glow. Opposite the sliding door was another door, the one by which John Young would step down on to the platform when we reached the great railway colony of Jamalpur at seven in the morning. This door was presently locked from the inside. Set into it was another of the shaded windows, and I saw darkness going past beyond the half-closed slats – darkness punctuated by whirling points of light that might have been fireflies or sparks from the track. To either side of the window was a cloth panel with a stitched design of fading pink flowers and green leaves. At the cloth panel end of the seat to the left was a four-foot-high cabinet with door closed. There was no cabinet in the corresponding place on the opposite side, but a heavy curtain of the same faded flower design as the panel. If you walked through that you came to the thunderbox and shower bath, both operated by dangling, knotted chains.

Contemplating the compartment, I was worrying about the shadowy spaces beneath the seats. Somebody had been leaving poisonous snakes in the first class compartments of the East Indian Railway, and this was a first class compartment of the East Indian Railway. I had checked every corner of my own compartment before settling down, and I only hoped that Mr John Young had done the same. I had a phobia of snakes.

On both seats were neat piles of newspapers and work papers

and these last, I saw, displayed the crest of the East Indian Railway: locomotive, palm tree and elephant, enclosed by a circular track – like a child's attempt to sum up India in a single drawing. There was also a carton of cigarettes: John Young smoked the same brand as me, Gold Flake, and the compartment smelt of these cigarettes and what I supposed was John Young's cologne.

We sat down opposite each other. John Young reached under his seat and I nearly said, 'I wouldn't do that if I were you.' However, he pulled out nothing more dangerous than the zinc tray in which the porter at Calcutta had placed an outsized block of ice. It was mainly water in the tray now, with some bottles of Evian rolling with the motion of the train. John Young handed me one, and we drank from the necks of the bottles. We both fell to staring at the electrical fan above our heads. It was revolving too slowly – slower even than the one in my own compartment, which was next door.

'It is doing its best, you know,' said John Young, smiling.

The indications were that he was a railwayman, so my lie would have to come in soon. The Anglos were all over the railways. As a rule they were loco men (drivers or firemen), or what they called 'traffic birds' (train guards, ticket collectors). But John Young was evidently a superior officer of the railway, and most of *those* were British. It sometimes seemed to me that almost all the first class passengers on the East Indian Railway were British officers of the Railway. Generally speaking few people travelled first class on the East Indian Railway. It was said you couldn't afford to grease the axles of the first class carriages from the receipts they earned. No, the third class man was the important one. Ninety per cent travelled third, paying about a third of a penny per mile, one-fifth the price of a British third class fare; and the first class numbers must have had fallen off still further as a result of the snakes.

John Young was smiling at me, wondering about me. There was a sheen of sweat on my face, and drops would periodically form and race towards my collar. John Young showed me up by his high-laced, well-dubbined boots, blue-and-white-spotted bow tie, and general smartness. He was about of an age with me – in the late thirties or early forties. He looked like me in other ways: a skinny sort, centre-parted dark hair, medium moustache. But he was semi-black, and he had a certain manner . . . Jovial – that was the word. It was how an Englishman was *supposed* to be.

I kept thinking about the bloody snakes. Several had been discovered in the past fortnight, and there had been two fatalities. First to die had been a Mr Herbert Milner, an Assistant Auditor with the Railway. On Tuesday 10 April he'd been bitten by a common krait when he entered an empty first class compartment at a spot called Asansol. That was about a hundred and forty miles from Howrah station in Calcutta, and on a different line to the one John Young and I were presently riding upon. Whereas we were heading north-westerly, Asansol was on the main, directly *westerly* line from Howrah, the 'Grand Chord' as it was known. Continue on that stretch, and you came to the capital, Delhi. Asansol was a place of railway works and coal mines – also great fuming mountains of stored coal, from photographs I'd seen. Herbert Milner had not closed his compartment door, and after killing him, the snake had moved into the corridor of the carriage, where it had been discovered by a train guard at the next-but-one stop, Dhanbaid, where the train had terminated.

The other fatality had occurred at Howrah itself. An Englishwoman, a Miss Schofield, had stepped into a first class compartment and the snake was waiting for her. She had not booked the compartment into which she had stepped, just as Mr Milner had not booked his. So neither she nor he was the intended target. Nobody in particular could have been the intended target, only the general category of first class passengers.

Miss Schofield *had* closed the sliding door on entering, so the snake was still in with her when she was discovered. The snake was a hamadryad, a king cobra. It was twelve bloody foot long, and it was possible that it had reared up a good five feet when she entered the compartment, so that its head would have been about level with hers. Being a king cobra, it would then have widened its ribcage below the head, extending its 'hood' as a warning. But it had not bitten her. It hadn't needed to. Miss Schofield had died of fright, which was most unusual, but she had had a weak heart. She was from Leamington Spa. She had come out to India to visit her brother, who was a managing agent for the British Indian Tobacco Company, and travelled about the country a good deal. I could not remember where her train was bound for, but that seemed hardly to matter, since no two of the snakes had been put on the same service.

John Young said, 'What do you say to a peg, Jim Stringer? I have a bottle somewhere about.' And I held my breath as he reached under his seat again.

II

'Do you know Leamington Spa at all, Jim?' enquired John Young, because we had been discussing the snakes as we drank our pegs.

He had produced from beneath his seat a bottle containing about five inches of Indian whisky, that is to say distilled molasses, that is to say *rum*. The label read 'Loch Lomand', whereas 'Loch Lomond' would have been closer to the mark. He had summoned his bearer from the servants' compartment – the foremost one in the carriage – and the fellow had equipped us with two glasses. John Young had asked where my own man was, and I had said I preferred to travel without, which he obviously found irregular. The lie was beginning to loom.

He had jokingly suggested that, in view of the snake attacks, we were brave men to travel in first class on the East Indian Railway. He had been reading about the attacks in *The Statesman*, and had been particularly interested in the case of Miss Schofield from Leamington Spa:

'It is in the county of . . . ?'

'Good question. Not sure.'

'But not in Yorkshire.'

'No.'

'. . . That being your own county.'

'That's right,' I said. 'I'm from York.'

'Now York, I believe, is the plum. I have read about the fine cathedral there.'

'The Minster, yes. Not a patch on yours in Calcutta, if you ask me.'

'Also the beautiful railway station. Principal junction of the . . . North Eastern Railway . . . ?'

'*London* and North Eastern. There was an amalgamation.'

John Young said, 'A very great railway, I believe.'

'*Fairly* great,' I said, grinning.

I was determined John Young should not overrate 'the homeland'. He would be happier if he settled for what he had: namely India, and the mighty enterprise whose metals we were riding

7

upon: the East Indian Railway. It was not to be sniffed at.

The London and North Eastern Railway came in at six thousand five hundred route miles, making it the second biggest show in Britain after the London, Midland and Scottish, which had about seven thousand eight hundred. True, the East Indian was only half that in route miles: there was not the British density of branches. But the Grand Chord of the East Indian – extending as it did from Calcutta to Delhi and beyond – covered a tract of country half as long as the distance from Land's End to John O' Groats, and its gross receipts from passenger and freight traffic far exceeded that of any British railway. This was mainly because of the coal traffic, since the East Indian sat atop the Bengal coalfield, which had begun to be exploited in earnest during the war, and had sufficient reserves to supply almost the entire world east of Suez.

But my companion was still dreaming of Blighty . . .

'I tell you what, Jim,' he said, leaning confidentially towards me, 'I would like to drink a fine glass of Scotch whisky in the dining room of York station.'

'You'll be lucky,' I said, picturing the dusty bottles of Bass on the shelf behind the buffet counter.

It wouldn't quite do to ask whether he had actually visited Britain. Some of the Anglo-Indians would speak of it as 'home' in a heart-breaking sort of way, even if they had never been. But John Young was not a typical case. He was a gazetted officer of the East Indian Railway, and he must have been a very bright spark to get so high.

He was taking out his pocket book.

'My wife and my boy,' he said, indicating a photograph, and handing the whole pocket book over to me. There were a number of hundred-rupee notes inside – at least four – but I was supposed to be looking at the photograph. John Young's wife was plumpish, pretty, looked perhaps less Indian than he did. The boy was rather wild-eyed, with a great deal of hair. He looked a bit delinquent.

'Anthony,' said John Young as I contemplated the picture. 'He prefers Tony, of course.'

'Good-looking chap,' I said.

'I daresay. But the boy is a worry.'

'On the railways, is he?'

'Regrettably, yes.'

Then the boy wasn't at one of the railway colleges; was not on course to be a gazetted man like his father. I wouldn't have pressed the matter, but John Young volunteered the information: 'He is a travelling ticket inspector,' he said, with some contempt. 'I am going up to Jamalpur to see if I can find a course of training for him.' He added that he himself was on the Commercial side, the department that solicited custom for the Railway.

I still held John Young's pocket book. I was now examining the metal warrant badge, set into the leather, and had put on my reading glasses to do so. This token entitled him to travel in first class on the East Indian Railway without payment. It was about the size of a half crown. The elephant and the circular track were engraved upon it, with John Young's name engraved above. I carried the equivalent in pasteboard, as befitted a temporary holder of the same privilege.

'A beautiful thing,' I said, handing back the pocket book.

From my own pocket book, I produced a photograph of my wife – Lydia by name – our daughter Bernadette and myself. It had been taken on the maidan – the main park – of Calcutta, on our first full day in the town: Saturday 7 April. Both Lydia and Bernadette wore cotton shirts and jodhpurs, and they had removed their sola topees so as to show off their hair: Lydia's was tied up in her usual quick but complicated way. Bernadette's blond hair was modern – that is, short. They were off for a riding lesson, and laughing about it for some reason. I was not off riding, only paying for the lesson; I was also beginning a really good 'go' of tertian malaria, and so my smile was rather dazed compared to those of the females, who were excitedly poised at the start of their Indian adventure.

Lydia's aim was the liberation of the Indian nation. Or – if that should seem a tall order for one person – the liberation of Indian *womanhood*. To that end, she'd spent the weeks before our departure corresponding with Indian or British women who ran the sorts of organisations that corresponded to the British Women's Co-Operative Guild, of which she was a paid-up official.

I indicated Lydia and Bernadette, adding, 'We have a son, but he's at the London University, and he didn't come out with us.'

Pointing at Lydia, John Young said, 'She looks almost . . .'

'Almost Indian? I said, 'Or Anglo-Indian?'

'Do you mind if I say that?'

'Not in the least. She'd take it as a compliment.'

I didn't much care for this conversational turn. It was becoming rather sticky.

'But the girl is not at all dark,' said John Young, concentrating now on Bernadette. 'What age?'

'Sixteen, nearly seventeen.'

'Trouble?' he said, looking up.

I nodded. 'Has been since she was about eleven. That was when she decided to change her name. Well, she took her second name, and made it her first.'

'And what was she first called?'

'Sylvia.'

'Why the change?'

I shrugged. My theory was that the name Sylvia was too like the name Lydia. The girl wanted to strike out on her own. Lydia had not approved. She had chosen Sylvia in honour of Sylvia Pankhurst, the famous feminist, whereas if any Bernadette was famous for anything . . . then I dreaded to think what it might be. I said something of this to John Young, and he rather shamed me by saying, 'Of course, there is St Bernadette of Lourdes, who had visions of the Virgin.'

I had forgotten about her. It struck me that John Young might easily be Catholic. Many of the Anglos were.

'In India,' John Young continued, 'people have lots of names.'

He resumed his examination of the photograph. Bernadette was rather cat-like in features, and her hair gave off a beautiful light, as could be seen even from the picture.

'A clever girl, no doubt,' John Young said.

'She got into the high school on a scholarship,' I said.

'Our boy, too,' said John Young. 'We thought it would be the making of him,' he added, but he was still studying Bernadette. 'And she's left the school now?'

I nodded again.

'Has she been finished off?' he said, grinning. For a moment I was minded to clout him, until I clicked that he was referring to finishing school.

I shook my head. 'We don't go in for things like that in York.'

Bernadette's new friend Claudine Askwith, whose father was top brass in the traffic department, and came from Hampshire . . . she'd been to finishing school. Apparently, the main thing it had taught her was how not to appear educated.

The train was slowing again, and none too smoothly. From beyond the closed curtain came a repeated clanging: most likely the flush chain on the thunderbox clashing against the carriage side. Presently we came to a complete stop.

'Is this the single-line working?' I asked after a while.

John Young was at the window. 'No, we've come into a station.' He invited me to look out.

'I am using the term loosely, Jim.'

The only sign of life was the haze of insects around each platform lantern. Nobody at all in the waiting shed. As a rule, you could expect some sleeping Indians, and any number of pi dogs. Then again, nobody had boarded or alighted from our carriage at *any* of the dozen or so stops we had made since Howrah. Someone out of sight blew hard on a pea whistle and we lurched away. I glanced down at my watch. Midnight, dead on.

John Young said, 'Are you in India on business, Jim?'

III

This was John Young's own country, and it was only fair I should provide some explanation as to what I was doing in it. To buy time, I offered him a Gold Flake. I lit it for him, and lit my own. I sat back. John Young was a likeable fellow, and so he would get the truth; but not the whole truth.

Some years before, the government of India had contracted the management of the biggest of the Indian railways – the East Indian Railway, headquartered in Calcutta – to a private company. Now the government was minded to run the show directly. The Company would be nationalised, this being the up-to-date method of running a railway almost everywhere except the homeland, and direct control of such a gigantic and important concern would help the government of India – that is, the British – to *remain* the government of India. It was anticipated that this transfer would occur a couple of years hence, in 1925 or so, and every man on the Company awaited the date with trepidation.

The government was proposing to invest heavily in the railway, so as to take advantage of the traffic boom occurring since the end of the war. But the money must be properly directed, so economies would be implemented, defects discovered and corrected. 'Rationalisation' – that was the word Stanley Harrington had used...

Stanley Harrington was a Secretary of the Transport Division of the India Office in London, and it was he who had recruited me to the Commission of Enquiry being conducted into the East Indian Railway. He had done so via my governor in the York railway police office, Chief Inspector Saul Weatherill. The chief had no end of contacts with the so-called intelligence agencies, and it was through him that I had been sent out to Mespot in 1917, to stew in Baghdad whilst keeping cases on a certain loose-cannon of a lieutenant colonel. My knowledge of secret police work and railways combined would make me the perfect man for India, Harrington had said.

Harrington knew the East Indian Railway inside out. On the face of it, the show was economically operated. What with all that coal to hand, together with cheap labour, working costs were a mere thirty per cent of receipts. But Harrington believed there was 'considerable laxity' in its operation, and laxity was something he knew all about, being a large, slow-moving man, and the almost permanent inhabitant of a certain Italian restaurant around the corner from the India Office, in which he consumed mountains of ravioli and ice-cream before settling back with a cigar and numerous coffees. Harrington took me there every day for a week (during which he put me up at the Savoy Hotel), and in the first of our luncheons he offered examples of the Indian laxity, some of which were officially sanctioned. For instance, even the European clerks would take off all the Hindu and Moslem holidays. But very often brazen illegality was involved. 'Would you believe that entire *elephants*, Captain Stringer, very often go missing from the marshalling yards?' There was much outright theft; there was fraud, and there was corruption at all levels of the Company.

In the subsequent luncheons, Harrington had explained about the three Schedules: A, B and C. The enquiries under Schedule A would relate to security arrangements in the yards, shops and works of the Railway. Those under Schedule B would touch on pilfering and corruption amongst junior staff – mainly Indians and Anglo-Indians. But it was Schedule C that was the ticklish one, and Harrington spoke of it in low tones even in the half-empty restaurant.

Schedule C enquiries related to corruption amongst the gazetted officers, that is to say the mainly British top brass of the Company. Graft was rumoured to be commonplace at this elevated level, but hard information was in short supply. One had to peer into the interstices of the accounting systems, looking for the discrepancy between passenger numbers on a certain route and receipts obtained, or asking why less coal was consumed than was apparently justified by the number of trains stated to be running, and so on. But assuming these discrepancies were explained by crime, how were the guilty men to be quickly identified? That was a matter of circulating in the burra clubs of Calcutta with eyes peeled and ears cocked. I would be equipped with an expenses budget that would enable me to keep cases on the top men, socially speaking. 'You'll be wanting a good Italian restaurant,' Harrington had said, 'and Firpo's on Park Street comes highly recommended. I believe you will recognise some of the puddings there as being similar to the ones served here. We can't quite run to the real luxury hotels,' he continued, 'but I think they'll do you pretty well at Willard's on Chowringhee.'

'Stayed there yourself, have you?' I enquired.

Harrington shook his head.

'And you've not eaten at this place, Firpo's?'

He had not.

I was on the track of an idea that had been growing in me since the first luncheon, and as we awaited the bill after the final one, I put the question to Harrington: 'Have you ever been to India?'

'My dear sir,' he said, 'it's a six-week round trip!'

It appeared he was too busy administering India to go there. Besides, as he explained, he had a young family to take care of – and at this, I made my swoop. Might I take out my own wife and daughter? He agreed to my proposition before I could ponder the wisdom of having made it. My secondment was to last six months. When asked what I was about in India, I was at liberty to mention Schedule A and I might, with discretion, mention the closely related matter of Schedule B (it would be widely assumed that I would be giving hell to the humble Bengali clerks and coolies in any case) but Schedule C was top secret. Only the senior men in the East Indian Railway Police force, under whose auspices I would be working, knew about Schedule C, and it was on no account to be mentioned to anyone else. The stakes were too high. The Railway Board in India would press for the severest penalties where corruption was found among gazetted officers, and that had already started. A year before, a certain British mechanical engineer of a small 'up-country' workshop was found to have been constructing boilers of a slightly lower specification than the ones he had been accounting for, and pocketing the difference to the tune of a sum in rupees amounting to not more than several hundred pounds. Even so, he – a married man with two young children – was now sweating out seven years in the Alipore nick, Calcutta, from which he would be lucky to emerge alive.

I would be assigned a colleague for my investigations, and the two of us would form an 'enquiry team'. This other fellow had only just been recruited. He would also be briefed by Harrington; he would sail for India just two days after me, and his name was Major Fisher.

'The brief is to examine the crime-prevention measures, and look for loopholes,' I said to John Young, after I'd told him some of the above.

'And that's why you're going up to the Jamalpur workshop?'

I nodded. 'Just a bit of a poke around.'

John Young was shaking his head, though still smiling. 'It's one *big* loophole, Jim!' he said. 'Take the goods side – consignors and consignees on the fiddle, almost always with the connivance of the railway staff. I tell you Jim, what's not lost to outright burglary goes in insurance frauds.'

He was rather squiffed now. The level of Loch Lomand was sinking fast, and it was his doing, since I'd been refusing his offers of a top-up. I was on quinine tablets to keep down the malaria, and strictly speaking I was supposed to lay off the drink altogether.

'Small things would help,' John Young was saying, pouring the last of the whisky into his glass. 'Elementary checks like locks and rivets on wagons. But where is this Major Fisher?' he added, for I'd mentioned my colleague Fisher.

I indicated with my thumb over my shoulder: 'Next-but-one compartment along. Did you not see him on boarding?'

John Young shook his head. 'Only from the back. And his blinds have been down ever since.'

'Have been since Howrah,' I said.

'Is he ill?'

I shook my head, thinking of Fisher. He was very far from ill. He'd served on the North West Frontier during the latter half of the Big Stunt, and seemed to have become inured to the Indian climate as a result. Accordingly, Major Fisher was able to expend a great fund of energy on the betterment of Major Fisher. A picture of him composed in my mind: a big, incredibly rude man, with a big, brown cannonball-like head, on which he wore an outsized, coal scuttle-like sola topee. He was on the make all right, with ambitions lying well beyond police work. He, like me, was a detective inspector with the British railway police who preferred to use his army rank. Before and after the war, he'd been on the force of the Southern Railway. Well, he was a Londoner born and bred, lived in a spot called Camberwell. Beyond these bare details, I could not go, because Fisher kept his cards very close indeed to his chest.

'You two don't get along?' John Young suggested.

I gave a slight nod.

'Then that is obviously his fault,' said John Young.

I attempted to convey nothing much by a smile.

'But the two of you must stick together! With this investigation of yours . . . you will be making enemies all along the line!'

While silently applauding his knack for hitting nails on the head, I could not afford to discuss these matters with John Young. I rose to my feet and extended my hand.

'I'm obliged to you for the peg,' I said. 'And I'll see you in the morning.'

IV

My own compartment was oven-like, even though the fan still toiled. I locked the sliding door from the inside. Anyone proposing to sleep on an Indian train would do the same, the instances of dacoity – banditry – being high. I then adjusted the levers of the window for maximum flow of air. Looking out, I saw that we were rattling past the silhouette of . . . not so much a hill as a great lump of rock, a giant meteorite, perhaps, that had long since crashed on to the dusty Bengal plain. There were a couple of telegraph poles at the top of it, leaning at crazy angles, together with what looked to be a half-ruined castle. I watched it until it was out of sight. I pushed up the armrests on one of the bench seats, and that was all that was needed to make the couch. Now for the bed roll. It would be stowed in the cabinet. I opened the door, and there was the white cotton bag with E.I.R. stitched in red on the side, and very *badly* stitched. The job had been done with sullen reluctance, and I knew where – in the workshop of Alipore Jail. I shook it about to wake up any snake that might be sleeping inside. Pulling out the not over-clean sheet, an idea broke in on me: perhaps there had been a snake in Fisher's compartment. Maybe it had done for him soon after we'd pulled away from Howrah, and that was why I'd not seen him since.

We'd boarded together at Howrah. He'd arranged the sleeper

reservations, and collected them in person from the E.I.R. main ticket office at Fairlie Place. 'Here's you,' he'd said, shooing away the sleeping car attendant who'd been trying to salaam and offer tea. 'Compartment two.' Fisher had then handed me the voucher for number two. As I'd settled myself, he'd hung about in the corridor smoking one of his Trichinopoly cigars and getting in the way of the attendant's attempts to greet *other* arrivals. I had noticed an oldish fellow crossing past my compartment to get into the next one along, number three, and I'd been vaguely aware of John Young taking number one. At the time, I had taken him for an Indian rather than an Anglo. Soon after we'd pulled away, Fisher had gone into the next-but-one from me in the direction of the engine, number four, and dragged the door shut and lowered the blind. There were only five compartments in the carriage, and I assumed every passenger had a compartment to himself (there not being much call for first class on the route to Jamalpur, which was mainly used by the young Indian apprentices heading up to the great workshops) . . . all except the servants in the servants' compartment, number five. There were two in there, I believed: John Young's man and another belonging to the old fellow in number three.

I sat down and broke open the Webley. Three cartridges in the chamber. I had another dozen in my portmanteau, but surely three was enough even for an Indian night train? Some guide or other I'd read 'For Young Men Heading East' had recommended nothing more than boiled water, aspirin and a mosquito net for a trip such as this. Then again, the young men in question had probably not been riding on a railway subject to snake attacks, or making enemies 'all along the line' by the nature of their work. Had Fisher and I done so with our investigation? We had only been underway for a fortnight, and most of that time had been spent taking delivery of the documents relating to Schedules A, B and C. So we'd hardly had a chance to make mortal enemies. We'd so far looked at only a fraction of the documentation assembled for us by our Indian clerk. The matter relating to Schedule A was mainly so many smudged plans of railway shops and sheds, with confusing dotted lines marked 'Guard Patrols'. Schedule B was a few bundles of letters: Indian railway clerks denouncing each other for being 'on the take' (in perpetuation of feuds that might have arisen decades before in the villages of Bengal), records of footplate men who appeared to keep a home at both ends of the line; records of any men connected to former employees sacked and convicted of offences against the Company, records of employees suspected of being sympathetic to the Gandhian nationalist agitation.

The Schedule A and B papers took up most of the office we'd been allocated in the East Indian Railway headquarters at Fairlie Place, Calcutta. The Schedule C material had originally consisted of only two files; but that was now down to one, and this was the result of a burglary having taken place in the police office. It had occurred four days ago, late at night on Thursday last, 19 April. What was in the stolen file? I couldn't say exactly. It had come by post that morning, in an envelope marked 'Railway Commission of Enquiry'. Fisher had been out of the office, doing I knew not what, so I had taken delivery of it. Inside had been in a pasteboard folder, sealed with string and wax, and with no accompanying letter or chit.

I had been in and out of the police office all day. At six o'clock, just before knocking off, I had broken the seal, to be confronted with perhaps thirty sheets of badly typed notes, the topmost headed: 'Pertaining to corruption amongst the officers of the traffic department . . . compiled by One Who Knows'. It seemed even money whether this would prove useful intelligence or merely the settling of scores by an aggrieved employee. I did not consider that it demanded my urgent attention. I had put the file in a desk drawer and quit the office. The door of the office was then locked by our Indian clerk. I had seen him do it. I had then walked down into the hot bustle of Fairlie Place with the man. Sometime in the night, that door was busted open, either by someone who didn't have a key, or wanted to look as though he didn't. Whoever had taken the dossier must have done so in the hope that I had not read it, but on seeing the broken seal they must surely have assumed I *had* read it. It might therefore be a good idea for me to lay hands on whoever who had so much to lose by the reading of the report, before they laid hands on me. The burglary left us with one remaining file in Schedule C, and that was nothing more than a mass of figures about the Company in which a trained statistician might be able to find some anomalies, but neither I nor Fisher fitted that bill.

It had occurred to me that Fisher had stolen the file, simply because I found him to be a generally suspicious character.

I thought of Fisher as I stood pissing into the thunderbox, the dark sleepers flickering past the bottom of the dirty tin hole. When we'd first teamed up, I'd thought I must have got across him somehow. But it seemed that everyone had got across him. Fisher was as rude to the railway officers as he was to the Indian constables. His mantra was 'You have a complaint, brother? Put it through the proper channels.' Or 'You know where the bloody complaints book is, don't you? Here, I'll fetch you a pen.' And yet he was learning Hindustani. He had a book on it; and in the two weeks I'd been walking about Calcutta with him, I'd seen him give money to beggars – whole rupees, not just a few anas. On a tour of the goods yards around Howrah, he'd suddenly broken away from our party and given assistance to half a dozen Indians trying to push a great bale of cotton up a ramp. 'Put your bloody backs into it, can't you?' he'd roared at them.

I washed my hands and face. The sound coming from the thunderbox hole was like a complaining voice from the underworld. I pulled the chain, watching the silver whirlpool form and die on the tracks as soon as it had formed. You couldn't say that Fisher was particularly guilty of what the wife called 'colour prejudice'. He was prejudiced against every bugger.

I stepped back into the shaking compartment. I stretched the sheet over the couch, and in doing so I knocked the cotton bag to the floor. There appeared to be something still inside it. It had struck me that the snake attacks seemed to have started at the same time as my arrival in India, but I did not believe the snakes could be connected to the Commission of Enquiry. The snakes were an attack on the railway rather than on those investigating the railway. Either way, I nudged the bag with my foot to make sure the 'something' was not something alive. I squinted inside, then fished out a rolled-up mosquito net: the kind you draped over yourself, like a shroud. I turned off the electric light; I retreated beneath sheet and net, and I commenced to sweat.

I thought of our daughter, Bernadette. John Young had guessed right there as well. She *was* trouble.

In her first week at the high school in York, she had been given the stick by the headmistress for laughing at a teacher, a Miss Brewster, who owned a motor car. Miss Brewster parked her car on the asphalt of the school yard, and it seemed that every time she climbed in, it sagged in the middle. The day after Bernadette had received her punishment, Miss Brewster had climbed into her car again; it had sagged again and Bernadette had *laughed* again, albeit this time outside the school gates. But she was given the stick for a second time, and that had confirmed her as a rebel.

She had been such a sweet girl too, and – aged five or so – keenly interested in railways. Lydia would deliver her to me at the police office, on the main 'up' platform at York station, and we would wander about. She liked the steam from the locomotives – 'train clouds' she called them. She would be hypnotised by the sight of a train arriving, and when it had left the station she would be bereft, calling, 'Come back, come back!' The train never came back, of course, and I explained that there would be a very great smash if one ever did. So then she wanted to go and see where the trains *lived* – that is, the sidings. I would walk through the sidings with her, being one of the few men in York with a pass that allowed me to do that, and we would traipse along between the high wagons to the point where I became quite bored. But not Bernadette.

One day I saw a fellow trying to break the seal on a wines and spirits wagon, and I ran him in – arrested him with Bernadette in tow. She wasn't frightened but the bloke swore like blazes, and when I'd handed him over to the duty constable in the police office, and taken Bernadette off for her regular treat of an eclair at the station hotel, she pronounced: 'I did not like that man.' It had been an important day in her life, as when the car had sagged for the second time. She'd been down on police work ever since, and down on railways as well. As she grew older, she would join Lydia in recommending different jobs to me, something swankier or – what was her other word? – ritzier. Might I not be a lawyer, attending the Crown Court, where all the briefs were so dashing in their long black robes?

In other words, she was on the way to being a snob, like her mother, but with not much sign of her mother's social conscience. Bernadette had other virtues though. She was a spirited girl, and very kind (to anyone who didn't stand in her way). One of her story books contained an illustration of a young girl walking in a ballet dress across the beautiful terrace of a country mansion; the girl held a little sparkling purse, and exuded a great sense of confidence and pride. The caption read 'On a Birthday Morning!' and that was Bernadette all over. That was just how she walked though our home village. She was blessed in some way that could not possibly last, so I was always on the look-out for signs of sadness and disappointment that might herald the start of a decline into the reality of the world.

I spoiled her, I suppose.

A flash of light came through the window slats; it threw five bars of light on to the compartment floor, and they commenced to move in unison over my bed, and up towards the luggage rack, where they remained for five seconds before being snatched away. We had passed another illuminated factory or insignificant station on the line to Jamalpur. I wanted to get to sleep before the single-line working, because if it was hard to get off on a moving train, it was harder still on a stationary one. But I couldn't sleep.

I thought again of Bernadette . . .

She had been given piano lessons from a young age, and she had stuck to them. In that triumphant year of her scholarship, she played the piano part in Schubert's piano trio in B flat at the York De Grey Rooms, and it was a particular source of pride to the wife and me that the other girls – violin and cello – were both five years older. Then Bernadette had met Philippe Gregoire. She met him through her literature teacher, Miss Starling. Philippe Gregoire was a black man from America – New Orleans – and he had written a book about *being* a black man from New Orleans that had won a prize. As such he was a great curiosity in York, and Miss Starling had asked him to give a talk at the high school. Afterwards, he had played the piano in the assembly hall, and he had shown the girls how to play in a special dancing rhythm . . . rag time, it was called, and Schubert went right out the window after that. The girls and Miss Starling had loved it, and the one who had *really* taken to it had been Bernadette.

She had been tipped off that American music was all the rage in Calcutta, and this had proved right. For Bernadette and her friends, the place was 'jumping'. She had fallen in with the daughters of two railway officers, Claudine Askwith and Ann Poole, and they spent all their time playing American music on the piano or playing the records on the 'gram', and practising existing dances or – as if there weren't enough dances already – making up new ones.

Then we had all gone to the May Ball at the Six O'Clock Club. It was our second week in Calcutta, and even though still malarial, I was dragged there by the wife. The very top railway people were there, keen to hobnob with the near-the-top army officers and Indian civil service types who were the other principal guests.

The dance was held in a regulation Calcutta mansion, standing in its own compound a little way north of Dalhousie Square. In the lobby, the sola topees of the arriving guests were stacked on shelves fifteen foot high, creating an effect of a sort of library of hats. Aside from the ballroom there were many anterooms, some set aside for 'games' and all with their squads of Indian bearers ready to serve glasses of the famous Six O'Clock punch. There wasn't an orchestra but a 'band', which was something racier, and they knew the American dances. It had been immediately obvious to me that they *would* know them, because when Lydia and I entered the ballroom, the leader of the band, an Anglo-Indian who had a great deal of hair kept down with a great deal of pomade, was smoking a cigarette and talking to a selection of the prettiest women. The ballroom had opened out on to a veranda, and that opened out on to the gardens, where stood little colonies of basket chairs and tables, all bounded by a crumbling and picturesque brick wall, with little lizards darting all over it. Into this wall were set alcoves illuminated by Chinese lanterns. And those alcoves spelt trouble.

Bernadette had slid away from us on arrival, and I believed she had helped herself to two glasses of punch before filling out her dance card. The filling out hadn't taken long. She had been, to my mind, the prettiest girl in the room and it turned out that one man – or boy – had booked three dances. He was an Indian, one of only half a dozen in a room containing perhaps three hundred people. The rule of thumb was that no Indian could join a Calcutta club, save for a couple of the clubs that prided themselves on their open-mindedness, and so would admit one or two Indians (provided they were millionaires). You would see more Indians attending the *dances*, but even here they had to be something special, and this young fellow's dinner suit was certainly beautifully tailored; it flowed about his slim form in a way you rarely see. His patent shoes sparkled, and there was something sparkling in his lapel, too. It kept collecting the shimmer of the room and sending it out in a silver ray. It did so as he danced with Bernadette.

The wife and I were not dancing, but looking on from the side. We had danced the previous: a waltz, and that had done nothing

26

at all for my headache. It had struck me, in fact, that a waltz is malaria set to music.

I asked about the silver ray.

'It's a diamond,' said Lydia. She had met the fellow before at an earlier dance, and was now watching him intently. 'He is the son of a maharajah, and he's considered holy. Well, he's a high Brahmin.'

'Where did she meet him?'

'At a game of musical chairs.'

The wife was telling me this with a note of pride. I said, 'You can't have a railwayman's daughter from York, dancing with an Indian prince.'

'On grounds of colour prejudice, would that be?'

'On grounds they might strike up a romance, and that can only end in tears.'

We watched them dance: the two were inexplicably of the same mind. Really it was like seeing a horse run or a dog walk – you couldn't make out how it was done, which was perhaps why it was called the foxtrot.

Lydia told me the young Indian's name. His first name was normal enough: Narayan. The rest I couldn't catch. She told me that, being the son of a raja, he was a rajkumar, and from then on he was referred to between us as 'The R.K.'

The dance came to an end, and the dancers became a milling crowd, with Bernadette and the R.K. milling within it. But then they disappeared. They would be in the garden – in one of the brick alcoves. I said to Lydia, 'Shouldn't we go and find them?'

'I will in a minute. There's no harm in a little spooning. She's nearly seventeen, Jim, and while I know you don't want to be here, the only reason you *are* here is because of her.' That was true enough. We had been invited to the dance by the Askwiths

27

on account of their daughter's friendship with our daughter. We wouldn't have made the grade otherwise.

As the next dance began, I said, 'She was booked with someone else for this one, and I can't see her.'

Lydia turned to me. 'Jim,' she said, 'you've gone yellow.'

'Don't change the subject.'

'You should go back to the hotel.'

She escorted me back to the lobby, all the time telling me not to fret about the R.K. He was only one of many sons of one of many maharajahs. Were there not about fifty pages of them in the *Calcutta Directory*? And this boy's father was amongst the smaller ones. He had only about a hundred and fifty square miles somewhere 'up country'; Lydia didn't know exactly where, only that you couldn't get there by the East Indian Railway. The place was called Suryapore, and it was mainly forest, but there was some coal, and a quantity of ruined temples. The boy's father, the Maharajah of Suryapore, spent a good deal of time in America. When he was in India, he was not entitled to a gun salute when formally received by the British and so, as far as the Indian aristocracy went, he was something of an also-ran. He was still worth a mint, however.

The wife was in two minds about the R.K. She could see the dangers of an association, but did not want to display colour prejudice by warning the girl off him. She also admired his looks, his money and his social position. After talking over the matter the next day, I had taken it on myself to speak to Bernadette. She'd blown up as soon as I'd mentioned the R.K.; I'd got cross in turn, and pronounced the ban: she was absolutely forbidden to see the R.K.

By my reckoning, she'd seen him three times since then, secure in the knowledge that her mother did not support the ban, as long as she was always in public when with him. It had been my fault to start with, of course. I ought not to have brought the two of them to India.

Judging by the clattering of every loose object in the compartment, the Jamalpur night train had hit full speed. The young dancers of Calcutta had a word for this loose shaking and I could not at first call it to mind. But it came to me at length: 'syncopation', and the small satisfaction of recalling it allowed me to drop asleep in spite of all.

V

I dreamt of a snake that generally carried itself in the shape of the 'and' symbol: 'ampersand' I believed was the word, and this snake could open doors by coiling itself around the handles. It seemed to be trying to open the exterior door of my compartment, the one by which I would step down on to the platform when we arrived at our destination, but how could it do that while we were flying along at top speed? I then heard a sort of slow gunshot, and I saw the flare of the gun at the same time, but that couldn't be right. It was the flare of other guns at other times that I had seen, but I believed the shot I had heard was real. I sat up and turned on the light.

All was as before. The fan was still turning, I was still alive. No bullet had been loosed in this compartment, but the train was at a stand, and I somehow knew it had been at a stand for some time. I opened the sliding door to the dark corridor; I heard a noise from the left, but I turned right, and walked into a man

29

lying on the floor. He was in his underclothes. I leant down. The corridor carpet was sodden with blood, the man's underclothes likewise. The man was John Young. The sliding door of what had been his compartment was open, and he was half in and half out of it. A man was standing behind me. I turned – a European probably in his sixties in ghostly white pyjamas that stood out in the gloom. He was the oldish fellow I'd seen on boarding. He had come from compartment number three. He said, 'What's wrong with his head?' and I saw what he meant: about a third of John Young's head was missing. Fisher now came out of number four compartment in white cotton trousers and braces but no shirt. He had on his boots with laces unfastened. There was an expression on his face that was hard to interpret.

The oldish man said, 'I heard a noise.'

'You *would* do,' said Fisher, indicating the body. 'He's been bloody shot, hasn't he?'

Behind Fisher, two sleepy-looking Indian servants were emerging from compartment five.

The oldish man half turned towards Fisher. 'Before that. I mean from outside.'

I said to nobody in particular, 'How did the shootist get into the carriage?'

I stepped over Young's body, and went into his compartment. I turned on the light.

'That's all the dabs on the switch messed up,' said Fisher, who was standing in the doorway. But I was not so concerned about fingerprints. It was more important to get the lie of the land. The compartment was much as I'd seen it when talking to John Young, except that his bed had obviously been slept in; or at least lain in. I looked down again at the body. His suit coat had been thrown over his lower legs, and the pocket book had been thrown down on it. Ten-to-one that was now empty of money, but it ought not to be touched.

'Dacoits,' I said.

'You going to open that?' said Fisher, indicating the door leading to the outside world. I unlocked it, and it swung open, disclosing the wide blue Indian night, the sound of a million crickets, and a smell like the interior of some great, hot barn. Under the blue light of a quarter moon, I saw an Indian on a stationary horse – might have been five hundred yards off. There were two other Indians on horses a few hundred yards further off again, and they were waiting for him. As I looked at the nearest man, he turned his horse and began riding away towards his fellows, going along the top of an embankment crossing a network of dried-out paddy fields. He was a raggedy-looking man in white; his thin arse went up and down like the ticking of a clock.

'That's bloody nice, isn't it?' said Fisher.

Behind Fisher, a uniformed Indian leant into the compartment from the corridor. 'What has been going on here?'

'Oh, good of you to turn up,' said Fisher.

The Indian was in white with a red turban and a wide leather belt around his waist. A long stick was wedged into the belt. He was a 'watch-and-ward' man, part of the force that guarded the trains. Fisher indicated the Indians riding away towards the horizon. 'There you are, pal,' he said. 'Throw your bloody stick at them, why don't you?'

The corridors of the train were not continuous. It was therefore impossible to get from one carriage to another while the train was moving. The watch-and-ward man had entered by means of one of the two doors leading down from the carriage at the ends of the corridor, and that was obviously how the dacoits had got into the carriage, and they had done so, of course, while the train was at a stop, or slowing to a stop.

I jumped down from the compartment; the dirty track gravel hurt my bare feet. The Indians were now gone from sight. I looked up at the outside of the compartment door. It was splintered near the lock. So the bandits had tried to come in to John Young's compartment this way before moving to the end door. I walked three paces over the track ballast, and looked up at the outside of my own, locked exterior compartment door, and my heart beat faster as I saw that it too was splintered. If anything, it was in a worse state than John Young's door. They'd tried to get into my compartment as well. I walked further along: none of the other compartment doors showed signs of any damage. All the doors looked high up from down on the ground with no platform, but you'd have no trouble getting at them while sitting on horseback.

Fisher had jumped down from John Young's compartment, joining me on the track ballast. Behind him came the watch-and-ward man, and *another* watch-and-ward man, for they always worked in pairs. Fisher commenced to light a Trichinopoly cigar.

I said, 'What stopped the train?' and it was the second watch-and-ward man who answered: 'Signal, sahib.'

We were at the single-line working, the site of a predictable stop, and any stopped train was a target for dacoits.

Chapter Two

I

Thirty-six hours later, the 'up' *day* train from Jamalpur back to Calcutta was being trailed by its own tall shadow, and the shadow of its steam. The train had the luxury of tracks, but the shadows had to make do with red stony ground. At a spot called Sahibgani, we had gone into the station restaurant to eat a 'Hindu military meal', meaning chapattis and curry with meat. I doubted that the Hindu soldiers went in for cheese and biscuits and a glass of port, but we had been offered that after the main course. I had turned down the port because of my quinine tablets, whereas Fisher had turned it down because he never touched a drop of alcohol . . . which always made me think he was saving himself for something, somehow. We had then boarded the train again.

Fisher had been reading as we ate, and he was reading still. Then, it had been the political supplement to the *Calcutta Yearbook*. Now, it was *The Hindustani Manual* by Lt. Col. D. C. Philpott. Philpott had the market in Hindustani manuals sown up. Lydia had *Domestic Hindustani* by the same fellow, and had taken very strong objection to the introduction, in which Philpott stated that this book was meant for ladies, and therefore confined itself to simple, everyday Hindu phrases. If Fisher was learning anything from this book, then it all went out the window the moment he came across any actual Indian. Then it was all

'You there', or 'Yes chum, I'm talking to you.'

I fell to looking out of the window. Now that the sun was over-head rather than coming in directly, we had the slats fully open. I pointed.

'Why is there a bridge there?'

'It's a bloody river, isn't it?' said Fisher, barely looking up.

'There's no water.'

'Come back in two months. It'll be a bloody torrent. Probably sweep the bridge away.'

. . . Which brought me back to my original question.

I thought back over the night before last. I had set down in note form the important data.

1. The Jamalpur night train of 23 April had come to a stand about three minutes before the shot was heard. It had been at a spot called Ghoga.

2. The train had been stopped by the adverse signal guarding the works on the line. Every night train to Jamalpur for the past two months had been stopped at this same signal, and the procedure was that the train waited until a pilotman was sent along by bicycle from the signal box a mile away. The pilotman would then put his bike on to the footplate, and guide the driver over the points and on to the opposite line, and stay with him until he was clear of the works. No driver was allowed to proceed until this man turned up. The line was slightly curved at the point where the train waited, so that much of its length was out of sight to the blokes on the footplate. It was known that this stop might make the train vulnerable to dacoits, and yet it was protected by only two watch-and-ward men, who were not armed, whereas

the dacoits who preyed upon Indian railway passengers always *were* armed.

3. In that three minutes, any number of people would have had a chance to come up to the first class carriage. For example, anyone from the rest of the train might have walked up to it by climbing down from their own carriage and entering via the end doors. There had been seven other carriages in all: four thirds and three seconds. Taken all together there had been about three hundred and fifty passengers on the train.

4. Reading from the rear of the first class carriage, the compartments ran as follows:

Number one: John Young's.

Number two: mine.

Number three: the one belonging to the elderly European, who turned out to be a churchman attached to St Paul's cathedral, Calcutta: Reverend Canon Peter Selwyn by name.

Number four: Major Fisher's.

Number five: the compartment occupied by two Indian servants – the man belonging to John Young, and the man belonging to the Reverend Canon Peter Selwyn.

5. The killer may have come from this very carriage. That is to say, he could have been any one of the above-mentioned men (except me). Yes, I had seen Selwyn, Fisher and the servants emerge from their compartments into the corridor, but any one of them might have shot Young, retreated into their compartment, then re-emerged looking surprised at developments. But it was odds-on the killer had entered

from outside, by means of the rearward end door, having failed to open John Young's exterior compartment door, and my own exterior compartment door. Most likely, the killer was one of the three horsemen seen riding away, and my money was on the one who'd been closest to the train when I'd looked out.

6. The nearest habitation to the line was a farm at a quarter-mile distance. This was east of the tracks. There was a ruined blockhouse about the same distance to the west. The horse riders I'd seen had been heading west, and had perhaps been making for this ruin, but nobody had been able to give chase.

7. On the face of it, the killing had been an act of dacoity or banditry of the sort ever more familiar on the railways of India. The likely scenario was as follows: the killers made straight for the first class carriage, where the richest pickings would be found. They tried a couple of exterior compartment doors at hazard, but these were locked and they couldn't prise them open, so they moved to the end door, which was not kept locked, and gave access to the corridor. Very likely John Young heard the entry, opened the sliding door of his compartment, and stepped into the corridor to come face to face with one of the dacoits. He had been immediately shot in the head, and had fallen on the threshold of his compartment. One or more of the dacoits had then stepped over the body, entered the compartment, removed John Young's suit coat from the peg on the wall and taken out his pocket book. From this they had removed all the cash I had previously seen in that pocket book, which I

had estimated at four hundred rupees, about thirty pounds. That would represent a month's wages for a British ticket inspector on the Indian railways; for an *Anglo-Indian* ticket inspector, it might represent *two* month's wages. For a dacoit – assuming the dacoit to be a peasant – that sum represented undreamed of riches, perhaps ten times more than he might expect to earn in a year by his normal labour. The dacoits had then made off on horseback.

8. I had verified the loss from the pocket book in the presence of Fisher. He had picked it up using a handkerchief so as not to disturb fingerprints. I told him that my fingerprints were already on the thing, and I told him of my conversation with Young, of which he seemed to have been unaware. He had been asleep throughout, he said.

9. Hovering in the doorway as I spoke had been the elderly Englishman, the Reverend Canon Peter Selwyn. Major Fisher had broken off from talking to me and turned towards Selwyn. 'Why the hell are *you* going to Jamalpur?' Fisher had asked him. Selwyn had replied, 'Now I am sure you can phrase that more politely if you try.' 'But I'm not going to try,' Fisher had shot back, and Selwyn *had* answered, but directing his words to me. It seemed he'd booked to preach in the railway chapel at Jamalpur. Perhaps we didn't realise that half the apprentices were Christian? Yes, they were mainly Catholic, and he was part of the Indian *Anglican* Church but Selwyn was a great friend of Father somebody or other, and his trip to Jamalpur was a very important part of the ecumenical mission of St Paul's. 'Is that so?' Fisher had asked with folded arms. He had then unfolded his arms,

and ordered everyone out of the murder compartment. It was to be sealed off until it could be examined by the fingerprint bureau of Calcutta C.I.D. (since the East Indian Railway force did not run to a fingerprint bureau of its own).

10. As for the two servants in the first class carriage . . . They were both Mohammedans, and both *called* Mohammed. They were both in the late fifties or early sixties, and they had been sleeping in the servants' compartment when they heard the shot. Both seemed decent sorts, and John Young's man appeared very cut-up about what had happened to his master. They could not be considered suspects to my mind.

11. Having sealed the murder compartment, Fisher had instructed the watch-and-ward men to walk the length of the train looking for any suspicious characters. They had reported back fifteen minutes later: 'No anti-social elements, huzoor.'

12. As regards the investigation of the crime, it would obviously not fall to Fisher and me, as Fisher knew very well in spite of all his shouting. We were witnesses merely. When the shot was fired, we were within the railway police district of Jamalpur. An Indian sub-inspector had been despatched by light engine along the line from there, and had arrived at about four o'clock in the morning – nearly three hours after the shot had been fired. When he arrived, he went into the sealed compartment and searched it, with Fisher shouting at him to beware of disturbing any fingerprints, at which the sub-inspector had coolly replied that he knew his job, and would do it much better without someone yelling in his ear.

13. The sub-inspector had been unable to find a bullet in the murder compartment. It had, he said, gone clean through John Young's head, and drilled into the wood of the carriage roof. It might never be recovered. The sub-inspector had then searched the other four first class compartments, and politely asked all the occupants to turn out their pockets and bags. In the process, he uncovered one gun: mine, with its three bullets in the barrel. I explained that it was my old service revolver, a Webley Mark 6, and that I carried it everywhere. I had assumed that Major Fisher did the same with *his* old service revolver. He certainly provoked enough people to justify carrying a gun. I could not swear to have seen Major Fisher's pistol, but I was sure I had noticed the bulge of it under his top coat when we had boarded at Calcutta. However, no gun of any sort was found in Fisher's compartment, and he was not asked about any gun.

14. As for Canon Peter Selwyn, he had apparently not much more than his overnight things and two books. One was the Bible; the other was called *By the Light of Uranus*, and it was not a book about astronomy. It contained some rather singular illustrations, and was stamped 'Not to be taken into England'.

15. The sub-inspector did know his job. He also knew that the searches were really just for form's sake. Everyone had been milling about outside the train for hours. Anybody could have got rid of anything just by pitching it into the dust, and I wondered why Selwyn had not tried this with *By the Light of Uranus*. Perhaps he felt the risk of being caught in the act to be too great.

16. One thing I myself noticed as missing when the sub-inspector came up was the reservation chart for the carriage. This was supposed to be posted up in a wood-and-glass frame on the exterior of the carriage, by either one of the two end doors. These charts listed the names of those who had reserved compartments. The compartment numbers were also written on the coupons given out with the tickets at the booking offices, and these numbers were supposed to correspond to those on the reservation charts. Therefore the reservation charts were to remind people of what they already knew, and prevent mix-ups in the crush of boarding. But there had been no crush on boarding the night train to Jamalpur, and I had not looked for the reservation chart at Howrah, so I did not know whether it had been there at that point or not. The glass of the cases was often smashed, and the charts were often lost en route, or never posted up in the first place, especially if there had been many late bookings or cancellations. Since the sleeping car attendant had got off at Howrah after seeing the passengers aboard, there was no one to ask about it during the stoppage except the train guard. He was Anglo-Indian, and more Indian that Anglo. He'd heard of the dead man, John Young: 'A fine fellow – example to us all'. The guard was sure dacoits had been responsible. They knew about the stop for the single-line working, and since it took place in a remote spot, the train was an easy target. 'I am betting you,' he kept saying. He could throw no light on the matter of the reservation chart.

17. The footplate crew of the Jamalpur Night Mail were Brit-

ish, and their engine was an Atlantic type, of British make. The driver was called Collins, the fireman Jackson, both covenanted men – that is, working for the E.I.R. for a fixed number of years before returning home. They were both late of the London and North Western Railway, where they'd been on a goods link. 'I got pig sick of Willesden Junction,' said Collins. 'Simple as that.' Now they were on expresses, albeit thirty-mile-an-hour ones. Reaching for Jackson's shovel, I asked if I could 'put a bit on'. I did so and, leaning over to inspect the results, driver Collins said, 'You've done that before, haven't you?' Even though the engine was stationary, they had to keep a careful eye on the fire, the Bengali coal being so poor. There'd been good Welsh coal in London, and no dacoits to worry about, but there *had been* Willesden Junction. The two had been warned of the danger at this red signal, but in the event they hadn't noticed the attack. 'I never saw nothing,' fireman Jackson said. Driver Collins was ten years older than Jackson, and would be returning home soon. He had a place lined up at Broadstairs, Kent. He had enjoyed his time in India. 'Signed on for five years originally, but that turned into a twenty-year touch.' He had married 'a half-Indian lass, my green-eyed princess', but she'd died ten years ago. 'I still miss her, and I'll tell you what else I'll miss when I get back to Blighty.' He nodded towards the shaking fire of the sun, which was beginning to climb above the horizon. 'That old bugger.'

18. After talking to Collins and Jackson, I had returned to the exterior of the first class carriage and looked up at the doors. Judging by the marks on them, the dacoits had tried

41

as hard, if not harder, to get into my compartment as John Young's, before giving up and going to the end door. Their aim might have been purely to rob, and that certainly appeared to be the case. But it was not impossible they meant to kill John Young, or any other man in the carriage. The facts were compatible with John Young having heard them boarding the carriage, and having tried to stop their progress along the corridor towards one of the other four compartments. There had been a scuffle; Young had been shot. The bandit, or bandits, had fled, pausing only to take the money from the pocket book. Why not take the whole pocket book? I could not say, and perhaps they could not either.

19. Other thoughts were hard to shake:

   a) I was probably deemed to have read a file that might have disclosed the sort of corruption that could earn a man twenty years in jail.

   b) It was Major Fisher who had suggested we make the trip to Jamalpur, and that we do so on the night train of 23 April.

   c) It was Fisher who had booked me into my compartment.

20. At five thirty in the morning, the night train to Jamalpur Junction remained stationary, protected by smoke bombs on the single track fore and aft. I was smoking a cigarette outside the first class carriage, and the yellow wooden destination board reading 'Jamalpur' seemed like a promise that would never be kept. The train did not move off again until six in the morning, by which time a riot was brewing in third class, and the heat had started.

We had arrived at the great railway colony and workshops officially known as Jamalpur Junction at 0900 hours on 24 April. The
Indian sub-inspector travelled back with us. On arrival, Fisher,
Canon Peter Selwyn and I were met by the sub-inspector's governor, an Inspector Hughes, who ran the police operation at
Jamalpur, and was also commanded the surrounding railway police sub-division. Hughes was equipped with a fine moustache,
and rolling North-of-England tones that I liked listening to.
(He'd cut his teeth as a detective on the Hull and Barnsley Railway before the war.) He walked us over to the great railway re-
fectory, which was empty just then –the apprentices' breakfasts
having all been served – and which smelt of curry and carbolic.
We sat down at one end of a long table, and a bearer brought tea,
toast, jam and soda. We were joined by the sub-inspector and a
new chap, also Indian. Our voices echoed as we talked, and we sat
in a tight blue cloud of our own cigarette smoke. Hughes said that
some of the bad lads who preyed on the trains were known, so an
arrest wasn't out of the question. The Indian officers then took
formal statements from the three of us, and we were very politely
fingerprinted.

The first class carriage in which the murder had occurred
would be quarantined throughout the day, then sent back on the
evening's 'up' Night Mail to Calcutta. Our statements would be
on that train as well, but Fisher and I would not be. We were to
overnight in Jamalpur, as originally intended, and it seemed that
Selwyn would be staying two nights with his friend, the Catholic
chaplain. When the statements reached Calcutta there would be
a tussle over whether the case should stay with Hughes and the

railway police or be taken over by the civil police. There was also an outside chance that the Calcutta C.I.D. would put its oar in, but Hughes thought this unlikely. It took more than an act of banditry – even a murderous one – for those grandees to stir themselves.

Fisher and I then got round to the job that had taken us to Jamalpur in the first place: touring the site. Neither Hughes nor the sub-inspectors came on this; instead we were assigned two constables, which was Hughes's way of saying he considered the whole Commission of Enquiry business a pantomime, and an impertinent one at that.

Anything metal at Jamalpur was too hot to touch, and all day long, the air was overcharged with black smoke from the foundry chimney. We were shown the railway barracks, the railway hostels, the railway college, railway cinema, railway sports grounds, and the railway golf course. We saw the railway workshops: iron foundry pattern shop, brass fitting shop, turning shop, erecting shop, carpentry shop, paint shop. Hughes said they made almost any part of a train on site except wheels, which seemed perverse of them. Wheels were supplied externally, principally by a company called Macpherson Trading of Calcutta, and we were shown a siding full of flatbed wagons, loaded with Macpherson wheels. Our inspection completed, Major Fisher had informed Hughes that there were two entrances to most of the sheds. Hughes had said, 'I know that.' 'There should only be one, shouldn't there?' Fisher had said. 'So you want to rebuild the whole complex?' Hughes had enquired, and Fisher had said that it would be cheaper than continuing to sustain the present astronomical losses to pilfering. Single entrances, manned by trusted guards, would help stop the leakage. Fisher said he would be recommending there be half as many guards at present, but that they should be paid twice as much. They would then be less liable to accept backhanders. Well, that put the kybosh on the evening. Fisher should have put forward his suggestions later on – preferably in writing from Calcutta, and with a few 'may-I-suggests' to sugar the pill.

At four o'clock we all went to tea at the mansion of the Chief Locomotive Superintendent, a fellow called Ryan, late of the Midland Railway. Hughes barely said a word, and Fisher was his usual gracious self. Consequently the grandfather clock in the Ryans' hot, dark drawing room seemed to have a very loud tick indeed, as I stood about eating Dundee cake and feeling spare. Mrs Ryan had tried her best to make things 'go'. Summoning a bearer, she'd said, 'There's Darjeeling or Assam tea, Major Fisher. Or will you take a glass of sherry? Do say yes.'

'No,' was all I heard.

After the tea party, Fisher performed his vanishing act again, retreating to his room in the hostel. Hughes suggested I might look in at the railway cinema, where a cowboy film was showing; he then cleared off. In the end, I watched some of the apprentices playing cricket. Evidently, these lads were so keen, they played right through the hot weather. Halfway through the game, it broke in on me that the clattering from the workshops had stopped, so that I heard only the spacious sounds of bat and ball, and the occasional shout of encouragement from the field.

I was given a decent room, but I hardly slept. I was thinking about the night train.

Fifty miles short of Calcutta, Fisher, having set Colonel Philpott's Hindustani guide aside, was reading . . . something else, while drawing on a Trichinopoly cigar. The Trichies were little, evil-smelling things, and he got through about forty a day. He appeared to be reading one of the engineering supplements of the *Railway Magazine*, but he held the thing folded in such a way that I couldn't properly see, and I knew I'd be in for a dusty answer if I asked. So I put a different question.

'Do you think the lifting of the Schedule C file had any bearing on the shooting?'

Fisher lowered his magazine slightly.

'You think they were coming after you?'

'Given the state of the door, maybe. It's not impossible, is it?'

'It's as good *as*. It was dacoits. You saw the buggers.'

'But they might have been acting on behalf of someone else.'

'Like who?'

'Whoever was named in the file.'

'And we don't know who that was, do we? *Since you didn't get round to reading it*.'

And he went back to his magazine.

The time scheme was about right, it seemed to me. The named man, or men, had got wind of the incriminating file. They'd stolen it on Thursday. Once it was in their hands, they'd concluded I must have read through the thing. It then became imperative to do away with me before I could put about what was in it. For all they knew, I might have already had a copy of the file typed up, in which case they would be wasting their time by killing me, but that was a chance they were willing to take. They'd had Friday and a week-end in which to prepare, and they'd come for me on the Monday.

Through the window slats, the dusty ground was a dazzling yellow. It was as if we were riding across the surface of the sun itself. I thought about Fisher. Which Calcutta hotel was he booked into? What, come to that, was his first name? Hang on, I *did* know that. I'd seen it on a chit delivered to him at the office: Noel. But therein lay another mystery. What had the chit said? I would have given fortunes to read it, since it was written in a very elegant hand. Was it to do with our investigations? I did not believe so. Perhaps it had been an invitation. Fisher, a single man in a city of dances and parties, must have had a social life of some sort, but to the best of my knowledge, the only club he belonged to was the Tollygunge, on the southern edge of town, which was famous for its golf course. I believed Fisher was good at golf. It was one of the subjects he would read books about, to-gether with the Hindustani language and odd aspects of railway engineering.

I leant forward and said to Fisher, 'When you play golf at the Tolly, *who* do you play?'

'Generally go round alone,' he muttered, from behind his magazine.

'What's the sub?' I said. 'Twenty quid a year, I've heard.'

'Don't make me laugh.'

Well, there wasn't much chance of *that*.

I sat back; a golden flash came through the window. I closed my eyes against it, and the syncopation of the carriage put me into a short dream. I saw Indian trains coming up with the sun-rise. I saw myself in a compartment, pointing a pistol at the head of John Young. How dare he drain Loch Lomond? The gun went

47

off, and the watch-and-ward men were in the compartment doorway: 'You are committing nuisance! It is strictly prohibited!' A moment later, that train compartment was a cell in the Alipore Jail and Fisher was pacing about outside. I heard him shouting, 'Get in there and watch that bugger!' But I wasn't bothered about Fisher; there was something called an electric rope on the floor of the cell, and I knew that at any minute, it would turn into a king cobra.

I awoke with alarm. I had not meant to sleep in the presence of Fisher. It was the noise of our compartment door being dragged open that had roused me. The train was hurtling along, and my sola topee was rolling quickly back and forth on the luggage rack. In the doorway stood a ticket checker, a European. He was staring at Fisher.

'Recognise me?

Fisher put down his reading and eyed the man. 'You're a ticket inspector.'

'*Chief* Ticket Inspector . . . Many countries but one empire!'

Fisher continued to eye the man.

'Why, it's the slogan of the Boys' Empire League!' said the ticket man. 'We're comrades, the pair of us . . . animated by that noble spirit of fair play that commands the respect of the world.'

After eyeing him for a little longer, Fisher said, 'Are you going to inspect our tickets or not?'

'You didn't recognise me,' said the ticket inspector. 'But *I* recognise *you*. It's Noel, isn't it? Noel Fisher. I'm Tommy Melrose! From the Peckham branch! Do you remember Bill Barclay? He's living on Lake Tanganyika. In a boat! And Dickie Watson? He's farming in New South Wales. You wouldn't believe how many sheep he's got. He doesn't even know himself. Only trouble is, it's mutton for breakfast, mutton for luncheon, mutton for . . .'

Fisher had removed his authority to travel from his pocket book. He passed it towards the ticket inspector. 'Warrant card for temporary staff,' he said, 'I think you'll find it in order. He has one the same,' he added, indicating me. The ticket inspector took the document.

'*Major* Fisher, is it?' he said, '. . . and travelling in first class. By the way, I hope you've checked this compartment for snakes?' He attempted a laugh, but it was difficult under the weight of Fisher's stare. He handed back the warrant card. 'I always knew you'd get on. What are you doing out here?'

'Never you mind.'

'Hush-hush, is it? You really don't remember me?'

'I do, yes.'

'Thank God for that. Thought I was going crackers for a minute.'

The ticket man turned to me. 'Always the man of mystery, was Noel. He once said to me that he meant to come out east and make a fortune, but when I asked how, he wouldn't let on. You don't hear much about the old BEL these days. Half a dozen of us founded the Peckham Branch; we had a concert – raised five pounds. The Mayor gave the vote of thanks, wished us every success . . .'

Fisher was staring out the window at passing palm trees. It was strange to hear the cockney voice in conjunction with those.

'You can find me any day of the week, Noel, in the running men's mess at Howrah.'

'I'll bear that in mind,' said Fisher, and the man dragged the door shut and departed.

It was now my turn to eye Fisher. As I did so, he lit a Trichinopoly cigar, and I believed it was to cover his confusion.

There were now chimneys among the palm trees, for we were approaching the Calcutta suburbs. Soon we would come to the sidings and godowns of the railway lands of Howrah, where many strange freights could be seen: the occasional elephant, or opium in special vans . . . but opium was packed and transported only when the weather was right.

Peering through the venetian slats, I saw goods yards, goods sheds, coal yards . . . women carrying coal in baskets on their heads; a tender waiting to receive coal with a ladder up its side. It was the easiest way to carry things – on your head. We ran past the two godowns and adjacent foreman's bungalow that had been burnt. That had been a famous scandal of a few weeks before my arrival, an outrage that had been put down to the 'Ghandi volunteers'.

Fisher did not leave off reading until we came under the roof of Howrah, whereupon he stood up and, reaching for his sola topee, said, 'Will your man be waiting for us?' I gave a nod, and we climbed down.

Howrah station smelt of past burning, like the ash pan of a dead fire – that and curry, of course. The light was the colour of dark gold. The sea of people swirled us past 'Refreshment Room, European'; 'Refreshment Room, Moslem'; 'Refreshment Room, Hindu Vegetarian', among other refreshment rooms. We showed our privilege passes at the gate, and came to the circulating area. Unfortunately not even the air was circulating, let alone the people. All around the booking offices, the shops, the tea and cake stalls, Indians were sitting or lying down, waiting. They *liked* waiting.

As we approached the ticket gate, I began looking out for 'my man'.

I had a Gurkha police sergeant – a havildar – assigned to me, name of Deo Rana.

Many of the best of the railway police constables were Gurkhas. Major Fisher had been offered his own man, but he'd found him 'a bloody clever dick . . . so he can go off and mutter behind somebody else's back.' I thought the true reason was that he didn't want anyone observing him closely, and finding out what he was really up to.

Deo Rana was a slow-burning fellow, good in a scrap I should imagine, and yet thoughtful with it. He spoke Nepalese, which was his native tongue; also Hindustani, some Bengali and some English. But he usually kept silence: his face habitually carried about as much expression as a block of wood, and when I spoke to *him* he would rock his Chinese-looking head from side to side, as though saying 'no', refusing my remark. By this, he didn't mean 'no'; he might even have meant 'yes', and whether this was a habit with all the Gurkhas or just Deo, I could not have said.

He'd been warned of our arrival, and he waited at the ticket gate, as I walked up with Fisher in tow. Making a brief bow, Deo Rana lead us to towards a police tonga waiting specially for us

As we climbed up, I said, 'I don't know if you've heard, Deo, but a fellow was killed on the train on our way out.'

'Killed how? Snake?' (Because he'd heard of the snakes like everybody else.)

'Lead poisoning,' said Fisher, lighting one of his bloody Trichies.

'Shot,' I said, by way of translation.

Deo Rana asked, 'Indian? English?'

'Blacky-white,' said Fisher.

'And how is?'

'Napoo,' said Fisher.

'Sahib?'

'Bloke threw a seven.'

'Seven?'

'He bought the bloody farm, didn't he?'

'Explain please.'

'Don't you understand English, man? He's copped it; dead.'

A bit later, when we were stopped in the traffic on the Howrah Bridge, Deo Rana spoke again: 'I hope it was one criminal, sahib, shot by police.'

I told him the victim seemed to be far from a criminal, and I gave him all the data we had.

I then looked out through the slats of the tonga window. Only the rickshaw-wallahs could find their way through the block – stick men, they were, whereas their passengers were almost always large Europeans, lying like so many giant babies in so many giant prams. I heard the bleating of a motorcycle horn. A native police team was coming up, weaving through the tongas and motors: sergeant and inspector, both in white, and with spikes on their sola topees.

On finally gaining the east bank, we turned right on to Strand Road. At the Armenian Ghat, thoughtful-looking Hindus stood waist-deep and fully clothed in the khaki-coloured water of the Hooghly River. A big ship was coming, just passing the High Court. They would have to open the bridge for that, and the blocks would be bad for hours after. The ship hooted, making a boom that had in fact seemed to be there all along, a combination of the rattling tongas, ticking rickshaws, roaring motors, street trader cries – a perfect headache of din and dazzle. The traders were all along the Strand pavements: mostly one-man outfits, a dirty umbrella to keep the sun off, an upturned crate with maybe oranges on top, maybe candles or home-made cigarettes. In York, all these blokes would be counted 'doubtful traders' and closed down by the council. I looked at them with a kind of morbid fascination. If those chaps could shift a matchbox or a candle every half hour, then perhaps, depending on what they charged . . . but then I would see their women, and their babies rolling in the road before them, and I would abandon the speculation as hopeless.

We turned into Fairlie Place, where we climbed down from the tonga. We were adjacent to the steps leading to the wide marble principal booking hall of the East Indian Railway headquarters. When I had first come to Calcutta, this place had puzzled me. Why locate a booking office half an hour's walk from the station it served? Actually, that was the whole point. The booking office was not smudged by the nearness of soot and smoke. This was *clean* travelling, with the centrepiece, behind the clerks: the giant pink, white and green tiled map of India. But that was only the public part of the giant Moorish-looking castle that was the East Indian Railway HQ, and Fisher now turned and entered the courtyard of the castle . . . while I remained in Fairlie Place with Deo Rana.

I asked him whether he'd been to the railway lands today. He shook his head, meaning yes, he had.

'See many dodges going on?'

'Many. And, sahib, I saw the snake men.'

I assumed he meant a squad of snake charmers. There were plenty at Howrah.

I said, 'Do you think the snake men know about the snake *man*? The fellow putting the snakes on the trains?'

'That is possibility.'

I said, 'I'd like to take it on, but it's not our investigation. I mean . . . if the villain were *sharping* the railway, instead of doing people in . . .'

'Sahib, snake men steal from the railway.'

'Steal what?'

'Rats.'

I eyed him. 'But the railway has plenty of rats to spare, doesn't it?'

'Snake men need many rats. Take, take all time – give nothing. They should give, sahib.'

'Give what?'

'Informations.'

'All right,' I said. 'We'll pay a call.'

'Go tomorrow, sahib. Soon.'

'Keen on snakes, are you Deo?'

'I like them very much, sahib. You will be bringing money.'

'Baksheesh?'

He shook his head, meaning yes.

'How much?'

'Ten . . . Fifteen.'

Fifteen rupees. That was more than baksheesh. Deo Rana gave a half bow and departed into the bustle of Fairlie Place. His working day was over, and he was going home. I believed that he lived on the police lines near the jute mill on the other side of the river.

I nodded at the police sentry in his box, one of half a dozen who took turns to guard the main entrance to the courtyard. Neither of the two who'd been on duty during the night when the Schedule C file was nicked had seen any 'stranger' enter the courtyard. But it was not unknown for them to make a bed of the table in the little guard house, and there were other ways into the castle for strangers and non-strangers alike who had the right keys or were in the know.

Some tongas waited in the cobbled courtyard, and two motors. Around the perimeter were palm plants in highly polished brass pots. Two of the courtyard walls had verandas halfway up and here stood white-suited Europeans in sola topees, men of the railway detective force. There were some uniformed men in addition, both Indian and European. A sort of late tiffin was going on up there, with bearers moving between the men. Punkas flapped above them, like so many giant birds trying to take off. It was amazing how many police a single railway could throw up.

In one corner of the courtyard was a rickety, hot iron staircase that seemed like an afterthought. *Its* potted palms were half-dead, and by the time you got to the top it was just stony soil in the pots, and a good many cigarette stubs. But this was the quickest way to the offices of the detective division. I climbed the staircase and opened the door at the top, entering a gloomy corridor with small scruffy rooms running off. All was khaki coloured, right down to the twirling fans, which were all thoroughly stained by cigarette smoke. Anyone might climb the iron stairs and enter the office of the detective division, since the door was always kept unlocked. I heard:

'Well you've got a bloody lunatic on your hands, haven't you?'

It was Fisher's voice, coming from an office whose door stood open. It belonged to Superintendent Christopher Bennett, who sat at a small, battered desk with Fisher facing him. Bennett ushered me into the room, and there was no spare chair so I leaned against the peeling wall. They were talking about snakes.

'It's the damnedest thing,' Bennett was saying. 'The day before yesterday, the information clerk came in here with a report of a snake bite in a first class compartment at Bally. The fellow went out, and he was back five minutes later with a second flash: "Another instance of same, sahib."'

'Where was the second?' I asked.

'Khana Junction.'

'Same train?' I said, because both of those were stops occurring early on the main westerly line of the East Indian Railway, the Grand Chord. Bally was the first station on the line, about seven miles after Howrah. There were some mills at Bally; otherwise it was the start of the paddy fields. As for Khana, that was more like seventy miles out: a railway colony. 'Different trains,' said Bennett, 'both terminating at Khana Junction.'

I asked, 'What *were* the snakes?'

'The first – the one at Bally – was a sawscale viper, a small snake. The victim died two hours ago. I've just had a wire from the Presidency Hospital. He was an American tourist, travelling alone, name of Walter Gill. He boarded at Howrah – hadn't booked the compartment—'

'Had *anybody* booked a seat in that compartment?' I cut in.

Bennett shook his head again. 'There are ten trains a day to Bally. There's no need to book. The second, the one at Khana, was another common krait. The victim was an old boy: a Colonel

Kerry, late of one of the Burma garrisons. The whole thing was seen by his wife, who was sitting opposite. The colonel got up take something off the luggage rack, and according to her, the snake was just suddenly there on the floor between them. The old boy for some reason leant down towards it, and put his hand out . . .'

'Bloody idiot,' said Fisher.

'Got a bite on the wrist. A photograph was sent up from the railway hospital at Khana.'

Bennett took an envelope from his desk drawer; he took a photograph from the envelope. 'That's his arm.'

It did not look like an arm.

'We don't have a photograph of Gill, but we do know he was paralysed by the bite before he died. His parents have been telephoning around the clock; they're proposing to take legal action against the Company.'

'Bloody Americans,' said Fisher.

'The common krait', said Superintendent Bennett, taking up his pipe, 'eats its own young.'

'How are there any *of* them, then?' I said.

'Not *all* its own young, Jim,' said Bennett, lighting the pipe.

Superintendent Bennett smoked for a while. I watched him do it, but Fisher had his arms folded and his head down; I could have sworn he was thinking of something else entirely. Bennett's tobacco was called St Julien. The lid of the tin carried an illustration of a man looking very like the superintendent: handsome, rather pink-faced, with swept-back fair hair. The slogan was 'Keep a cool head.'

'So that's four deaths,' I said. 'Two by the common krait.'

'Thanks for reminding me, Jim.'

'What does a common krait look like?'

'Not as pretty as a *banded* krait,' Bennett said, blowing smoke. 'Or so I would imagine. In *The Jungle Book*, a banded krait is the enemy of Rikki-Tikki-Tavi.'

At this, Major Fisher looked up: 'Who's he, when he's at home?'

'Rikki-Tikki-Tavi is a mongoose, Noel. He whispers, "Be careful, I am death."'

I said, 'You'll be getting in the snake experts, I suppose.'

Bennett smoked at me in the approved St Julien manner.

'Try the zoo,' I said. 'Reptile house.'

'Now there's a thought,' said Bennett, smiling, I assumed because he'd had that thought already.

Fisher said, 'Is whatsisname back from leave?'

By 'whatsisname', he meant our assigned clerk. An Indian clerk was a 'babu', and this label had somehow got tangled up with our man's name, so that he was Babu Jogendra Nath Bhattacharji; but I had discovered that it would be equally polite to call him Jogendra Babu for short. Just then, the man himself walked past the open door.

'Oi!' called Fisher, and with the briefest of nods to Bennett, he was out of the door and after him.

Christopher Bennett smiled. He *was* keeping a cool head. Well, he was an easy-going sort, but he was a man under pressure, and the news of the killing of John Young would add to it. Copies of the statements made by Fisher and myself and Canon Peter Selwyn concerning this event were on his desk. Bennett was the coming man of the East Indian Railway force, everyone knew that: detective superintendent at thirty-five or so and bound to be detective chief super before long, which would make him the top man. And he seemed to be progressing without making waves. He was supervising our enquiry team, but it seemed he'd carry that off without putting too many backs up in the Company, especially since not many knew about Schedule C. Bennett was popular with his men. They respected him as a gent, as captain of the police polo team, and as a product of Cambridge University. He was an intellect, and he didn't go in for bull or undue formality. He said that his dealings with his senior men should be – what was the word? – 'collegiate'. There were no boastful certificates of merit on the walls of his office, no print of *The Midnight Steeplechase*, no sporting photographs (even though he *was* captain of the polo team). Apart from the portrait of the King-Emperor, the only 'picture' that hung there was a framed scrap of Indian cotton that was of historical interest in some way. Most Oxford and Cambridge types went in for the Indian civil service, and only ended in the police if they failed the exam, but Bennett had got points for *choosing* the police, and the railway police at that.

'Will the C.I.D. take an interest, you reckon?' I said, nodding towards the statements.

'They've been sent copies, of course,' he said.

I took out my cigarettes.

'Mind if I?'

He could hardly object, given the fug he was blowing my way, 'cool and fragrant' though it may be.

'I think they have their hands full with revolutionary plots,' said Bennett.

The nationalist agitation was taking an ever more violent turn. The trouble at Amritsar had brought it on. And then there was Mr Ghandi – the Mahatma. He himself was *non*-violent – a sort of black Jesus in glasses. The wife was always talking him up when she considered she was in progressive company, and sometimes when not. I'd had to warn her about that; she could queer the pitch for me as a copper. Of course, she'd taken not the slightest notice. A chap had recently been drummed out of the Tolly-gunge golf club for being too easy on the Mahatma. But secretly, I thought he was right. We had our patriotism, why shouldn't the Indians have theirs?

Bennett said, 'It was good to see you at Firpo's on Saturday, Jim.'

I nodded.

'A very good "do", sir.'

Firpo's *was* a good Italian restaurant, as Harrington in London had told me, and Bennett had booked it for a supper dance to celebrate his marriage: a party for those who had not been at the wedding, which had been held some weeks before my own ar-rival in Calcutta. It was all at the instigation of his new wife, Mary, who was very pleased indeed to have married Detective Superin-tendent Bennett, and wanted the world to know it. I hadn't much enjoyed the occasion. I'd spent the whole time fretting about the burglary of the Thursday.

Firpo's was the 'in' place for a celebration. Bernadette and her friends spent half their lives there, eating astronomically expen-sive ice-cream. Their famous Desert Sunrises were heavenly. Sud-denly everything was 'heavenly' with Bernadette; that was when it wasn't 'septic' . . . or some people were 'lethal' (boring, that meant).

From along the corridor, I heard an Indian voice at the end of its tether: 'But Major Fisher, that is impossibility!'

'You'd better go and see what's happening,' said Bennett.

V

Fisher and Jogendra Babu were in a dusty room full of files. This was our office. Since the burglary, a sign had been put on the door: 'Private', but the door now stood open. Fisher was studying the shelves and muttering to himself, and the clerk sat at a table piled high with ledgers. Fisher's outsized sola topee was also on the table. Seeing me in the doorway, the clerk made a half salaam and began his complaint.

'He is wanting occurrence books for all similar incidents going back years.'

'Jogendra Babu,' I said, and he gave a half nod, as if to say thanks for at least trying to get my name right, 'similar to what?'

Fisher answered from over at the bookshelf.

'Gun attacks by dacoits on trains in the Jamalpur sub-district, what do you think?'

It seemed he was more interested in the Jamalpur shooting than the snakes, but he was only dabbling in it. Our job was the Commission of Enquiry work, not finding killers. Jogendra Babu removed his wire glasses. He was a chubby, round-faced man with what I supposed had to be counted very beautiful skin. His elderly mother had recently died, and he gone 'up country' somewhere to attend to the funeral. 'Stringer sahib and Fisher sahib,' he said, in a tone of great exasperation, 'there is no such category as "gun attacks", any more than there is "putting snakes".'

'Forget the bloody snakes,' Fisher cut in

'There is murder, there is assault, there is robbery, there is un-licensed transportation of an animal; there are no gun attacks.'

'Tell that to Mr John bloody Young,' said Fisher, who now collected up his sola topee, and made ready to quit the room.

Judging by his face, Jogendra Babu could hardly believe his luck at this development. He had told me that he found Fisher 'extremely overbearing', and he used to repeatedly ask whether I was in charge of Fisher ('Who is sahib?' he would say, or 'Who is running show?') in hopes I might bring him to heel. But I had to explain that Fisher and I ranked equally in our enquiry team.

'What are you up to tomorrow?' I asked Fisher as he marched out.

'*I* don't bloody know, do I?' he called over his shoulder. 'Probably be back here playing hunt the bloody thimble.'

When he'd gone, Jogendra Babu removed his handkerchief from his top pocket, and wiped his spectacles. He lived in a world of spectacles, ink, ledgers, dust. The golden sunlight that continually flowed into the rooms in which he worked – and that was coming through the window now, with a soft evening tone – seemed entirely wasted on him. In the corner of the room stood his black umbrella, neatly furled. He carried it against the sun. Shortly after meeting him, I had asked whether he would also use it against the rain, come the monsoon. 'Yes, yes,' he had said, 'it is very versatile.' He folded his handkerchief, and replaced in his top pocket. Jogendra always wore a tight black suit coat above loose white trousers, but then there was a reversion to formality at ground level with the black patent shoes he wore. 'I am having enough on my plate with Commission of Enquiry,' he said.

'I shouldn't worry,' I said. 'We're not meant to be investigating the shooting. That's for Hughes at Jamalpur.'

Jogendra Babu nodded; he knew that. 'Or the C.I.D. might come in . . . do you think they will?' Jogendra shrugged; he might know more about this than he was letting on. 'If Fisher starts his own enquiry,' I continued, 'he'll be stood down from it in short order.'

'Yes,' said Jogendra. 'It is to be hoped.'

'All that being said, though . . . Could I get hold of a copy of the reservation chart for the carriage?'

'Why do you require it, sahib? The reservations are known. Yours, Fisher's, cathedral man, shot man . . .'

'But I just want to see if any late change was made.'

'Booking office is incinerating those lists.'

'Sounds a bit drastic. When?'

'Quickly. They are not long retained.'

'But I would like to see it.'

'Yes. I will see.'

Looking about the room, there seemed to be more files than ever relating to Schedules A and B. I said as much to Jogendra. 'Sahib,' he said with a sigh, 'it is endingless.'

I said, 'I was sorry to hear about your mother, Jogendra Babu.' I had thought about saying 'Babu-ji', because 'ji' was something you could add – a sort of endearment.

'Oh,' he said, after a moment. 'Yes. She was very aged lady.' He resumed his tidying. 'So sorry, I was dreaming miles away just then.'

'Away with the fairies, as they say.'

Jogendra Babu looked up at me and smiled: 'Away with Fisher sahib and incorrect stipulations!'

I walked over to the desk from which the file had been stolen and quickly pulled open the drawer in question, half expecting the file to have been put back. Jogendra knew exactly what I was about, and again he smiled at me. The drawer, of course, was quite empty.

Calcutta had stopped being the capital of India in 1911, the honour having gone to Delhi, but it did not seem in the least discouraged by the fact. Motors, tongas, electric trams, horse-drawn trams, rickshaws – you were just about safe from them if you kept to the pavement, or at least to the inside edge of it. But even there you had the traders to contend with: 'I have emporium, sahib, only little walk this direction', and they would try and take you down some alley. 'Not buy, sahib, but only look – only *look*!' And that last word often said with a real anger that made you think the government couldn't keep the lid on this for much longer. Half the buildings were grand but falling down, the white-painted fronts crumbling and stained brown as white-painted buildings on a seafront sometimes are, only here it was the sun, not the sea that had rotted them away.

The doorways of the buildings usually stood open, and they showed dark hallways, and battered brown staircases, leading up to offices. Many Indians conducted their business on these staircases, Indian doctors especially. One plaque I always read:

PHTHISIS SPECIALIST. Surgn R. P. N. Ganguly, B.Sc., M.D. D.P.H., European and American trained renowned specialist. Cures hopeless cases, Consumption, Asthma, Diabetes, Heart, Nerve and Private Diseases.

This was on a doorway at Old Court House Corner, just north of Chowringhee, in the very centre of town, and it piqued my interest every time I walked past. As to 'private diseases', I could make a hazard, but what was phthisis? Was this man Ganguly a quack? Couldn't be, with all those letters after his name. The main problem was what, if any, connection Dr Ganguly had with the plaque below, which read, 'Massage. Genuine Japanese Speciality. Miss Hatsuyo.' Next to this brass plate was lodged a small framed photograph of the woman I took to be Miss Hatsuyo, and a real peach she looked: her gaze was half averted, in a way that made me think the Japanese speciality might be very much to my liking. The fact was that I had only noticed Doctor Ganguly because I had noticed Miss Hatsuyo beforehand.

I walked on. I turned from the din and chaos of Dalhousie Square into the din and chaos of Chowringhee Street. The sun was going down rapidly, but I was sweating freely. Every electric tram advertised Lifebuoy Soap, and you could see why. The whole city was in need of the stuff. I turned off Chowringhee, and the chowkidar bowed at me as I walked through the gates of our hotel. I intended to have a cold bath and one bottle of Beck's beer. Then what? There was nothing 'on' for the evening, no party or dance in prospect as far as I knew.

Willard's Hotel was better than the Bristol, also on Chowringhee, but not quite up to the standard of the Great Eastern or the Grand. It was famous for its forecourt, which I now traversed: the little botanical gardens, with fountain, fish-pond, potted palms, dangling birdcages and coloured electric lights woven into a canopy of bamboo, in which many tiny lizards chirruped. Under the canopy were tables and chairs for drinks on the terrace.

I paused to light a cigarette, hearing:

'The zoo animals are really all very friendly. They come up to be scratched.'

'Not the tigers, though?'

'Of course not! If the *tigers* came up to be scratched, I'd want my money back.'

I saw Lydia with a glass of lemonade at a corner table. As I approached her, I heard:

'What do female Sikhs look like?'

'Search me.'

'Because I mean, it's not as if *they* wear turbans, do they?'

Lydia had also heard this exchange, and she rolled her eyes at me as I approached.

She stood, and we kissed. She wore a rather slight white dress, which made her look very brown.

'I hope you found a lot of criminality at Jamalpur, Jim,' she said, pushing back her hair, which had come loose behind. I sat down. A bearer was approaching, but he was delayed by a European who was standing his way and lighting a cigar. The bearer bowed at the man as if to acknowledge that this one of the most ridiculously big cigars ever seen.

I said, 'Tell you about it in a minute. Where's Bernadette?'

'Oh, where do you think? At a tea dance.'

'A tea dance where?'

'The Wednesday Club.'

'But it's not even Wednesday.'

'It *is*, Jim,' said the wife, leaning forward. 'It's been Wednesday all day. It's just a little affair,' she added, smiling. 'Dancing to the gram.'

The Wednesday Club . . . that was in a pavilion near the cathedral, a five-minute tonga ride along Chowringhee. 'She's with the girls?' I said.

'Of course she is.'

Her two new best friends: Claudine Askwith, daughter of

William Askwith, Traffic Superintendent of the East Indian Railways, and Ann Poole, daughter of Douglas Poole, Deputy Assistant Traffic Manager (Goods). The waiter came up and I ordered a lemonade.

'Not having your beer, Jim?'

'I'll have it when Bernadette comes back – when we go through to dinner.'

'Now,' said the wife. 'The trip to this Jamalpur place. Spill.'

'Spill' was one of Bernadette's words. It meant 'tell all'. The wife was expecting an account of the factory visit, but what she got was an account of a murder, albeit presented as the work of dacoits, which is what it almost certainly had been.

'So you're blaming the Indians?' she said.

'That's about the size of it.'

'You look exhausted, Jim.' The wife put her left hand on mine, and raised her right for the waiter. 'A Beck's beer for my husband, please,' she said.

'I'm quite happy with lemonade.'

'You're *not*,' she said. And it was true that I hadn't actually touched the stuff.

I said, 'Don't tell Bernadette about it,' and the wife nodded.

When the beer came, Lydia said, 'It's known to be dangerous, isn't it? That stretch of line?'

'How do you know?'

'William Askwith called earlier this evening. He said, "I hope's Jim's all right." Well, not in so many words. He said, "I trust Captain Stringer had a safe and satisfactory journey on the down express."'

'Hold on,' I said, 'How did Askwith even know I was going there?'

'I suppose Bernadette must have told Claudine, who told *him*.'

'And why was he telephoning anyway?'

'Oh, just to say that Eleanor would be collecting the girls from the dance and bringing them here.'

My mind swung back – as it always did at mention of William Askwith's name – to the theft of the Schedule C dossier. Before its loss, I had gleaned that it referred to corruption or embezzlement in the traffic department, and William Askwith was the *head* of traffic. Did he seem crooked? No. But then those public school and Oxford types (or was it Cambridge in Askwith's case?) never did. That was the whole purpose of their education: to stop them coming over as the rogues they frequently were. That said, Askwith was worth a mint, and there was something odd about him: he was too formal in his speech, talked like a copy book. He was like a sort of parody of a swell. And he seemed to have no *face* to speak of, just a white oval beneath his sola topee. His light blue eyes appeared to be too small, but not as much too small as his nose or mouth. He had no hair to speak of either, and looked as though he never *had* had any. His wife, Eleanor, seemed all right to me, although Lydia thought her a snob. She was a rather elongated, worthy woman, not quite beautiful, and that went for her daughter, Claudine, too. Their faces were medieval somehow, like the faces of women on paintings in churches. Whereas their daughters had formed an instant, if competitive, friendship, Lydia and Eleanor Askwith had got off on the wrong foot. To the best of my recollection, Lydia had been on the edge of a group taking tea in one of the hotels, and Eleanor Askwith had been at the centre of the group. She had been ignoring Lydia (according to Lydia) and had said, 'If only we had one other person we could play bridge.'

'What about me?' Lydia had asked me later on, 'I was "one other person".'

'But you can't play bridge,' I had said.

'*She* didn't know that, you clot! For all she knew, I was a demon at it.'

All three of the Askwiths were intellects; read a good many books, and did everything right in a social way. Lagged for twenty years in Alipore Jail, William Askwith would be able to get on with his reading; but I didn't think he'd take very well to it otherwise.

From the first, I'd thought that if William Askwith had been named in that dossier as being on the take, then it must have been Douglas Poole – the father of Bernadette's other best friend in Calcutta – who had done the naming. Douglas – commonly known as Dougie – Poole looked like Dan Leno: that is, like a sad-eyed superannuated jockey. As with Leno, his clothes always seemed too big, and his hair had to be kept firmly plastered down, otherwise it would do God knew what. Dougie Poole wasn't as funny as Leno of course, but he was good company with a mournful sense of humour. He also had a whimsical streak, and a taste for the bottle, and so on the face of it it was incredible he'd ended up a senior traffic manager. His wife, Margaret, was a cheerful, competent sort who seemed to laugh off her husband's drinking. She was pretty or not according to the expression on her face, and she had a great deal of frizzy and colourless hair, as did her daughter, Ann. The Pooles all spoke with slight London accents and were generally looked down on by the Askwiths. In fact the two families would have had no social connection at all were it not for the friendship of their daughters.

It was rumoured Poole wasn't up to the job of Deputy Assistant

Traffic Manager (Goods), and that must have been on account of his tippling, since he seemed bright enough to me when sober. As the head of traffic overall, William Askwith was Dougie Poole's boss, and known to be a hard governor. With the present push for far-reaching economies, it seemed to me that Dougie Poole must be in a perilous position, and he may only have been saved from the push by his daughter's connection to the Askwiths. Surely, therefore, if Dougie Poole had anything at all on William Askwith, he'd use it. The only trouble with this notion was Poole's apparent amiability: he wasn't the cagey, backstairs sort who'd split on another chap under cover of anonymity.

From inside the dark, hot hotel lobby came the tinkling of a clock chime. It was now seven. I asked the wife, 'You're sure they haven't gone "on"? They're not with that bloody maharajah, are they?'

'Bernadette says you've got a complex about him.'

'You haven't answered the question.'

'Whether the R.K.'s there or not, Bernadette will be brought here in minute by Eleanor Askwith.'

'I expect he'll be hanging around. He's made a dead set for her.'

'He's got beautiful manners, and they both like dancing. She calls him Raju – I think that's rather charming.'

Lydia ought to have been up in arms for the girl. Instead she seemed at this moment to be encouraging a romance.

'No doubt he's *heavenly* as well.'

'He's charming, handsome, intelligent.'

'Well, I've warned her off.'

'. . . Which of course will have the opposite of your intended effect.'

'How do we know he's clever anyway?'

'He went to the North Indian equivalent of Eton. It's in the Himalayas. His English is absolutely perfect, practically.'

It was now five past seven. Our usual dinner table was booked for eight. Whenever Bernadette was even slightly late back from an event, I thought of organising an immediate police sweep of the city, and I would make my own mental sweep of it. On the face of it, Calcutta resembled a steaming hot London. The maidan was perhaps the equivalent of Hyde Park, but there were jackals on the maidan that would scream at night. Yes, the High Court was like the Houses of Parliament from the front; but the back of it was falling down, and propped up by bamboo scaffolds, and the river running before it contained dead bodies.

I ought not to have brought the girl out here.

I had now finished my beer; Lydia had fallen silent. Before long, the clock in the lobby would chime the quarter hour. I said, 'I'm just off out front for a look,' and Lydia did not say I was becoming needlessly agitated. I walked from under the canopy, and through the gates on to the hard standing where the tongas and motors for Willard's Hotel would pull in from the Chowringhee traffic. The light was fading fast, if not the heat. There were palm trees over the road, like giant dark stars on sticks. Beyond them, the maidan had become mysterious, like a sea. There were some low, burning . . . somethings on it, like stars that had crashed to the ground. Tongas and the occasional motor hurried past – all apparently making a point of ignoring Willard's; and now a rickshaw was coming. The rickshaw-wallah was like a man running for his life; he was clearly about to expire, and yet the European fellow sitting up behind was just staring into space. They too ignored Willard's Hotel.

The pavement on this side of Chowringhee was a market, and

the stallholders were beginning to pack up. At the nearest stall to where I stood, a man sold leather belts from underneath a green storm lantern. There were flies all around the green light, and the belts looked like so many dead snakes. A little way beyond him was the Elphinstone Picture Palace, whose lights were beginning to blaze in the darkness, but I didn't glance that way because I knew I would see the projecting advertisement for *Reported Missing*, 'a comedy in six reels'.

The wife had chosen her words carefully. Eleanor Askwith would be collecting the girls from the dance. In other words, she was not there with them. There was no chaperone. It was true that Claudine Askwith, at seventeen, was a year older than Bernadette, but she didn't count.

Where was the R.K. staying? He was putting up at a hotel with his father, the maharajah, who was in town on business. It would have to be the Grand or the Great Eastern. I would go there and ask him to give me back my daughter, or tell me where she was, and if he didn't I would do the bastard in. But one of the Austin taxis was approaching. It looked somehow promising, and I almost put out my hand to stop it even though its roof light was not lit. It pulled up before me anyhow, and there was Bernadette laughing in the back with Claudine Askwith; and Claudine's mother, Eleanor, was in the front passenger seat. The green night-fog of the city swirled in the taxi headlights.

Bernadette stepped out, calling out, 'Bye, Claudine, love!'

She wore one of her many dresses that wasn't long enough, one of her hats that wasn't cheap enough, and a cashmere wrap I believed to be her mother's. Eleanor Askwith did not get out, but wound down the window. 'Here she is Captain Stringer, all safe and sound.' On her lap was a novel, and inside the novel, some

72

leaflets. She took a couple out and passed them through the open window. 'Have you had these already? And do give one to Lydia.' The leaflet read:

St Dunstan's Fund … Buy Happiness for Others! Many poor children, their bodies wasted with want and neglect … Rs 25 monthly will feed, clothe and educate one child. We have no paid workers. Purely a voluntary effort.

'Thanks very much,' I said. She smiled at me and the taxi pulled away. Could such a woman really be married to an embezzler?

'Have you caught the snake man, Dad?' said Bernadette.

'It's not my job to catch him. Why do you ask?'

We were walking back through the hotel gates.

'The snakes were the hot topic at the Wednesday,' said Bernadette. 'People were saying they would stop going on the trains until he's found.'

'All the snakes have been in first. So they could always go in second.'

'Some of them were saying they jolly well *would* do.'

'Was that flipping R.K. there?'

'I don't know why you're so rude about him. He's a "friend of Britain", Dad. His father sent troops to the war.'

'He's a friend of *yours*, that's what bothers me. I want to know if he was there.'

'If I say yes, you'll blow up, and if say no, you won't believe me.'

'I've told you not to see him. For those blokes, a girl is marriageable at aged eight. How many wives has he got already?'

'Lay off, Dad.'

Under the canopy of leaves, Lydia had another lemonade on

the go. When she saw us, she stood up at her table and waved.

'Dad?' said Bernadette.

'What?'

'The trains to Darjeeling are on a different line, aren't they?'

'Different to what?'

'To the snakes.'

'Different line, different company.'

Trains to Darjeeling and 'the hills' were operated by the East Bengal Railway, from Sealdah station on the other side of town from Howrah. No snakes had been found on those trains as yet.

'When we go up there,' said Bernadette, 'I'll need some clothes.'

'You'll need a good thick sweater.'

She laughed. 'I'll need some chic little party dresses.'

The trip to Darjeeling, to escape the heat, was one of the two big events on the horizon. The first was the East Indian Railway Debating Society dance coming up on Saturday. Lydia and Bernadette would be travelling up to Darjeeling on the following Monday, and I was to join them on the Wednesday. They would be staying for the best part of a month, whereas I would be there for only a week. Lydia had taken a house up there. She had booked it from a classified advertisement in *The Statesman*. Cedar Lodge, it was called: Lydia had had visiting cards printed with the name on them. That was how things went on in the hills. You posted your card through the letter box of people you wanted to know – 'dropping' your card, it was called – and waited in agony to find out whether they wanted to know *you*.

Lydia kissed Bernadette and we all agreed to walk straight through to dinner, but the happy mood was interrupted when I produced Eleanor Askwith's leaflet.

'She's been feeding the poor again, has she?' the wife said, rather bitterly. It seemed to me that she resented the amount of time Eleanor Askwith spent among the destitute children of Calcutta – which was not really all that much time. From what I could make out, she gave a few days every year to this effort called the St Dunstan's Fund. The wife called this 'Lady Bountiful stuff'. It was a different sort of do-gooding to her own. Lydia was involved with an outfit called the Women's India Association. She had become an honorary member of that club, in her role as an emissary of the Women's Co-Operative Guild, Yorkshire division. At these meetings, co-operative credit schemes were discussed (whatever they might be) and plans for the education of Indian females. It seemed to me that these enlightened women had their work cut out, given the approach of India's religions to women.

We walked through the lobby of the hotel, which was dark but not heavy, the chairs and tables being mainly bamboo, and interspersed with many plants and even small trees in copper pots. There were cushions scattered about the place, but you didn't get much in the way of upholstery in Calcutta; and the floor was a matter of rugs on bare wood rather than continuous carpet. On the walls were paintings of picturesque Indians looking happier than was needful, given that they were only carrying water pots or beating clothes; and there were dried snake skins hanging from the walls as well.

We were shown to our table by a bearer, who went off to get the menus. The wife called after him what sounded like 'Shook-ree-yah', which was Hindustani for 'thank you' or so she thought. As we waited for his return, I said, 'How rich are the Askwiths?' and both Lydia and Bernadette piped up, for they were very interested in this subject.

'Their flat is unreal,' said Bernadette.

75

'Parquet flooring throughout,' said Lydia. 'And they won't be renting in the hills. They've bought a place up there.'

'It has a paddock and a pony for Claudine,' Bernadette added.

'Is she a good rider?'

'That's the queer thing. She doesn't ride at all. Says it makes your sit-upon too big.'

'Bernadette!' That was the wife.

'I'm only saying', Bernadette continued, 'they just don't know what to do with all their dough.'

'And how does Askwith get on with Ann's dad?'

'Mr Poole's a lovely man, but he's a rummy isn't he? Everyone knows that.'

'Does he ever talk about his work?' This was to Bernadette specifically, since she spent more time with the Askwiths.

'About the railway you mean?'

'About his particular line of work.'

'Well, he's a top box-wallah, isn't he?'

'Yes, in traffic.'

'What's that, exactly?'

'Movement of trains. Keeping tabs on the whereabouts of carriages and wagons so they're always in the right place at the right time, and scheduling them for cleaning and periodic running repairs.'

'Sounds *lethal*.'

Chapter Three

I

Early the next morning, I ran into both Askwith and Poole.

I had woken at six in the hotel, and I went down to a *chota haziree* of anchovy paste on toast and a pot of tea. I took it on the terrace, and even though the heat had started, the teapot was wrapped in a thick, knitted cosy. As I ate, I watched a squad of Indian police doing physical jerks on the maidan.

The wife and Bernadette were still sleeping in our suite of rooms. After dinner the night before, Bernadette had complained of a headache, and Lydia had given her two aspirin, which had sent her off. I reckoned she had been drinking pegs at the dance. Lydia and I had then revolved the idea of lovemaking, but even though Bernadette seemed deeply asleep, she might wake at any moment and walk through the door connecting our room with hers. We had had relations only once since coming to India, and that had been exactly a week before, when Bernadette had stayed overnight with the Askwiths. It had been a perfectly satisfactory ride (at least, *I* thought so) and we had ended in a bath of sweat.

A bearer brought some more toast, also that morning's copy of *The Statesman*. The snakes were all over the paper, whereas the shooting of John Young did not feature and, I believed, *had* not featured at all, possibly because it had occurred too far 'up country'. A press communiqué from the East Indian Railway was quoted to the effect that all possible steps were being taken to safeguard passengers. Carriages, especially first class, would be thoroughly inspected by Company personnel when trains were made up, and a reward of five thousand rupees was to be offered in return for information leading to the apprehension of the culprit. But in light of the two further fatalities, the paper asked, 'How long before the masses will abjure travel on the line?' (In common parlance, the East Indian Railway was always 'the line.')

I decided to walk to the office.

Anyone who didn't know the way from Willard's Hotel to the East Indian Railway's castle in Fairlie Place would only have had to fall in with the flow of bicycling clerks. What started as a trickle on Chowringhee became a flood on Esplanade Row: first clerks, second clerks, *acting* first or second clerks, record keepers, cashiers, draughtsmen, subordinate ledger clerks, upper subordinate ledger clerks, temporary upper subordinate ledger clerks. In every case the bicycle was black. Pay grades ranged from about forty rupees per month (three pounds) to four hundred, and these last would have an attaché case dangling from one side of the handlebar, and perhaps a tightly furled black umbrella dangling from the other, like a mobile scales of justice.

The bicyclists were not allowed to take their machines into the courtyard of the castle, so they parked them in the racks by the hot and mustardy river. Between seven and eight o'clock, the clerks who'd parked their bikes clashed with the clerks yet to do so, and chaos resulted in Fairlie Place. The superior European officers would add to this chaos by pulling up in tongas and motor taxis, and, as I turned into Fairlie Place, I saw one of the latter fighting its way through the massed clerks. The taxi stopped a little way short of the courtyard entrance and William Askwith climbed out. In doing so, he coincided with his more junior colleague, Dougie Poole, who'd been walking with clerks. Askwith's suit was of white cotton tweed, which kept the creases out; Poole's was of white linen, which did not. His suit looked about two sizes too big in addition. Askwith carried a calfskin briefcase. I knew the kind: it was hand stitched and there would be special compartments inside for everything from ink bottle and paper knife to visiting cards and railway tickets. Dougie Poole made do with a bent valise, carried under-arm. Askwith saw me first.

'Good morning to you, Captain Stringer,' he said, touching his sola topee.

'Morning there,' I said, because I never knew whether to risk calling him William.

From behind him, Dougie Poole nodded at me and flashed a rather pained grin. Then, as Askwith began to speak, Poole embarked on a huge yawn.

'According to Eleanor,' Askwith said, 'the girls had a lovely, if rather strenuous, time at the Wednesday Club.'

'Bernadette did seem tired,' I said. 'I'm not quite sure why.'

'They were learning some silly, but evidently rather involved, new dance. Had a thoroughly ridiculous name, something to do with—'

'The banana glide,' Dougie Poole put in. 'It's considered "hot socks" at the Wednesday.'

'I gather you encountered a spot of banditry on the Night Mail?' said Askwith, ignoring Poole.

'A fellow was killed,' I said. 'A Company man: Anglo-Indian.'

'Yes,' said Askwith, 'a very poor show.'

I wondered how he knew of it. So I asked him.

'We had special orders about the return of the carriage,' he said.

'It was to be kept sealed. I saw a copy of the wire last night.'

A reasonable answer, even if this seemed a minor bit of business to be crossing his desk, given that he was head of traffic. Presumably he had known nothing of the trouble when calling Lydia to explain the arrangements for collecting the girls. We spoke for a while about the attack and the death of John Young. 'What a country that can produce such horrors,' said Askwith, in his blank way.

I asked him how things were in his department.

'The traffic's expanding all the time, so we must work hard to keep up with the operational and maintenance requirements. But as with your police work, Captain Stringer, our main attention focuses on the coming change, and the rationalisation. It's certainly keeping us all on our toes, isn't it Douglas?'

But Dougie Poole could not give an immediate answer, having embarked on another yawn. It was becoming increasingly hard to talk in that fast-moving sea of black and white clerks, and now Askwith and Poole gave themselves up to the flow and, with a tipping of hats on all sides, allowed themselves to be swirled away from me, and into the courtyard.

I lingered on the pavement, being occasionally buffeted, and watching the motor taxi that Askwith had climbed down from, and which had still not managed to leave Fairlie Place. I had heard that he would never on any account use trams or tongas in town, but only taxis, and according to Lydia this was because he'd had a brush with the Gandhi-ites . . .

In the year after the war, the Mahatma had organised a protest campaign against the security measures of the Rowlatt Act. The Act was meant to keep the revolutionists in check, but had only succeeded in creating an army of them, the protests against it having resulted in the killings at Amritsar. There'd been bother on the streets of Calcutta. Indians had stopped the trams, and made Europeans get off and walk. Evidently, William Askwith had been on one of the stopped trams, and the protestors had not only made him walk, they'd also confiscated his sola topee, exposing his head, which was bald, to the strongly raying sun. Evidently, Askwith himself did not like to recall the event.

Five minutes later, I had gained the office I shared with Fisher and Jogendra. Fisher's enormous and sweat-stained sola topee was on the top of a filing cabinet, and Jogendra's umbrella was propped in the corner, but there was no sign of either man. After checking the drawer to see whether the stolen file had been returned (it had not), I began looking over the Schedule B files concerning graft among junior employees. I was after one particular letter that touched on a certain interesting store room at Sheoraphuli station, which was one of the early stops on the Grand Chord, only about fifteen miles out from Howrah. I fished out the letter and folded it into my pocket book. A visit to Sheoraphuli was on the cards, but I doubted I would get round to it today, for I would be spending most of my time on the railway lands in company with my Gurkha colleague, Deo Rana.

I spent a further hour on the files, until the rising sun discovered the one window in the office, and began raying in ferociously. I called a passing bearer, and he brought me a cup of sweet and milky tea.

I resumed my reading of *The Statesman*. A 'communal riot' had occurred in the district of Faridpur, wherever that was. These were a regular occurrence in Bengal. The phrase meant fighting over religion, generally – in fact always – between Moslems and Hindus, and here was the British Imperialist argument on a plate:

if we left, civil war would break out. But I did not think it such a good argument. If we'd gone into India to stop a civil war in the first place, then it might have been. I had moved across the page to an arsenic poisoning case, when Superintendent Christopher Bennett walked in.

'Would you come through to my office, Jim?'

I followed in the wake of his pipe smoke. He sat down at his desk, and I sat down opposite. There was still nothing on his desk save the tin of St Julien tobacco, and I was beginning to think there *should* be something on it. For example, a dossier about the dangerous snakes of Bengal. I admit there was some devilment in my question: 'Have you seen the paper, sir?'

'Yes,' Bennett said. 'Middlesex beat Surrey by three wickets.'

He removed his pipe from his mouth and he smiled, but it was a rather crooked smile. I said, 'Have you been on to the zoo?'

'Oh,' he said, 'I think they've got their hands full giving elephant rides and chimpanzee tea parties.'

Not in the reptile house they didn't.

The snake trouble was testing his amiability to the limit, but he wouldn't let on. He was the type who would mop his brow with a *folded* handkerchief however fast the sweat rolled down. I told him I was about to go off to the railway lands with Deo Rana. 'He tells me there are snake men there, stealing from the Company.'

'Snake charmers, you mean?'

'Not exactly sure.'

'From what I can see,' said Bennett, 'these incidents have done the charmers no end of good . . . the snakes seem more exciting.' He spoke in a drawling way that I thought rather forced. He sat back, clasping his hands behind his head.

'Haven't you and Fisher got rather a lot on without troubling about the snakes? I really do think you can leave those to the regular chaps.'

By which he meant himself. I had know from the 'off' that the investigation of the Night Mail shooting would not fall to me, and I was now being warned off the snakes as well. But the snakes interested me, and it seemed to me they did fall within Schedule A of my brief as officially defined.

I heard a rumble of heavy boots on floorboards, and a raised voice from the end of the corridor; it sounded like Fisher.

Superintendent Bennett said, 'Jim, I'm afraid a certain Detective Inspector Khudayar Khan of the C.I.D. would like to see you about the Jamalpur business.'

He was glad to be able to give me some bad news, I thought, in the light of my forward remarks about snakes.

'When?'

Bennett removed a chit from his desk drawer. He read it over, replaced it.

'Seven o'clock today if that's all right.'

It had clearly better be.

'Is he seeing Fisher as well?'

Bennett nodded. 'At *six* o'clock. Khan's in the Writers' Building, you know.'

The Writers' Building was a long palace that took up the north side of Dalhousie Square, a mixture of government offices and swanky private apartments. The main tram stops were all in front of it.

'Where's Fisher now?'

A trace of a smile returned to Bennett's face. I turned to see Jogendra Babu standing in the doorway. He said, 'Fisher Sahib away outside. He is having a jolly good cooling off.'

83

Judging by the yellow blaze of sun at the window of Bennett's office, I doubted that.

Bennett said, 'Major Fisher has invited Jogendra Babu to make a formal complaint.'

'About what?'

'Himself, sahib,' said Jogendra Babu. 'And this I will most certainly be doing.'

He salaamed and continued along the corridor.

Bennett said, 'Fisher was rather put out because everything to do with the shooting was sent to Jamalpur. He wanted to get his teeth into it, just like you.'

'But that wasn't Jogendra Babu's decision.'

'It was mine – not that there was any decision to be made. The jurisdiction is with Hughes at Jamalpur.'

'But now the C.I.D.'s coming in.'

'Not necessarily, Jim. They might just want to hear your side of the story. By the way, Major Fisher asked me something about you. Requested some data. Thought I'd better tell you.'

He smiled: he was enjoying this as well.

'He wanted to know if you were going up to Darjeeling. I said I assumed Lydia would be – and your daughter. But I didn't know about you. He said he wondered whether you would like some company, if you were travelling alone.'

'With all due respect sir, I don't believe you.'

'He didn't quite couch it like that, no.'

Bennett was looking at his pipe.

'I think he proposes to accompany you, anyhow.'

'Are *you* going up?' I asked Bennett.

'Mary will go. I had meant to go with her, but business might keep me here.'

He meant snake business.

I quit Bennett's office, and returned to my own, where Jogendra Babu was hunting up a file.

I said, 'Did you manage to get hold of the reservation chart from the Night Mail, Babu-ji?'

He gave a half nod, began fiddling with his wire glasses.

'Is it available?'

He thought about this for a while. Then he nodded, and said: 'Is indicated.'

'What is indicated, Babu-ji? When will it be available?'

'In the fullness of time, sahib.'

'Well,' I said, 'it *is* a murder investigation.'

'But one you are not undertaking, sahib?'

'Not officially, no.'

I tried a grin on him; it didn't really work.

Jogendra Babu said, 'I *am* official, Stringer sahib.'

Perhaps by this, he meant that the chart had been sent to Hughes at Jamalpur Junction.

'But you will see what you can do, Babu-ji?'

'I am seeing, I am seeing.'

Evidently I had been laying it on a bit thick with the addition of the affectionate 'ji'.

II

The main part of the Armenian Ghat took the form of wide steps going down into the river. Be-robed Hindus stood on the steps, immersed to varying degrees, watching the wide, brown river and sometimes pouring it over themselves. Fisher stood on the very top step, his boots well clear of the water. He stood with his hands on his hips, and a Trichinopoly cigar in his mouth. I was watching him from behind – from Strand Road – but I could tell about the cigar from the smoke flowing about his enormous and globe-like head. I imagined the smoke as coming from inside his head, for I supposed he was fuming as usual. But I did not believe he was *really* put out by being blocked from investigating the shooting. I remained watching for a while, and he remained staring fixedly ahead. Not once did he reach up and touch the cigar; he smoked it only by sucking and blowing with his mouth. A sacred cow – or at any rate a cow with ribbons on its horns – was descending the steps to take a drink, and for a while it stood right next to Fisher, looking at the water, and obviously thinking hard, just as Fisher was. But he never gave it a glance.

Presently he spat out the cigar stub, and turned so that I saw him side-on as he walked past the small quays, mooring posts, and riverside godowns. He came up on to the pavement where he passed by one of the thin sadhus or holy men, a fellow sitting on a green square of cloth, who seemed to have bathed in ash before daubing himself with some streaks of orange paint. The fellow was not begging – he occupied some other world altogether – but in passing him, Fisher trickled some coins into his lap.

Deo Rana came up beside me. He gave a small bow.

'Good morning, Deo. Where exactly are we going?'

'Backside of station, sahib.'

We decided to walk, but we had to wait to cross the Howrah bridge because the centre of it was being floated away to let a ship go through. In the blazing heat of the day, I wondered that the sailors could be bothered to sail the ship, and that the bridge men could be bothered to accommodate them. Once on the Howrah side, we skirted the front of the station and the stampede for tongas and taxis, and we went past the first clock tower, which said eleven fifteen, and the second clock tower of the station, which said not quite the same thing.

We traversed the waterfront, and the barges being unloaded by derricks that spat out black smoke and made a machine-gun rattle as they strained to lift the swinging white bales of cotton, jute and tobacco. The crane operators and dockers kept up a constant shouted commentary on the transportation of the bales, rising to a peak of agitation as the loads dangled between barge and bank . . . or perhaps they were speaking about something else entirely. On the right side stood the railway lines, leaving the road at right angles, with low, red one-storey buildings in between, some with the benefit of a platform to raise them above the black ash, and all with wide green doors open to receive or discharge goods. On the lines were wagons – 'mixed goods' they'd be called in Britain, but all goods in India were mixed. The contents were sometimes branded on the sides. I read 'Kerosene', 'Sugar machinery', 'Tea', 'Copper wire'.

We were walking alongside a train. The bales loaded on to it put a spicy haze into the air that made you want to sneeze. Still with the train to our right, we climbed up on to one of the platforms, and walked past the open doors of one of the low red houses. Men sat around a rough table drinking tea from a big brown pot. There was a stone sink with a tap, empty gunny sacks folded on the bare wooden floor, and framed photographs around the walls showing cricketing scenes; also a sign reading 'ALWAYS TAKE CARE'. The men looked out at us with moderate curiosity, but not enough to check their talk. A white-suited sahib and a railway policemen – they probably thought I was someone making a complaint about theft of goods. We descended from the platform, and carried on, still shadowing the long train. It had been made up, yes, but there didn't seem any question of it going anywhere, and when we got to the end of it, I was not in the least surprised to see there was no engine.

Beyond the train, and beyond the other waiting trains, the tracks curved away right towards Howrah, but Deo Rana was leading me left, where the goods yard began to fade. There might be tracks in this territory but they went nowhere in particular, and there might be engines, but they were likely to be crocks. I had my eye on a little saddle tank with no cab, just a pressure gauge on top of the boiler like an eye on a stalk. There were two men on the back of this queer-looking bug, and I thought they must have been in the process of dismantling it, but then it coughed into life, ejecting one foul ball of smoke like a man spitting phlegm, and it clanked away towards the Howrah main line, becoming bent as it disappeared into the heat haze.

Deo Rana was leading me towards one of the long red loading bays. It had a platform, but not any tracks. Over the wide door, a sign said 'Trainlighting Office', but it hadn't been *that* for a while. Some mill or factory over to the left was making an orange cloud, and beyond that was the native city of Howrah, the Black Town, a maze of shacks and litter, with hundreds of crows circling above. Indicating the loading bay, Deo said, 'Snake men.' There were two, sitting on the platform. Another two came out of the train-lighting office as we approached. The snake men looked like men in a Bible story. One – the governor, I supposed – came down from the platform and salaamed to Deo, who turned to me and said, 'Baksheesh, sahib.'

I took out my pocket book and gave the fifteen rupees to Deo who gave it to the snake man. By filling out three forms, I had got the money from the petty cash guarded by one of Jogendra Babu's men, but the sum was not *so* petty. The head snake man reminded me of the Arabs I had seen in Mespot, resembling a sort of scarred hawk. Having safely stowed the money – he had a cloth purse rolled into his dhoti – he spoke again in Hindustani (I assumed that was the lingo) to Deo Rana, who turned to me and translated: 'You will take one tea?'

I had been eyeing the dark interior of the trainlighting office, hoping to go in there and escape the sun. But we all walked over to a smouldering fire at some thirty yards' distance – a fire made of railway sleepers bleached and worn down to something like driftwood. Tea was made and the snake men rolled cigarettes. I declined the offer, but lit a Gold Flake. Deo Rana did smoke but never on duty. Indicating the trainlighting office, I asked the head snake man, 'Do you live there?' and I looked to Deo to translate. The answer that came back via Deo – 'We don't live anywhere' – couldn't have been quite right.

I said, 'Are you gentlemen snake charmers?' and the question, when put by Deo, caused amusement. The answer came back: 'Sometimes, sahib.'

I was about to ask where all the bloody snakes had got to, when a small Indian boy came running over the ash from the edge of the Black Town. He wore a European shirt and shorts, and he was fairly clean, but he knew the snake men all right. He was laughing, and calling out to the head snake man, indicating a certain spot in the ground. All the snake men got up, and went towards the kid, and Deo Rana turned to me, saying, 'Hamadryad.'

'A king cobra?'

'The king yes,' said Deo. 'Very long, much poisonous.'

The kid, dancing in the dust a hundred yards off, was laughing fit to bust. The king cobra was in a hole in the ground in a patch of grass a hundred yards from the red house. It wanted to hide, you could tell that, but it couldn't hide because it was too long to fit into the hole, and its back end stuck out. As the kid laughed and pointed, the snake kept wriggling to try and fit a little deeper in. It turned out that one of the snake men – not the governor – had some English because, indicating the snake, he said, 'He is great rascal!' but it seemed to me the snake was perfectly blameless so far. As for the top man, he was crouching down and rubbing his hands in the ash. I realised I had seen something similar done before . . . prior to a performance . . . the strongman at the circus as he prepared to lift the heaviest dumbbell. The top snake man approached the snake, and his English-speaking comrade stood behind, holding a stick that I now saw was forked. He saw me eyeing it. 'Hold neck,' he said, grinning and gesturing with the stick. He seemed confident that things would go according to plan.

The snake man was bending down over the twitching tail of the king cobra. Then he began pulling, hauling it in like a bloody sailor on a hawser, and with six feet of snake out of the hole, he was still hauling. At twelve feet he was still hauling, and I had dropped back from the snake gang, so that I was standing twenty yards away from them and contemplating a dash to safety. The English-speaking one, with stick poised, turned to me and called, 'You are afraid of the worm of the earth?'

'Yes,' I called back, and then the head came out, and he leaped at it with his stick.

The boy was jumping about, shouting 'Wah-wah!' The snake's mouth was wide open, showing the pink interior that looked like I don't know what. Behind the trapped base of the head, the hood swelled out and shrank back repeatedly, like a pair of bellows. The snake was growling like a bloody dog. The snake man had grabbed its neck, and was bending low over its head, speaking to it. The one who spoke English said, 'He will soon be our friend.'

The governor had lifted the snake by its neck, and the others got hold of the rest of it, and they carried it at shoulder height, like men carrying a roll of carpet, towards the trainlighting office. I followed at a distance. Deo Rana, who liked snakes, was walking by the side of the governor, and they were talking about the beast in their own language. As we reached the red house, Deo, indicating the snake, said, 'He destroy a man in thirty . . . forty seconds.'

Indicating the governor, I said, 'Will he kill it?' and the English-speaking one said, 'Nay, huzoor, we do love it.'

The governor continued speaking to Deo as we entered the trainlighting office. Deo turned to me, saying, 'It is against his dharm to kill snake.' I think I knew what that meant. The universe would be put out of balance, and he would lose points, lose merit.

The trainlighting office was dark and smelt of piss. I saw a wooden crate stamped 'Burn & Co.' and there was wire mesh nailed over the top. It held living rats. Alongside it against the wall stood a row of baskets of various sizes, all in the shape of urns. All had lids, and one of the lids was roped down. Also in the gloom I saw a snake charmer's pipe, firewood, a canteen of water, a shotgun, and a tea caddy decorated with a picture of a fox hunt going through pretty English countryside. The governor knocked the lid off the endmost basket, and with a co-ordinated heave, the men tossed the king cobra inside. The boy then clamped the lid down and sat on top of it. The governor had picked up the tea caddy. He was again speaking to Deo Rana, who said to me, 'They have another snake. Same.'

'Oh Christ.'

'They show you,' said Deo, and he was pointing, of course, to the roped-down basket.

But the governor was brandishing the tea caddy.

Deo asked, 'You take one tea?'

'Fine,' I said. 'I mean thanks. And then will they tell me about the train snakes?'

The English-speaking one had heard.

'That we know,' he said, 'we *say*.'

III

This time the tea had condensed milk in it, and a spice of some kind. There were chapattis as well, brought over from the Black Town by the boy, and filled with soft cheese. We ate and drank sitting on the platform. Again, the snake men offered their black tobacco for hand-rolled cigarettes, and I was starting to think I might be getting my money's worth as a sort of excursionist even if I had not so far uncovered any new data touching on the snake attacks. But then Deo Rana, who had been speaking to the governor, turned to me, saying, 'Baksheesh, sahib.'

'But he's already had his bloody baksheesh.'

Deo Rana put this point to the governor, who at first said nothing, staring straight ahead towards the heat-dazed train movements of the Howrah goods yard. Then he spoke, and Deo Rana transalated: 'That was morning baksheesh. Now afternoon.'

I said, 'I have no more money.'

'You have ten rupees,' said the English-speaker. This was true; I did have ten rupees in my pocket book. I eyed Deo Rana. He shook his head, so he was telling me to give it over. I handed the ten rupees to the governor.

'Now I need information,' I said.

Deo Rana spoke to the governor, and the response came back, 'Soon informations. Music first.'

The boy was coming out of the trainlighting office holding the charmer's flute and one of the smaller baskets. The basket was placed in front of the governor, who squatted in the dust and began to play. His flute had a bulge in it, as though someone once blown so hard that it had inflated. The governor took one hand away from the pipe, swiped off the top of the basket and the snake was there, standing up and swooping with the movements of the pipe. It was another cobra – I could tell by the hood – but not a king. It was so much smaller than the king that I felt confident about moving a little closer to the basket. The English-speaker, who stood with arms folded behind the governor, looked up and said, 'You are not safe, you know that.'

So I moved back again.

The snake continued to dance. I said, 'It likes the music,' and the English-speaker shook his head.

'Snake deaf,' he said. 'All snakes deaf.'

'Really?'

He threw up his arms as if to say he was amazed I didn't know.

'Where ears?' he said, laughing. 'Only . . . feel shaking. On ground.' He stomped his bare foot.

'Vibration,' I said. 'They feel vibration.'

'Yes, huzoor.'

The music had stopped, and the snake fell back into its basket. If they couldn't hear the sound, the snakes must be interested in the motion of the pipe; it also struck me they liked being cooped up. I put that to Deo Rana, and he put it to the governor as the boy carted the basket away. The reply came back: 'Snake feel safe in small place,' and it seemed wrong that the snake should be the one to worry about feeling safe.

The boy was now coming out of the trainlighting office carrying the largest of the baskets. It was about as big as he was, and the ropes were off. The snake men and Deo Rana were all now squatting or standing near the edge of the disused platform, and I was standing opposite them, about twenty yards from the platform. There was a strong mood of afternoon. The crows circled more lazily over the Black Town, the cloud of smoke and dust from the mill had turned a deeper orange, and the noise from the Howrah goods yard had become a continuous and distant drone. I was exhausted from my day in the heat. I wanted to be back at the hotel in my iced bath with my Beck's beer.

I watched the boy, marvelling at his energy in the heat of the day. He commenced climbing down from the platform edge while holding the basket, but the basket was too big for him. One of the snake men called out just as the kid fell and the lid rolled away, and the bloody thing came racing out. It moved like an arrow towards me; everyone else was behind the snake; only I was in front of it. I turned and ran but I would not beat the snake; I turned to see how close it was and I fell as the snake – six feet away from me – began rising into the air. The snake was swaying over me, it was like the fucking Indian rope trick . . . and then it was being rapidly withdrawn over the dusty ground. The governor was pulling its tail, and then the English-speaker stepped in with his cleft stick. The snake was trapped again. Everything stopped, and I was able to think. Something had not happened that should have. The snake, now being returned to its basket, had remained dust-coloured all along its length. In spite of the accident, the egg had not cracked. The snake had not opened its mouth. The English-speaker was now shouting at the boy, and chasing him about the platform in a half-serious way. A third snake man – one who had so far kept in the background – was on the platform, and holding up a darning needle in one hand, and a roll of fishing line in the other. As I sat in the dust, he waved them at me.

Whilst I could now think, I could not speak for the beating of my heart. When I *could* speak, I said, 'They stitched up the mouth.' Deo Rana was walking towards me. 'How will it eat?' I said.

Deo Rana replied, 'Snakes not need food for long time. Many weeks, not need. Soon, they will open mouth, get poison part and cut, cut.'

Then they would sell it to a charmer, I supposed. You could cut a dash with a king cobra. All the ones I'd seen so far had used the standard sized ones. I wondered why they needed to stitch the mouth in the first place. To weaken the snake perhaps, demoralise it.

It was time for some hard facts.

I said to Deo Rana, 'Do they know about the snake attacks?'

He talked to the snake men, and came back with: 'Sahibs come. Buy snakes.'

'Who?'

'Not know names.'

'They speak to these buyers; they sell them snakes. But they don't know their names?'

'They not sell. Their brother sell.' He corrected himself. 'Not brother . . . uncle . . . very bad man.'

'Their uncle is a very bad man?'

'Terrible man.'

More talk between the snake men and Deo Rana, who said, 'Uncle is deaf.'

'So the snakes are deaf, and the uncle who sells them is deaf?'

'Yes, huzoor. Both deaf.'

'For Christ's sake,' I said.

A wind was getting up, bringing the dust cloud from the jute mill closer, and making the sleepy rattling of the goods yard seem further away. I felt myself to be a very small and unimportant part of India as I asked, 'Does the *uncle* live anywhere?'

From what I could make out, he did not. Even so, he was 'away'. This much I gleaned from the English-speaker, who then went into the trainlighting office, and came out saying, 'We have photograph.'

He showed me a picture of an elderly Indian wrapped in snakes like Harry Houdini wrapped in chains. If he was not quite as wild and ragged as a sadhu, he was getting on that way.

'When is he coming back?'

He would be back soon, and they would say where he could be found – in return, no doubt, for another twenty-five rupees. I was tired of the snake men; I was even tired of Deo Rana, who had promised more than he had delivered. Perhaps the snake men had heard of the Commission of Enquiry, and feared that a clean sweep was to be made of the railway lands. They would then be *ejected* from the railway lands. But not if they had something to offer the police. As we all stood in a semicircle in the hot, dusty wind, I gave Deo Rana one last question to translate: 'Do they think their uncle's customers include the man who puts the snakes on the trains?'

Deo Rana put the question, and turned back to me with the answer. 'Yes,' he said. 'They think it.'

Chapter Four

I

As the sun descended towards the railway lands, I headed for the Railway Institute. I walked alone, Deo Rana having returned to Fairlie Place. The 'Insty' was the club for the Anglo-Indians, their home-from-home, but there was nothing official about that; any railwayman might drop in (except for the pure Indians, who had their own Insty). It happened to be the nearest source of cold beer to the house of the snake men. I also wanted a glimpse of the world John Young had inhabited.

The Insty stood within its own grounds, beautifully kept, with big flowers that looked wrong-coloured, as though painted by an over-imaginative child. A gardener, or mali, was weeding the beds. Two peacocks paced the garden. They did not bother to do their display for me, but the gardener salaamed, and I tried to do likewise back. I was not good at salaaming. I ascended the steps of the Institute.

The lobby was like an English church hall, with bunting in the rafters. Not only were there photographs of the King-Emperor around the walls, but other members of his family too. And there were pictures of trains, jumbled up with notice-boards on which advertisements were pinned: 'Shalimar Paint and Varnish', 'Detachable Boiler Insulation', 'Thornycroft: Service Counts', 'Carbon Means Expense'. There were bookshelves, holding the

Locomotive Journal, *Railway Carriage & Wagon Review*, the *Railway Gazette*; but also the *Encyclopaedia Britannica*, and stories like Robin Hood and King Arthur in Bumper Books – these to keep the Anglo-Indian boys on the straight and narrow.

Beyond the lobby was a long wooden corridor with more bunting, more photographs. I gave my hat to a butler and entered the corridor. The rooms off were indicated by little signs sticking out of the corridor, like railway signals. I could hear the sound of table tennis being played, and played well. It was one of the games the Anglos liked, along with darts, badminton, and housey-housey, which was their bingo – village hall sorts of games. The children liked to play hopscotch, or perhaps their parents made them play it, as being the right sort of game: un-Indian.

The corridor photographs showed mainly Anglo-Indians presenting each other with prizes at social occasions. Sometimes Europeans were involved, but not often. Indianness fluctuated amongst the Anglo-Indians just as the levels of drink fluctuated in the glasses they held. The young women were always beautiful – the older ones too, come to that. Their beauty detained me on my way to the bar, thirsty though I was. A young Tommy would come out to India, and get himself an Anglo-Indian girl. She was a prize to him because she was so beautiful; he was a prize to her because he was white. He would then enter the Anglo-Indian world, or he would if she had anything to do with it. Therefore she was like a siren luring him . . . But that would suggest there was something wrong with being in the Anglo-Indian world, and I did not believe there *was* anything wrong with it, except that the European snobs would look down on you, and try to keep you out of the top jobs, and imitate your 'chi-chi' accent behind your back.

I was aiming for the sign reading 'Bar'. Before it was a sign reading 'Function Room'. In there, I saw half a roast chicken, the remains of a trifle, cheese and biscuits on a long, decorated table. Anglo-Indians avoided curry, I believed. It was the end of an afternoon party, half a dozen guests lingering. I heard, 'You'd come off the regulator by the banyan tree' – a driver speaking to a fireman perhaps.

I walked on to the bar, where a smartly dressed Indian sold me a cold Beck's beer, whereas the Anglos drank wine and water for preference, called it 'grog'. I took a belt on my beer. Yes, I did fear the worm of the earth, and I knew that nightmares awaited me as a result of my encounter with the king cobra. I looked at the notices beside the bar: 'Steamship tickets to Europe', 'Oxygen gas of high purity'. I read, 'Have you considered white spirit's advantage over vegetable oil and turpentine as a solvent and thinner of paints and varnishes?' I had not. And there was a poster showing a steel wheel on a short length of rail. 'Macpherson Trading', I read. 'Wheels, Tyres, Axles, Fish Plates and Permanent Way Rails. We at Macpherson's specialise in making these products, at our large steel works, which possesses advantages conducive to rapid and economical production.' As I had learnt at Jamalpur, this outfit was the principal supplier of wheels to the E.I.R.

The overhead fans in the bar rocked as they revolved. There were more fans than drinkers. Besides myself, there were two other men; they sat in the corner. One was pure British and big, the other Anglo-Indian and small. The British fellow was at least twenty years older than the Anglo – probably in the late fifties. He had a gravelly voice of the kind you heard in the burra clubs, so what was he doing in the Insty? He talked the talk of the burra clubs as well.

'. . . heads the list each year for the numbers of tigers killed,' he was saying. 'I know of no place where you are more certain of getting tiger. During a single fortnight, Colonel Marsh got . . .'

I had two hours until my appointment with Detective Inspector Khan of the C.I.D. What did he have in store? No doubt another snake would come slithering out of another basket. The big sahib in the corner had moved on from Colonel Marsh to himself. It was impossible not to hear him.

'I tell you, Freddie, I thought it was a cloud shadow that moved across the short grass to my left, but I realised, as he stepped into the dusty path, that the big cat had arrived. His flanks were swinging gently, his tongue lolling, his tail was carried high with a dinky little upward curve at the top. The big paws came down without a sound. The powerful brute within thirty yards of me might have been walking on air. He froze into a perfect statue.'

'Gosh,' said Freddie, or something like that, and more out of politeness than astonishment.

A boy had come into the bar. I had seen this boy somewhere before. He came up to me directly – too directly, the kid was drunk – saying, 'Who are you, and what are you doing round here?' He was John Young's son, Anthony, and I had seen his photograph. I told him who I was, and I offered to buy him a drink.

'You were the one talking to my dad?' he said. (He would have been given a rough outline of the murder of his father by one of Superintendent Bennett's men.) 'So you were the fellow with the gun. Listen, did you shoot my dad?'

'Of course I didn't.'

'But hold on, you're a cop yourself. Are you looking for the bloody darkie who shot him?'

'You've just said *I* shot him. The investigation is being conducted from Jamalpur.'

'Being conducted, is it? Who by?'

'A man called Hughes.'

'You know, I'm rostered up to Jamalpur from time to time. Maybe I'll go along and see him.'

'You're a travelling ticket inspector.'

'That's me – railway boy! How do you know, anyway?'

He kept moving his hair back from his forehead; there was a great deal of it.

'Your dad told me. I had quite a long talk with him.'

Anthony Young shouted, 'Boy! Another beer for the sahib. I can see you like beer,' he said, indicating my empty glass. 'Where's that one gone? It's evaporated, man!' When the drink was poured, he said to the barman, 'Put it on the funeral bill.'

I said, 'You drink it.'

'No man, I've been drinking all day. You know what's been going on through there?' He indicated the function room, the place where I'd seen the afternoon party. 'What's it called when you have a bloody good drink up after a funeral?'

'A wake.'

'Dad's wake. We buried him today at the church . . .'

'Which church?'

'Holy Joe's. St Joseph's.'

'You're a Catholic.'

'Do I look like a bloody Hindu?'

'Why do you think I shot your father?'

'I'll be honest with you: I think you had an argument with him.' The boy leant against the bar, becoming conspiratorial with me. 'I've been asking around about you. You're on an investigation of corruption by the railway lot, so listen . . . You thought my dad was on the take. Commerical man, working on big contracts. You know how that could go.'

He certainly was a sharp kid. It was almost as if he knew about Schedule C. I said, 'I liked your dad.'

'Come on, man, of course you say that!'

'If he thought *I* thought he was on the take . . . Then he would have been more likely to shoot *me*, wouldn't he?'

Silence for a space.

'So now you get amused at me? My dad – carrying a gun! Listen, you had an argument with my dad. You know . . . all that whisky the pair of you knocked back. My dad had the top education of India, but he was a booze-ard like you. And he would blow up, man.'

I said, 'He told me he had a lot of arguments with you.'

'He did, that's right. What else did he say?'

'That you were wasted as a ticket inspector.'

'You think I want to be like him? I loved my dad, but do you know what I called him? Nowhere man. Too big for the Insty, too small for the big clubs. But not really too *small*, man – too black. Do you know how many other top men came to see him off?'

'You mean gazetted officers?'

'Six.'

From the corner I heard, 'Anyhow, I ducked just in time to give Stripes a free passage.'

'Sounds a fair number for a small funeral,' I said.

'And how many of those came back here, do you think? Two. You should have heard them. "Oh, you people have made such a lovely job of your Institute, we must come here more often."'

'I doubt they said that. Not in so many words.'

'What are you doubting, man?'

'They wouldn't say "you people." Is your mother still in the other room? I'd like to go through.'

'Why?'

'Pay my respects.'

'Keep your respects.'

The big Englishman who'd been talking about tiger hunting was approaching from behind Anthony Young, who turned aside, indicating the man, saying, 'Here, you will like him. Another booze-ard.'

The boy then quit the bar.

II

'His father would have given him a clip round the ear,' the big Englishman said, 'or indeed a belt. A very good man, John Young.'

We were sitting in basket chairs on the veranda of the Institute. The Englishman had introduced himself as Charles Sermon, and on hearing the name I realised I'd heard of him. He was an officer of the East Indian Railway, and quite famous for being British and yet haunting the Railway Institute. I accounted for my own presence on the Company payroll in the manner approved by Harrington in London, mentioning only Schedules A and B of the enquiry. He nodded blandly at this. I made it clear that I was not investigating the killing of John Young, and Charles Sermon made no reaction beyond saying, 'They've a sound chap on the job, I hope?'

Sermon was a traffic manager, quite high up on the passenger side. I mentioned Askwith as being the father of my daughter's friend and he gave a respectful nod. 'My boss,' he said, looking across the garden. I waited to see whether there would be any advance on this. As there was not, I mentioned Dougie Poole, and his name brought a smile to Sermon's face. 'Dougie's on the goods side. Great fun is Dougie, but it would be wrong to take him for a lightweight.'

'How do you mean?'

'Oh, I don't know, but he's an interesting chap, bit of dark horse . . .'

I seemed to me that Sermon would neither be on the take, and nor would he finger anyone who might be. These actions would be insufficiently romantic for him. I supposed that he was perfectly good at the complicated work at the traffic department, but that his true mind was elsewhere: in the mofussil.

The mali was now stringing some up some empty kerosene cans. Charles Sermon explained that they would rattle against each other, and so keep the fruit bats off the mangoes. Since the mali spoke no English, Sermon pointed out some of the flowers to me.

There were orchids of various kinds, sunflowers, red dahlias, carnations, African daisies. We sat among the scent of these flowers, with just a hint of manure. The garden was beautifully kept, except for a couple of bushes close to where we sat that looked half dead, with leaves only on the uppermost parts. But they must have been meant to look like that; they would not have been tolerated in that condition otherwise. Sermon offered me a good Turkish cigarette from a good silver case, and we smoked in silence for a while, gazing towards some wagons being shunted in a cloud of golden dust, with the sun setting beyond, and occasionally sipping our drinks. Anthony Young had called Sermon a 'booze-ard' but there was a good deal of water in his whisky, and I was on lemonade.

'You like it here,' I suggested to Sermon.

'I do,' he said. 'I'm tolerated by the regular crowd; they serve a proper glass of whisky, the provender is excellent, and it's just a short stroll over the bridge from my place off Strand Road.'

But not as short a stroll as the burra clubs of downtown Calcutta would be.

He was an old India hand, and his white drill suit was of a Victorian cut. It was of good quality, but slightly grubby, or at any rate not as white as the flower in his buttonhole, which was not like any I could see in the garden. I believed it was a white carnation, whereas the carnations in the garden were of other colours. He wore old-fashioned horn-rimmed glasses that clashed with the rough redness of his face, and seemed to signify the descent from outdoorsman to box-wallah.

'Do you think he did it?' I said. 'Do you think the boy did his father in? Or arranged for it to be done?'

Charles Sermon seemed quite shocked.

'The two of them would have rows, and they would have rows in *here*,' he said, indicating the Institute, 'but I don't think it would ever have come to that, old man.'

'What did they fight about?'

'Politics primarily, I think. The father was a great loyalist, like most of the Anglo-Indian chaps. The son thought that was rather craven of him, I suppose.'

'But surely no Anglo-Indian supports the nationalists. They'd be worse off under the Indians than they are under us.'

Charles Sermon shrugged, reached for his whisky. 'Anyhow,' he said, 'he was killed by a bandit wasn't he? I've seen a lot of that myself up country . . .'

On the face of it, he was a man for the mofussil, the countryside, and it was the devil's own job to keep him off hunting, yet from what I could work out he'd long since stowed away his shotgun. He was now just an ink-spiller in the traffic office . . . although not for much longer. I had gleaned that Charles Sermon was coming up for superannuation, and the return to Blighty.

He was saying, 'Talking of dacoits, I was up with my old shikari pal, Clive Webster, in the Mandlabaju block in the Central Provinces. Now whilst the majority of villages in that territory are—'

'Do you have a place lined up for when you go back home?' I said, cutting him off.

'Oh,' he said, because he didn't seem to mind being cut off, 'your neck of the woods: Scarborough.'

The coast. I should have known. After years of humidity, the old India hands wanted sea air.

'The Esplanade?' I suggested, because I knew Scarborough, and I could see him in a flat there, overlooking the floral gardens, the funicular railway and the sea. Every evening at six, he'd go to the Esplanade Hotel for his peg. There'd be people in there who'd listen to his hunting stories. Well, they'd *have* to. I myself had always hankered after the Esplanade: the grand white houses seemed to capture and hold the sun. But no; Charles Sermon wouldn't be on the Esplanade . . .

'Few streets inland from there, old man.'

We drifted on to the snake attacks, and I told Sermon of the photographs I'd seen. Midway through my account, Sermon stood up to help the mali with the kerosene tins. When he sat back down he was wheezing somewhat. He was slightly out of condition.

'Compare death by tiger bite,' Sermon said, returning to his seat.

'Compare it to what?'

'Snake bite. Ever seen Stripes take down a buff?'

'A what?'

'Buffalo, old man. Tiger on a buffalo. Straight to the neck. The buff doesn't know what's hit him. A lightning death – almost pleasant in the absence of pain. I recall—'

I told him I was very sorry, but I had an appointment at the Writers' Building. Sermon seemed to regret my departure. He sent a bearer to collect my hat, offered to accompany me to the garden gate of the Insty. We looked out over the railway lands, which were strangely peaceful under the setting sun: the marshalled goods wagons to one side, the passenger coaches to the right, all patiently waiting – and Horwah still further to the right. Charles Sermon said, 'There's only one man to speak to on the snake front . . .'

'Is he at the zoo?'

'He practically *is* the zoo. Professor Hedley Fleming. Cleverest man in Calcutta.'

And he shook my hand warmly.

III

The electric lights blazed from the windows of the Writers' Building, and the trams moved back and forth in front, shuffling their advertisements for Lifebuoy Soap like cards in a pack. Their motors whined and their bells tolled, but inside the office of Khudayar Khan all was silent.

The room was green. The window blind – half down over the window – was also green, and there was a brown scorch mark in it. I wondered if the sun alone had done that. No electric fan twirled, and yet Khudayar Khan wore a tightly buttoned double-breasted top-coat, and his white tunic shirt was tightly fastened at the neck with a gold pin. As a Moslem high up in the elite police, Khan was a very rare bird indeed, and he seemed to know it. He was handsome in a bony kind of way, and very commanding with his silences, during which he was usually smoking. I had never heard of his brand before; it was called Advantage.

A constable had brought us a cup of sweet tea, and I too smoked.

Khudayar Khan began by asking about my life and police work back home. I was determined to put our interview on an equal footing – we were men of the same rank, after all – and so I in turn asked him whether he had visited Britain. He reluctantly admitted that he had attended London University for a while, and I told him my boy was there at the present time.

He said, 'And your daughter is here?'

'She is,' I said, 'She is enjoying the social life.'

'An expensive business,' said Khudayar Khan, and I felt I'd fallen into a trap. 'When I was in London,' he said, after watching me through smoke for a while, 'I lodged in a place called Somers Town.' He then spelt it out for me. 'Not "summer" as in fine weather: that inference would have been grotesque.'

'It rained all the time, I suppose.'

'Of course it did, yes. It was a sort of hostel I was staying in. A terrible place.'

I felt like saying, 'Don't blame me for London; I'm hardly ever there.' Instead, I observed: 'It's near King's Cross station.'

'The trains made a dreadful racket as they came out.'

'Well they're working against the grade—'

'I'm sorry. They're doing what?'

'Going uphill. So you'll get the cylinder beat. I think it's one in a hundred and seven through Gasworks Tunnel, and much the same through Copenhagen Tunnel. That's quite steep for a railway.'

He drained his little teacup, watching me carefully.

'But it levels off at Finsbury Park,' I added.

'We haven't got the results back from the fingerprinting,' Khan said.

'You'll find my prints all over his compartment. I was in there talking to him for a good while.'

'Talking and drinking whisky.'

'Sort of,' I said.

'What do you mean?'

'In the first place, it was only "sort of" whisky . . .'

He didn't like that. It was an implied criticism of his country, although as a Moslem of course Khudayar Khan would not touch a drop of alcohol.

'. . . And in the second place, I personally only had one glass of it.'

'Are you saying he was drunk?'

'No. My prints will also be found on the warrant badge in his pocket book,' I added.

'Why?'

'He passed it over to me to look at – as I said in my statement.'

I assumed he'd read the statements. There were no papers on his desk, nothing on it but a black statuette of a horse. Come to that, there was no picture of the King-Emperor on his wall.

'John Young was shot with a high calibre pistol,' said Khan.

There was a period of silent smoking on both sides.

'You were found to be in possession of such a pistol.'

'As would about half the former army officers in India.' But not Major Fisher. Why not? Should I disclose my suspicions of him? Should I ask what Khudayar Khan had made of the man? Instead I remarked, 'The reservation chart was missing.'

Khan was now putting out his cigarette.

'They're always missing,' he said, 'or very often. Shall I tell you something, Captain Stringer? The Youngs live out at Tollygunge. Three months ago, the police – the civil police, I mean – were called out to deal with a row between the father and the son.'

'It had become heated?'

'Violent.'

'What was it about?'

'Money.'

'Are you saying the boy is a suspect?'

But my question was met with a question: 'You saw a dacoit riding away? He was in Indian clothes?'

I nodded. 'There were two others with him, but further off. They wore, you know, pyjamas.'

He didn't quite like that, either.

'Shalwar,' he said. 'Loose, light trousers, wide at the top, narrow at the bottom, and then kameez – a long shirt or tunic. The two together are called shalwar kameez.'

'Yes, that fits the bill.'

Had any such outfit been found among the possessions of John Young's son, Anthony? A search of his house might have account-ed for the agitation he had shown at the Institute. It should be simplicity itself to find out whether Anthony Young had been on duty as a ticket inspector on the night of the murder, and if so where. Should I let on about my encounter with the lad? I decided against. I was not meant to be investigating. And for all Khudayar Khan's interest in Young, I felt I would be lucky not to graduate to the position of suspect myself, in which case I should not be seen to be throwing blame elsewhere. Nor would I mention my suspicion that I had been the intended target. Khan would think that self-important of me, and he would think me incompetent for losing the file. But it was as though he read the drift of my thoughts.

'You are on a railway Commission of Enquiry, or something,' he said, and I started in on an explanation of my work, which he cut off halfway through, saying, 'This whole country needs a Commission of Enquiry.'

Not quite the remark of a fully paid-up loyalist, I thought.

Chapter Five

I

The next day was Friday. The thermometer was nudging the ton, but most of the senior railway police at Fairlie Place were 'gate-happy', being about to leave for Darjeeling and the hills.

That morning, Superintendent Bennett went into a conference with two of his detectives about the snakes. The news was all over the police office. Overnight another common krait had been found in a first class sleeping compartment of the night train from Howrah to Moghalsarai. Moghalsarai was on the main line, the Grand Chord, from where passengers changed to the branch for Benares, that city full of Hindu temples (and factories). Moghalsarai was a long way out, about three hundred miles. The snake had been under one of the two lower berths; it had been discovered in the middle of the night, and beaten to death with a cane by a man called Watkins who was the chairman of Blakeborough & Sons, hydraulic engineers of Calcutta. The other men in the compartment were from the same outfit; their trip had been made in relation to a contract with the Railway. I had heard that, after leaving Howrah, the train had made two stops on its journey to Moghalsarai, but I did not know where.

A communiqué had been out to say the reward was being increased from five to ten thousand rupees. Immediately before he went in to the conference, I had collared Bennett and told him of my experiences among the snake men of Howrah. Bennett had heard me out politely, but had not taken a note, and when I finished, he said, 'This snake charmers' uncle . . . don't you think he sounds rather mythological?'

'He might hold the key,' I said.

'The key to losing another twenty-five rupees, would that be?' Bennett said, lighting his pipe. I nearly asked whether the common krait was not becoming rather too common on the trains of the East Indian Railway. I was becoming rather sick of Bennett. His charm had worn thin, and who was St bloody Julien anyway?

I said, 'You have a few leads of your own, I suppose, sir?'

'I'd rather not say just now, Jim.'

All this enigmatical stuff wouldn't wash. It stood to reason that if he was closing in on the culprit, he wouldn't have increased the bloody reward.

An hour later I was looking over some papers in the office when I heard – by the banging of some doors – that Fisher himself had pitched up. A little while later I heard muffled shouting, followed by Jogendra Babu's raised voice: 'Fisher sahib, kindly shut up!' A door opened, and now the voices were clearer. Fisher said, 'Any more of that, pal, and you'll be out on your bloody ear.'

'As for rudeness,' Jogendra Babu said, 'I recommend to read your own Bible, and story of mote and beam.'

'Yes,' said Fisher, 'I'll go off and read it now. Nothing I like more than thumbing through the bloody Old Testament.'

'Parable of mote and beam is in *New* Testament.'

The gloves were off between these two. Another door was slammed, then another; then Fisher came into our office with papers under his arm. He sat down, lit one of his Trichinopoly cigars, and began leafing through the papers. After a while, I said,

'You saw Khan yesterday in the Writers' Building?'

Fisher nodded.

'Me too. What did you make of him?'

'Typical bloody Indian, wasn't he? Trying to blame Europeans for everything that goes wrong in his bloody country.'

'He tried to blame *you*?'

'Wanted to know why I thought it was dacoits. I said, "How about this? They were known to target that stretch of line. The thing had all their hallmarks, and we saw one of them clearing off on his horse."'

'What did he say to that?'

'Not much. Then he said, "You're the masters now, but we'll be running the show before too long." I said, "Good luck to you, pal. I'll be long gone by then."'

'And where will you be?'

'I don't bloody know, do I?'

I noticed a singular sort of squirming happening beneath his brush-like moustache. To all appearances, he had now abandoned his interest in the shooting of John Young. As for the snakes, it seemed he'd never had much interest in them in the first place.

'All set for tiffin?' he said.

We were to have a meeting about our fact-finding with a chap from the Railway Board, and it was to happen over tiffin.

The fellow turned out to be called Ross Sinclair and to have one of those soft Scottish accents that nearly puts you to sleep. Our meeting took place on the veranda, beneath the creaking of a hand-pulled punka, and with rather inadequate shade. It was a rather rambling affair. The meal over, Sinclair suggested to us that the Railway would recruit a better class of employee if it advertised the posts in the railway journals.

'Then you'd attract the railway hobbyists,' I said, '. . . train watchers.'

'Nutcases,' said Fisher.

At this point Bennett joined us, together with his pipe.

I suggested a perimeter fence be erected around the railway lands of Howrah. I also put forward a theory I'd been developing about a certain type of twelve-ton covered goods van commonly used on the railway that had a small trapdoor in the side meant to allow a yard man with a torch to check on the contents . . . but which also allowed easy access to those contents for any suitably skinny villain.

'Fair suggestions, Jim, but both a good deal too expensive.'

That was Bennett. He was definitely down on me, but he mustered a smile when Fisher started in on how he'd discovered that some storekeeper's clerks were doing the job without pay.

Bennett said, 'Perhaps you think some hidden advantage lurks in the holding of the appointment, Noel?' Fisher had also come across a weighing machine inspector who owned a racehorse, and Bennett had a good chuckle at that: 'Now I'd like to have a look at *his* post office savings account.'

But he was obviously still thinking of the snakes.

Ross Sinclair brought up the subject of Darjeeling. Fisher fixed his eye on me, and said, 'You're off up to the highlands, aren't you?'

Bennett, re-filling his pipe, said, 'It's called having a change to the hills, Noel.'

I nodded.

'Got your tickets yet, have you?' asked Fisher.

'Put in for them, yes.'

I'd put in for privilege bookings to Darjeeling through Jogendra, and they had been available to collect for some days since. It was the East Bengal Railway that ran that way, but it was possible to book for that line at the East Indian Railway booking office. And Jogendra had said it was regrettably necessary that I should go down to the booking office and pick up the vouchers myself, since they had to be signed for. It appeared that Fisher was yet to apply for his own booking, and he intended to do this directly and in person at the booking office.

'Go down later and do the business together shall we?' he suggested, lighting one of his Trichies.

It was just about the first instance of normal and friendly behaviour that he had shown towards me, and I didn't like it one bit.

II

Mindful of what had happened the last time I'd set off on a railway journey with Fisher – that is to say, I had come close (I believed) to having my head blown off – I had resolved to travel apart from him on future occasions. But I had a morbid curiosity about his intentions. I could always make sure to stay awake in his company. And I would not be putting Lydia and Bernadette at risk, since they would be travelling separately.

Therefore, at three o'clock that afternoon, I was standing next to Fisher in the queue marked 'Staff Tickets' in the great marble booking hall of the East Indian Railway.

All the queues were long, the poojahs being in prospect. Most of the white sahibs waited in line with the Indians, but not all.

Some would push to the front. They would say something like, 'Excuse me there,' but would not look at the men or women they had pushed past. If any Indian had objected, the queue jumper would have called in one of the two constables who stood in the doorway. They were Anglo-Indian, and they would side with the sahib, which was why folk of that persuasion would get short shrift from the Indians when independence finally arrived. If it did come to a row, the queue jumpers would not say, 'I'm white so I must be allowed to go to the front.' They would more likely say they were an officer from some important department, and it was essential for the smooth running of society that they get their ticket in double-quick time. I believed that, if Fisher had been in a hurry in the booking office, he would have shoved in front of a white as readily as a black.

He said, 'When are you going up?' and since he'd asked point blank it was hard not to give a straight answer.

'I reckon next Wednesday,' I said.

'With the wife and the missus?'

'They're off up beforehand.'

I eyed him narrowly. Was he glad that I would be travelling alone?

'Taken a house, have you?'

I nodded.

'What's it called?'

'Can't remember,' I lied.

I asked Fisher, 'Where are *you* putting up?'

'Hotel,' he said.

'Got a name, has it?'

'Hotel Mount Everest.'

'Sounds cold.'

'They should do me all right there. They have a French chef.'

There was a picture of the little Darjeeling train behind the booking clerks; it advertised *Tickets Touristiques*.

'I wouldn't bother with those,' said Fisher, seeing where I was looking.

'Why not?'

'No roof on the bloody things.' And I believe he very nearly smiled again. He said, 'I was reckoning on next Wednesday as well.'

I didn't believe him. He'd simply taken his cue from what I'd told him.

'Glad we're not in that bloody line,' said Fisher, indicating the queue next along, which was hardly moving, and was for refunds. The rule on the East Indian Railway was: 'For refund file an application at place of issue.' It took an age to get a refund, but they were given in full up to twelve hours before the booked time of departure, so it was worth the effort. The fellow dealing with refunds was being assisted by another chap, and there was a notice in front of him: 'Clerk under instruction. Your patience is appreciated.' It was like the signs people put on their new motor cars: 'Running In.'

We now arrived at the front of our own queue. I collected my bookings. When it was Fisher's turn, the Indian clerk, having seen us talking, asked, 'You gentlemen will be sharing?'

Fisher said, 'Spot on, brother.'

So we were booked into the same first class compartment for the first leg of the journey: overnight to Siliguri, which lay at the base of the hills. On the second part – the little hill train – there could be no shared compartment, the carriages being saloons. So the trip to Siliguri was the worry. But at least there could be no anxiety about snakes. So far, they had all been on the trains of the East Indian Railway, operating from Howrah, and none had been on the East Bengal from Siliguri.

III

Fisher went off after we'd got hold of the bookings. I watched him as he headed towards Dalhousie, through the floating blue smoke made by the street vendors as they fried their multi-coloured foods. I then turned and looked towards Strand Road. There was a snake charmer near the Armenian Ghat. It was nobody I knew. He had an ordinary cobra. Alongside him was a sleepy-looking man selling cigarettes. If I were that man, I'd have moved a few feet to the left, but perhaps he knew the poison had been cut out of the snake. I returned to the office, where Jogendra came up to me with a form to fill out. Nothing unusual about that, but this was a form special to him personally: his written complaint against Major Fisher. It was so beautifully handwritten that I couldn't bear to read it, but I caught sight of 'ceaseless persecutings'. A complaint would be taken more seriously if another officer had witnessed the bad behaviour, and Jogendra was asking me to sign up as having observed the rudeness of Fisher. I decided to do so; Jogendra was certainly in the right. Fisher had regularly suggested he make a complaint, and it was now time to call his bluff.

After I had signed, Jogendra bowed. He then handed me two chits, as though by way of a reward.

The first was from Charles Sermon, the new acquaintance I had made at the Insty. He was sending me his best wishes, and the telephone number of a Professor Hedley Fleming herpeto-logist, of the Calcutta Zoological Gardens. Sermon had already had a word with Fleming, and he would be willing to speak to me, whether on a formal or informal basis, in connection with the train attacks. Sermon said he couldn't think why Fleming hadn't been called in up to now, since he was 'the top snake man in Bengal'.

The second chit concerned the other investigation I wasn't supposed to be pursuing. It was from the churchman who'd been on the Jamalpur train: Canon Peter Selwyn. He had something to tell me – something that might have been 'nothing at all', but there seemed to be a degree of urgency attached, because the chit ran on: 'Perhaps come to evensong at the cathedral this evening – it's a short service! – and we can go over the road after to my club, the Bengal.'

I sent a runner to say I would be there.

IV

The service of evensong at St Paul's Cathedral was *not* short. As on my visits with Lydia to York Minster, I marvelled at the way the choir managed to make the Magnificat – nine short lines on paper – last a quarter of an hour. The cathedral was white and cool. The congregation was black and white, mainly the latter. The presiding vicar – not Peter Selwyn – was white. A curi-ous feature of the cathedral was that it was full of bright green birds. As the congregation took its place they had been swoop-ing about all over, and I somehow thought they would be well-mannered enough to stop when the service began, but they did not, and their swoops became ever more daringly low over the vicar's bald head. He ignored them; everyone ignored them except me. I spotted Selwyn halfway through the service. He looked slightly bored, and was fiddling with the silver crucifix on a long chain around his neck. I walked up to him in the cathedral compound after the service. We shook hands, and he asked whether I had enjoyed the service. I said I had enjoyed the birds: 'I thought they were beautiful.'

'And you mean the Reverend Fuller is not?'

On his home ground, the fellow was more like his true self. He had it all laid on here. Close at hand were all the best things in Calcutta: the cathedral, the Victoria Memorial, the maidan ... and the bar of the Bengal Club. This was a stately place of wicker sofas, potted palms, and flitting, white-turbanned bearers. The chiming of several clocks harmonised pleasantly with the tinkling of glasses as the pegs were served. Selwyn knew our white-turbanned bearer very well, and seemed on the best of terms with him. He took his whisky with soda and ice, which was not considered good form in India – only water was meant to be added. Selwyn said, 'They say ice spoils the taste of the whisky, but then I don't much care for the taste of whisky.' He leant forwards, 'Left entirely to my own devices, I'd have it with lemonade.'

We sat back.

I asked, 'What exactly is a canon?'

'Well, first of all, it is spelt c-a-n-o-n, not two ns in the middle, yes?' I nodded, sipping my drink. 'It's just that you sent your chit confirming this appointment to "honorary c-a-n-n-o-n Peter Selwyn".'

'Thanks for pointing that out,' I said. 'I'll know next time.'

'I think perhaps there had better not be a next time. Nothing against you personally Captain Stringer, but we don't want to seem to be conspiring.'

'Conspiring about what?'

'Well, I don't think there's any point having a conspiracy unless it's *against* someone.' He was grinning. 'I refer to your peculiar friend Fisher. He never comes here, does he?' he added, looking about.

I shook my head. 'His club is the Tollygunge. For the golf.'

'How grotesque.'

'He's only a temporary member.'

'Yes, because he would certainly be blackballed if he applied to become a full one. There is a vestige of civilisation, even among the committee men of the Tolly.'

Selwyn was now signalling to his friend for another peg. 'I'm essentially a half-retired vicar with certain administrative duties in the cathedral chapter. I still do the odd bit of preaching . . .'

'Which is why you were on the train to Jamalpur Junction.'

'. . . Which is what I want to talk to you about. I formed the impression you didn't quite see eye to eye with Major Fisher even though he's a colleague of yours, and I thought you might like to know about something I saw when the train was at stand and everybody was wandering about in the flipping desert.'

'I would.'

'It's very simple. Fisher had something in his hand; he dropped it into the dirt, and kicked some more dirt over it. After he was so rude to me, I was naturally very keen to catch him in some indiscretion – anything would have done really, but ideally something that implicated him in the crime . . .'

'And would get him hanged.'

'Well . . . no. Something that would embarrass him, I suppose, because I don't think he could really have *shot* the poor man, do you?'

'I don't know. I certainly don't see *why* he would. I don't think John Young had an enemy in the world, except possibly . . .'

'Who?'

'It doesn't matter. But what did Fisher drop?'

'When he'd moved away, I went over to see if I could find out, but perhaps I'd misjudged where he dropped it . . . Anyway, I could find nothing, and by now *he* was watching *me*.'

'Do you think he knew you'd seen him drop it? Whatever it was?'

'Possibly.'

'Well,' I said, 'what do you *think* it was?'

'I think it was some sort of canister, a silvery metallic tube. That mean anything to you?'

'Not immediately, no. What size was it?'

'Perhaps six inches long . . . half an inch in diameter.'

'You're sure he was hiding it? Not just throwing away some bit of flotsam.'

'Pretty sure he was hiding it.'

'And you never mentioned it in your statement?'

'When that statement was being taken down at Jamalpur, he was sitting about six feet away. Anyway, I've said my piece now; I shan't do any more about it.'

I said, 'Have you been interviewed by an Inspector Khan of the C.I.D.?'

'Who?'

He had not, then.

We discussed the shooting for a little longer; we then moved on to the snakes. Selwyn said that suspicion must fall on a rail-wayman, somebody who often rode on the network, or at least knew it very well. I told him something of my encounter with the snake men of Howrah, in company with Deo Rana.

'Snakes – nagas – are symbolically important to the Hindus,' Selwyn told me. 'Of course you know Lord Shiva wears a cobra around his neck.'

'I did not know that.'

'And of course you know that the serpent, Shesha, is the king of all nagas. Lord Vishnu rests on him.'

'Is that so?'

'All around Calcutta, you will see the manasa tree, sacred to the little goddess of that name. She's the sister of Vasuki, king of all the serpents.'

'Really?'

'It gives protection to the planter from snake bites. It's a horrible-looking thing really, a sort of springwort. The branches appear dead at the lower levels, where you'll see a crudely carved figure of the goddess.'

That was a turn up. Surely I'd just seen such a half-dead bush at the Insty? Two of them, in fact. But there had been no carved figure beneath.

'Snakes are important for the home team as well, of course,' said Selwyn.

'The home team?'

'The religions of the Book,' he said, indicating the crucifix around his neck. 'In the Garden of Eden, the snake is death – death or the devil. Something bad anyway. One way or another, you have to come to terms with the snake.'

Silence for a space.

'That said, there aren't many snakes where I will be going next year,' Selwyn said.

'Back to Blighty?'

It appeared that Peter Selwyn, like Charles Sermon and the driver of the Jamalpur night train, would soon be sailing for Liverpool.

'I did think of staying on, but you can't *dwindle* here. You're either running the hundred-yard dash or you're dead, but in the little town of Southwold in Suffolk, dwindling is the number one activity. Everybody's at it.'

Southwold was on the coast, and so once again the need for bracing sea air.

'When are you going?'

'January. I was jolly lucky to be left a little cottage near the harbour.'

'There's a small gauge railway in Southwold,' I said. 'Goes to a spot called Halesworth. Main traffic is fish.'

'Tell me more about that Gurkha chappie of yours. I like the sound of him.'

I conveyed to Peter Selwyn my high opinion of Deo Rana.

'I wish I had a Gurkha to help with my work in the cathedral,' he said

'They're mainly known for their skill at hand-to-hand fighting.'

'That's exactly what I need! Shall I tell you a joke about the Gurkhas?'

'Go on then,' I said, rather warily.

. . . Ten minutes later, after we had said our goodbyes amid the bowing servants of the club lobby, and I was standing on Chowringhee looking for a tonga, I decided it would be worth re-telling that joke, but that I had better be very careful where and when I did it.

Mainly, though, I was thinking about Fisher.

Chapter Six

I

What the men of the East Indian Railway ever found to debate, I did not know – argue over, yes, but as to formal debating, I had never seen any sign of it. As far as I could tell, the Debating Society committee existed mainly to organise the Debating Society supper dance, which was the number one jamboree of the season for railway officers, and quite famous in Calcutta. It was the occasion when the Company repaid favours, or tried to make new friends – so the guest list extended beyond the Railway.

On the morning of the dance – Saturday 28 April – I took a turn on the maidan with Lydia. She would actually be spending half her day on the maidan, since she would be going riding with Bernadette later on. We walked over the light brown grass in our light brown sola topees, the burning sun seeming to make an additional weight pressing down upon our heads. As we left the town behind, the sound of the Saturday traffic was replaced by the sound of music. We approached a military band playing in a bandstand that surely didn't belong here, but must have been whirled by some international tornado from Hyde Park . . . In which case it had crash-landed, because it was slightly broken down. Wooden chairs with peeling paint were scattered around the bandstand, where an audience of sorts had gathered, consisting mainly of red-faced men of the Charles Sermon type, who came to hear the marching music. Then there were some middle-class Indians, who seemed more detached.

Somebody had left a newspaper behind on one of the seats; it was not *The Statesman*. I picked it up, dividing the pages and giving half to Lydia. The first heading I read was 'Another Snake Attack'. The battle of the men of Blakeborough & Sons with the latest krait was detailed, even though it had occurred three hundred miles out of town. The piece concluded:

> Since the attacks have occurred at numerous locations, and since all the trains concerned in the attacks originated from Howrah, responsibility for the investigation rests with the Calcutta Division of the East Indian Railway Police. The investigating officer is Superintendent Christopher Bennett. At the time of going to press, no statement was available from the Superintendent.

The music had stopped; I looked up. The conductor of the band was holding a conflab with a trumpet player. I wondered whether Superintendent Bennett had read that article. It would take the edge off his enjoyment of the Debating Society dance if so. I looked over to Lydia, who appeared to be reading about the motion pictures being shown in town. *Reported Missing* was still playing at the Elphinstone, but I fancied *The Adventures of Tarzan* at the Tiger Picture House.

The programme of music had ended, but the band weren't quite done yet. They struck up with 'God Save the King', a rather rusty version, and it did strike me that they had a cheek playing it, the King being so far away. I looked across at Lydia, and she was still reading, not standing for the King. But then again we were on the outermost chairs, not really included in the concert. Of those in the seats close to the bandstand, about half were standing, whether European or Indian. The others were walking away. But one man, I saw, was walking *towards* the bandstand from the direction of Chowringhee: Detective Inspector Khan. He was beautifully be-suited, and of all the many hats available to him he wore a Panama at an angle that was the opposite of rakish. The man's life, I thought, must be like a hall of mirrors. As a C.I.D. detective, he was a prop of the empire, yet it was not his empire, either as an Indian or, still less, a Moslem. Perhaps he was not a *practising* Moslem, and certainly he wore Westernised clothes, but the few middle-class Moslems in Calcutta generally did dress that way, as far as I knew. In a way, he beat the British at their own game. For example, he was a sight more elegant than most of them, and better spoken. He almost had what was called an 'Oxford voice', but perhaps his real allegiances were apparent from the man who tailed alongside him: a Moslem servant in white skull cap. This servant carried a canvas kit bag over his shoulder.

'God Save the King' was in its dying strains as Khan came up to the bandstand. He paused, and for a moment I thought he was actually standing to attention for the King-Emperor. But in fact he was lighting a cigarette. Having accomplished this, he walked on, and it seemed to me that whether God saved the King or not was a matter of very little account to him. I pointed him out to Lydia.

'That's the C.I.D. fellow who quizzed me yesterday.'

'Really?' said Lydia, and she put down the newspaper and watched him for a while.

Something about her attitude made me ask, 'What do you make of him?'

She said, 'He's heading for the stables,' by which she meant the gymkhana on the maidan, the very place to which she and Bernadette would shortly be going. 'He's riding out,' she said.

'Riding out to where?'

'Oh, come on, Jim,' she said. 'Riding out means *riding*.'

'And the servant is carrying his tackle.'

'His *tack*, Jim, his riding gear.' She snorted once with laughter. 'Tackle indeed ... He's not going fishing, is he?'

By now, Khan and his man were small in the distance, and the members of the band were picking up their music sheets prior to quitting the bandstand.

II

I had a kind of preview of the Debating Society dance before it occurred. At 1 p.m., I was sent by the wife to call Bernadette to tiffin. Walking through the lobby of the hotel, I heard the strains of what I suspected was 'syncopated' piano, which I followed downstairs to the music room of the hotel, where Bernadette and her good friends, Claudine Askwith and Ann Poole, were whiling away the hot afternoon. The door was half open, and as I approached it, the music stopped.

'Claudine, you warphead!' Bernadette was saying. She was holding on to Ann Poole, and had been dancing with her to the piano as played by Claudine Askwith, and evidently not played *properly*. Claudine struck up again, and Bernadette and Ann started dancing again, Bernadette counting all the while: 'Two-ho step, two-ho step.' Still dancing, Bernadette said, 'Raju believes that all life is a dance of Shiva.'

They were talking about the R.K.

'Or so he *says*,' Claudine shouted, over the sound of her own piano-playing.

'I doubt he *really* believes it,' said Ann. 'I mean, nobody would, would they?'

'He has forty temples to the God Shiva in his kingdom,' said Bernadette.

'His kingdom! You make him sound like a man in a fairy tale,' Claudine shouted. 'I thought it was thirty temples anyway.'

'What's ten temples give or take?' Ann put in.

'He's very philosophical anyhow,' said Bernadette. 'He has a different attitude towards time.'

'That's because he's got so much flipping money,' said Ann.

'He believes that time is circular,' said Bernadette.

'Like a clock, you mean?' said Claudine, still playing.

'Claudine,' said Bernadette, 'you are being simply impossible today.'

As she danced, Ann Poole caught sight of me over Bernadette's shoulder. 'Hello, Captain Stringer! Bernadette-ji, it's your pater.' They now revolved in the course of their dance, so that it was Bernadette who was looking at me over Ann's shoulder: 'Clear off, Dad,' she said happily.

'It's tiffin.'

'All right – at the end of this number.'

But then Claudine, at the piano, made another mistake and the dancing stopped.

'For crying out loud!' said Bernadette.

'Ever so sorry, loves,' said Claudine. 'I'm just so excited, what with the dance coming up, and our new house.'

Over tiffin, I asked Bernadette whether this new house of the

Askwiths was the one waiting for them up in Darjeeling, or some other.

'She found out just today,' said Bernadette. 'It's a new house here in Cal. They only had a flat before.'

'Where is it?'

'Park Road South.'

Then it would be an enormous villa, requiring a squad of servants.

Bernadette left the table early. When she'd gone, I asked Lydia: 'Will the R.K. be at the dance tonight?'

She replied, 'I'm not his social secretary, Jim', which of course was not a denial.

III

The Debating Society dance was held at Wright's Hotel, adjacent to the beautiful St John's Church, and near enough to the river to make the hot night air brackish. Lydia, Bernadette and I went there in a two-horse tonga with the Pooles. Dougie Poole was already 'a bit squiffed' as Margaret cheerfully informed us. She was a pleasant woman, but it was possible that she didn't have any imagination, and so couldn't see what her husband was doing to himself.

Uniformed Indians made a guard of honour as we stepped down from our tonga on to the gravelled forecourt of Wright's. They formed two ranks, and in between them stood William Askwith. As a physical specimen he looked so featureless that he displayed his fine dinner suit almost to advantage.

'Our host awaits,' said Margaret Poole, peering through the

tonga window.

'Why's he the host?' I whispered to Lydia. 'He hasn't bought Wright's Hotel as well, has he?'

'He's president of the Debating Society. You twit.'

Askwith greeted the three of us very graciously, and in the absence of any other tongas rolling up just then, we embarked on a little chit-chat.

'What does the Debating Society actually debate?' I enquired.

'Well, let me see now,' said Askwith. 'We had one only last week: "The motor car is the future of passenger transport, and railways must act accordingly."'

'I hope the motion was defeated.'

'I'm delighted to say that it was defeated resoundingly, Captain Stringer.'

'And all those who voted against will be sacked,' put in Dougie Poole, which Askwith did not like, and tried to ignore. 'But our gatherings do not always take the form of debates,' he continued. 'We have lectures as well. Last month, Mr Joseph Miller from signalling gave us "The Lighter Side of Block Telegraph Working".'

'Went down a storm, he did,' said Dougie Poole.

Askwith inclined his blank white head towards me. 'Perhaps, Captain Stringer, you would care to entertain us on the subject of . . . Well, how about "Railway Police Work at Home and Abroad"?'

I eyed him. There was no expression on his face; then again, there never *could* be any expression on his face. The Pooles had already gone into the hotel, and taken Bernadette with them. Askwith was turning to Lydia. 'You look are looking absolutely lovely, Mrs Stringer.'

Lydia had wrestled the cashmere wrap back off Bernadette;

and she wore a short, silvery dress she had been rather uncertain about. She'd been turning over the problem for days: could she carry it off? I thought so, and evidently so did Askwith, but now another tonga was rolling up, with a motor taxi chugging impatiently behind it, so we stepped into the hotel.

'Well, it would be a shame if he was proved corrupt,' said Lydia as we walked through the lobby, 'given that he was so nice about my dress.'

'Hold on,' I said. 'Who's trying to prove him corrupt?'

'I should say that was the theme of your incessant questions about him.'

'You realise it's essential he doesn't get wind of my suspicions?'

'You think he already has done.'

'You seem very confident about reading my mind.'

'One doesn't exactly have to be the Martian Girl.'

'Who's the Martian Girl?'

'A very famous mind-reader on the halls.'

'I've never heard of her.'

We had already waved away two bearers offering champagne, and I wished we could explain that Lydia was teetotal, and I was on quinine, because they all looked so disappointed.

Lydia said, 'You think he staged that attack on the train and the wrong man was killed by mistake. And you think your Major Fisher might have been involved.'

'That's pretty unlikely, isn't it?'

'But it's what you think.'

This particular dance floor was chequered black and white like a chessboard, and the spirit lights on the white tablecloths were all glimmering pinks. The French windows were open on to the dark lawn, where pink and white Chinese lanterns hung from the trees, before the blackness of St John's churchyard took over.

I had a waltz with Lydia. Afterwards, we separated, and I saw Askwith entering, having presumably greeted all the important guests. He was deep in conversation with Superintendent Christopher Bennett. Naturally the two would know each other. They were talking in low voices, and Bennett looked glum, in contrast to his wife Mary, who was following behind and talking excitedly to a woman I didn't know: 'We did think of the Great Eastern for the reception, but in the end it had to be the Grand. I mean, you only get married once, don't you? One hopes so anyway!' She appeared to have found the one woman in Calcutta who hadn't heard all about her wedding.

I turned towards the dancing. Claudine, Ann and Bernadette all had partners, none of whom was the R.K. I became aware that Dougie Poole was swaying by my side, whisky in hand.

I said, 'I'm told the Hindus believe all life is the dance of Shiva.'

'Yes, but Shiva dances to destroy the world,' said Poole, 'so it's not quite as light-hearted as it sounds.' He took another sip of his peg. 'There's Shiva the destroyer, Vishnu the . . . preserver, Brahma the creator. You can remember it because . . . no, it's gone.'

'How's life in traffic?' I said.

'Oh,' he said, 'the goods traffic is increasing constantly, but the more goods traffic you have, the more goods *wagons* you have to keep tabs on.' A photographer and his assistant were photographing the dancers, perhaps for the *East Indian Railway Magazine*. 'You know the trouble with goods wagons?' said Poole. 'They've got *wheels* on 'em, so they're liable to go just anywhere. But how's everything going on in the police department, Jim? Any ideas about this snake blighter?'

'Well, that's not my investigation.'

'Lucky you.'

I looked about until I located Superintendent Christopher Bennett. He was trying to light his pipe in the garden, just beyond the French windows.

'It's his,' I said.

From his appearance it was odds-on that Bennett *had* read the snake report in the newspaper. He attempted a smile when he looked towards me though. I turned again towards the dancers. Lydia was in amongst them. I did not know her partner, but he was old and grey enough not to be counted a rival. It was accepted between the two of us that dancing was not my strong point. Dougie Poole had drifted away. He was hunting up another peg, and every so often he appeared to be buffeted by a strong wind that didn't exist. Why did he drink? He would be on a good wage, perhaps fifteen hundred rupees per mensem; he had a flat full of servants; regular trips to the hills, and his daughter, Ann, had been to good schools in England and Calcutta . . .

Lydia and Bernadette came up, and they were excited after the dance, as if they'd come off a fairground ride. I raised the question of Dougie Poole.

Lydia said, 'Did you notice his dinner suit?'

'What about it? It's too big.'

'Yes, and he's wearing a white dinner jacket.'

'We all are.'

'And a wing collar with it. That's wrong.'

'I don't see anything wrong with it.'

'I know. That's why I had to return the wing collars you bought in Port Said.'

'Mr Poole's lovely really,' Bernadette put in. 'Ann adores him, but he's a bit nuts, and practically always blotto. Claudine told me that *her* dad's warned Mr Poole about his drinking.'

Lydia turned away to take a fruit punch from a bearer.

'I wonder what's eating him,' I said to Lydia. 'Poole, I mean.'

'He doesn't get on with India; never has done since he came out here the year after the war. *This* year, he went down with prickly heat in February – before it was hot. You know it was Margaret who dragged him out here?'

'That's it,' said Bernadette. 'It was the only way they were going to get a reasonable number of servants.'

'You see,' said Lydia, 'Margaret's father had been in the Indian Army and he loved the life – very social, you know, and played all sports, whereas poor old Dougie's a duffer at everything like that.'

'He's originally from a spot called Walthamstow,' Bernadette put in, 'and Claudine says he's Walthamstow all over and that's why Ann has a London accent.'

'She probably says you have a Yorkshire accent,' said Lydia.

'Of course she does.'

'Any more gossip about him?' I said.

'*Yes*,' said Bernadette. 'We were talking about the snake attacks this afternoon, and Ann just happened to mention that her dad had kept snakes as a boy, and he'd written away to one of the boys' papers about them.'

'Why?'

'Asking advice. The letter was printed in the paper, anyhow.'

'What paper?'

'I don't know. Why don't you ask him?'

I would do. I had thought that if Poole had any involvement in the bad business going on around me, it might be that he'd sent in the dossier complaining about corruption in the traffic department. I certainly had not fingered him as the loony putting the snakes on the trains.

I found Poole again a few minutes later. He'd got hold of a bottle of champagne, and was scrutinising the label. When I came up to him, I looked at it as well. It read, 'Dry Elite.'

'*That's* a misnomer,' he said.

Dougie Poole had himself brought up the subject of the snakes just a moment before, so I felt at liberty to wade right in.

'What do *you* reckon about the snakes?' I said.

'I reckon it must be the nationalist Johnnies going after all the top box-wallahs in the first class carriages,' he said. 'The snake would be a good weapon for them. Comes from the soil of India. So it's like turning India itself against the imperialist enemy.'

Having finished his glass of champagne, he was pouring himself another one.

I said, 'I've heard *you* had an interest in snakes, when you were a lad?'

'I kept a snake,' he said at length.

'What sort?'

'Oh, grass snake.'

'Of course, they're not poisonous.'

'Venomous, Jim, venomous. No, they're not that. And they're beautiful as well. Greenest thing you ever saw. Like jade. I became very attached to him.'

'I believe you sent away to a certain paper about the snake?'

'You *are* well up on all this.'

'I had it from the girls, you know.'

'Yes. Well, when he was dying I sent away . . . for advice. To the captain.'

'Captain who?'

'*The Captain*, Jim. Paper of that name.'

'Really? I had that as a boy as well.'

'Did you really Jim? Did you love "Tales from the Indian Railways"? "Founded on fact", they were . . . I don't think. By H. Hervey, "illustrated by the author". Did you notice how all the stories in *The Captain* were "illustrated by the author"? I think they must have been hard up. But "Tales of the Indian Railways" . . . What about that runaway train load of elephants with the monkey driving? Implausible in itself, but when you add in the *other* runaway trainload of elephants, coming the opposite way on the same line, also with a monkey driving . . . Bit hard to credit, even when you're ten.'

'What did they say about your snake?'

'They said the snake was likely too cold, so I put it in the cupboard with the airing tank.'

'Do any good?'

He looked at me with his sad, down-pointing eyes.

'Not a bit. Didn't last more than another two days.'

The guitar man in the band started making that chugging noise; another of the speciality dances was getting underway. I looked into the garden. There were as many people out there as in. It was backstage, so to speak: men smoking, women adjusting each other's dresses and scanning their programmes. The church beyond was just a dark silhouette. Near the French windows, I noticed, one of the white-clad servants was presiding over a table on which stood not food or drink but a display of fancy, tasselled photograph albums. Dougie Poole having embarked on another of his weaving walks through the crowd, I approached this table, and I took out my reading glasses as the bearer presented one of the albums for my inspection. It showed past dances of the East Indian Railway Debating Society, labelled with the dates. The first dance had been held in 1904, so this present one was the nineteenth, not a very notable anniversary. Back in 1904, tails had been worn. As I leafed through the pages, I saw how these became ordinary dinner suits, and the women's hair and dresses got shorter, the latter quite excitingly so. A woman was beside me. She said, 'That was my husband,' and she was pointing down to the page I had open, which was the page for the previous year: 1922.

She was a woman in early middle age, beautiful in the Anglo-Indian way, and she wore black. She was one of the very few Anglo-Indians in the room. I looked again at where she pointed and saw photograph of a smiling, handsome man of medium features and perfectly symmetrical moustache. It was the late John Young. The woman introduced herself as Sonia Young, and over the sound of the band, I tried to commiserate with her loss, and to say something of my close involvement in her husband's final hours. But she already knew. She had caught sight of me at the Institute.

'I should apologise for my son. He was belabouring you.' She looked slightly less Indian than her husband, but had a slightly *more* Indian way of speaking. 'He is always *resenting*.'

'I should think he's entitled to a few resentments,' I said, 'after what happened.'

'No,' said Sonia Young, 'because this world is open to him.' She indicated the dance. 'His father made sure of that. But he chooses to plough his own furrow.'

'He is not in here then?' I said, indicating the book.

Sonia Young shook her head. 'John and I though – plenty of times.' Taking the book from my hands, she leafed through the pages, and the years. 'We were quite a bit thinner then,' she said, smiling. She was a very straightforward person.

I said, 'Perhaps your son sees a different India emerging.' It was a strange thing to be saying, with the Elephant Glide or whatever it might be, yo-yoing away in the background, and Sonia Young didn't think much of my suggestion because she said, 'No . . . It is only a question of his temperament. He has a poor temperament. He gets it from me.'

'Now I don't believe that for a minute,' I said.

'You are calling me a liar?' she said, with a raised eyebrow.

'Not a bit of it,' I said.

'You've met John. You saw *his* temperament. You know it's not from him.'

'Of course not.'

'So what *are* you saying, exactly?' she said, laughing.

'That's a good question, that is,' I said, putting the photograph album back down, which caused the Indian in charge of it to bow at me.

Sonia Young said, 'Do you think it was these notorious criminal tribes, then, that killed my husband?'

'The evidence points that way,' I said.

Mrs Sonia Young didn't seem convinced about the criminal tribes, but at least she didn't appear to think that *I'd* done it.

The music, and therefore the dancing, had stopped. The band members were leaving the stage for a breather, pushing towards the French windows and lighting cigarettes. To my left, I could hear Mary Bennett saying, 'The bouquet? That was red roses, just as if we'd been marrying in Surrey! The cake was done at Firpo's. Well of course they *are* the best.'

Her prized husband, Superintendent Christopher Bennett, was standing about three feet away from her and looking spare. Once again, he acknowledged me, raising his hand in greeting. I thought he might be coming over, and so I turned to Mrs Young, saying, 'This is a colleague of mine, Superintendent Christopher Bennett.'

'I'm sorry, who?' said Mrs Young. She still had half an eye on the tasselled album, and the photographs of the life she'd lost; and Christopher Bennett wasn't coming over anyway.

IV

Moving through the ballroom, I heard, 'The city engineer won't walk under that veranda, so I'm dammed if I will.'

Walking further, I heard, '. . . the ladies' hockey season, that amusing prelude to the season of masculine hockey . . .'

And then I heard, 'There was this couple dancing at the Trocadero . . .'

Dougie Poole was embarking on the Gurkha joke, the one Canon Peter Selwyn had told me in the Bengal Club. It was evidently doing the rounds.

'Why the Troc?' someone asked.

'You'll see,' said Poole, and he paused, frowning. 'No you won't. They were dancing *somewhere* anyhow, somewhere in London . . . So they're waltzing away, and the woman says to the man, "Do you come here often?" and he says, "No, not often because I'm in the army out in India, and I'm just home for a while on leave."'

A dozen sahibs and memsahibs were clustered around Poole, who was leaning against a food table. They all looked very worried as he pressed on with the joke: 'So *she* says, "Oh, you're in a good regiment, I'm sure," and *he* says, "It's a Gurkha regiment actually." She says, "Really? But I thought the men in the Gurkhas were all black," and he says, "No dear, only our privates are black."'

142

Two of the memsahibs departed at this point – and sharpish. The band leader was announcing some new speciality, and Poole had to shout to be heard above him: "'But my dear,' says the woman, "how simply marvellous!'"

One man laughed.

Somebody had alerted Margaret Poole, and she came fast across the room. She took her husband by the shoulders, by which time all his listeners had moved away. 'Douglas,' she said. 'You've had enough,' and she turned towards me, saying, 'Of course, he'd had enough an hour ago.'

Two hours ago would have been nearer the mark, but she didn't seem very upset. Margaret Poole spoke to her husband as if he were a child: 'A peg is one part whisky to five parts water, dear. Not the other way round. And you have to get up early to go to Asansol.'

There was a look of amusement on her face, if anything. Margaret Poole was rather tanned and capable-looking. Her frizzy hair might have been colourless but it sprouted very healthily. Dougie Poole had never felt the 'Call of the East'; his wife had felt it. She was the sort of Englishwoman who was born to be on the back of an elephant. I asked a bearer for a glass of iced water, and, murmuring something about the great heat, I passed it to Margaret, who passed it to Dougie, whom she had now placed in a chair. It was pretty obvious that she cared for him, which perhaps made things worse for him, since he might be wondering why, and not finding a reason. I wondered why Poole had to go to Asansol. It was the best part of a day's journey. Probably for a meeting about coal traffic: Asansol was a great centre for that. The meeting would likely be on Monday, and he would be travelling there tomorrow – on the Sunday – so as to arrive in good time.

Leaving Dougie Poole in the capable hands of his wife, I resolved to seek out the bottle of Beck's beer to which I was entitled. I found one at a corner table, where I lit a Gold Leaf. Blowing smoke, I thought ahead to the business *I* had in hand for Monday: an early visit with Deo Rana to a certain storeroom at the spot called Sheoraphuli, followed by an appointment with Professor Hedley Fleming of the Zoological Gardens; and I tried to see how the snakes, the Night Mail shooting and the possibility of corruption in the traffic department might all fit together. I hadn't got very far, when a long-faced, rather religious-looking woman said, 'Have I already given you one of these?' It was Eleanor Askwith, and the leaflet concerned her charitable effort, the St Dunstan's Fund.

'You have actually.'

At this rate, I might have to make a donation. She turned aside as the music stopped, and I saw that the band was vacating the stage to make way for her husband, William Askwith. He thanked us all for coming to the Nineteenth Annual East Indian Railway Debating Society dance. He told us how such occasions as this celebrated the fellowship of the Railway, the most important in India. These were difficult and uncertain times for the Company, with the government about to take over, but we in this room were united in a single aim: to serve the public. He then put in a word for that part-timers' corps, the East Indian Railway Regiment, in which he was a major (new recruits were always welcomed), and also for the St Dunstan's charitable effort, whose patroness was his wife, and which was a purely voluntary effort, with no paid workers, and much in need of donations. There was then a toast, and three cheers for the Railway.

After the speech, I went to the palatial Gentlemen's, where I drained off the Beck's beer. When I returned, a new dance was in progress, but I could not see Lydia or Bernadette on the floor. I had also not seen them during the speech. I circulated the dance floor and, walking past the French windows, I heard Lydia's voice, slightly raised, coming from the garden. As I approached her, I heard Mary Bennett: 'Well, in the end common sense prevailed, so I wore the white charmeuse trimmed with diamante and sprays of...'

Lydia stood in a group of people clustered under the branches of what I believed to be an ebony tree. Pretty Chinese lanterns hung from the black branches, but the conversation had taken a heavy turn.

'Of *course* socialism can work in India,' Lydia was saying to a railway officer.

'My dear lady, I beg to disagree. It is quite incompatible with the religion, as all these Congress-wallahs are most uncomfortably aware.'

'Which religion?' Lydia enquired. 'Hinduism?'

'Naturally, yes. We have our classes, they have their castes – it's much the same.'

'Caste is fading.'

'Is it my dear? Tell that to the untouchables sleeping in the gutters of Chowringhee.'

'There is a great principle of egalitarianism in the religion,' said Lydia.

'Of *what?*' enquired her opponent.

'Of equality,' said Lydia. 'In Hindu philosophy we are all manifestations of God. We are all sacred.'

'*I'm* not,' said one old buffer lighting a cigar.

'It is held that we are all one,' the wife pressed on, and her opponent eyed her thoughtfully. Perhaps he was thinking her rather beautiful, as I was just then. He said, 'You would have only one class only on the trains, I suppose?'

'Classes on trains are neither here nor there,' said Lydia, and the man eyed her for a further interval. He was trying to work up some sort of conclusion.

'We all have to *stick together*,' he said slowly. 'But we are not all *one*.'

The group began to break up; Lydia turned to me.

I said, 'Have you seen Bernadette?'

'She's around somewhere,' she said, waving vaguely in the direction of the dark churchyard.

She did not seem to care for the job of chaperone, which surely did fall to the mother of a girl. I followed a line of white lights to the low railing that separated hotel from churchyard. The air was soft and thick and hot, and full of the chirping of crickets. I walked once around the church, which had a low yellow light burning inside it, and coming round to the far side, I saw a couple lying on the grass. They embraced while lying on their sides in a sort of horizontal dance hold. The woman was looking at me, so I said 'Good evening', and she replied politely, just as though she were not practically in the middle of the sex act. I stepped back over the railings, then back into the ballroom, where a speciality dance was in progress; what they called a 'spot dance', with a small number of couples showing off in a circle of admirers. Ann Poole was in there, so the Pooles had not gone home, in spite of Dougie's condition. Ann danced with a regimental type – his shoes were exceptionally shiny, at any rate. Claudine Askwith was also there, also equipped with what appeared to be a young officer.

It was then that I saw Bernadette. She was dancing with the

R.K. She seemed to keep pushing him away to contemplate him, and after every contemplation, she would whirl him around, then pull him tightly towards her, as though highly satisfied with the result of her examination. I wondered how differently this would look if they were in love. I believed it would look more or less the same. I could see nothing but a world of trouble waiting for the girl, and so, when the music stopped, I walked directly over to Bernadette and took her by the arm, peeling her away from the R.K., who was beginning to make a salaam of some sort towards me.

I said to Bernadette, 'I have to speak to you urgently.'

'*What?*'

'In the garden.'

Quite surprisingly, she did follow me out, and Lydia was there on the lawn. 'We're going home now,' I said to the two of them.

'We are not,' said Bernadette. '*Why* are we?'

'Because the dance has ended.'

'No it hasn't.'

'For you, it has.'

'This is ridiculous,' said Bernadette.

'It is *slightly*,' said Lydia, folding her arms and eyeing me. Well, they were in it together. Bernadette made a move back towards the dance floor.

'We're going!' I shouted after her, at which she veered off towards the black tree. She picked a Chinese lantern off the tree branch as though it had been an apple, and spun around hurling it towards me. The little candle inside flew out through the top and made a falling arc of light, a small shooting star, before extinguishing itself on the grass. I was hit by the paper concertina and a spray of hot wax.

Tempting though it was to land her a clout, I knew that was out of the question – had been since she was nine or ten. I stood red-faced, pointing to the French windows. Lydia took her, holding on to her arm; I followed, and as we grimly skirted the dance floor, the band struck up. On the hotel driveway, two tongas were waiting. Bernadette was shouting about how we must be 'screwy' if we thought we could stop her seeing whoever she wanted to see; and how she hated all the 'flat tyres' she met at the 'lethal' supper dances at the De Grey Rooms, and the 'grungy' tea dances at Terry's Emporium, these being the social highlights of York life that she had sampled and found wanting.

We got her into the tonga anyway, whereupon she fell silent, as the prisoners do when you put them in the Black Maria. She knew the game was up – at least for now. It was only when I took my seat in the tonga that I saw, through the window, William Askwith standing outside the front door of the hotel. He had resumed his hostly position, and was inspecting his pocket watch, albeit with face blank as usual. Who was he waiting for, now that the dance was almost over? As our tonga rolled away over the gravel, another was approaching. Both vehicles were going at a lick, and so I only had a fleeting glimpse of a large head slowly turning.

I believed it had been Major Fisher inside the tonga.

Chapter Seven

I

I woke shortly before dawn on Monday. I dressed in the bath-room so as not to disturb the wife. All ready and laid out on the cabinet were cigarettes, pocket book, revolver. I exited the suite as quietly as possible, and put my boots on outside the door. As I walked through the dimly lit lobby, I was surprised to see sever-al of the uniformed bearers sleeping on the couches or the floor, and to hear snoring coming from behind the reception desk. I found the chowkidar sleeping in his lodge, and I had to wake him so that he would open the gates of the hotel compound and let me out. I stepped out into the soft green darkness of Calcutta, where the first market stalls were being put up on Chowringhee, but the trams had not yet started, and nor had the heat . . . so I could walk fast. There were some cyclists about, but not the or-derly bicycling clerks. The early chaps were weirder. One came out of the gloom on a tricycle with two chairs belted on the back. Then came another, with another two chairs, followed by a *pair* of tricyclists carrying between them the table corresponding to the chairs. They all turned into Esplanade Row, and the latter two shouted as they co-ordinated, but they did not wake the little sepoys who slept on pavement mattresses, like so many toy sol-diers fallen over.

Fairlie Place was quiet. For the first time, I saw no bathers on the Armenian Ghat, and no traffic block on the Howrah Bridge. But by the time I had crossed the river, there was light in the day; my hat had become heavy, and Howrah was fully alive, with the cranes swinging over the barges at the jetties, the men shouting, tongas arriving and departing, and the air full of the burning of Bengali coal. I entered the station. On the concourse, the crowds swirled while the engines waited, fuming beyond the platform gates.

I made for gate three, where a stopping train for Moghalsarai was about to set off along the Grand Chord. It would be calling at the spot called Sheoraphuli.

Deo Rana was waiting at the gate as arranged. He saluted and handed over a square leathern case about eight inches by eight. I lifted the lid of the case. Inside was a bit of kit called a Mandelette Picture-Taking Machine. 'Easy to operate?' I said, and Deo Rana shook his head.

'Buggeration,' I said, until I remembered that in Deo's case this meant yes.

'Even for little child,' he said.

Beyond the gate, the train was being boarded by means of the usual free-for-all.

'Would you care to come in first class with me, Deo?'

'Thank you, sahib, I would like.'

By agreeing, he was putting himself in the way of the snakes; and that was exactly *why* he had agreed. We located the one first class carriage and climbed up. We had not booked, and it appeared we could take our pick of the seats. Walking along the hot, dusty corridor we passed one compartment after another with not a soul inside. The whole carriage, in fact, was empty. I dragged open one of the doors, and as I was stepping in, Deo

Rana said, 'I first, huzoor.'

'Nonsense,' I said, and so we split the duty of checking the compartment for snakes.

We took our seats, and Deo Rana said, 'Webley gun, huzoor. You have?'

I took the piece from my shoulder holster and handed it over.

'Comes very handy,' he said. Deo Rana liked guns – guns and snakes.

After finding all in order with the Webley, he returned it to me, and we sat back.

We waited for the sound of the pea whistle. I checked my watch: it was six fifteen, and we had been due away at 6.12. We waited a further minute.

'They are not hurrying up at all,' said Deo.

I had thought I heard raised voices from the platform, and now they came again. Telling Deo Rana to sit tight, I quit the compartment and stepped down on to the platform again. A party of Europeans with bags and suitcases were rowing with the Indian train guard. Their leader was a young English fellow.

'Yes, I daresay first class is, as you say "most height of luxury" but we don't want to go in first.'

'But you are having tickets and bookings for first itself.'

'But we want to travel in second, and we want you to find us an empty compartment.'

'But there *is* no empty, sahib.'

Now a woman stepped forward from the party: 'Look we're quite happy to go in third class if necessary. We just don't want to get attacked by poisonous snakes, is that so unreasonable?'

A conference was taking place between another two of the males in the part, and they now took the guard aside, and began a low muttering with him. One of the Europeans took out his pocket book. They were offering baksheesh; offering to pay not to go in first . . . and being turned down by the looks of it. Either way, the original fellow had now lost patience. He strode over to the guard, shouting, 'Look, you go and take some bloody Indians out of second class and put them into bloody first!'

'Sahib, that is impossibility.'

'What are you talking about, man? They'll jump at the chance to go first class.'

'Sahibs, train is late. I am blowing whistle.'

And as I leapt back up, he did so, and the train began drawing away, the locomotive barking violently, and giving a long, shrieking whistle as though from annoyance at the delay. Regaining our compartment, I told Deo Rana what had occurred, at the same time as opening the window blinds to verify that – yes – the Europeans had remained on the platform rather than risk the snakes. I wondered how many other, similar scenes had occurred at Howrah in recent days. It occurred to me that if the perpetrator put even one serpent in second or third, then he might single-handedly start to reverse the tremendous increases in ridership seen over the recent years; but he – or they – seemed to be fixated on first.

As we pulled away, I sat down and began to inspect the picture-taking machine. The big feature was that it could take pictures without the need of plates, films, printing or dark room, and so no third parties need know what you'd photographed. Fisher and I had been equipped with one apiece, and he'd already used his, I believed, to take pictures of unguarded entrances to certain railway properties. This was the first time I'd used mine, and I was doing so at the suggestion of Deo Rana, who'd booked the thing out of the police office stores on my behalf. You pointed it, and pressed the button (there was only one), and the image came out on what resembled a postcard: one of a dozen or so held in the cartridge attached to the back of the contraption. The thing was fully loaded anyhow, and there was a flash bulb attachment. I set it aside, and began looking out of the window. Deo Rana was doing the same, and his face betrayed no expression as he contemplated the ragged people who made their homes on the margins of the lines, and who at this time of day could be seen breakfasting on low-loaders parked in sidings, or making their ablutions on the track ballast.

On aggregate, the Grand Chord headed west, but it curved north in its early stages, and we were running a little way inland of the milky morning river, over which the sun was climbing. After a while, the factory chimneys of Calcutta gave out, and we were into a region of scrub and paddy fields, with occasional thickets of palms, and crumbling blue or orange buildings that looked temple-like to me. But then the factories (jute mills in the main) resumed, with the mercury climbing steadily all the while, so that I had to mop my brow, causing Deo Rana to turn towards me with what might have been the beginnings of a smile. 'Too much of heat, sahib,' he said.

After twenty minutes, we called at Bally, where the American tourist, Walter Gill, had been found dead in company with a saw-scale viper. Half an hour later, we climbed down at Sheoraphuli, and the sound of the train pulling away was replaced by the sound of gulls circling overhead. They – and the hot breeze blowing over from the river – made the place seem like the seaside. The station was small, and quiet. The main part of town, and the river docks, lay beyond the opposite platform, which could be reached by a dusty footbridge. There was no local man to greet us. Well, we had not been expected . . . but we *had* been seen, and the door of a station office closed further along the platform on which we stood. We walked along the deserted platform, passing a drinking fountain on which was posted a sign: 'Help the Railway to Help You', and below was a list of instructions, such as 'Do not take a bath in the drinking fountain'. Beyond the platform buildings, and the door that had closed, we turned left into a station yard: a square of hard mud. In one corner was a cow; in the opposite corner, a man sat on his haunches, smoking elegantly. Near the cow was the place to which I had been directed by the anonymous letter: a small blockhouse, with padlocked door. There was a sign on the door, and Deo Rana read it aloud in a thoughtful way, as he liked to do, to practise his English: 'Please Knock'. With one kick, he smashed down the door, and we entered the blockhouse.

The first thing I saw inside the blockhouse was a pasteboard box, on which appeared the words 'Whisky, when it is good, is the embodiment of progress and happiness'. It was full of bottles of Dewar's whisky. The room was crammed full of boxes and crates, about a third holding types of whisky, and it was all the good stuff: Dewar's, White Horse, Old Smuggler, and none of your 'Loch Lomands'. There was a good deal of brandy into the bargain, mainly Hennessy's. There was an ice chest in the corner, and that was full of bottles of Beck's. There was no ice in the chest, and the bottles were somewhat dusty, but they were highly saleable nonetheless. There were cigars and cigarettes, mainly Piccadillies. Behind me, Deo Rana cried 'Watch, huzoor!' and I tensed and turned with gun in hand, but he was only indicating a supply of silver plate watches, made by the Imperial Company of Calcutta. Some of these goods might have been the legitimate possessions of the East

Indian Railway. The whisky might, for example, have been purchased for station dining rooms, but even the items so acquired
did not belong in this dark and dusty lock-up, and most of the
booty here had simply been lifted from the private-owner wagons
entrusted to the railway for transit.

I commenced to photograph the stuff, as Deo Rana stood
guard outside. Across the yard, the squatting Indian remained at
his post, although he had now tossed away his cigarette stub, and
was grinning broadly. I had pressed the button of the picture-
taking machine for the third time, when a great clattering came
from the direction of the station. Setting down the camera, I
ran, with Deo Rana, on to the 'down' platform on which we had
alighted. The footbridge was shaking violently, and resounding
to the clatter of boots. They belonged to some functionary or
other of Sheoraphuli station – I only saw the chap fleetingly as he
came off the bridge and exited the station on the opposite side.
He was the guilty party anyhow, and the long and tedious business of running him to earth would now begin, but that would be
for others to do, and they would be armed with my report. I had
no intention of chasing the fellow through a foreign town with
the temperature at a hundred and five degrees. But Deo Rana, I
sensed, was disappointed not to be able to do so.

II

On the afternoon of that Monday, I rode a tonga to the Calcutta
Zoological Gardens. I arrived early, with half an hour to kill before my appointment with Professor Hedley Fleming. As in London Zoo, which I had once visited, there were queues at all the

entrances, and elephants wandered about with grinning children on them. But whereas in London the elephant drivers wore blue uniforms with brass buttons, the elephant men here – mahuts by name – wore hardly any clothes at all. Also, an electric railway ran through this zoo. It ran too fast, like a toy that was about to break. It emitted a whirring noise that could be heard even when it was out of sight, and made the heat of the afternoon seem hotter.

In the reptile house, there was a different kind of humming – from its own electricity generator. It was a hot, dark blue hall. There were ornamental trees, ornamental ponds, and long benches. Glass panels were set into the walls, and behind these were snakes, if you could spot them, but many of the glass cases presented an apparent puzzle: find the snake. Most seemed asleep, buried under sand or bits of log, but when one of them did move, it was thrilling, on account of the winding and unwinding occurring simultaneously. In their oddness the snakes were on a par with the elephants, but elephants knew they were odd, and so they had a kind of resigned look about them, whereas the snakes had absolutely no expression at all. Like the worst of the villains I had come across, they were in some parallel world. All sorts of people you knew looked like elephants, sheep or monkeys, but a snake . . . You might say a snake looked like a small, bald, bad-tempered man whose face had been made worse by having been in a bad house fire.

Hedley Fleming's office was attached to the reptile house, and at half past three a scientific-looking Indian in a white coat took me from the office into a dark passage, which was the service corridor for the snake enclosures. This was closed off to the public, and the many black doors set into the right-hand wall were bolted shut. In the gloom ahead of me I could see another man in a white coat. He was closing and bolting one of the doors like a prison warder, but he also had alongside him a trolley of the kind used in hospitals, and I had learnt from the *Calcutta Directory* that Hedley Fleming had practised as a medical doctor in London before coming out to India. He turned towards me. He had a thin face, curly blond hair, pale blue eyes behind round wire glasses. He looked like the cleverest boy in the form. He shook my hand without really looking at me, Meanwhile the Indian who had introduced us did not depart as I expected, but took hold of the trolley and pushed it along to the next door. The trolley squeaked badly. Upon it was a mix-up of odd-shaped glasses and bottles, some rubber tubing, a pump-like thing, and what I slowly realised was an outsized single white canvas glove – a glove for the hand of a giant: his left hand. Two of the bottles, I saw, had treacly yellow stuff in them. In the semi-darkness, we walked past some metal boxes with holes in them. They'd been put on the left side of the corridor. Thick black cables that were themselves snake-like ran along the floor of the corridor. On the right side, the next doors were coming up, and these were padlocked. The squeaking of the trolley stopped, because the scientific Indian had left off pushing it. He wasn't overly chatty, this fellow, and nor was his governor. But Professor Hedley Fleming did now turn to me, saying, 'One more call to make, Captain Stringer, then you will have my full attention.'

He was unshackling one of the two doors we stood alongside – the bigger of the two. As befitted his junior status, the Indian was unshackling the smaller one. The doors did not come right down to the ground, but were more like hatches. Professor Fleming stepped back as he swung open his door, and there was heap of gravel, a grey log and, some three feet beyond that, a pane of glass. I was on the wrong side of that pane of glass. On the right side of it, but still looking horrified, was a small Indian boy, a paying customer of the reptile house. His head just came up to the level of the glass; his mouth opened and closed twice. I could not hear him, but I thought I knew what he had said: 'Wah-wah!' Observing that the boy had taken a single pace back – and that with the safety of the glass between him and whatever was in the enclosure – I took *two* steps back. The Indian had got the smaller trapdoor open, and the professor was putting on the single glove. As he did so, a snake's head came into view from the right-hand side of the rectangle of light revealed by the open door. The snake's head was not on the gravel, but about four feet above it, and therefore near the top of the rectangle of light. It was a king, and here was the rope trick all over again.

Beyond the glass, the Indian boy had now turned sideways on, and was shouting at the top of his voice through two cupped hands for someone he knew – mother or father, no doubt – to come and take a look. If he wasn't careful, a keeper would come and chuck him out for making such a racket, but on my side of the glass, I couldn't hear him at all, and nor could the king, the king being deaf. The king was moving his head up and down. The other, smaller door must have given the Indian access to king's tail end, and the Indian was busying himself at the trolley again, pouring water into a saucer. He then put this into the aperture revealed by the small door. The king's head was still swaying about in the bigger rectangle. The king's hood was open wide, and I was hypnotised by its weirdness. It was like a case of flat mumps. A hood should be above, not below, your head. It was as though the snake had been lying down on one of the dusty roads of Bengal when a motor car had come along and run it over just behind its head, so flattening out the neck.

Professor Hedley Fleming stuck his left hand – the hand with the big glove on it – into the enclosure, and held it in front of the snake's head, like a policeman stopping traffic. The snake looked at the glove, then smoothly pulled its head back out of the rectangle of light so that it was lost to my view. The Indian was now looking through his own opened trapdoor with folded arms. His posture suggested . . . not pleasure exactly. It was more that something had occurred that did not surprise him. I walked over, took up position behind his back, and looked. The snake's head was at *this* end now, and it was drinking the water from the saucer. But the scene was soon interrupted, for both men were now shackling their doors. The Indian then walked over to the trolley, and began pushing it back to the door by which we had come in, with Professor Fleming following. The trolley squeaked loudly.

III

I put it to Professor Hedley Fleming that he had trained the snake.

'I wouldn't put it quite as strongly as that,' he said. 'The king cobra knows that if he turns away from the raised glove, there'll be a drink of water waiting for him.'

'A drink of water is enough reward?'

Fleming nodded.

I said, 'Do you think you'll be able to build on that – take the training any further?'

'Unlikely.'

I wanted to observe that snakes seemed to have blanket policy of doing nothing appealing. They ate the worst possible food (rats or other snakes), and in killing people they caused the worst possible sorts of death. But Hedley Fleming was glancing at his watch. It was the second time he'd done it since we'd come into his office. He'd been willing to see me, just as a doctor is willing to give an appointment, and as with the doctor's appointment the time for chit-chat was limited. He had not offered me tea.

'About the poisonous snakes on the trains,' I said.

'Venomous,' he said. 'Poison is ingested. There are a couple of snakes in South America that have poison glands on the backs of their heads. If you ate one of those, then, yes, you'd be poisoned. Where the snake bites *you*, it's venomous.'

'I see,' I said. It was the second time I'd been corrected on this point.

Fleming's desk was in the middle of the room. Beyond it was a sort of laboratory table, and on the wall beyond that was one of those university photographs that clever people have on their walls to remind everyone how clever they are. It showed the massed ranks of their particular year of a particular college at Oxford or Cambridge, but Fleming's was too far away for me to make out the detail.

Hedley Fleming asked, 'Are you the officer investigating these cases? That wasn't clear from Mr Sermon's chit.'

'Not directly.'

'What does that mean?'

'I'm assisting a colleague.'

'Formally?'

'Yes,' I said, and so he had brought a lie out of me. 'The head of the investigation', I continued, 'is Superintendent Christopher Bennett. Do you know him?'

'Why should I know him?'

'Socially. Evidently six hundred people went to his wedding.'

Hedley Fleming eyed me. I didn't much care for him, and he didn't much care for me.

'You say "evidently",' he said. 'Weren't you there yourself?'

'It was before I came to India. He gave another party later, and I went to that.'

'Well *I* didn't, Captain Stringer. Now how can I help about the railway cases?'

I said, 'Is this the first you've heard of snakes being used as a weapon?'

'I've heard of it in native vendettas. Snakes put in people's houses.'

'Never on trains before?'

'Of course not.'

I said, 'We don't know exactly where in the compartments the snakes have been placed. I mean they must have been of sight, otherwise the victims wouldn't have entered the compartments in the first place.'

Hedley Fleming said, 'The logical place would be under the seats, wouldn't it? There's usually enough space there, from what I can recall.'

'Why would that be logical?'

'Snakes live in holes in the ground. They feel safer in a dark, restricted space.'

'Would they prefer to be in a restricted space with hard edges, or in a cloth bag or a rolled-up coat or dhoti?'

'In a restricted space with hard edges.'

'Even a restricted space where one side is open, like the underneath of a railway seat?'

'Yes.'

'And when you say "happy", what do you mean?'

'I mean the snake would stay there for a while.'

'Long enough to let a passenger come in and sit down?'

'Yes.'

'So a snake is quite happy in a snake charmer's basket?'

'Quite happy. Tell me, what was the latest death?'

'There were two on Monday. A sawscale viper killed an American tourist at Bally, and a common krait killed a retired colonel at Khana Junction. Is there any real difference in the effects of those two snakes?'

'The viper causes a very protracted and unpleasant death, which should appeal to the sadist.'

'What happens?'

'Extreme anaphylactic reaction.'

'Go on.'

'Within twenty minutes you'd be bleeding from every orifice. After a couple of days you'd have turned yellow and your organs would be shutting down.'

'If you were bitten on the arm, say, and you applied a tourniquet immediately, could that save you?'

Hedley Fleming looked at his watch again. He evidently didn't think much of the tourniquet idea, because he didn't even mention it. 'If you severed the arm immediately, you might have a chance.'

'And if you didn't?'

'Look, you're going to die anyway. If you mean what would happen to the arm, it would be three times its normal size after a few minutes.'

'And as for the krait . . .'

'The krait, like the cobra, is an elapid. It's a faster death, but still more unpleasant.'

'How?'

'The central nervous system shuts down completely after about ten minutes so you're fighting to breathe, but you're paralysed.'

'And on one occasion the *king* cobra was used.'

'For theatrical effect, no doubt.' Professor Fleming leant forward and for the first time there was a trace of animation about him. 'The king cobra is a most remarkable beast, Captain Stringer.'

'Why?'

'It's . . . enigmatic.'

'All snakes are enigmatic aren't they?'

'The king is a cut above, capable almost of a degree of . . . magnanimity.'

'He wasn't very magnanimous to Miss Schofield of Leamington Spa.'

'But she wasn't bitten, was she?' That was true, and it seemed Hedley had been following the cases in some detail, after all. 'A king has been known to merely . . . strike a man with his head, to give a kind of punch.'

'As a warning.'

'Exactly.'

I was revolving the idea of telling him about my own encounter with a king cobra, when Fleming said, 'I'm afraid I have a social engagement this evening, and I really must prepare for it.'

As we both rose, I said, 'What is the appeal of snakes? Is it a sort of morbid fascination?'

'No, Captain Stringer, it is not. About twenty-five thousand people a year die of snake bites in India, the majority in the central provinces of Bengal. There is at present no effective antivenom of any kind. It is in the hope of assisting in the search for one that I came to this city.'

So that was me told.

Coming out of the Zoological Gardens, and signalling without success for a tonga, I headed north for a minute, before crossing the ornamental bridge that seemed embarrassed to traverse the sunken green water of the crumbling canal called Tolly's Nullah; then I walked past the Telegraph Stores, and the Police Training School, coming to the junction with Lower Circular Road, where I contemplated the square mile of burnt grass that made up the race course and polo ground.

A motor car came up to the junction with all its widows down and I looked inside. The driver was Indian. In the rear seat sat Hedley Fleming in a white dinner jacket, and this set up a clash between his clever schoolboy aspect and the world of adult party-going, so that Fleming seemed caught halfway between scientist and socialite. I believed he saw me as the car paused, but either way, it drove on, turning left on to Lower Circular Road and making a spiral of dust in its wake.

An approaching tonga stopped for me, and this small success was accompanied by another. I had seen Hedley Fleming – in the guise he presented in the car rather than at the zoo – on a previous occasion, and not in the flesh, but in the photograph albums displayed at the Debating Society dance.

IV

An hour later, I was in the stifling lobby of Willard's Hotel, looking over the novels in its bookcase. I picked up *Plain Tales from the Hills* by Kipling. I thought I might take it downstairs to the basement music room, where I knew that Bernadette was practising dances with her friends, Ann Poole and Claudine Askwith. In a couple of hours' time, Bernadette would be *leaving* for the hills, so I could suggest she take the Kipling with her. It might begin the bridge-building after the disastrous ending of the Debating Society dance. I might also ask if they wanted some lemonades sent down.

I began to descend the staircase leading to the basement, but halfway down, I froze. I had heard a loud wail. I darted forward; the door of the music room was closed. I opened it, and Ann Poole was screaming into Bernadette's shoulder. They were in an embrace, and Bernadette was facing towards the door. Claudine Askwith was sitting at the piano, half turned towards Bernadette and Ann. As I entered the room, Ann continued to scream.

'What the hell's going on?'

From the piano, Claudine said, 'Ann's father was bitten by a snake. We've just had the news.'

'Is he all right?'

Bernadette eyed me for a while. It was the first time I had addressed her since the end of the Debating Society dance.

'He's absolutely fine,' she said at length, and Ann's scream redoubled.

'Was he on a train?'

Claudine nodded, and played a couple of notes. She said, 'He was going up to that place – what's it called again?'

'Asansol,' said Bernadette. 'The coal place. For a meeting. The snake was in the compartment. The first class – it was under the seat.'

'Where did it bite him?'

165

'On the foot.'

I had meant where on the line.

'On the boot, she means,' said Claudine. 'The top of his boot. The venom came out, but it just ran down the leather of his boot.'

Ann screamed again.

'Obviously she's very upset,' said Bernadette.

'Although we don't really know why,' added Claudine.

At this, Ann broke away from Bernadette to explain.

'It's just that Dad's been in very low water recently, and this coming on top of everything else. It was all too much.'

It had *been* too much. Now, it appeared, everything was fine. She did not seem tearful; she had simply been making a great deal of noise. I had always had her down as a level-headed girl, and now she was reverting to type.

'Ann,' I said, 'it is very important that your father makes a statement to the police. Has he done that?'

Ann nodded, and I got the following from her . . .

Her father, Dougie Poole, had been bitten on Sunday late afternoon as the Asansol train came into Ondal, which was two stops before Asansol itself. Poole assumed the snake had been in his compartment since Howrah, albeit sleeping or biding its time. This must be the case, he thought, because no other passenger had come into the compartment since departure from Howrah. Therefore nobody could have deposited a snake in the compartment. But then again, Poole himself had been asleep for much of the time – and no wonder, I thought, after the amount of drink he'd put away the night before. The snake had been identified as an Indian cobra, not a king. The deputy station master at Ondal had then killed it.

Poole had waited until this morning – Monday morning –

before telephoning through to his wife with the news. Ann herself had only just heard of it.

'You can go now, Dad,' said Bernadette.

'Well, if you're sure she's quite all right.'

Somewhat slower music recommenced as I walked back along the corridor. I reflected that, if the snake man had been going after employees of the East Indian Railway in particular, then here was his second direct hit, after Herbert Milner, the assistant auditor, killed at Asansol itself, and the very first person to die.

I realised I still held *Plain Tales from the Hills*.

Chapter Eight

I

Whereas Howrah station sits directly on the west bank of the Hooghly River, Sealdah station is a mile inland of the east bank. In that station, the light of day was trapped and dying, but all the *heat* of day – the day that had been Wednesday 2 May – remained. I carried only a tiffin basket containing biscuits, potted meat, a bottle of Beck's beer, and a kit bag I had containing my revolver.

On the Monday evening Lydia had taken up most of the luggage I would need for the hills, or what she thought I would need. This included my golf bag, my dinner suit, the new Duxolite oiled silk cape she'd bought me (because it might be raining up there), and the new cotton tweed suit she'd bought me (because it would also be cooler). These were stowed in the new cabin trunk she'd also bought from the North West Tannery Company of Calcutta at a cost of well over two hundred rupees (it was the one the elephant stood on in the newspaper advertisements). Lydia and Bernadette would be in Darjeeling by now – ought to be, at any rate, dropping and, it was to be hoped, receiving calling cards. Lydia had not telephoned or wired to say she had arrived safely but I wasn't unduly worried because, whilst I had asked her to do that, she had not actually *agreed* to do it.

I had arranged to meet Fisher at 8 p.m. by the ticket gate, and I saw him through the colourful crowd before he saw me. He stood beneath a flickering electric lamp, beside a flower stall. That was all wrong: Fisher wasn't the flower-giving type. He had his own kit bag, tiffin basket and a traveller's portfolio. It seemed he meant to do some office work on the train. He had exchanged his cream linen suit for brown cotton twill, and he had a lightweight top-coat over his arm. He had polished his shiny black bulbous boots and, it seemed, his moustache. As I closed on Fisher, I was study-ing his suit coat, trying to make out the bulge of a pistol in a shoulder holster.

'All right?' I said.

'Tolerably well,' he said. 'Yourself?'

Here, I thought, is a man with excitement in prospect, and there was more to it than simply a holiday in the hills.

I asked him if he'd heard about Poole. He had done; he didn't express any interest, but said, 'There'll be no bloody snakes on this trip anyhow. They've all been on the East Indian.'

They'd all been on the *main line* of the East Indian Railway as well, but that might just have been the law of averages, since most trains departing from Howrah went that way. As Fisher and I walked through the ticket gate, I thought of the statement made by Poole, which had been forwarded to Fairlie Place. Most of it I already knew. Poole had been travelling to a meeting with a rail-way officer whose title was Traffic Supervisor (Coal) at Asansol, and he'd been asleep. He'd also been having a nightmare, which he did not describe in the statement. As a result of the nightmare, he'd woken to see the snake crawling on to his boot. He'd tried to kick it off, and it had struck, but only at the boot itself, and this had occurred just as the train pulled into the spot called Ondal, two stops before Asansol.

Fisher and I went through the gate with a crowd of people who seemed to be carrying every article they owned. Most boarded second or third class carriages, but we approached one of the two firsts. This time, the reservation chart was in place on the side of the carriage, but the typing was badly smudged, and in the dirty evening light of the station, I couldn't make it out without my reading spectacles, and they were stowed away. As I peered at it, Fisher climbed up.

'Excuse me.'

I turned around to see a European holding a portmanteau. He was a little bloke with a little triangular beard.

'Are you boarding in first?'

I nodded.

'Well, if I were you, I'd think twice about it. A sawscale viper was found in a first class compartment of this service yesterday.'

'But . . . I would have heard of it.'

'The Company's seen all the trouble on the other line. So they've hushed it up.'

I said, 'How do *you* know about it?'

'I've a friend who works for this lot.'

I immediately thought of the wife and Bernadette, and the lack of a telegram. 'No snake was found on Monday, was it?'

'Not as far as I know. My friend would have said.'

'Anyone hurt?'

He shook his head. He was clearly rather disappointed that no one had been hurt.

'I'm off along to second,' he said, 'and I recommend you do the same.'

I said, 'I'll have a word with my pal,' which was a funny way of referring to Fisher.

Little-beard headed off along the platform, and I climbed up into the airless first class corridor, where the attendant was showing Fisher into a berth that was little more than a light blue tin box, with light blue bunks already made up. It had none of the battered grandeur of the Jamalpur Night Mail, but there was a good fan, spinning fast. The first thing I did was look under the seats for snakes, at which Fisher said, 'What's your game?' But the attendant knew what I was about. He said, 'This train very safe, sahib,' which told me the bearded man had been telling the truth. Without a by-your-leave, Fisher climbed on to the top bunk, so I threw my bag on the bottom bunk, and lay down upon it with that day's *Statesman*. I called up to Fisher, 'A snake was found on this service yesterday. Sawscale viper. The Company's keeping it under wraps.'

'Leave off,' said Fisher, or something very like. He'd apparently decided to just ignore the snakes. They wouldn't dare get in the way of *his* programme, whatever that might be. But it seemed perfectly logical to me that a snake would finally turn up in first class on the East Bengal Railway. It was now the poojahs for the first class types of Calcutta, and they were off up to the hills by means of the East Bengal line.

Presently, I saw Fisher's legs hanging over the side, since he was sitting on his bunk. He then commenced *swinging* his legs into the bargain, like a boy sitting on bridge over a stream. Then blue smoke began to loop down towards my bunk, so Fisher was now smoking a Trichie as well as swinging his legs.

I said, 'You turned up late at the Debating Society dance, I noticed.'

No reply. The legs kept swinging, but more slowly.

'Fancied a bit of a jig, did you?'

'That's it.'

'Of course, by then the "do" was about finished; only one dance left, I would have thought. You *can* dance, can you?'

'Is should think so – all the bloody mess dos I've been to.'

The swinging legs regaining some of their speed now.

'You didn't come with a partner, though . . . So who had the pleasure?'

'I don't know. Some bloody woman.'

'What was the dance?'

'A fucking waltz, wasn't it?'

'You weren't there to meet anyone in particular?'

The legs had stopped swinging. There came a knock on the door.

'Enter!' I shouted.

An Indian dragged open the door: a steward. He was proposing to collect our booking for dinner, to be taken at a twenty-minute stop somewhere down the line.

'Nothing doing,' said Fisher. 'We've already eaten.'

'Then order for drinks, sahib?'

'Sling yer hook,' said Fisher, and the man bowed and closed the door. Fisher's legs recommenced their swinging.

I did wonder at Fisher's reasons for wanting to avoid interruption. It was true that we had both eaten, and it was a great palaver to order a meal on the Indian railways. It was always a rushed job, and there was no end of people to tip. So perhaps that was the beginning and the end of the matter. In any case, it would be futile to resume my questioning about the dance. I checked my watch: five minutes until the 'off'. I took the Webley out of my kit bag and slid it under my pillow. That would come in handy against any snake as well. I put my one bottle of Beck's in the ice tray.

I opened my paper, and my eye fell upon a report that some outfit known as the Swaraj-something-or-other had been declared illegal by the Governor of Bengal. Ghandi-ites of some kind. I turned over the page: 'Fierce Fight at the Zoo.' A tiger had attacked two leopards. The tiger had pulled up the iron drawbridge of its cage by yanking on a chain with its teeth. This had occurred on the Monday – the very day I had seen Hedley Fleming at the zoo. I turned the page, and with a great crash Fisher jumped down from his bunk. He took off his suit coat, revealing a sweat-soaked shirt tunic. No shoulder holster. But the pistol might be in his kit bag, or in the pocket of the suit coat, which he now hung on a peg by the window. He ducked into the little washroom, pulling the curtain behind him. I heard the clunk of the lavatory seat being raised or lowered. Fisher was paying a call of nature – a call of the longer sort, I suspected, from certain ancillary sounds. I eyed the suit coat. Fisher wouldn't come out of the washroom without first pulling the chain on the thunderbox. You weren't meant to do that in a station – the prohibition applied even here in India where all railway lines doubled as latrines – but Fisher wasn't a man for such niceties. His suit coat hung lower on one side than the other. I stood up, put my hand into the lower pocket, and there was the piece: a Webley, like my own. I broke open the gun, and there came the shriek of the platform guard's whistle. The cylinder was fully loaded. We lurched away, and Fisher threw back the curtain as I thrust the gun back into the pocket. He had not pulled the chain; he was in his undershirt, and he held his unbuttoned trousers loosely about his waist. We were running clear of the station now and rattling over a bridge. Fisher was eyeing me.

'What are you playing at?' he said.

173

'Nothing.'

He seemed willing to let it go at that. I didn't believe he'd seen me touch the gun. He eyed me for a while, then delved into his kit bag and found a blue-and-white package: Bromo water-closet paper. He returned to the thunderbox and closed the curtain. But then he immediately threw the curtain open again, plucked the suit coat off its hook and took it in with him. So perhaps he *had* seen what I was about. But surely he couldn't shoot me with a revolver in a compartment of a fully occupied railway carriage – not if he hoped to escape detection: the report would be too loud. I had heard the shot fired on the Night Mail to Jamalpur, but that had apparently been fired by a wild dacoit about to make off on a thoroughbred horse. If Fisher planned to loose off a bullet in the compartment we presently occupied, then he would need . . . It came to me at last: the word that should have been on my lips when I spoke to Canon Peter Selwyn in the Bengal Club. To shoot someone on a crowded train, Fisher would need a *silencer*: a silvery metallic tube about six inches long and half an inch in diameter – surely the very article that Selwyn had seen in Fisher's possession.

Ten minutes later, we were lying on our bunks again, and I had my Beck's on the go. I didn't like the look of the meat paste in my tiffin basket; I believed it had curdled in the incredible heat. Fisher was addressing me from the top bunk; he was speaking of 'the last lot': the war. I knew nothing of Fisher's own war, save that he had been in France, then on the North-West Frontier of India. I believed he had served in both the Royal Engineers and the Military Police, but when asked he'd only say, 'That's all ancient history, isn't it?'

He said, 'You were on the little trains. In France.'

'Two-foot gauge.'

'But it's not *quite* two foot, is it?'

'One foot eleven and five eighths, if we're splitting hairs.'

'But the mountain railway – the one we'll be taking to Darjeeling. That really is two foot, isn't it?'

'Dead on,' I said. What the hell was he driving at?

I heard Fisher lighting a cigar.

'You were running arms to the forward lines. Petrol-electrics, I suppose?'

'Steam. Baldwins. Made in America.'

'Up to the job, were they?'

'Not bad. The boilers were set rather high.'

'So they were unstable?'

'That's it.'

Paddy fields beyond the window slats. We had left the city behind.

'Blow over in a breath of wind?' Fisher suggested.

'Breath of wind from a nine-pound crump, yes.'

'But you came through all right?'

'I'm sitting here talking to you, aren't I? Lying here, I mean.'

I had half a hundredweight of iron in my left thigh but I didn't go into that. Nor did I mention the bad blood within my own unit that had arisen from one capital crime and resulted in another.

'You didn't pick up a medal, then?'

I shook my head, forgetting that Fisher couldn't see me. I had received some private congratulations for sorting out the bad business, but only after I'd nearly swung for it myself.

It had also earned me a posting to Mesopotamia, and the privilege of keeping tabs on the lieutenant colonel of dubious morals.

'But you got your commission?' Fisher said.

It was as though Fisher was trying to work out how much of a loss to the world it would be if he shot me dead.

'For what it's worth,' I said, taking up my copy of *The Statesman* again.

On the top bunk Fisher had control of the light switch. He now turned it out. In the rattling darkness, I paid my own visit to the washroom. As I emerged from it, we ran through a station, and an arc of electric light swung through compartment, illuminating the side of Fisher's face. He was silent, but not asleep. Before regaining my berth, I peered through the window slats at the endless paddy plains of North Bengal. Here and there were the beautiful silhouettes of palm trees – they looked better in silhouette – and of wooden contraptions used for irrigation. The mysterious orange sparks from the engine held my gaze. I closed the slats, and retreated to my bunk. Eventually I dropped asleep, in spite of my best intentions. Some time later, I was aware of a voice: it said, 'Someone's coming.' It was Fisher's voice. For a while, nothing happened, and I half believed I had dreamed it

I was awakened by the compartment door being pulled open. The train was moving slowly. Some light spilling from the corridor illuminated two faces: an Indian railway official and a European. The train began to gain speed. We must have made a stop, where this European had boarded. The official entered the carriage and began making up the opposite bunk, creating a good deal of din in the process.

'For Christ's sake,' Fisher muttered, after enduring a minute of the din, and then the European was about installed. The official quit the carriage, pulling the door to behind him. The European settled himself quickly, but then he got up and went into the washroom. He was in there for a good while. He came out to the accompaniment of the roaring flush of the thunderbox, then he went over to the window and opened the slats. All was darkness beyond, but he continued to peer through.

'Get to fucking bed,' said Fisher, and the man turned his head somewhat in the direction of Fisher. The man did not stir himself unduly, but he did close the slats a few seconds later, and climbed into his bunk. Half an hour later, I could still not be sure he was asleep, but I was pretty certain on another point: whatever Fisher's plan might be, he could not shoot me now.

II

The European did not appear to speak or understand English. I put him down as Italian or Spanish or something, going by his responses to the bearer who came in with tea and toast at half after five in the morning. I opened the window slats: more paddy fields, now with pale orange sunlight burning the mist away. As I moved back from the window, the track began to curve, and I immediately looked again. What I had taken for a great bank of cloud was in fact a great bank of mountains, and it appeared that we were approaching the very perimeter wall of India.

Siliguri station was located at the base of the five-mile-high mountains, and it stood in the same relation to them as a doorstep to a tall house. It was as if this weird situation had sent everybody mad, and the sidings around the station contained engines and wagons of two sizes: full-sized and half-sized. A half-sized train was made up and waiting for us on the platform opposite to the one we'd come in on. Another little train waited behind it, and both together made up the Darjeeling Mail. In other words, what was billed as one train was really two. Well, I supposed it was better for a short train to fall off the mountain than a long one.

Fisher, it turned out, had a good deal more luggage than what had accompanied him in our compartment. He engaged two porters, and shouted at them continuously as they carried two cabin trunks, a shotgun sling and golf clubs across the platform from full-sized to half-sized luggage vans. The tip he gave must have made up for the abuse, since it caused the Indians to bow very low. *Were* they Indians, in point of fact? They looked oriental, like Gurkhas, and we would be heading towards the territory from which Deo Rana and his fellows had originated.

The little engines were four-coupled saddle tanks, bright green in colour, and overrun with engineers. Three blokes were crammed on to the footplate, a further two sat on the coal bunker, which straddled the boiler. As I looked on, two more blokes climbed up on to the buffer beam, so the engine was now practically smothered by the men who operated it.

The carriages offered a variety of accommodations within each class. Our tickets allowed us to travel in any marked 'First'. Fisher selected a saloon of the second train. This was an open carriage (no compartments), which suited me, as it meant I wouldn't be closely confined with Fisher. The carriage held couches, basket chairs and occasional tables, as though furnished from a house clearance, and as we boarded three European women and their assorted children climbed up, together with their three ayahs, or maids. All turned and smiled at Fisher and me.

'Room for us all here, I think?' said the first and boldest of the women. Half rising to my feet, I nodded and smiled. But Fisher remained seated. He lit a Trichinopoly cigar.

'I say!' said one of the women.

The bold woman said, 'The children don't care for your cigar smoke.'

'If truth be told,' said Fisher, 'I'm not very keen on it myself.' He then fixed his bulging gaze on the children, one by one. 'I mean, it's only a cheap cigar,' he added.

It was to the children's credit, I thought, that none of them flinched under Fisher's gaze. But at this point of maximum rudeness he gave ground. Rising from his chair, he said, 'Best for all, I think, if my friend and I adjourn to the smaller saloon.'

He was indicating a narrow corridor at the south end of the saloon that, as it turned out, led into a supplementary space holding nothing but two basket chairs and an ashtray on a stand.

So I was trapped with bloody Fisher again.

We sat down opposite each other in the basket chairs. Fisher had his Webley in his suit-coat pocket, and I had my Webley in mine. I now also matched his Trichinopoly cigar with my own Gold Flake. Beyond our seats, a glass door gave on to a carriage-end balcony, or veranda. From the platform, the pea whistle blew. It was extremely shrill, and I wondered whether it was half-sized, like everything else. We pulled away, and the glass in the veranda door began to rattle. We were trundling along the high street of the town, past tumbledown hotels, and men going past the other way on slow horses. The window glass was clear, no venetian slats. I stood up and walked through the door on to the veranda, and the moment I reached the open air, the town ended and we were into jungle, where the sunlight could not break through. There was a kind of underwater light, and the creepers came down through the trees like anchor chains. Occasionally white tombstones flashed past in the dark tangle of the jungle floor. We were not yet climbing.

The engine exhaust roared and crackled. I could hear but not see the little loco. Presently we came into a jungle clearing, and a station. We stopped. We'd been going for half an hour, and we were in for a six-hour trip. There'd be a good many stations before Darjeeling, and if Fisher wanted to do me in so that corruption in traffic may not be investigated, he would have to time his move carefully. We were aboard the second of the two trains, so if he stepped out on to the veranda, shot me, and pitched my body on to the track I'd lie undiscovered for a while. But even though it had been Fisher who had picked the second train, he could not, surely, have predicted the arrival of the ladies which had caused us to remove to the supplementary saloon.

We began running past the corrugated iron shacks of a bazaar. The shack roofs were painted light green and the sky above was the palest blue. We ran around a curve and, by leaning over the veranda railing, I could observe the little engine. The two blokes on the tender would pick up lumps of coal and pass them around the side of the cab to the fireman, who would inspect them, as if considering their suitability, but he never in practice rejected them. He just put them on the fire. As for the two men on the buffer beam, I believed they were laying down sand so as to increase traction – and we *were* now beginning to climb. I looked though the glass door at Fisher on his basket chair. He had got hold of a newspaper, and he was opening and closing the pages with great rapidity, as though trying to catch the news by surprise.

It seemed perfectly possible that he had meant to shoot me with a silenced pistol on the night train to Jamalpur. But silencers were fiddly bits of kit, and something had gone wrong, so he had fired with an unprotected Webley, but he had done so in the darkness, and it was John Young who had taken the bullet. But no pistol had been found on him; and what about the Indians who'd been galloping away on horseback?

We were running through thinner forest; pine trees were appearing among the bamboo, and India was beginning to be below us. The train went into a tight curve on the edge of the hill, and it *kept* curving through a short tunnel. While we were in this tunnel, the other train was on top of the tunnel. We were looping the loop, as on a fairground ride, and at the end of the loop we were much higher. The plain of paddy fields lay below: the giant chessboard on which the British played their game of empire.

We came into another station. A painted board said 'Rangtong' and there was nobody there but the station master, who stood on the platform looking mightily pleased with himself. As we pulled away, I heard the rattling of the glass door. Fisher came out on to the veranda. He leant far out over the back railing.

'Come here,' he called, still leaning over the side.

'Why?'

'Something queer about the track.'

Was he really interested in small gauge railways? We were now approaching a second curve, a second loop. The train gave a lurch, and as we continued our curving progress, with the right side of the train now overhanging the edge of the drop down into the plain of Bengal. The veranda railing protecting us from this drop – a drop of some two thousand feet, I thought – was somewhat lower than waist height, so while the drop was big, the railing protecting us from it was small. The train curved and curved, and then we were two thousand two *hundred* feet above Bengal, and still overhanging the drop as we rattled across the face of a mountain.

'Come *here* and look at *this*,' Fisher demanded again.

Remaining behind him, I said, 'Look at bloody what? I'll look at it from here, if it's all right with you.'

'The track,' he said again. 'Something's missing.'

The train hit another curve, which swung us sharply to the right, projecting us yet further over the drop. Could it be there really was something amiss with the rails? The carriage did seem to be rattling badly – and there were women and children inside. I inched forward so that I was alongside Fisher. We watched the unwinding of the little track. The outer rail was two feet from the edge. If you fell on to that track and rolled even slightly you'd be gone, falling away into thick clouds, the plain of Bengal having now been replaced by a damp mist.

'*What's* missing?' I said.

Fisher turned to face me, his eyes bulging, his moustache fluttering in the backdraft of the little train. It was the first time I had seen it move. Behind us the glass door rattled. We both turned. One of the women was there, and one of the children: a boy. The woman was holding her hat against the breeze with one hand, while the other hand rested on the shoulder of the boy. He stepped over to the railing of the veranda and gave a polite cough. He was being sick into the cloud. A case of either motion or mountain sickness.

I turned back towards Fisher. 'What did you want to tell me about?'

He pointed down, and for a while he didn't speak, and we watched the rails.

'No track shoes,' Fisher said, at length.

'That's right,' I said. 'The rails are screwed directly on to the sleepers.' It was an economy measure permissible on small-gauge railways, where not so much 'give' was needed in the rails. I said as much to Fisher, but I did not believe he listened.

The boy had stopped being sick, and he looked to be benefit-ting from the colder air. He was eyeing Fisher curiously. Fisher put his hand into his suit-coat pocket, and I was on the point of knocking him over the veranda when I realised this was not his gun hand that he was reaching with, but his left. Out came a paper bag. He held the bag in front of the boy, who took from it a boiled sweet.

The woman was the person who had clashed with Fisher be-fore, and she could not conceal her amazement at this develop-ment.

'Now what do you say?' she asked the child when she finally found her voice.

'Thank you for the humbug, sir.'

Fisher eyed the boy. 'It's not a flipping humbug, is it? It's a comfit.'

III

The tropical forest had given way to oaks and rhododendrons, and the Indian summer had become an English spring, albeit a misty one.

We were beyond the halfway point, and Fisher and I were back in our little anteroom to the main compartment. After the loops, the train had performed some other tricks. For example, it had climbed for a while by running hard uphill into a dead end, then reversing over points on to a higher ledge than it had started from, then running hard uphill again, so progressing by zigzags. The first time the train made a reverse, one of the women in the main saloon had screamed, probably imagining we were running out of control down the hill. The train had then started chasing its tail again: another loop.

At a spot called Tindharia we had been besieged by tea-wallahs. It had been distinctly cool there, and the women had put woollen sweaters on the children. On emerging from that station, we had been able to look down on the workshop of the mountain railway; it came and went through swirls of cloud, like a factory that had died and gone to heaven. An hour later, at a spot called Kurseong, we had all taken a meal in the station restaurant. Then the children from the first class carriage stood on the platform and watched what looked like an organised entertainment by a troupe of monkeys. I almost expected the monkeys to bring round a hat afterwards. Kurseong was a vertical town, with tea plantations all around. As we pulled away from it, the clouds became strange, with whirlpools of vapour ascending and descending inside them. My ears clicked.

'Why the interest in narrow-gauge railways?' I asked Fisher. We were back in the little saloon, smoking at one another.

Silence for a space.

'I saw an advertisement in the paper. Small-gauge kit being sold off . . . Thought there might be money in it.'

'Who was selling?'

'Bombay . . . Port Authority.'

A further silence.

'What paper?'

'*Statesman*.'

'When?'

'I don't bloody know, do I? Couple of weeks back.'

I was a faithful reader of *The Statesman*. At three anas, it was very good value. I had seen no such advertisement.

The window was wide and clear. Beyond it, I saw that we were beginning to coincide with a road: the Cart Road, I believed it was called. It was going the same way as us: to Darjeeling. The queer-looking mountain people walked along it, some carrying baskets strapped to their foreheads. We shuffled into a place called Tung, all steam and fog. The houses of Tung were made of wood, with triangular roofs, like so many cuckoo clocks. Long tattered streamers flew from flagpoles in the gardens, where grew willow trees, cherry trees and red flowers that blazed brightly in the haze. We rolled past some Gurkha-like men digging up the road, and the locomotive rang its bell at them. One man looked up from his work, grinning. They all wore big gold earrings, like pirates. An ox cart was approaching them, and behind the ox cart a motor. The very rich did prefer to motor up; I'd seen a number of cars on the road, and plenty of petrol bunks. This motor was long and blue, almost as long as our railway carriage and I believed it was the kind they called a 'Continental'. The driver was uniformed. A dark-suited and middle-aged Indian sat beside him. On the rear seat, looking over a newspaper, sat a handsome young Indian in tweeds. It was the R.K.

Our train swayed towards the car, and he was looking through the window, looking my way, and it seemed that he didn't know quite what to do. He half raised his arm, just as Fisher, in the chair opposite to mine, raised his paper to his face. Well, it was clear as day. The two were acquainted; the two were in league, and didn't want me to know it. It wasn't Askwith Fisher had been going to meet at the Debating Society dance; it was the R.K. I continued to watch the Continental as it overtook the train. The golf clubs, fishing rods and gun bags bristling from the rear matched Fisher's golf clubs and gun bag. He was going up to the hills because they were going up to the hills – and yet he had wanted to *travel* up with me.

If the murder of John Young on the Jamalpur night train had been the result of a bungled attempt to do away with me, with Fisher as a conspirator, then the instigator need not have been William Askwith, or whatever traffic officer feared being exposed as corrupt. What if the instigator was the R.K.? He was presumably a man used to getting what he wanted. It appeared that he wanted my daughter, and I was the barrier standing in his way.

Thinking of Bernadette, I willed the train on. I didn't want the R.K. to arrive in Darjeeling before I did, but two minutes later I saw him again. His Continental was parked behind another motor, just as big, possibly a Rolls. Its European occupants had stepped out on to the road, and a gush of steam was coming from the radiator. The cars had no choice but to attack the hills, and it was too much for some. The R.K. and his two companions were stopping to assist. It seemed I would beat him to Darjeeling after all.

Fisher was still reading his paper, or pretending to.

'Why have you come up here?'

'For the bloody social gaiety, why do you think?'

We had come to a place called Ghum. We circled a wide, flattish hill for no apparent reason, and with infuriating slowness. But then, finally, we were bearing down on the terminus.

IV

Darjeeling was a town falling down a mountain, and this mountain had turned its back on India, and the plain of Bengal. Instead, it faced a blue-grey valley patrolled by clouds. On the other side of this valley were 'the snows', the Himalayas, which were, at the present moment, buried treasure, merely a whitish gleam behind bands of grey cloud. The sun was big in the sky, like a painting of the sun, and it gave off little heat. Most of the European men boarding the tongas, or walking along the principal road – the Mall – were *dressed* like mountaineers. Thick knickerbockers, guernseys and pipes were the order of the day. The women's coats were sometimes fur-trimmed. The air held the smoke of a hundred coal fires and the dark light of impending downpour. Taken all together, I felt that I was in the Scottish Highlands, some time either side of winter.

Fisher was delayed behind me in the station, mustering his goods and marshalling some servants for the short run to the Hotel Mount Everest. The queue for tongas was too long, so I engaged a rickshaw. I showed the man a hand-drawn map, given me by Lydia, on which Cedar Lodge was indicated . . . and the rain began to fall as we ticked our way along the Mall.

After the station, the Mall became a bazaar, with stalls on the road. Next came bigger buildings, including the clubs of the town, set back from the Mall, and with British-looking gardens. Thereafter, the Mall became a pleasant avenue running through a park, with overspreading cedars and white railings against the steep drop, and well-dressed strollers, all now holding aloft umbrellas that were shiny with rain.

We came to Cedar Lodge, prettily located in the park. It resembled the station master's house at Grosmont in Yorkshire. I hurried along the drive, to be greeted by the middle-aged married couple who were caretakers of the house and servants to its occupants. They were not mountain people but from the plain, and their English was good. Their names were Ajit and Sahira.

They were the sole occupants of the house. Where were the memsahib, and the missy memsahib? I wanted to know. Ajit said they had gone out to some sort of tea. So they had not been killed by a snake on the 'down' train from Sealdah. Ajit asked whether I myself wanted tea. The cup was delivered to me by Ajit in the living room. His wife was looking on anxiously from the door-way, and I believed that Ajit spoke for both of them when he said, 'The house is kept just as the memsahib likes it.'

'You mean it is a mess?'

'No, sahib,' he said simply, but he did mean that, and I was sure his wife had asked him to point out that the mess wasn't their fault.

I walked around the house, cup in hand. The rooms were small and solid, with wooden floors, red turkey rugs and tartan blankets. The place put me in mind of Christmas. A log fire was laid in every room, and a *coal* fire was lit in the main room. All the coal scuttles except the one in the main room were empty, and I concluded there was a shortage of coal in town, about which I would be proved right.

Where Cedar Lodge differed from the station master's house in Grosmont was that it was clean. But it was littered with the betokening signs of female social ambition: three dresses thrown across the bed of the master bedroom, and there was a copy of a book by Annie Besant, who had had helped found the Congress party of India. This was the reason the wife admired Annie Bes-ant, and also the reason she resented her: Lydia would have liked to have founded the Congress party herself. A pile of calling cards lay over-toppled on the bedside table. 'Captain and Mrs Stringer . . .' I couldn't bear to read the continuation of it. That 'Captain' was such a slim branch for Lydia to hang it all on, whereas her daughter might have the chance of an Indian prince. Half a dozen shimmery evening dresses hung in the wardrobe, which was more than I recalled Lydia having, but perhaps a few were Bernadette's: the two had begun to merge in that way.

I saw that, once again, a communicating door would connect the master bedroom with Bernadette's bedroom. There would be no marital relations here either, and my mind swung back to Miss Hatsuyo of Old Court House Corner, and her Japanese speciality.

There were two portable gramophones in Bernadette's bedroom, and disks scattered around them. Her brand-new travel case was on the bed with its contents spilled over the thick counterpane, including more rouges, hand mirrors and bottles with bulb sprays than I liked to see. A torn envelope disclosed a note of some kind. It surely could not be from the R.K. He had only just arrived, and this note had been opened and read some time ago. Yet the paper was of good quality and 'For the attention of Miss Bernadette Stringer' was written in a very fancy hand. I moved towards it, but stayed my hand. I ought not to look.

I moved towards the window. I was thinking how quiet this place was compared to Calcutta, when I heard the rattle of an approaching vehicle. A single horse was pulling a carriage of the kind called a dandy through the trees and the rain.

I switched on the electric light in Bernadette's room. On the dresser lay a catalogue of some kind: it was called *Beauty Shop*. There was also a slumped pile of silk hats on the dresser. Bernadette called ordinary (but expensive) silk hats 'useful hats'; then there were 'charming' hats, and the newly fashionable material for these was lizard. But here was something else again: a leather hat. It looked like a racing driver's hat, only there was a band of lace across the front, so it was really for the female *accomplice* of the motor-car driver. It had not been worn, and the price tag was still inside. Thirty rupees. The cost of a decent cotton twill suit; or two months' wages for an Indian labourer, depending on which way you looked at it.

On the pillow a magazine lay open and I saw the heading, 'Powder Puffs in the Balance'. Being unable to credit that such a headline could generate what appeared to be several pages of small print, I picked it up. I put on my reading glasses: 'One must admit that the heat of ballrooms and the ardour of dancing are foes to the complexion . . .'

I returned to the living room. A large brass clock ticked; the coal fire made a similar sound. It was now almost eight o'clock. What type of tea continued until eight? Of course, they might have 'gone on'. In India, a tea party often followed a tea party. Yes, the two of them had been expecting my arrival, but the social round was more important.

At eight thirty, I asked Ajit and Sahira whether they could expand upon the memsahib and the missy memsahib having gone to 'tea', and they disclosed that the tea had been 'on the Mall'. Well, everything was 'on the Mall'.

At eight forty-five, I stepped out of the house, and lit a Gold Flake under the blaze in a lamp that was in turn under the branches of a cedar tree. The great valley lay beyond the trees. I wondered whether, come morning, there would be a view of 'the snows' through the trees and across that valley, and at that moment I heard the sound of a motor. This could be them, I thought. They had gone for a spin in someone's car, and were now being returned; but it was a motorcycle that came through the trees, a native constable riding upon it. I dropped my cigarette and stood upon it. Was he the sort of constable who brought bad news? I put my hand out to stop him.

'Sahib?' he said, and that was hopeful. His tone suggested he couldn't have been looking for me.

'Were you looking for Cedar Lodge?' I said, indicating the house.

He shook his head. He wore a white turban and a long white cape against the drizzling rain. He was a handsome chap; he looked like a sort of motorised angel, and on the petrol tank of his bike was written the word 'Zenith'.

'I am worried about my wife and daughter.'

He cut off his engine, and I felt strangely light-headed in the sudden silence, there in that illuminated woodland high in the sky. Nobody could climb Everest, the highest of 'the snows', on account of the lack of oxygen. Maybe it was in short supply at this lower level too. The constable was taking out his notebook . . . but I could now hear the rattling of a tonga, coming from the direction of town. 'Hold on,' I said to the constable. The tonga was coming on fast. I was practically praying for it to stop outside the little wicket gate of Cedar Lodge, and when it did so, and Bernadette jumped down, followed by the wife, who stepped more carefully on to the muddy ground, I heard myself saying to the constable, 'I need not trouble you any further, thank you.'

V

'A lot flat tyres,' said Bernadette, who was 'curled up' on the sofa, in the manner approved by the young ladies' magazines. She meant that the guests at the tea had been a lot of bores. The last of the coal burned in the grate.

I was drinking a peg; the wife held a glass with a green cordial of some kind in it.

She said, 'You'd think that if someone had just been attacked by one of the most dangerous snakes in the world, and then they gave a tea party, that you would *go* to it.'

'Well, you did go to it,' I said.

Bernadette said, 'The Askwiths didn't.'

The tea had in fact not been on the Mall, but at the small hotel on Victoria Road where the Pooles were putting up. They had given the tea, in their modest way, in a private room of the hotel. It was by way of celebration of Dougie's escape from sudden death, but it had unfortunately coincided with another tea, given by His Excellency, the Governor at his summer residence. The Askwiths had been at this grander event, and Lydia was affecting to be put out on the Pooles' behalf when in fact she was put out at not being on the Governor's guest list herself.

'He hasn't suffered any ill effects then? Dougie, I mean.'

'Nor any good ones,' said Lydia.

'He's still a rummy,' said Bernadette.

'At tea you are supposed to drink *tea*,' said Lydia.

'Did he talk about it? The snake attack, I mean.'

'I thought you'd read the statement he gave,' Lydia said, crossly.

But I wanted to know if there was any discrepancy between the statement he gave and what he was saying now.

'He said he knew very little about it,' Lydia continued. 'He told us that if he'd been wearing his elasticated boots he'd be dead – if the teeth had gone through the elastic.'

'The *fangs*,' said Bernadette, with great relish. She, in contrast to her mother, was in a good mood about something, and I thought I knew what. The arrival of the bloody R.K. She'd expected it, or got wind of it somehow.

After an interval of silence, I began to ask about their journey up. 'Was the weather clear? Did you get any views?'

Lydia said, 'It's not "views". Only in Yorkshire do people have "views".'

'It's *scenery*,' said Bernadette, looking up from her magazine.

The wife's chain of thought was perfectly clear: she would never go to the best tea parties if she was married to a man who said 'views', and in this she was quite right.

Chapter Nine

I

Breakfast was served by Ajit and Sahira at nine o'clock, by which time no further visiting cards had been returned. Therefore the wife's edgy mood continued. She was very polite to Ajit and Sahira, not so polite to me. The business of the calling cards was certainly not to be joked about. All the Calcutta party-going was supposed to have been a preparation for her month in the hills, so she was like a footballer who had trained for a cup final, only to discover that he had been left out of the team. After breakfast, Lydia went upstairs for a bath. The rain still fell, and all the coal was gone. In the living room grate a log burned, giving a sweet smell. Bernadette and I took the armchairs either side of the fire.

'How many cards have been dropped, and how many returned?' I said.

'Mama dropped about ten. She then sent me out on a bike to drop another five. We've had two returned, if you include the invitation to the Pooles. The other was from the Askwiths, but that's only because I told Claudine to tell her mama and papa to get a wiggle on.'

'And does *your* mama know that?'

'Yes. She figured it out.'

It was a bad lookout, but there was nothing further to be said on the matter of the cards. 'What are you going to do today?' I asked Bernadette.

'Read. Drift about.'

'Got any balls to go to?'

'Not 'specially. There's a fancy dress at the Amusement Club.'

'But you haven't got a costume.'

'Anyone who's got a kimono, a Chinese hat, some kohl and a pair of silk slippers can go as Aladdin.'

'And have you got all those things?'

'Probably.'

'Aladdin's a man,' I observed.

'Mmm . . . sort of. There's a tea *dansat* at some church hall or other. We might crash that.'

'Who's "we"?'

'Me and Ann and Claudine, obviously. The big blow is next Monday – at the Gymkhana Club. You're coming to that.'

'Am I?'

'Mama said.'

'Since when have you been calling your mother "Mama"?'

'Since about three weeks.'

Silence for a space.

'Dad.'

'What?'

'Would you like me to teach you the shimmy? Well, not the shimmy, but the foxtrot. All you ever do with Mama is waltz.'

'I don't see myself shimmying. I've got six inches of metal plate in my leg.'

'There's no reason why you couldn't be a good dancer.'

'I'm too old.'

Silence for another space.

'Will you be seeing the R.K. here?' I demanded.

'How should I know?'

'I want you to steer clear of him.'

'I know you do.'

She appeared quite calm, which made me the opposite.

II

That morning I went for a walk alone, carrying an umbrella with a broken spoke. There was a mass of rolling cloud down in the valley, like a silent, foaming sea. On the Mall, a fellow in the dark recesses of a blacksmith's forge called out, 'You will be wanting to see about your umbrella for the monsoon!' Behind him, another man was hammering away at one of the curved Ghurka swords. But presumably they ran to fixing umbrellas as well. It was hardly the monsoon yet. A light rain fell, but not so as to disrupt the holiday mood of the Europeans who sauntered about the narrow lanes. It was all 'Compliments to the air!' and 'It's set fair for this afternoon, I believe!' and 'Oh, but you must come to ours!'

I walked for a good while about Darjeeling. The fixtures of the municipality were like their British equivalents, but there was something playful about them, as if they were in a children's story. The town hall tried too hard to look serious; the post boxes were bright red and gold, and the roof of the goods shed, next to the station was, I noticed for the first time, sky blue.

I was standing near the taxi rank of the station when I spied the long, blue car, the Continental. The chauffeur was in the process of taking down the roof canopy, the light rain having now stopped altogether. The chauffeur regained his place at the wheel; the dark-suited, businesslike man sat in the front alongside him.

On the back seat sat the R.K., and there was a new man along-side him: Fisher. Here was the connection proven beyond doubt. The car was now moving slowly through the wandering crowds, and when Fisher saw me he spoke to the R.K., who tapped on the shoulder of the businesslike man, who spoke to the driver, who stopped the motor. They were twenty yards off. Every man in the car was looking at me. After a further word between Fisher and the R.K., these two climbed down from either side of the car; they convened at the radiator where, after a further conflab, they began walking towards me.

Fisher was slightly in the lead as they approached. He was bet-ter dressed than I had ever seen him, in a good suit of green tweed. He said, 'Jim,' and it was the first time he'd called me that, 'I'd like you to meet a very good friend of mine: His Highness, the Rajku-mar of—'

'Huzoor,' the R.K. said, cutting him off, and making me a smart bow. He was smaller than I had thought, and slightly older, perhaps in the late twenties. He wore a suit of still better green tweed that Fisher's. He was holding out his hand. How should I address him? I wasn't at all sure Fisher had been right in calling him 'His Highness': that was perhaps why the R.K. had cut him off.

I settled on: 'Pleased to meet you, Rajkumar sahib.'

I did not think that Hindus (especially high-born ones) went in for handshaking; they believed the touch of a foreigner might defile them in some way, but this fellow had a good, firm hand-shake. Then again, he wore a diamond in his right earlobe.

'I am delighted to meet you, Captain Stringer. I have heard a great deal about you. How are you enjoying it here? I hope you don't mind the rain too much?'

'Not too much.'

'It's what we're all here for, I suppose . . . Major Fisher tells me I always spend too much time on the niceties, Captain Stringer, so I will come right out with it: since I'm told you don't go in for shikar, what do you say to a round of golf?'

'What, *now*?'

He didn't seem to hear that. He was turning towards the businesslike man, who had also stepped out of the car, and was standing, un-introduced, about ten feet behind us in the road.

The R.K. said, 'Captain Stringer, I am proposing . . . ' He looked back at the businesslike man again. 'What's that thing called? A three-for-all, or something?'

The businesslike man gave the politest of shrugs while remaining ten feet away, so I answered the question: 'Do you mean a three-ball?'

'Ah, Captain Stringer. I can tell you are practically a scratch man.'

In fact, I just hacked my way around the railway course at York, usually alone, and gave up when I'd lost all my balls. I said, 'I can hardly play at all, I'm afraid.'

'But you should see me,' the R.K. said. 'I am always distinctly over par. They all averted their eyes when I teed off at the Tolly-gunge Club. Apparently my stance alone foretells doom. My secretary informs me that I swing outside the line – which is all very well, but *what* line?'

'I don't know,' I said. 'Have you considered having lessons?'

'I am a lost cause, I fear,' said the R.K., 'but I love the game even so. Did you say you will join us?'

'Well,' I said, 'I mean . . . is there a course?'

Fisher spoke up. 'Of course there's a course. His Highness

wouldn't be asking otherwise, would he?' The R.K. winced. 'His Highness' had definitely been wrong, but the two were in close alliance, no question of it.

'The course is out at Tiger Hill, Captain Stringer,' the R.K. said. 'Only a few miles away, and only nine holes. I'm afraid the greens are in a shocking state, but then again you can see Mount Everest in favourable weather. Might we collect you in the motor?'

'When?'

'The prognosis is excellent for tomorrow, Saturday.'

What prognosis? It hardly mattered. I was going to play golf with him. It was simply inevitable, but I did not want him at the house, because then he might run into the girl that I was sure he had fixed on for a wife: namely my own daughter, and I did not want her to know about any of this. I said, 'That will be rather out of your way. Let's meet outside the railway station.'

'The station it is then,' said the R.K. 'Say, two o'clock?'

He put out his hand, and we shook again.

'Confirm by messenger?' the businesslike man – I assumed he was the secretary – suggested from his distant post.

'No, no,' said the R.K. 'All these dammed chits flying about all over the place – not necessary.'

The three of them walked back to the car. On the way, the businesslike man raised an umbrella and held it over the R.K.'s head, since the rain had started again. Fisher was close enough to the R.K. to get some of the benefit of the umbrella. Somehow, I did not think that Fisher would ever be returning to work on the East Indian Railway Commission of Enquiry. After they had driven off I remained in the road, pedestrians, tongas, ponies and ox carts flowing by on either side of me, my mind in a whirl. I had been not so much flattered as practically *flattened* by the boyish charm of the R.K. His charm lay partly in the fact that his English, while good, was slightly 'off'. It lay also in the enthusiastic briskness with which he conducted his business.

But why did he want to play golf with me? And why was he associating with Fisher?

III

I resumed my walk, and at getting on for midday I found myself on what I believed was called Auckland Road looking at a notice fixed to the double doors of one of the bigger chalet-like buildings. It read, 'Bertram's', and there was a list of the amenities inside, including post and telegraphic office, games room, liquor bar, reading room and lending library. Well, I was an honorary member of Bertram's. It was one of the clubs you could join in advance for the length of your stay. Lydia had arranged it for me, and looking at the notice I saw a chance to take up a line of enquiry I'd been meaning to pursue since the evening of the Debating Society dance.

Bertram's was a matter of polished wooden floors, green notice-boards, bookshelves not confined to library and reading room, and sodden umbrellas sprouting everywhere. There was quite a crush of steaming, damp Englishmen in the bar, so I gave up on the beer and walked directly through to the reading room-cum-library, a chilly place, the fire in the great fireplace being unlit owing, as I supposed, to the coal famine.

The fact that the place ran to lending books had made me think they would have *children's* books, and they had plenty, including volumes of *The Captain*. It was one of the principal boys' papers, and it was 'for Old Boys too', as the covers always proclaimed.

Dougie Poole was in the middle forties. He would have been thirteen in about the mid-nineties. I picked out the volume for the collected *Captains* of 1896–7, and began looking for the 'Naturalist's Corner', an item that occurred regularly, along with many a 'Cycling Corner' and 'Athletic Corner'. While flipping the pages, I took the volume over to the long centre table, where two other readers sat, both looking over the sporting papers. 'Naturalist's Corner' was advertised as being 'conducted by Edward Step, F.L.S.' The queries from the young naturalists were printed in bold, and Step's answers were given in ordinary type below:

H. P. Pearson (Hendon) declares himself 'an ardent collector of birds' eggs', and he wishes to know . . .

William Lessing (Devizes) wishes to know the average age of the common spider . . .

F. Dixon (Doncaster) desires to begin a collection of dried plants this spring . . .

I skipped further down the column on which this last appeared – it was page 33 of the March 1897 issue – and there was the name I was looking for, but not quite the query I had been lead to expect:

Douglas Poole (Walthamstow) wants information respecting the keeping of an adder.

An adder: a poisonous – or rather a venomous – snake, and not the harmless grass snake that Poole had mentioned as being the subject of the correspondence.

Edward Step, F.L.S. replied:

I am not sure it is such a very good idea to keep an adder as a pet. The snake is a small but true viper, and known to be irascible. Adders may strike without warning when handled, and human envenomation from adders results in about a dozen fatalities a year, while deaths among pet dogs run into the many hundreds. I cannot imagine where Master Poole found his adder. In the wilds of Walthamstow presumably, since they are not sold in any pet shop of the normal kind . . .

Further down the page, Mr Step did stoop to answering the question, albeit briefly, as if washing his hands of the matter:

The snake wants a sunny house, floored with gravel, and with bathing arrangements.

I heard a loud 'How's tricks, Jim!' from the doorway, and Dougie Poole himself was walking, somewhat erratically, towards me. I hastily flipped over the pages of *The Captain*, so that he found me something on 'The Stamps of Japan', or so I hoped.

'Your girl's over at our place,' he said, as I stood up and shook his hand.

'Oh,' I said. 'Good.'

'Glass of fizzle? I've a bottle on the go in the liquor bar. You a philatelist on the side?' he enquired, as we made for the door of the reading room.

'Come again?' I said, and then I clicked: the Japanese stamps. 'Passing interest, you know.'

*The Captain*s had been bound in blue, whereas I had usually seen them bound in maroon, and they had not been loudly announced as collected *Captain*s, but only by small gold lettering on the spine. Therefore Poole might not have stumbled upon the name of the publication I was reading.

'Philately will get you nowhere,' Dougie Poole said, and he smiled rather sadly as we took our seats in the ram-packed bar. Half the bottle was left; Poole signalled for another glass. He was no advertisement for champagne-drinking, and I insisted he give me no more than *half* a glass.

'What's the celebration Dougie?' I asked.

'Oh, life itself. Being alive, you know.'

'And not being . . . envenomated.'

He pulled a mournful face worthy of Leno himself. 'Why did we colonise a country that had *those* bloody things in it? All wrong, Jim, all wrong.'

'But you know snakes,' I said.

'Oh,' he said, 'when I was a boy I had a vivarium.'

'A what?'

'Just like an aquarium, Jim, only without water. A harmless little ringed snake I had in there, I think. One and six from a shop in Seven Dials.'

At the Debating Society dance, he'd said it was a grass snake; and on the pages of *The Captain* that I'd looked at a moment ago it had been an adder.

'What did you feed it on?'

'At first, newts. But that was an accident. I mean, I kept the newts in a vivarium, and Gregory ate them.'

'Hold on. Who was Gregory?'

'The snake. Then I got in frogs.'

'Where did you find the frogs?'

'In spring there's plenty of frogs all over the place, Jim. You go to, you know, a *pond*.'

'But the rest of the year?'

'The shop in Seven Dials. About thruppence a piece – far too much for a frog if you ask me. Fortunately, snakes don't need much feeding; go without for days on end. They're rather ascetic chaps; don't even need much air. Perfectly content just being in your pocket for a day, and that's where I kept him.'

Whether by accident or design, he was muddying the waters. I decided to make my shot. 'But you wrote to a magazine about snakes, you said?'

'I was forever writing away for enlightenment when I was a lad, Jim. Did you ever read the *Sunday Strand*? There was a fellow in there called the Old Fag or some such thing. Back page. You'd write to him for advice.'

'On what subject?'

'Life. He was an expert on life, Jim. So I dropped him a line. I'd be fifteen or so. It was after I got my start on the railway, anyhow.'

'Which railway, Dougie?'

'Oh, London, Brighton and South Coast. I found office work rather slow, so I sent in a card to the Old Fag saying I'd always fancied myself doing something else: acting, for preference, or writing books. Well, he came down like a ton of coal on the acting. A wandering and uncertain life, dubious company; engaged for three months, and out for six, and so on.'

'And the writing life?'

'He said, if you're a born writer, you'll write a book – won't be able to help it.'

Dougie Poole hadn't written a book as far as I knew.

He now rose to his feet. 'Just going to drain off, Jim,' he said, and he began pushing his way through the liquor bar crowd. The moment he was out of sight, I stood and followed. Did he think I'd got the drop on him? If so, he would go into the reading room instead of the Gentlemen's, and he would check on whether I'd been looking at *The Captain* in order to get on the trail of his true interest in snakes. I was closing on the exit door of the bar just as Poole was pushing his way through it. In the corridor, he approached the open door of the reading room, where the bound volume of *Captain*s that I'd been reading lay undisturbed in the long table. He looked into the room, but did not go in; he continued on his way to the Gents'. Had I been saved from discovery by the colour of the binding?

I myself then ducked into the reading room and set the volume back on the shelf, before regaining our table at the liquor bar, where Poole joined me a moment later.

'How's the missus getting on with the cards?' I said.

'What cards?'

'Hasn't she been dropping cards?'

'You make her sound butter-fingered, Jim.'

'You know what I mean. Has she been giving out calling cards?'

'A few, yes.'

'And how many have been dropped on you?'

'Oh, not many. Shouldn't think. We're no great socialites.'

'Does Margaret mind?'

'Maggie doesn't mind about anything much. She's a good girl.'

You could say this for Dougie Poole: he'd made a good marriage. He was no fool, either. He wouldn't have risen so high in traffic if he had been; but he certainly was a rummy, and with the arrival of the second bottle in prospect, it was time for me to leave him to it.

IV

The Continental motor car was silent, as was its driver. The dark-suited secretary, who had been introduced to me as Mr Chakraborty, was likewise. Major Fisher had done little more than grunt as I climbed into the car at the railway station, and the R.K. himself had fallen to reading some document after greeting me, which he'd done this time with a salaam and not a handshake. Perhaps his religious calendar dictated that on this day he – or more likely I – was untouchable. In order to read, he had put on wire glasses. Observing him in the rear-view mirror, I saw that they did not in way lessen his youthful good looks, but made him look clever in addition.

After leaving town we had been driving, for most of the time, in a wooded valley. There was no rain, but a light morning mist. It might have been an English wood, except that the trees were too big, and there were tattered flags by the roadside. They had been brightly coloured but were now faded, as though a great celebration had been held some years ago: the prayer flags of the Buddhists. There were more Buddhists in Darjeeling than Hindus. We passed a snow-white waterfall and now all the trees gradually became pine trees. They gave off the same scent as the fire that had burned in Cedar Lodge when I had taken my early breakfast.

We turned off the road, and roared quickly up to a wide log

cabin: the clubhouse of the course, evidently. We all climbed out of the car. Something more than a game of golf lay in wait, I was sure of that. In order to delay the moment of its starting, I took out my cigarette case. The R.K. watched me do it.

I said, 'Care for a cigarette, Rajkumar sahib?'

'Please,' he said. 'Take one of mine,' and he trumped my battered silver-plate cigarette case with a solid silver one of his own. I helped myself to a cigarette – they were fat Turkish ones – and the R.K. lit it for me with his Dunhill lighter.

'My name is Narayan, Captain Stringer,' he said. 'And I am a very bad Brahmin, as you can see.' After a pause, he added, 'But not bad in everything. When I marry, I will do it in the correct way. I will marry the one who chooses me, and I will seek to satisfy the requirements of the bride's family.'

So that's his game, I thought: he's going to break the news that Bernadette has chosen him. Well, I would put him off, and I would not mince words in doing so. If trouble flared, I had my Webley in my golf bag (it being impossible to make a golf swing while carrying a revolver in one's suit-coat pocket).

There were two other cars parked before the pavilion, but no other golfers to be seen. We bypassed it anyhow, walking directly to the teeing ground. That is to say, Fisher, the R.K. and I walked there while Mr Chakraborty and the driver remained loitering by the car; I assumed that one or other of them would go into the clubhouse to pay the green fee and find some caddies.

The course was nine holes only, ranging over a series of bright green hummocks that were dotted with little copses, and funny looking conical shelters, which might have been viewing posts, for these green hummocks marked the very edges of the Darjeeling uplands. Beyond was the great gorge in which lay a jumble of smaller hills that began to climb again at a distance of a hundred miles or so, and there the ascent culminated in the Himalayan range, but that white barrier in the distance was currently patrolled by greyish clouds.

On the teeing ground, it was obvious that I was the worst-equipped player, but I had expected that, and the discrepancy was not as great as I had-feared. I had made my knickerbockers by tucking my twill trousers into my thick green stockings, but the R.K. and Fisher both sported the genuine plus-fours. My golf bag was, like Fisher's, made of ordinary brown webbing, whereas the R.K.'s appeared to be made of white calfskin. But he, like Fisher and I, carried only half a dozen clubs, and none of us wore the speciality hob-nailed golf shoes. I was hatless. Fisher and the R.K. wore those wide, round jobs that I always thought resembled dustbin lids, and that I associated with newspaper pictures of sporting Americans. The R.K. must have been somewhat Americanised because he announced that the first hole was a 'par-four', whereas the English term – or at any rate the term always used at Hob Moor Railway course at York – was 'bogey four'. On the teeing ground, Fisher was making ferocious practice swipes with his driver. 'Let's get off while we have the place to ourselves,' he said.

It was the kind of remark that made me glad of having brought the Webley. This course was in a lonely spot, and I was sure there would be many precipitous places in which an inconvenient Englishman might be done away with. Also, it appeared we were not to have our bags carried by caddies, which the R.K. apparently called 'cadets'.

'They are available by prior booking, Captain Stringer,' he explained, while unwrapping a ball, 'but they are generally off-duty Gurkha soldiers, and they tend to glare rather horribly when one addresses the ball. The consequence is that one usually misses entirely.'

So it appeared that this member of Indian royalty would be carrying his own bag.

'Will you have the honour, Captain Stringer?' he said.

I nodded in thanks, and stepped up. 'Stroke play or match play?' I asked, and nobody seemed to know, or care.

'Just get on with it, will you?' said Fisher.

'We'll play just for fun,' said the R.K. 'And do take your time,' he added, with a glance of reproach at Fisher.

The green was four hundred yards off, at the end of a fairway pinched in at the middle by two copses. As I made my own address, Fisher was still making his practice swipes.

'Major Fisher will now *stand still*,' said the R.K., and this he did.

I took my usual three-quarter swing, the theory being that this was a quarter less likely to go wrong than a full swing. The ball made a hundred and fifty yards, approximately straight.

'Trouble free,' the R.K. said, pleasantly. He invited Fisher to play next, and he sent the ball fifty yards further. He was a decent hand at the game. Then the R.K. drove with a quick, short swipe of the ball . . . directly into the trees on the right.

'Sliced it,' he said, simply. 'Why do I play this game?'

As we walked at a lick towards our three balls, Fisher said to the R.K., 'Your stance is too open, isn't it? Remember the invisible line that runs—'

'Stop!' commanded the R.K. 'Or I shall be blinded by science.'

Fisher and I made our second shots, while the R.K. looked for his ball in the trees. He found it on the margin of the trees, made his address, and committed the same fault as before. 'More of the same,' he said, as he watched the ball land in a bunker to the right of the green. 'It's that world-famous Chinese torture, Captain Stringer,' he said, as we marched on. 'Death by a thousand slices!'

I looked back and saw two men – both Europeans – on the teeing ground behind us. Against all expectations, we had company on the course. Fisher had seen them. The R.K. enquired, 'What is your home course, Captain Stringer?'

'Oh, just the Hob Moor course in York, Yorkshire,' I said, and he was nodding as though he knew it of old.

'It's the railway course,' I said. 'It's on Corporation land, so it's open to the general public. In practice that means people walking aggressive dogs . . . or small boys. The boys cricket on the greens when golf isn't being played – and when it *is*.'

'Oh dear,' said the R.K. 'This Hob Moor place is sounding worse by the minute!'

'The clubhouse is an old carriage,' I said.

'Well, that's charming at least,' said the R.K.

He wouldn't think that if he saw it.

We had now approached his sliced ball. The R.K. flashed at it. 'That's how to do a slice,' he said, watching the result. 'Just in case you didn't know.'

And so it was for the next three holes. Fisher played reasonably well, and kept silence. The R.K., whether using brassie, mashie or niblick, would slice the ball to the edge of the fairway or clean out of bounds, and after each of these fluffs he would make some self-deprecating remark in his English that was good but ever so slightly 'off'.

'Mmm . . . misplaced,' he would say, or 'Misguided', or 'That transcended a joke.'

On the fifth hole, the R.K. was in a fairway bunker, having *hooked* the ball for a change. He selected his jigger. 'My father is endeavouring to build a course in Suryapore,' he said, 'but we can't get the right grass: the bent grass, you know – for the greens.'

The R.K. was looking over my shoulder as he spoke. 'There is Mount Everest, by the way,' he said. While clouds were gathering above our heads, the ones at that far distance had cleared sufficiently to show a mountain in between two other mountains – and rather smaller than them, being further away, as though shyly hiding.

But I would not continue the pretence of being on some pleasant tourist outing.

I said to the R.K., 'I believe you know my daughter.'

'Bernadette,' he said, in a perfectly even tone after making his shot. 'Friend of Ann and Claudine. I have danced with all of them, but Bernadette is the best dancer. I have danced three or four times with her, and I have heard her play piano as well. She plays like . . .' I thought he might say 'an angel', but instead he said, 'an earthquake . . . I love the sound of it. I was discussing this charming girl, and Major Fisher mentioned that you were her father.'

Fisher, having played his own second shot, had now positioned himself directly alongside the R.K., dwarfing him in size. I thought he must be 'the heavy': that *must* be it. Fisher and the R.K. had their backs to the green; my back was to the teeing ground.

'It was then that I determined to meet you,' the R.K. continued, 'and hence my invitation to golf today.'

I heard a loud thump behind me, and a golf ball came to rest three feet behind my heel. The two men following had not waited for us to move out of range before teeing off.

'That's bloody rude,' said Fisher, and he knew all about rudeness. He looked furious, whether because of the arrival of the ball or because of what it had interrupted I could not say.

'We will let them play through,' said the R.K., so we waved the two behind to come on, while we backed on to the semi-rough. The pair did not thank us as they walked up to their second shots. They were Englishmen all right. I heard one say to the other, 'It was a cram exam, and I'm a good crammer.'

When the two had played a pair of decent approaches to the green, I said to the R.K., 'You were saying about my daughter?'

But he was still watching the two Englishmen. 'We will let them get well ahead,' he said, before turning towards me once more.

'My daughter,' I repeated. But it had commenced to rain, and the R.K. said, 'Let's take refuge in that cadet shelter.'

V

The shelter was a little way inside the trees. It resembled a turret that had become detached from a castle. Close by was a guru's tree, with painted lower trunk, and candles set into the roots. Affecting to be interested in this curiously placed shrine, I urged Fisher and the R.K. to go on ahead of me towards the shelter, saying I would catch them up in a moment. The tree had perhaps been chosen because of the dreamlike flowers that grew from creepers in its branches: giant khaki-coloured blooms that I believed were orchids.

I observed the caddie shelter. When Fisher and the R.K. were inside it, I took the Webley from my golf bag, and put it into a pocket of my suit coat. I then made my own way through the dripping trees to join them. The interior was unlined bricks with sacking and cigarette stubs on the floor. In the semi-darkness, I could smell the fustiness of the sacking, and a hint of the R.K.'s cologne. He removed his cap, and dabbed his brow with a good handkerchief. He smiled at me. Fisher, meanwhile, was fumbling inside his suit-coat pocket. He removed a metal tube, about six inches long – the very item, surely, that Canon Peter Selwyn had seen him attempting to conceal after the shooting of John Young. Fisher eyed me as he detached the end of the tube, and he removed from it a cigar. It was nothing more than the expensive sort of cigar retainer, made of silver plate or silver. It seemed that his days of smoking the little Trichies were over.

The R.K. was saying, 'When Major Fisher pointed you out to me at the dance, he mentioned that he was your colleague on the enquiry team; he also said you'd worked on the narrow gauge railways in France. But excuse me – am I to speak of narrow, small or light railways?'

Major Fisher was sniffing his cigar.

'Havana,' said Fisher, when he saw me eyeing him.

I hesitated. The R.K. had asked a question about railways. Not about my daughter. I started in about how 'narrow' and 'small' gauge were interchangeable terms. A railway designated 'light' could be either, or it could be a railway of the standard gauge, but either way it would have been given certain exemptions by the Ministry of Transport as regards signalling, fencing, level crossing and so on. 'But I am speaking of Britain,' I added.

'And *I* am speaking of the tiny Indian state of Suryapore,' said the R.K., 'where my father wants to build a railway – a light railway – to carry from our two small mines of coal to our principal river, which is in fact our *only* river, for onward shipment. I am employing Major Fisher here to implement this project.'

'But Major Fisher works for the East Indian Railway,' I said, eyeing the man once again.

'Not for long,' said Fisher.

I asked at random one of the numerous questions swirling in my mind: 'Where did you two meet?'

'At the Tollygunge Club,' said the R.K. 'I was told Major Fisher was in the railway business somehow, and I resolved to engage him in conversation . . . I like a challenge, you know.'

We both looked at Fisher, who lifted the cigar to his lips and viciously bit off the end.

'You shouldn't do that with a Havana,' I said.

'Stow it,' he said.

I turned to the R.K., asking simply, 'Where do I come in?'

The R.K. said, 'You will be returning to Britain at the end of August. Major Fisher and I wonder whether you would be willing to act as our agent in the mother country. It would be a short commission, but well worth your while in the monetary sense. We would want half a dozen locomotives, perhaps twenty covered goods wagons and a small number of coaching vehicles. We have settled on the two-foot gauge, and so you would be required to hunt up the war-surplus stock.'

'Can't you find the two-foot gauge in India?' I said.

'If I were you,' said Fisher, who was finally lighting his Havana cigar, 'I wouldn't look a gift horse in the mouth.'

'Some of the British war surplus did come out here, Captain Stringer,' said the R.K., 'but it has often been badly tampered with. It all seems to have been through something much worse than a mere war . . . and so we look to the homeland.'

'Right,' I said. 'Well, I'll be happy to try and help.'

'Good,' said the R.K. 'We can refine the details over the coming weeks. This is for you, Captain Stringer, to seal the deal.'

He removed a silver hip flask from his golf bag; he passed it to me. In sheer relief, I took a sip of what was probably excellent whisky before thinking about it, and then – also before thinking about it – I passed the flask back to the R.K. He managed to refuse it by smiling and bowing.

'But you must have it back,' I said.

'Oh, but you will never manage to *give* it back,' he said, still smiling. 'You are stuck with it.'

Of course, no Hindu would share in that way. I coloured up, but that didn't matter. He wasn't asking me to visit his home state, and he wasn't asking me to take Bernadette there. He did not seem particularly interested in Bernadette: she was just a dancing partner, and I found myself, in spite of everything, a little put out by that. But on balance I was greatly relieved. Fisher had not acted in concert with the R.K. to kill me on the night train, and it appeared that he had not been carrying a silencer on that train either. Rather, he had been carrying an expensive cigar in an expensive cigar tube, both purchased on the strength of having hit the jackpot with the R.K. I assumed that he had wanted to ride up with me to Darjeeling in order to sound me out on small gauge railways, and make sure I was the man for the job.

Fisher had now stepped outside the caddie shelter. It had stopped raining; there were golden gleams of sun in the sky, and the guru's tree looked much prettier and less sinister to my mind. I covertly returned the Webley to the pouch in my golf bag.

We resumed our game on the sixth hole, a dogleg. I played a safe, short shot with my mashie. The R.K. attempted the same. I didn't see where his ball went, but he made another of his curious observations after the hit: 'I am in the artificial sand.' He meant another bunker. Fisher took out his driver. He meant to try and cut the corner.

'Hold this,' he said, handing me his cigar.

He succeeded in his attempt.

As he reclaimed his cigar I said, 'I fancy a couple of these.'

'Yes, well, you can buy your own can't you?'

'Where from?'

'I had this from Hatzopolo's on Lindsay Street.'

'In Calcutta?'

'That's the only Lindsay Street that I know of,' he said, and we all walked on at our habitual fast pace.

Behind us, the two Englishmen were mounting the teeing ground. They had been off taking their own shelter from the rain, and were now to the rear of us once again. Mine was the first ball we came to. I hit a bad hook, and it clattered into the trees. There was no point looking for it. I took another ball from my bag, unwrapped it, and this time found the apron of the green. The R.K., meanwhile was frowning in the sand trap.

'I'm half buried,' he said. 'I don't think my jigger will do the trick.'

Fisher took a club from his own bag, and carried it over to the R.K.

'Will that one fit the bill?' asked the R.K.

'I should bloody hope so,' said Fisher, blowing smoke. 'It's called a bloody "sand wedge" after all.'

I was thinking, 'Is that any way to talk to royalty?' when some sensation, the cause of which I was not immediately aware, made me turn to see a golf ball flying towards my eye at a hundred miles an hour; I rocked back. I had escaped practically certain death by two inches, and I had done so because Fisher and the R.K. had given a joint shout of 'Fore!' in the very nick of time. The ball had been struck by one of the two Englishmen behind, and he was approaching now as I picked myself off the ground, 'Sorry about that, old man,' he was saying. 'I was trying to cut the corner. By rights it would have gone miles over your head, but I rather topped it.'

'I don't think it is quite within the spirit of the game,' said the R.K., with folded arms. 'Not etiquette.'

'Well, now,' said the Englishman, 'as to that . . . I have apologised sincerely, and I do not think I need further instruction in what is, after all, a game invented in my home country.'

He was English and golf had actually been invented in Scotland. But what he meant was that he wouldn't take instruction from an Indian.

'Faults on both sides,' suggested the other Englishman.

Fisher walked fast towards the first Englishman, and belted him hard in the face. 'There are now,' he said.

I had known the fellow was for it, simply because Fisher had dropped his good cigar and trodden on it before making his advance. I could see the Havana now, flattened and dead in the semi-rough. The R.K. was shaking his head and looking down at the ground. The two Englishmen, one of them bleeding heavily from the nose, were hurrying back to the clubhouse with Fisher staring after them. For them, and for us, the game was over.

Chapter Ten

I

The hall at the Gymkhana Club was more like a gym*nasium* to my mind: a bare, echoing place with a viewing gallery running around the top. At least, that had been my impression at seven o'clock. Come eight o'clock, the place was no longer bare, but packed with perspiring dancers who moved under an ever-thickening cloud of cigar smoke and whisky fumes.

Lydia and I had had two waltzes, and had eaten the supper that had been served at ten. It had been a good dinner, involving a transparent soup with shredded meat in it, a haddock in cheese sauce, and lamb chops – but all in *French*. We now stood side by side on the gallery, looking down at the dancers. It was like looking down on a fairground, with multiple little coloured revolutions occurring. The dancers included Bernadette, Ann Poole and Claudine Askwith, and the music was one of the American specialities, which the lead bandsman called 'jass'. Bernadette, Ann and Claudine were all about the familiar business of embracing their partners, holding them out for inspection, approving of what they saw, and so embracing them again. Each danced with a young subaltern, or at any rate men in white mess jackets and sparkling shoes.

The R.K. was present, or had been, and he and I had chatted pleasantly about small-gauge railways. He had then danced one dance with Bernadette, and he may now have left for another social function entirely. Bernadette, twirling away below me, did not seem to be missing him.

This could be accounted for as follows . . .

After the golf game, I had returned to Cedar Lodge to find Lydia in but Bernadette out on a call with her friends. I had explained about the game to Lydia, and I had given her my insights into the character of the R.K. I had told him of the commercial offer he had made me, and I said I'd found him a thoroughly pleasant and sensible young fellow, almost completely European in his ways. I doubted very much that he kept a harem, and so on.

Eventually Lydia cut in, saying, 'Tell Bernadette all that.'

'But it would only encourage her,' I said.

Lydia, who had been sitting on the sofa and drinking a beef tea made with milk (she had been drinking no end of that revolting concoction recently), had made no answer to this, except to slowly shake her head before taking another sip of her drink. Darjeeling, it seemed, was not doing her any good at all.

When Bernadette was delivered back to Cedar Lodge, I proposed that she and I go for a walk. She said she didn't want to come; she had a jigsaw to be getting on with. I told her the jigsaw could wait. She said, 'No, it can't.' I said I wanted to tell her about a game of golf I had just played with the R.K., and at this she had put on her coat again directly.

We walked, through failing light, towards that part of town called Chowstra, a pretty little colony of chalets and trinket shops. We walked into a wood-smelling tea shop, and I bought Bernadette a cup of cocoa.

'I bet Raju's ripping at golf,' she said.

'He's very nearly as good as me,' I replied.

'But you're atrocious at golf.'

The observation was grist to my mill, so I kept silent.

'You talked to him about me, I suppose.'

'The moment I mentioned your name, he immediately knew who you were. He said, "Yes, she's the friend of Ann and Claudine."'

Another silence.

'I don't believe you,' Bernadette said. 'You're just trying to make me think less of him.' And there were tears in her eyes.

I said, 'I am being completely honest.'

'Swear on your mother's grave.'

My mother had died at the moment of my birth, as Bernadette well knew. She had often called on me to swear on her grave, and I did so again now. 'And I am being completely honest when I say I found him a thoroughly likeable young chap. I'm sure he doesn't keep a harem, and it was ridiculous of me to think that he did.'

'Yes. It was.'

'He and I hit it off pretty well. Did you know he has a keen interest in small-gauge railways?'

Bernadette was looking sidelong; but she was rallying, I could tell. There would be no more tears.

'He's planning to lay out one himself,' I continued, 'in the two-foot gauge. He and his father are more like company directors than minor royalty, and they run Suryapore very much on business lines, but also with one eye on the interests of the people. They pay their taxes as you said, and they give no trouble. They're a model of the kind of rulers that the government wants to encourage. Now I don't know how things stand between the two of you, but if you wanted to have him around for tea or something, then I for one would make no objection. In fact, I'd very much enjoy the chance to have another chinwag with him.'

Bernadette was looking at her empty cup. At length, she said with utter disgust, 'A *chinwag?*'

As we walked back to Cedar Lodge, she said, 'He has an interest in railways, you say?'

'Little ones, yes.'

And we walked on in silence.

I did not believe that I alone had been responsible for Bernadette's cooling towards him, but my approval of the chap had apparently sealed his fate, and I believed I had rescued my daughter from what could only have been a painful entanglement on both sides. But if the wife was pleased about this outcome, then she had not said so. She had appeared indifferent. Her gloomy mood had continued, and she was silent as she stood beside me now, on the gallery of the Gymkhana hall. Presently, she did a half-turn towards me to say something. I couldn't hear above the pounding of the 'jass', but she moved away from me directly after. As a rule, the wife never gloomed for more than a day, and I was starting to think there was more to this than the matter of a return of cards.

I wandered down from the gallery, and through the hall. The band members were taking a breather, so I could hear the talk of the guests.

I heard, 'They've overdone the servants. You can't see the bloody wood for the trees.' And I heard, 'Do they ever go out and about, the purdah ladies?'

I stepped outside, and lit a Gold Flake. The evening was mild. Rickshaws awaited, and a couple of motors, but not the R.K.'s. Yes, he must have left already, and Fisher had not shown up at all. I crossed the road, from where I could look out over the downward portion of the twinkling town. It was a beautiful spot, but it had made my wife miserable – or *something* had.

I tossed away my cigarette stump, and re-entered the hall, where I saw Dougie Poole taking a drink from one of the tables that lined the hall. He was wavering somewhat as he moved away with it, and I wondered whether he had sobered up even for a moment since I had seen him last. I then clapped eyes on William Askwith. He was saying to a big, lobster-like man, 'You get rather a mixed bag up here, now,' and he was eyeing Poole all the while. In spite of the blankness of Askwith's face, it was pretty clear to me that he thought Poole an unfavourable specimen. Askwith's eye now fell on me with, perhaps, a different sort of blankness on his face. He approached with hand outstretched, and every appearance of amiability.

'Captain Stringer,' he said. 'Delighted to see you here. I hope the mountain air is clearing your mind of any Commission of Enquiry headaches with which you may be afflicted?'

It was difficult to know what to say to that.

'As a loyal servant of the Company, it would be quite wrong of me to suggest that you have been enjoined to clean the Augean stables, Captain Stringer, but—'

'There's a lot to be getting on with,' I said, 'yes. But I know you're pretty hard-pressed in traffic as well.'

'Quite so, and to continue the equine train of thought, we are rather changing horses in mid-stream. You may have heard that we had considered putting in to the Board for substantial new orders of rolling stock.'

'Passenger or freight?'

'Oh, both. We had conducted the necessary surveys, and armed ourselves with a pretty watertight case . . .'

'But surely', I said, 'there's no shortage of passenger carriages at least. At any one time there are hundreds standing idle around Howrah. A carriage might be there for a couple of months between runs, surely? And they're not properly guarded, hence all this snake trouble.'

Askwith's expression did not change, because it could not change.

'The Board might well have made that very same point, Captain Stringer, had we proceeded with our application. It is likely they would also have trotted out the familiar line that when Indian passenger carriages are overcrowded, the Indians simply resort to travelling on the roof!'

I gave the half smile that seemed to be required.

'Such observations are always likely to be made by those unacquainted with the plans and diagrams from which we work. Nevertheless, in consideration of the economy drive presently underway, we propose to withdraw our application for supplementary stock, and I will propose instead a more scientific system of rotation.'

Askwith was raising his glass in greeting to someone over my shoulder.

'And how would that work?' I said.

'In essence, the periodical repairs ought to occur after a certain number of miles rather than a certain period of *time*. That way, the number of running miles would be kept permanently in view, and in place of a mass of irrelevant documentation I would like to see introduced a new and simplified distribution card – a universal document, you see – for every rake of carriages or wagons, these to be filled out by the running men, and also used as a record by the traffic managers.'

'I see,' I said, because I almost did.

But now the woman who'd been signalling to Askwith came up and claimed him, and I went looking for the wife, while revolving all that Askwith had said, and wondering above all why *why* he'd given me all that technical stuff. I knew I'd found Lydia when – during another pause in the music – I heard an aggrieved male voice saying, 'You seem awfully keen to get the British out of here.'

He was in a sitting-out room together with Lydia and half a dozen others. The speaker was somewhere at the top of the Boss Class, a friend of Askwith's. His name was Kendall, I believed, and he had public school written all over him.

'I don't wish to be rude,' he said to Lydia, 'but you could make a start by leaving yourself.'

'My passage home is booked for 30 August on the P&O line,' Lydia said, which was true enough. 'On returning, I will be giving a series of talks to some organisations I am involved with, and I will speak of the charm, politeness, modesty and forbearance I've met out here.'

'She means from the natives,' somebody said, rather bitterly.

'I mean from the *Indians*.'

'They're not all forbearing,' said Kendall. 'There are people at this dance who've been the victims of revolutionists.'

'Who?'

'Major Askwith,' said Kendall. 'He was riding on a tram in Calcutta, and he—'

'Had his hat removed, yes.'

'He could have had a sunstroke.'

'Yes,' said Lydia. 'But instead of that, he walked into the Army & Navy Stores and bought himself a new hat.'

'I was talking to him at the Governor's tea party,' said Kendall.

'Do you know what that man does to bring on young Indians in his department of the railway? Damn it all, we're here for their own good.'

Lydia said, 'So British India is one big charitable endeavour?'

Silence for a space.

'You could say that, yes.'

A clever-looking old woman in a long Victorian dress gave a snort at that. She very delicately took a thin cigarette from a silver case and lit it. She was enjoying herself no end.

'As Christians,' Lydia said to Kendall, '... we *are* all Christians, I suppose..?'

Somebody said, '*Rather*.'

'... *As* Christians,' Lydia ran on, 'we're not supposed to assert our moral superiority.'

'Who says?' enquired Kendall, genuinely baffled.

'John 8:7.'

'Well, I daresay...' said Kendall, who'd gone a bit vague.

'"Let he that is without sin cast the first stone",' quoted the man who'd said 'Rather.'

The shrewd-looking old lady pointed her cigarette at Lydia and said, 'I think *you've* just asserted *your* moral superiority.' It was a blow struck on Kendall's behalf, but he didn't seem to have noticed. He was lumbering along some distance behind.

He said, 'I'm not asserting my *own* moral superiority...'

'Anyone who knows Mr Kendall knows that would be ludicrous,' said the old woman.

Kendall said, 'I'm asserting the moral superiority of the British state over the condition of anarchy.'

Somebody said, 'I think we lost the moral high ground after the Amritsar massacre,' and everyone turned towards the new speaker, a young subaltern by the looks of him. This was a very unexpected – and strong – intervention on Lydia's side.

Kendall said, 'You are speaking of the Ajnala incident?'

Lydia said, 'When they kill us it's an "outrage", when we kill them it's an "incident".'

'Who is your husband?' the old woman suddenly asked Lydia. She seemed to keep switching sides – just to keep trouble brewing.

'I don't see what that's got to do with anything,' said Lydia, but somebody pointed to me, saying, 'There he is.'

Kendall looked my way: 'You're a railway officer, I think?'

I explained that I was a police detective, seconded to the East Indian Railway Commission of Enquiry.

The man who'd pointed me out (whom I'd never clapped eyes on before), said, 'You're on a sort of busman's holiday, I suppose. No offence meant.'

'I've nothing against busmen,' I said.

Half turning towards me, Lydia said, 'I should imagine my husband fought alongside plenty of them in the Somme Battle.'

I could have kissed her for that, especially since she looked so miserable. As a rule, this sort of ding-dong would do wonders for her.

The doughty old woman said, 'Can't see why anybody would mind an investigation. Unless they were on the take.'

Kendall, who had coloured at the Somme remark, coloured further at that.

Lydia stood up and looked across the room at me, with a sad half-smile that I could not understand.

Bernadette too was silent in the tonga as the three of us rode back to Cedar Lodge. But whereas the wife's silence was unfathomable,

Bernadette's was less heavy and more thoughtful. I was convinced that her infatuation with the R.K. was over, and so I had scored a victory on that front. I also felt that the question of Fisher had been satisfactorily resolved. All, or most, of his mysterious behaviour could now be accounted for, and I intended to reward myself by spending my last full day in 'the hills' doing little or nothing.

Back in Calcutta, Lydia and Bernadette had booked a programme of cross-country horse rides, and these would start tomorrow, from some stables at Ghum. Perhaps the exercise would do something to buck Lydia up, or maybe it would take my own departure to do that. I was an anchor to the wife's social ambitions, and she might float free without me.

There were no returned cards waiting for her at the Lodge, but as Ajit took our coats, he handed me a small and more official envelope that had arrived for me only an hour earlier. It was from the duty sergeant at the Darjeeling police office on Auckland Road. Detective Inspector Khudayar Khan of the Calcutta CID was in town, and he would be obliged if I would get in touch as soon as practically possible so that arrangements could be made for a further interview regarding the shooting of John Young on the night train to Jamalpur.

II

The arrangement made was that the detective inspector would come to Cedar Lodge. It happened that the door was opened to him by Lydia, and I heard her speaking rather merrily to him as I came downstairs. His presence seemed to have a galvanising effect on her, even though I had warned her that he could be out to fix a murder charge on me. She was holding his Panama hat as she said, 'It seems a shame to sit chattering over teacups in such a very beautiful place.' I did not catch his murmured response. He did not need to say much, looking as he did: blue twill suit with military cut, starched white collar.

I took him into the living room, closing the door firmly on Lydia. He was not a man for chit-chat, and I was in no mood for it. Inviting him to take a seat, I said, 'What progress has Hughes made at Jamalpur?'

'None whatsoever.'

'No dacoits have been identified?'

'They have not,' Khan said, taking from his suit-coat pocket a little leather notebook. He made a heading in it.

'Have you come up to Darjeeling just to see me?' I enquired.

No reply.

'You haven't come for the views, I take it.'

'The views are occluded today, as you will have seen for yourself.'

'I suppose it would bother me somewhat if I thought you'd come three hundred miles just to see me.'

'I have other business here as well. Half of Calcutta is here, as you know.'

'Including Major Fisher. Will you be interviewing him again?'

No reply.

'I don't know the whereabouts of Canon Peter Selwyn,' I said. 'I haven't seen him up here. Will you be interviewing *him*?'

'Detective Inspector Stringer,' said Khan, 'the fingerprint results have been returned from the bureau. Your prints were found all over John Young's compartment, and all over his warrant badge.'

'Yes,' I said. 'I told you they would be.'

'You were in there talking with him.'

'Yes.'

'Talking and drinking whisky.'

'You see,' I said. 'You know it all.'

Khan did not like that, but he was the same rank as me, and I would not kowtow to him.

'When we talked,' I continued, 'he passed his pocket book over to show me some pictures of his family. I took an interest in his warrant badge, which was set into the pocket book in the usual way – held by leather tabs.'

'The money was taken from that pocket book.'

'I did not rob the man.'

'Of course not, and ten years ago the matter would have ended with your denial.'

'Because I work for the imperial power.'

'We both work for the imperial power, which is why we must not appear to be in collusion. Remind me why you were touching his warrant badge.'

'I was curious about it.'

A pause while Ajit brought in the tea.

'Let me assist you,' said Khan, when Ajit had departed. 'It is an aesthetic matter for you. You consider these tokens beautiful.'

'I suppose so.'

'But you have one yourself. You can study your own.'

'Mine is temporary. It's made of pasteboard. You see, I am what some people call a "railwayac".'

'A what?'

'A railway maniac – shortened to railwayac. I have an annual subscription to the *Railway Magazine*. I am a member of the

Railway Club.'

'That is in London.'

'The headquarters of the Club, yes. But it's famous all over the world.'

'I have never heard of it.' He eyed me for a while. 'Tell me,' he said, 'have you ever stood on platforms with the intention not of catching a train, but of writing down the number on the side of the engine?'

'As a boy, yes.'

'When I was in London, I saw individuals doing that at King's Cross station – grown men as well as boys. I never thought I would meet such a person.'

Silence in the room. He had not touched his tea.

'I have not seen it done in India,' he said, 'this number-taking.'

'Well, you never know what's happening on Indian railway platforms. They're generally teeming. There are people *living* on the platforms.'

'Living and dying, Detective Inspector Stringer,' Khan said.

He had used my police rank to remind me of its equivalence with his own; to remind me this was a war between the two of us. I had previously done the same with him. How much did he care about John Young? If I read the man right, Khan was a nationalist who saw the Anglo-Indians as the lackeys of the British. Therefore he did not care for John Young. But it would suit a man like Khan very nicely if I could be proved to have *shot* John Young. The Anglos were one of the mainstays of British rule, and certainly of the railways. The killing of a high-ranking Anglo-Indian by a British policeman would go some way to wrecking that alliance.

'It's too easy for non-travellers to get on to Indian railway platforms, and railway lands generally,' I said. 'It is very much the sort of thing I'd like to see reformed.'

'Is it now?'

After a further interval of silence, I asked, 'Has there been another snake attack?'

'I don't believe so. Possibly. That is not my investigation.' He hesitated. 'Tell me,' he enquired at length, 'would your railway interest extend to . . .'

'To what?'

'No matter.'

Kahn eyed me – then glanced down at the fireplace, which was unlit.

'There is no coal,' I said.

'I know.'

'Does my railway interest extend to *what*?' I said.

'Nothing,' he said, rising to his feet. 'It doesn't matter.'

This sort of reversal wasn't like him at all; therefore it must be significant. In moving towards the door, he saw the book by Annie Besant, which Lydia had been reading, and which she had left on the sofa.

'You're interested in Besant and the Congress?' enquired Khan.

'My wife,' I said. 'She's something of an Indian nationalist. There aren't many of those around here,' I added.

'More than you might think,' he said.

'Where are you staying?'

'In a guest house by the police station. My expenses don't run to the good hotels.'

And on that gloomy note, our conversation ended.

III

In mid-morning of the next day, Wednesday 9 May, I arranged for a railway bearer to collect my kit bag, golf clubs and a portmanteau full of other items that Lydia wanted taking back to Calcutta. He took them to the left luggage office at the station. I myself was not due there until five past four, departure time of the Siliguri 'down' train. Some people I didn't know came round for what we at Cedar Lodge were apparently calling luncheon. Lydia and Bernadette had met them on the train up. The man was a doctor with a practice in Calcutta, the woman was a do-gooder. They were both very interested in feeding the poor, but were not connected to the St Dunstan's Fund of Eleanor Askwith. In fact, they disapproved of that for some reason, which was probably why Lydia had dropped a card on them in the first place. The woman was a good deal younger than the man, and – against all odds – rather a peach. I began thinking again of Miss Hatsuyo of Chowringhee and her Japanese speciality, and then of the adjacent plaque of Dr Ganguly and his own peculiar speciality. As Ajit and Sahira took the main-course plates away, I asked the doctor sitting opposite me, 'Do you know what phthisis is?'

'I should hope so,' he said. 'It's pulmonary tuberculosis.' He proceeded to describe this, until his until his wife told him to stop, since he was ruining everyone's enjoyment of the pudding.

After luncheon, Lydia and Bernadette went off to their horse riding. I kissed them goodbye and said I would see them in three weeks' time. If anything came up, they were to go to the telegraph office, from where they could telephone to me at either Willard's Hotel or Fairlie Place. When they'd gone, I drank a cup of tea and smoked a Gold Leaf before the living room fire in which the scented logs burned. Ajit told me they were deodar wood. He also said that a delivery of coal would be made around the town that afternoon.

At two o'clock, I quit the house. I had a free hand – literally since I had no bags to carry. I used that free hand to smoke further cigarettes while walking along the Mall. I was making for the Hotel Mount Everest, where Fisher was staying. My own suspicions of Fisher had fallen away after the golf game, but I intended to ask him whether Khan had interviewed him for a second time. I also wondered whether Khan had found anything on the two Mohammedan servants. He was a Mohammedan himself, so perhaps he would go easy on them, even if he did suspect. And then there was the Reverend Canon Peter Selwyn, churchman and Uranian. Was he a practising Uranian, or merely a student of the literature? Perhaps I had not thought enough about Peter Selwyn.

It was a steep uphill walk to the Hotel Mount Everest, which was only right, given the name. It stood on Woodlands Road, and was raised up again from that on an elevated walkway with railings to stop you falling over the edge. The exterior was white with black wood beams; the lobby was decorated with photographs of the actual Mount Everest . . . and Major Fisher was not in. He had left his keys at the reception, and gone out some hours before. A bearer was called over, and he verified that he had carried Fisher's golf clubs to a waiting taxi. Fisher had a nerve, I thought, going back to the Tiger Hill golf course, scene of the assault he had committed. But then he *was* a man for the bold stroke, and it was beginning to seem to me that he was quite often rewarded for it.

I wandered from the Hotel Mount Everest to the telegraph office, from where I sent a wire to Jongendra Babu at Fairlie Place, giving the time I was due in at Howrah, and asking that Deo Rana be sent to meet me. I drifted back west to some precipitous gardens built on terraces. A weak sunlight was now filtering through the clouds. Some Chinese-looking children were sitting on a bench, kicking their legs and singing 'Clementine', apparently with no adult anywhere near. The gardens – oriental children apart – reminded me of the gardens on the cliff top at Scarborough, and I thought of Charles Sermon, the traffic man who frequented the Railway Institute in Calcutta. He was due for retirement, and had fixed up to live in Scarborough, but he hadn't seemed very pleased about it. You shouldn't try to *live* in a pleasure ground. It would not deliver the goods – perhaps Sermon knew that in advance. Lydia had found it out about Darjeeling.

I looked at my watch. Forty-five minutes to train time.

I climbed higher, and the gardens gave way to a recreation ground, where some other Chinese-looking children were playing football. The goalkeeper, aged about ten, bowed a salaam to me as I walked past. I returned the bow from the touchline, but so awkwardly that the lad dashed off his goal line to greet me in the manner to which he thought I would be more accustomed. But as we shook hands, a shot was fired into the vacated goal, and there was an uproar from his teammates.

On the other side of the football pitch, I glimpsed a small European man. I thought it was Dougie Poole, but he did not return my wave, and quickly disappeared behind a wall with roses growing over it.

Twenty minutes later, I was walking along Auckland Road, which consisted mainly of big villas and sleepy-looking gardens. The police station was here, with its own front garden, just as sleepy as the rest. There was not only a monkey puzzle tree in the police garden, there was also a monkey. It walked like a man I had once arrested.

Alongside the police station was a villa advertised by a sign on the front lawn as Rockville Guest House. Khan had said he was putting up near the police station: this must be the place.

I walked along the crazy paving that led to the front door, which stood open. It gave on to an empty hallway. No bearer or chowkidar of any kind stepped out to greet me. I read the breakfast menu, posted in a display case on the wall. 'Sausages and curried eggs,' I read. The tea was 'finest Darjeeling'. Well, it would be. There was a high desk to one side – the kind you stood up to work at, a green ledger sitting upon it. The handwriting in the ledger was of perfect clarity: Mr Khan had booked into room 4. Half a dozen keys, with wooden tokens attached, dangled from the underside of the desk. Six keys, but eight hooks. The guests who were in residence retained their keys; the ones who were out hung them here. Branded into the wooden tokens were numbers, and key number 4 was present. I pocketed it; I bounded up the wide stairs.

I knocked on the door of the first-storey room marked number 4. If Khan answered, what would I say? I would say that there was no servant in the house; that I had discovered his room, and that I wanted an urgent word. I knocked for a second time. An urgent word about what? About the Jamalpur Night Mail, naturally. I would confide my suspicions of . . . my suspicions of Canon Peter Selwyn. He was of the Uranian tendency – in short, queer – and such fellows were sometimes in desperate straits and driven to desperate actions. I left off knocking. The house was unbelievably silent. It could not remain so for long.

I took out the key; I opened the door.

The few contents of the room were beautifully ordered: a folded copy of *The Statesman* on the neatly downturned counterpane; a book on the bedside table written in . . . what? Bengali? Hindustani? To my eye, all Indian lettering looked like the picture of the little dancing men in the Sherlock Holmes story. An oilskin hung from a peg on the door; a pair of highly polished patent shoes waited in shoe trees. There was a wastepaper basket, and inside it a folded brochure for a certain Walter Bushnell, optician of Calcutta. His spectacles would cure your headaches. I was glad to see that Khan needed glasses, this signifying a weakness in his armoury. I stood still. The window overlooked silent Auckland Road. But in the room, a clock was ticking very quickly . . . a small alarm clock propped in its own red leather case. On its face, the word 'Ego' was written in gold plate, and I somehow knew that this item would be Khan's all right, not the property of the house. It was a quarter to four. I had twenty minutes to train time. I was currently about *ten* minutes from the station, but I had to allow time to collect my baggage from the left luggage office. On the mantelpiece stood an unopened tin of cigarettes, Advantage brand. There were golden cuff links in a clean ashtray, a new and unused box of matches, Cutter brand.

I looked down at the grate. I crouched down. There was kindling in the grate, and crumpled paper, ready to burn, but there was no coal in the room – no coal in the town. Some of the paper had handwriting on it. As I reached out towards the paper, I heard a great roaring coming up from the street. I sprang over to the window to see a soot-blackened steam wagon rolling along Auckland Road. It was burning coal for its own engine, and it was *bringing* coal to Darjeeling town. A squad of tough-looking mountain men were hauling sacks of coal from the back of the wagon, and carrying them into the front gardens of the villas. All the houses were taking delivery; Rockville would be no exception, and then the coal would be put on to the fires that were made up and ready to receive it. I looked again at the handwritten papers in the grate. They had not been put in the wastepaper basket. Khan had meant them to be utterly destroyed. I plucked up the handwritten papers – it turned out there were two pages – and I quit the room.

There was nobody on the stairs, nobody in the lobby. I replaced the key on its hook below the high desk, and dashed into the garden. A European woman in gumboots stood near the gate; she was dead-heading flowers while waiting to accept a delivery of coal. I turned sharply right, and doubled back around the house, where I climbed a high embankment, which lead up to a hedge I could not get through. I tracked along the hedge until it was fashioned into an arch over a gate. I went through the gate, and I was now in a lane bounded by the hedges of numerous back gardens. If I missed the train, I would pay no greater penalty than having to stay on in Darjeeling, but I had mysteries to solve, and the answers lay in Calcutta. I began to run.

IV

The 'down' train was two trains, just as the 'up' had been.

I boarded the last carriage of the foremost one with a minute to spare. A little out of breath, I sat down on a cane chair in the final carriage. It was still the time of year to be arriving at Darjeeling rather than leaving it, and my only companions in the saloon were an elderly couple, both with books on the go. They must have been old hands on the mountain train, because they never looked up as the whistle was blown and we began to creak away. I lit a cigarette, at which the woman *did* look up, and pretty sharply, so I walked through the glass door at the carriage end, and on to the veranda. We were slowly embarking on the first loop – the one that ran around the flat-topped hill at Ghum.

We began to coincide with the Cart Road, and I saw coming up a big villa with stables attached. Before the gates of the property stood a collection of riders and horses. The light was already fading, and the riders were dismounting, or milling about with horses in tow. Most were women in jodhpurs, and among them would be Bernadette and Lydia. At a slight distance from the main crowd, an impeccable Indian was descending from his horse while a woman in a long coat – not riding clothes – held the head of his horse. We were now running practically alongside the pair, and I saw that the woman was Lydia, the man was Khan. Well, I had known he was a horseman. I watched them talking – he looking much livelier than he ever did when trying to pin the John Young murder on me – until they were out of sight.

I then transferred my stare to the engine of the train that was following our train.

I walked back to my cane seat, and resumed staring, this time at the descending dusk beyond the window. Trees passed by, gradually becoming darker. After a while, I saw nothing but my own haggard face. I looked malarial and old. No wonder Lydia had not troubled very much about the connection between Bernadette and the R.K.: she had an eye for the bloody Indians herself. It was perfectly clear to me now that Lydia was what they called 'sexually frustrated'. The condition went with being a progressive woman. If they were not frustrated, there would be no point in being progressive, they would just settle for what they had.

Why had Lydia not been riding, but just standing about and spooning with Khan? She'd told me she was going riding with Bernadette. I assumed that Bernadette *had* been riding, but it occurred to me that I now had no reason to believe anything Lydia might say to me. I reached into my pocket, and the silver flask the R.K. had given me was still there, still full of good whisky. Sod the quinine pills. I unscrewed the top and took a long pull, then a second one. The elderly parties in the saloon were deciding they had a 'wrong 'un' in the carriage with them, but I was trying to banish the image of the scene I had observed. It took me a further three pulls on the flask to arrive at the thought that, just as there had been nothing in it between Bernadette and the R.K., so there would probably be nothing in this. And if there was, then she could bloody well have him. She could be the star of her own scandal. It wouldn't prove so very much of a social advance, since Khan was only a detective inspector like me, and, being Indian, unlikely to rise much higher in the Calcutta C.I.D.

I took from my pockets the two bits of paper I had rescued from the fireplace of Khan, and opened them up. I contemplated the dancing men. They might have been perfectly innocuous: chits written to a tradesman, for all I knew. I looked over at the elderly couple. They looked like a pair of intellects; perhaps they understood this lingo? The odds were against. I thought of the office door in Fairlie Place that bore the faded letters: 'Convert to English'. I would take the papers there. Whatever they amounted to, these notes would throw some light on something. I made further inroads on the whisky. It had become too dark for my elderly companions to read, and they were both staring into space. I slept a little, then for a longer time.

I awoke in bright light. The carriage lights had been switched on, and we were in a station. But the station itself was all in darkness. I could just make out the wooden station house some way along the platform. Passengers were drifting into it from the train, and the two who had been in the carriage with me had already left. This must be Kurseong, the halfway point, where the supper break would be taken. I was not hungry, but I decided I would benefit from a breath of air, so I stepped on to the wooden platform, where I stood quite alone in the gloom. The station house was at some twenty yards' distance, a faint orange light at the window. I could hear the throbbing of the petrol engine in the generator wagon: it had been attached to the rear of the train at some earlier stop to give the light for the carriages. Beyond it stood the second train, and that too seemed empty of passengers. From the jungle rising above the station came a repeated animal scream, then came the fast clattering of some bigger beast running through the trees. I could see the dim outlines of the engine men on the platform. They were attending the generator wagon, which was giving trouble in some way. I heard a footfall close behind. There came a sudden blaze of orange light, illuminating a sad-eyed little man.

'It's Dougie Poole, Jim,' he said.

What had occurred was that the engine men had connected the generator to the *station* lights, and Poole now stood revealed beneath one of the platform lamps.

'Clever,' I said, indicating the lights.

'What would be clever, Jim,' he said, 'is if they could light the train *and* the platform.' And it was true: the little train was in darkness once again. The generator could illuminate either one or the other, but not both. Poole was for once not drunk, whereas

I was groggy from the whisky.

'You coming through for the supper?' he said.

'Hold on.' I said. 'Were you at the recreation ground in the town?'

'Took a stroll that way, yes.'

'I saw you.'

'I never saw you, Jim.'

Had he been tailing me? Had he finally worked out that I knew of his interest in venomous snakes?

'Where are you off to?' I said.

'Calcutta, of course.'

'Where's Margaret?'

'Staying on in the hills,' and he indicated the steep forest rising beyond the station.

'So's Lydia,' I said, grimly.

'There you are, then,' said Poole. 'No danger of the social round coming to an end. You all right, Jim?'

'I'm half cut,' I said, producing the silver flask. 'Fancy a belt?'

Poole shook his head. 'I'm off the drink,' he said. 'And for good.'

'What's brought that on?' I said.

'Come on, I'll stand you the supper.'

The little dining room of the station looked like an English tea rooms, right down to tea cosies and chequered tablecloths. But the only food going was no-meat curry.

'I've been given the chuck, Jim,' said Poole.

'Eh?'

'Askwith – at the dance. He took me aside, said I ought to be considering my future.'

'That's not the same as giving you the chuck.'

'Yes it is. Game's up.'

'Was it to do with the new system?'

'Eh?'

'Askwith told me he's bringing in a new system of traffic control,' I said.

'He said that, did he? Well, it hardly matters. Point is, I was canned at the dance, and he said he'd seen me in a bad state too often. India was clearly doing me no good, and I'd be better off going home. I wouldn't qualify for the full pension, but he'd see me right financially, and give me a good character. He said it wasn't too late for me to start again in traffic – said he had connections in the London and North Eastern set-up.'

'Decent of him, I suppose.'

'I didn't put up a fight, Jim. You know why? It was meant to happen. The snake had tipped me the wink, so to speak. An omen. Get out while you can. You know what the Hindus call fate? Karma. I was locked into it Jim, but now I've escaped, and *that's* called moksha. Release, letting go. I'm letting go of India,' he added, as a platform guard came in and announced we had five minutes to finish up before the train departed. There was no time for pudding. Poole picked up an orange in lieu of his.

'So you were fated to escape your fate?' I suggested, when we were back on board the little train. Poole had joined me in my carriage. We sat on opposite cane chairs, with the elderly parties reading once again in the background.

He nodded. 'That's very well put, is that, Jim.' (But you never quite knew when Dougie Poole was joshing.) 'Askwith's right. I'm not cut out for India. Look at me: I'm halfway up a bloody mountain and I'm sweating like a pig. Can't ride, can't shoot . . . I'm not moaning about it, Jim. I mean there's very few from Walthamstow who *can* ride and shoot. I'm generally not up to the mark as a

242

sportsman, apart from the funny sports. You know . . . egg-and-spoon in the Company revels on the maidan . . .'

'Good at egg-and-spoon racing, are you?'

'Not particularly, no. But you're *meant* to lose at that, aren't you? Also, I'm not particularly clubbable . . .'

'Oh, I don't know.'

I heard a rattling sound. It was the door leading to the veranda. Poole didn't seem to hear it. He'd removed the orange from his pocket, and was cutting into it

'And it's all clubs here. You're practically clubbed to death, Jim.'

A dark station floated past. Poole blew out his cheeks, and fell silent. His sad eyes glittered. I took a belt on the whisky in the flask. Interesting though Poole's news was, I couldn't stop thinking of Lydia and the infernal Khan. Were they conducting a liaison? It couldn't possibly be. She wasn't that sort. In all the time I'd known her . . . Well, there was Major Briggs in our home village . . . We often bumped into him on the riverbank with his numerous dogs. That was because he owned the riverbank, or a long stretch of it, and I believed that was half the reason Lydia like to walk there – on the off chance of meeting him, and she always blushed when he raised his hat to her. I took another pull on the whisky.

'Sure you don't care for a drop?' I asked Dougie Poole, and he shook his head. I ought not to be tempting the fellow, but it didn't seem companionable to drink alone on a night train.

We looked through the window. At Kurseong, the two engines had lit giant searchlights mounted on their boilers, and the light from the rearward engine would occasionally show cliff walls, giant trees or jungly depths of an unnaturally bright green. The female of the two elderly readers was now snoring; her book had fallen shut beside her couch, and her husband had done nothing to save the page. Douglas Poole was eyeing me with a curious expression.

'Oh, go on then,' he said.

'What?'

'I'll take a drop.'

I passed over the flask.

'The trouble with me,' said Poole, after he'd glugged for a good ten seconds, 'is I've very little in the way of character.'

He'd just been saying how his encounter with the cobra had *given* him character, stiffened his resolve to get out of India and start again in Blighty. Slurring my words somewhat, I pointed this out to him.

'Oh, I'm a changed man, all right. Just not quite so much changed as I might have said before. Everybody's going to see that.'

'*What*, for God's sake?'

'How changed I am.'

I heard again a rattling from the glass door at the carriage end.

'Before I quit this country,' said Poole, 'I'm going to find out who's leaving these bloody snakes lying about. That way, I'll be on the boat with an achievement under my belt. I'd give worlds to find out who this snake man is.' He looked up at me. 'I'm dead set on finding out.'

'Got any leads?' I said, eyeing him.

'Well, Jim, the real snake fanciers – I mean the *real* boys – are a breed apart. Chilly customers. Cold-blooded, I suppose. Did I ever tell you about the fellow who ran the pet shop in Seven Dials?'

'Where you got the over-priced frogs?'

'He was a rum cove, Jim. He'd sit inside the door of the shop with . . . well, never mind a fur boa, Jim – this bloke wore a boa *constrictor* over his shoulders.'

'Didn't that put people off going in?'

'Of course it did. But the fellow just sat there staring at the window glass with the thing crawling all over him. Daring you to come in, I suppose.'

'Rum,' I said.

'He wore glasses, Jim, and what with the tropical conditions in the shop they were always steamed up; but he didn't bother about that either.'

I thought of Professor Hedley Fleming. I then thought of Peter Selwyn, William Askwith and Charles Sermon. I asked Poole, 'I think you know a fellow called Sermon? He's in traffic, I believe.'

He nodded. 'Nice old boy, long-service medallist with the Company. Old India hand . . . Probably got a tiger skin for a bath-room carpet. Something of a war hero too, I think. Lied about his age to get in to the army; I mean he said he was *younger* than he was, Jim.' Having completely drained the flask, Dougie Poole set it down on the carriage floor. '. . . Sermon was commissioned into the Transport Corps – did two years or so in France. Practic-ally ran Boulogne Docks single-handed by all accounts. Got the D.S.O. for it, I think.'

'He haunts the Railway Institute.'

'That's right. Comes into the office early; does his turn, goes off there for his peg in the late afternoons.'

'Why?'

Poole shrugged. 'Cheap whisky? I've been there with him on a couple of occasions. Interesting controversialist. Is that the word?

Conversationalist. If you can keep him off tiger hunting.'

I then asked Poole a question I would not have asked had I been sober.

'You ever get wind of any funny business in traffic? Corruption, embezzlement or the like?'

Poole fixed me with his sad eyes for a second. 'Funny you should say that, Jim. We had a fellow in the department called Harry Jebb. He thought there was some queer business going on.'

'He told you that?'

'In a roundabout way.'

'Name names, did he?'

'Not a bit of it, Jim. A very discreet chap, Harry Jebb.'

'He's not dead, is he?'

'Not exactly *dead*. He's living in Eastbourne. Sailed for Blighty in mid-April sort of time.'

'Why?'

'Retired.'

I had received the dossier by post on Thursday 19 April.

I was pondering further questions about this Jebb when the end door of the carriage crashed open, and the elderly female sprang awake. But there was nobody there. Douglas Poole merely turned in his chair, while I rose unsteadily. Standing in the doorway was a monkey, and it was looking for trouble. It must have been on the veranda, and it had somehow managed to turn the handle of the glass door. Poole was indicating the monkey: 'Do you suppose he has a first class ticket?'

The monkey commenced to urinate with great force.

'Honestly,' said Poole. 'This bloody madhouse.'

And unfortunately there was no more whisky left to make it go away.

Chapter Eleven

I

'King Sol', said a giant advertisement on the platform we pulled into at Sealdah station. It was for a brand of beer, but it might have been advertising the sun itself, and I was glad to step out of that shadowy, thronging station and into the full glare. It was eight o'clock in the morning on Thursday 10 May. King Sol didn't do much for my hangover, but he was a plain dealer. I had grown tired of the damp, blue mists of Darjeeling, which seemed to symbolise the fogs in which my mysteries were mired.

I ought to visit the telegraph office at the front of the station to wire my safe arrival to the wife, but she could bloody well whistle for it. Smartly uniformed, Deo Rana waited for me with a police tonga – I should have married *him*.

I would have offered Dougie Poole a ride into town but I had separated from him at the foot of the mountains, in Siliguri. He hadn't had a ticket for the Calcutta Night Mail, and he'd had to queue for it in the booking office. I'd had a compartment to my-self, and I'd slept all the way back.

As the tonga drew into the Howrah bridge traffic block, Deo Rana put a copy of that morning's *Statesman* into my hand. I looked at the place indicated. Yet more 'illegal associations' – no, that wasn't it. He was pointing to an item headed 'New Snake Death'. R. P. Biswas, Indian barrister-at-law, travelling on East

Indian Railway business, had been found dead the previous mid-day at Rannegunge, one stop before Asansol. And so we were back – snake-wise – to the East Indian, and the Grand Chord. The corpse of Mr Biswas had been discovered sharing a first class compartment with a snake called a Russell's viper. On the face of it, that crime could not have been committed by anybody who had been in Darjeeling at the time; but *only* on the face of it.

'We must go and see the snake men's uncle,' I said to Deo Rana.

He shook his head vigorously, meaning he agreed absolutely: 'We are overdue for him. I have found place.'

'His address?'

'Not address. *Place.*'

He handed me a fragment of a Calcutta street map. A fairly central location was circled. I was surprised to see that it wasn't in the Black Town. Would more baksheesh be required? Evidently not: the snake men we had encountered on the Howrah railway lands were now acting out of revenge. For some reason or other, they had it in for their uncle, and so they had told Deo Rana that he would be discovered holding court, and no doubt selling snakes, in this particular spot on the afternoon of Monday 14 May. He would be there at what Deo Rana called 'three-four o'clock' on that day.

At Fairlie Place, Deo Rana went off to other duties, while I dispatched a coolie with my luggage to Willard's Hotel; then I stood alone for a moment on the steps of the booking office – alone, under the strongly raying sun, in the shifting crowd, wreathed in smoke from street cooking, incense and cigarettes. I turned and went through the courtyard arch. I climbed the hot iron steps to the police office.

I found Superintendent Bennett in his office. He looked like what he was: a man who had missed a holiday . . . and his office was changed. On the wall, besides the framed scrap of artistic cloth and the picture of the King-Emperor, there was a photographic portrait of his wife, Mary. There were now papers on his desk, and cigarettes had joined the tin of St Julien tobacco. I knew what the man was about: he was trying to own his office; trying to stay *in* it.

'How were the hills, Jim?'

'Mostly occluded. I had a visit from Khan of the C.I.D.; can you think why?' Bennett commenced to light his pipe. I said, 'I believe he thinks I did it.'

'Nonsense,' said Bennett, shaking out a match. 'I don't want to traduce a fellow officer, but by seeking you out for an urgent second interview, he could claim an expenses-paid trip to Darjeeling. The fellow does have a social life, I believe, against all the odds.'

'Yes,' I said bitterly. 'I think he does. Have you heard from Fisher?'

'Had a wire yesterday,' said Bennett. 'Fellow's quit. Had a better offer elsewhere.'

I had started in on an explanation about Fisher and the R.K., when a voice came from the doorway: 'Major Fisher is leaving us in the lurch?'

It was Jogendra Babu, and he was beaming behind his spectacles. He bowed to me: 'Please come through to my office when opportunity arises, Stringer sahib,' and he walked on.

Bennett produced a pasteboard folder from his desk. 'Recommendations for your enquiry from the man Sinclair. Looks like you'll be pursuing them on your own – or not at all, of course. They're only recommendations.'

Even so, it seemed positively evil of Sinclair to have been for-mulating proposals over that lazy tiffin of Friday last. Bennett pushed the papers towards me, but I would not be party to any attempt to make everything seem normal. I said, 'I've just read about the barrister, Biswas.'

Bennett nodded.

'. . . And the Russell's viper,' I added.

Bennett gave me a warning look, but I made my plunge. 'The question, if you ask me, is when was that train made up? I mean, when was it cleaned and prepared for the trip?'

'I know what "made up" means, Jim,' said Bennett, and he was studying the etching of the calm man on the tobacco tin, as though seeking inspiration. 'Naturally, we asked the traffic de-partment about that. That rake of coaches was thoroughly cleaned and prepared ten days beforehand.'

And that was before Dougie Poole had gone to Darjeeling. It was before almost anyone had gone to Darjeeling.

Bennett said, 'We've put on more patrols around Howrah, and it's not as if the carriages are standing there in the sidings with their doors gaping. You'd have half the beggary of the city sleep-ing in them if that were the case. The doors are all locked at all times except when the sweepers are in there.'

'But they're standard locks and standard keys aren't they?' I ob-served. 'Any man on the railway can lay hands on them. For ten clear days those carriages were available to the snake man. He knew they'd be used to make up a train eventually, and he knew they wouldn't be checked over again before that happened. From what I understand, most snakes will be happy to lie in a semi-dormant state for days on end without need of food or drink. The next thing they know, some great human has interrupted their slumbers and is threatening to bloody stand on them.'

Bennett had laid down his pipe. He was, at last, frankly angry.

'Thank you for your speculations, Jim. I would hate you to think I had not come to exactly the same conclusions myself. I'd have to be very stupid indeed not to have done so.' He sat back. 'You are required by Jogendra Babu, I believe.'

It was perfectly clear that I could not disclose to Bennett my appointment with the snake men's uncle. I stood to go, and as I did so, he relented somewhat. 'I have been slow off the mark, Jim, I will admit. It was the nature of these murders. I was taken aback by the sheer . . .'

'The brutality?' I suggested. Because snake bite did seem to be the worst sort of death.

'Not quite. More the sheer the ungentlemanliness of it.'

'I see,' I said, not seeing.

'But we are about to make our move, Jim. We are about to make our move.'

II

In his small and perfectly ordered office, Jogendra Babu handed a paper to me. It was the reservation chart for the first class carriage of the Jamalpur Night Mail of Monday 23 April. At least, that's what was written at the top, but this was not the document that might or might not have been posted on the carriage side, for this was handwritten in perfect, violet-coloured copperplate. I read:

Compartment 1: Mr R. P. N. Ganguly.
Compartment 2: Captain J. H. Stringer.

Compartment 3: Rev. Canon P. L. W. Selwyn.

Compartment 4: Major N. Fisher.

Compartment 5: Servants belonging to Mr Ganguly and Rev. Canon Selwyn.

My mind whirled. Was John Young really called Ganguly? Did he really have the same surname and initials as the doctor who shared a staircase with Miss Hatsuyo? Couldn't be. I had seen his warrant card; I'd spoken to his family. Far more likely was that John Young had booked into his compartment late, the original booking having apparently been made in the name of the phthisis specialist, and having been cancelled.

. . . And yet he was not down as *Dr* Ganguly, and so a different thought came . . . It must be a different Ganguly, albeit with the same three initials as the doctor. But while it was easy to imagine that there must be many Gangulys in Calcutta, how many R. P. N. Gangulys could there reasonably be?

Jogendra was highly amused. He said, 'I will explain, please?'

'If you don't mind.'

'This,' he said, indicating the paper, 'not official.'

'How do you mean? Are these the actual bookings as made?'

'Yes, yes, actual bookings. But not original paper.'

'No. Because the original would have been typed. Where is the original? Burnt?'

'Not burnt. Taken from booking office files by one man. But I must not disclose name.'

'Why not?'

'Because I am stealing from this gentleman.'

'You *stole*?' I was glad, but amazed.

'From under nose!' said Jogendra, and he was laughing, but also shaking his head.

All he had stolen, I discovered after further questioning, was the *data*. The Indian booking office clerk who had been required to give up the original document to the mysterious third party referred to by Jogendra had memorised the chart, it obviously being of the greatest importance for some reason or other. The clerk was a friend of Jogendra's, and he had dictated the names to Jogendra, perhaps persuaded by the prospect of baksheesh.

I said, 'This fellow who wanted the original . . .'

'You are permitted to speculate.'

'Fisher?'

'Further speculations are permitted.'

'Khan of the C.I.D.'

'Further speculations not required. You are hitting the nail on the head!'

'Do you suppose he wanted to know who was on the original list, or keep others from knowing?'

'That is beyond my comprehension, sahib.'

'I'm obliged to you, Jogendra. Is there anything I can do for you in return?'

'You are doing it already.'

He meant that I had signed the complaint form against Fisher – a complaint that was no longer necessary. I explained a little of the circumstances of Fisher's departure to Jogendra.

'Then he is out of my hair for ever,' he said, touching his bald head. 'It is red letter day in every way.' It was apparently a red letter day for me as well, because Jogendra had something else to show me. He stooped from his chair, and with considerable effort he lifted a heavy green volume from the floor. He had marked a place with a clean, folded handkerchief. It was the *East Indian Railway*

Police Occurrence Book (*Calcutta District*) for the year 1919. He indicated a certain entry, and sat back, mopping his brow with the handkerchief.

'Earlier instance of same,' he said.

The handwriting was tiny, and I did not have my glasses about me, so Jogendra leant forward, and helped me get the gist. 27 September 1919: a king cobra had been discovered in the first class carriage of a train about to depart from Howrah. No further details. Jogendra turned the page. 28 September 1919: a Russell's viper discovered in the first class corridor of a train just arrived at Serampore, ten miles out of Howrah.

But it seemed this was the end of a heroic paper chase on Jogendra's part, and not the start of it. He had not been able to discover supporting witness statements or first-instance reports in connection with these entries, possibly because the appearance of the snakes had not been taken at the time to be the result of criminality.

'I know you've already done a great deal for me, Babu-ji,' I said, 'but might it be possible to know what was going on with the Company at that time?'

'A terrific amount is going on, unfortunately.'

'Nationalist attacks?'

'A regular occurrence, sahib.'

It was the year of Amritsar: the massacre – that had been in April, I believed.

'Strikes?'

'Likewise equally. In year of 1919, everybody is at it. Even top sahibs.'

'The top sahibs went on strike?'

'Not really *strike*. You will see. I will assemble documents. But it will be hitting and missing.'

I rose to my feet, and bowed a salaam to Jogendra Babu, saying, 'I think we have both probably seen the back of Fisher for good.'

'He is liability.'

'He *was*, Babu-ji; he *was*.'

I walked along the corridor to the door marked 'Convert to English'. It was closed, and it turned out that it was also locked. A passing clerk said, 'Poojahs, sahib.' It seemed all the translators were on holiday. I thought about doubling back, and asking Jogendra Babu if he could translate the notes I had lifted from Khudayar Khan's room in Darjeeling, but it was unlikely that he would know the dialect, and I decided that he had already taken enough risks on my behalf.

III

I still wore my heavy Darjeeling suit, and by the time I reached Chowringhee it was soaked in sweat. The town had become sluggish in the great humidity; even the trams seemed to move slower, and to stand for longer at the stops. On the crowded pavements, many of the street vendors had adopted a horizontal posture, and all the dogs were sleeping, often in the middle of the road. Only the rickshaw men ran, as through determined to die, to escape this life and go on to the next one, which might prove better. *Reported Missing* had gone from the Elphinstone Picture Palace. Now showing was a 'Special Holiday Programme', which in practice meant a film called *Intolerance*.

I came up to the open doorway signified by the two brass plaques: Dr R. P. N. Ganguly and Miss Hatsuyo. I entered the hot gloom, and climbed the stairs; the place smelt of singed dust. Ganguly's rooms were on the first floor (as were Miss Hatsuyo's). I knocked, obtaining no reply. I knocked again with the same result. I tried the door: locked. I knocked one final time, and it was the door *behind* me that opened: Miss Hatsuyo's door. I caught a glimpse of the lady as she let a man out. He was a European, and upon seeing me, he bounded down the stairs, red-faced. But I was not concerned with him; I was eyeing Miss Hatsuyo. She was real; she fulfilled all the promise of the photograph, and she had perhaps smiled at me through the chink in the door before closing it. I lingered at the top of the stairs. Lydia had had a tussle with Khudayar Khan (perhaps); why should I not have one with Miss Hatsuyo? Make an international effort of it, League of Nations sort of thing. However, I descended the staircase slowly, lingering again when I regained the street, staring at the photographic portrait of Miss Hatsuyo and wondering about her Japanese speciality. It had certainly brought colour to the cheeks of her late customer.

I looked along Chowringhee, searching for the retreating form of the customer; instead, I saw the *approaching* form of another man altogether, Canon Peter Selwyn, walking fast, with a sheen of sweat on his pink face, silver crucifix bouncing about his neck, and some unknown violet-coloured flower in his buttonhole.

'Captain Stringer!' he said, and he took me by the elbow. 'Kindly follow me.' He was glancing in all directions as he took me through a broken gate, into a passageway running between a gun shop and a motor-car showroom. There was a pile of tyres in the alleyway, and somebody had lately ignited a heap of newspapers in it, or perhaps the newspapers had ignited themselves in the great heat.

'I assure you that I am not in the habit of asking men to accompany me down dark alleyways,' said Selwyn, 'but I believe we were overseen when we talked at the Bengal Club.'

'Who by?'

Cinders from the newspaper fire floated between us.

'The rather forbidding Detective Inspector Khan, or an agent thereof. Such a mysterious man as him must have agents, don't you think? At any rate, he summoned me on Wednesday last. Wanted to get from me everything I knew about the killing of Mr Young on the Jamalpur line.'

'That's fair enough. The wonder is he hadn't called you in before then.'

'But that's the whole point. I don't think he would have called me in at all – he would have been perfectly happy with the statement I made to Hughes at Jamalpur – but for the fact he'd seen me speaking to you.'

'But we spoke on the Friday. So he let five days go by before he called you in. Did he *say* he saw you speaking to me?'

'No, but he asked if I'd had further discussions about the case with anyone who'd been involved in it. I said no.'

'And he didn't contradict you?'

'Not verbally, but by the look he gave me.'

I offered Selwyn a Gold Flake. He refused it.

'What would you have done if he'd pulled you up?' I asked. 'I mean, if he said he *knew* you'd talked to me at the Bengal Club?'

'I would have said I didn't regard you as being involved in the case. But basically what I said to Khan was a direct contradiction of the ninth commandment.'

I frowned.

'"Thou shalt not *lie*", Captain Stringer.'

'Did he ask you about the metal tube you'd seen Fisher throw away?'

'Again not specifically. He asked if I'd seen *any suspicious behaviour*.'

'And you didn't mention the tube?'

'I mentioned that to *you*. I didn't want to say anything to Khan that I hadn't mentioned in my statement.'

'Did he ask about the . . .'

'What? Spit it out, man.'

'Well, the book you had with you on the train.'

'I assume you mean the Bible.'

I smoked with eyes averted. 'No,' I said.

I meant the other book, which had not been astronomy. I could not imagine that Khan would take very kindly to the activities of Uranians.

'Well now, Captain Stringer, I don't see how that could be a factor in the case.'

'No.'

'. . . Any more than the young Japanese lady whose advertisement you were studying with such interest just now.'

I gave that the go-by. Certainly Miss Hatsuyo could not be a factor in the case of John Young's murder, whereas her neighbour, Dr R. P. N. Ganguly, might very well be.

'But what about that metal tube?' he said. 'Did you find out anything more about it?'

'I believe it might have been a cigar holder.'

'Oh.'

'I can tell you that Major Fisher has now left the police service.'

'That must be a great relief for you.'

'He has gone to work for a maharajah's son in one of the native states. He is to build a railway.'

'What? Single-handedly? I must say, I'm clearing out myself. I sail for Blighty next month.'

'You've brought the date forward, then,' I said (because his original plan had been to sail in the New Year).

'It is the effect of Khan. He is an excellent advertisement for Suffolk.'

And off he went.

I lingered on Chowringhee, trying to get inside the head of Detective Inspector Khan. He had interviewed Selwyn on the Wednesday; he had come up to see me in Darjeeling the following Tuesday . . . Was there any connection? It seemed more likely to me that he had come up to Darjeeling having heard that Jogendra had been sniffing around about the reservation chart. From where I stood, I could see the sides of the trams as they clanged past: Lifebuoy Soap . . . Lifebuoy Soap . . . Lipton's Tea . . . Lifebuoy Soap. I drifted towards the junction with Dalhousie Square, and from here I could see the destination blinds on the *fronts* of the trams: Tollygunge . . . Lower Circular Road . . . Zoological Gardens. It was about to pull away. I walked – then ran – towards it.

I liked being on the tram. I sat with my hat on my knee. The lower deck was dark, and it gave shade; the bell was mellow like a church bell. As the tram moved south along Chowringhee, it would occasionally muster a burst of speed, so that the air moving through the window slats chilled the sweat on my shirt front.

But in the Zoological Gardens, all was slow again. The electric train was out of commission, as signs hanging from the little picket fence guarding the track repeatedly announced. The few visitors moved exhaustedly between the enclosures, or sat on the benches in the pagodas, sleeping, or fanning themselves with their hats. An ambling elephant crossed my path. In a moment, I thought, all movement will completely cease, as when the reel gets caught in the projector at the picture houses, then a sudden flame will eat us all away.

IV

In his office adjacent to the reptile house, Professor Hedley Fleming stood by the laboratory table, where he was pouring a slow-moving yellow liquid from a test tube into a glass jar. He had been at it for an age, as I sat by his desk smoking a Gold Flake. I had been admitted to his office by his Indian assistant, but only, it appeared, for the purposes of watching the professor at work. The yellow liquid moved like honey. I believed it to be snake venom, but Professor Fleming was not letting on. I had twice enquired, and he had merely said, 'I'll be with you in a moment, Captain Stringer.' He might be showing off. He was like the boy at school who will not let you copy his work but makes it plain that he is getting all the answers right. He really did look like an over-grown schoolboy – It was the curly hair and the golden glasses that did it. They had made him seem an alien presence in the photograph of him attending the Debating Society dance that I had seen *at* the Debating Society dance. I wondered who had been his partner on that occasion, because no adult went to that dance unaccompanied . . . except for Major Fisher, of course.

Finally, the pouring was over.

'I have five minutes, Captain Stringer,' Fleming said, sitting down opposite to me at the desk.

'Well, first of all, thank you for—'

260

'*Literally* five minutes, Captain Stringer.'

'Has Superintendent Christopher Bennett of the East Indian Railway Police been to see you?'

'About what?'

'About all the snakes that have been killing people along the line. You are the top snake man in Calcutta, are you not?'

'Captain Stringer, I am still somewhat baffled as to whether you come here in an official or an unofficial capacity. I think you admitted to me last time that you were not directly assigned to this investigation.'

'I am officially concerned with security, and that is being breached in spectacular fashion.'

Professor Hedley Fleming was contemplating my sweat-soaked form. Over his right shoulder I could see on the wall the university photograph, but I still could not make out the inscription. For all his appearance of being an overgrown schoolboy, Fleming must be about of an age with Superintendent Bennett. Bennett was a Cambridge man; Fleming either Oxford or Cambridge. Either way, there was an excellent chance that they had coincided in Britain or Calcutta. They *must* have done so, and yet both appeared to be denying any connection.

'Perhaps you think *I* am responsible for leaving these snakes on the trains,' he said.

I said, 'I would simply like your opinion. If I could just remind you of the facts . . .'

I took a scrap of paper from my pocket book.

'Five minutes, Captain Stringer.'

'Early in April,' I said, reading from the paper, 'there were a couple of incidents that did not result in fatalities. Then, on 10 April, a fellow called Milner, an employee of the Railway, was killed by a common krait at Asansol, about a hundred and forty miles out from Howrah. At about the same time, a Miss Schofield died of fright at Howrah station itself after an encounter with a hyderabad.'

'*Hyderabad*', said Fleming, 'is an Indian city. I think you mean a *hamadryad*.'

'Sorry, yes. A king cobra. Then, I think on Monday 23 April, a sawscale viper killed Walter Gill, an American tourist, at Bally, seven miles out from Howrah. On the same day, a common krait killed a Colonel Kerry at Khana.'

I hesitated. All the Ks made it ridiculous. Fleming was looking at his watch.

'Khana is *seventy* miles out from Howrah,' I continued. 'On Thursday 26 April, some men of Blakeborough hydraulic engineers beat to death another krait near Moghalsarai, about three hundred miles out. On Sunday 29 April Douglas Poole, employee of the Railway, was given a glancing bite by an Indian cobra at Ondal, two stops before Asansol. He was unharmed. On Tuesday 1 May a sawscale viper was apparently found in a first class compartment of an East Bengal train departing Sealdah station for Siliguri. Nobody was harmed, and it was removed from the train.'

Fleming frowned. 'That one wasn't reported.'

'No,' I agreed, 'it wasn't. Yesterday a fellow called Biswas, a lawyer travelling on Railway business, was bitten at Rannegunge, one stop before Asansol, by a Russell's viper. All but one of these attacks occurred in first class carriages of the East Indian Railway, on trains departing from Howrah, and I was wondering whether the attacker might have a grievance against the Railway, perhaps arising from his own employment on the Railway. Perhaps he was – or is – in the traffic department. He would then know something about where the trains are stabled at Howrah, and where they are going to, and he himself would have a first class pass that would allow him to board the right parts of the trains at any time and place anywhere along the line.'

Hedley Fleming hesitated for a moment. Then he said, 'Is the man Poole in the traffic department?'

I nodded.

'Are you saying he was bitten by a snake that he himself had taken on to the train?'

'I don't know.'

'From what you've said, I don't think there would have been any need for anyone to go along the line. All the snakes on the East Indian could have been put on at Howrah. '

'How do you make that out?'

'The biggest snake, the king cobra, was discovered immediately, at Howrah itself. Well, that's no surprise. A snake of that size couldn't remain concealed for long. The sawscale viper is an aggressive character, and so it attacked early, at Bally, just a few miles out. You say it was a sawscale that was found on the East Bengal, and it was discovered at the originating station there as well. But to go back to the East Indian, the snake coming to light at the furthest distance, at . . .'

'At Moghalsarai.'

He nodded. 'That was a krait, a relatively small snake, which might easily remain undiscovered for hours if tucked away beneath a seat. And there was another krait, you say?'

'That struck at seventy miles out – at Khana.'

'Even so, that's after a good distance. The Russell's viper would bide its time as well, and it struck towards Asansol, again after a good while.'

'But what about the ordinary cobra? That bit Poole at Ondal, just two stops before Asansol – so more than a hundred miles out.'

Professor Hedley Fleming shrugged. 'That is perhaps slightly anomalous. I might have expected an Indian cobra to strike before then if put on at Howrah.'

'So it could have been put on later, at a stop after Howrah?'

'All the snakes discovered after Howrah *could* have been put on after Howrah; I'm only saying they might not have been.'

He was rising from his seat. My time was up. He was no doubt relieved to see me putting the list of snake casualties back into my pocket book, and he was no doubt annoyed to see me take out another paper. It was the scrawled map showing the location of the head snake man. I handed it over to Fleming, saying, 'I believe that a man operating from this spot is selling poisonous – I mean venomous snakes.'

'Selling them to whom?' he asked, returning the map.

'The general public.'

'Well, why don't you go and question *him*, Captain Stringer?'

'He's not there at the moment. He's somewhere up country, no doubt collecting the snakes. He'll be back next week, and I'm going to turn up on his doorstep then – if he's got a doorstep.'

'Good luck to you,' said Hedley Fleming. 'Although I must say there's no reason to go outside Calcutta in order to turn up snakes.'

I had hoped to trigger some reaction by my mention of the snake man, but all I got was the glint of Fleming's glasses. Before closing the door on me, however, he asked, '*When* are you going to pay your call?'

'Monday,' I said. 'Three-four o'clock.'

264

'*What?*'

'Between three and four o'clock.'

I had put my cards on the table, in hopes that Fleming would do likewise. He eyed me as he closed the door. By all appearances, he'd gone back to thinking me an idiot, if indeed he had ever stopped thinking this.

I was escorted some of the way towards the gates of the zoo by Hedley Fleming's Indian assistant. As before, he was more or less silent, and when I asked, 'Was Professor Fleming at Oxford or Cambridge?' he confined himself to one word: 'Cambridge.' When I pushed my luck by asking, 'What college?' he gave a shrug. As we closed on the main gate of the zoo, we passed a giant birdcage, with two giant birds inside it. A small man stood before the cage, watching the birds, but I could only see his back. A tonga waited conveniently at the gate. As I climbed up, I looked again towards the birdcage, and the small man was still there, but half turned away. He appeared to be lifting a hip flask to his lips, and taking a drink. As the tonga rattled away, the suspicion grew on me that the fellow might have been Dougie Poole.

I rode the tonga back towards the middle of town, watching the sun crash down over the maidan, and thinking of the wife. Had she telephoned or wired to the hotel? I would not bother to check. I would not be beholden in that way – not after what she might have done. But I would be told anyhow if she *had* left a message.

I alighted from the tonga at Dalhousie Square. Should I try Dr Ganguly again? His premises were only a short walk away. But I was too exhausted, and I decided to walk straight back to the hotel. My way took me past a row of grey-haired Indians who conducted office work on the pavement. They sat on folding chairs at folding tables, typewriting away. They would compose and type letters for you; or read the letters that were sent *to* you. There were half a dozen of them, and they all wore spectacles, and they were all typing all the time . . . but only in the evenings, since they very sensibly avoided the heat of the day. Everyone knew the service they provided, but one of them advertised an additional skill, for a pasteboard sign propped in front of his typewriter paraded the famous phrase 'Convert to English'.

I positioned myself before him. I removed my sola topee and mopped my brow. The man was typing like a maniac. If he was impressed at having a rare European client he certainly did not show it; in fact, he put his head down and redoubled his typing speed. Another Indian came up to me. It appeared that he was a sort of secretary or agent for the typists.

He said, 'What is it you want, sahib? This man is busy.'

'Conversion to English,' I said, holding up the two crumpled papers I had taken from Detective Inspector Khan's unburnt fire. I passed them to the man, and he turned away from me while reading them. The fellow then began walking fast away from me. 'Hold on a minute!' I called out, walking after him, but he was only going to the end of the line of outdoor clerks, where he spoke to another individual who was connected to the enterprise but not typing. He then turned back to me.

'These wrong men,' he said, indicating all the typists. 'Come here tomorrow.'

He handed back the papers.

I asked, 'Are they not written in Bengali?'

He shook his head.

'Not Hindustani?'

He shook his head again. 'Tomorrow you will see.'

On returning to the hotel, I was given no message to say Lydia had got in touch. I had an iced bath, and then went out into the terrace, where I drank a bottle of Beck's beer and smoked a cigarette. I then walked back to the reception and asked whether Mrs Stringer had left word. No, nothing from the memsahib. I went back the terrace, and ordered another beer while looking out over the road. Having crashed down on to the maidan, King Sol was now bleeding all over it.

Chapter Twelve

I

I was in the police office at seven the next morning, which was the morning of Friday 11 May. The heat had started an hour before. Lydia had left no message at the hotel overnight. On my way to Fairlie Place, I had passed the plaque announcing Dr Ganguly, but it was too early for him, and in fact the exterior door was closed, the first time I had seen it so.

Lydia had left no message at Fairlie Place either, and there was no sign of Bennett or Jogendra at the office, but the latter had left on my desk some piles of documents relating to the affairs of the Company in September 1919, towards the end of which month a king cobra and a Russell's viper had been placed on its trains. A bearer brought me jam on toast and tea thick with sugar and condensed milk; I put on my spectacles and began to read.

At eight, I moved to the opposite side of the table, because the sun raying through the window was beginning to dazzle, and the blind was broken. At half after eight, Jogendra came in with some more boxes.

'Much obliged to you Babu-ji,' I said. 'The more the merrier.'

Each flimsy paper that I picked up fluttered under the revolving fan, as though panic stricken at what it might disclose, but after two and a half hours I was starting to think I was wasting my time. I had read of the doubling of certain tracks, and the temporary implementation of single-line working on others, because it was a time of big expansions; I read of a new batch of tank engines released from the workshops at Jamalpur, which had taken on more apprentices than ever in the previous year. No new light was thrown on the snakes of September 1919.

There was a lot on the social side, as disclosed by that month's edition of the *East Indian Railway Magazine*. September seemed to be the season of weddings within the Company, and not only in Calcutta but at the out-stations along the line also. There seemed numerous instances of accounts clerks or permanent way inspectors marrying the daughters of engine drivers or signalmen. '. . . Dancing was indulged in to the strains of excellent music supplied by Starlight Juvenile Jazz Orchestra . . . After the reception the happy couple left by train for their honeymoon.' There was always dancing, the couple was always happy, and they always left by train, of course. These would mainly be Anglo-Indian weddings. You could tell by phrases such as 'The reception was held at the Railway Institute', or 'Many European staff members attended.' That would have been taken for granted, and would not have needed stating, in the case of a *European* wedding.

With many men returning from the war there was also the biggest programme of sports yet seen, and page after page in the magazine was given over to the Company's Annual Sports on the maidan, probably because, being a mixed event with all pay grades and all races represented, this gave an impression of harmony within the Company. I read not only of long jump, high jump and all the running races, but even of events down to ladies' throwing the cricket ball, hoop bowling, obstacle race, potato race, egg-and-spoon race, three-legged race, open bicycle slow race.

'An event which caused endless amusement', I read, 'was the

Invalids' Race won by A. Tweedie and Mrs P. Turner.' 'Another event which evoked great fun', I read, 'was the bun-and-treacle race for boys, the winner of this event being loudly cheered as he reached the tape half blinded with treacle and pieces of bun sticking all over his face.' There seemed a determination on everyone's part to put the war behind them by means of dances, comic sketches, tennis-at-homes, whist drives, or fancy-dress balls. ('Mr West won the prize for most original. He went as "the House that Jack Built".')

I turned to a thin volume that Jogendra had presented. It was entitled *The East Indian Railway: A Short History of the Line*, and it was by 'P. T. Wallace C.B., C.M.G., D.S.O., and Friends'. It began, 'The history is not encompassed in its entirety, of course . . .' It certainly was not. Even with the assistance of his friends, P. T. Wallace had produced little more than a pamphlet. Jogendra had marked a certain page. I read fast down it:

It would hardly have been natural if the long strain of the war had not affected the Superior Staff in ways which worked very greatly to their disadvantage . . . But it must have been apparent to those in authority that disaffection was brewing. The cost of living had risen enormously. This was happening all over the world, but it struck one more in India than in England . . . The price of necessities, and the cost of servants, beer, whisky and food of all kinds seemed to have doubled . . .

In 1919, the position reached a climax. A large number of Supervising Staff entrusted to one of their number the formulation of a memorandum to the Directors praying for an improvement in their salaries and conditions of service. In the whole history of the E.I.R. nothing like this had ever before happened: a petition from the officers was unheard of, without precedent, and this is partly why I talk of a 'climax'.

The precipitating cause was undoubtedly the war. Those Officials had taken leave to serve in the army had found themselves returning to pay grades that were – *de jure* or *de facto* – lower than those obtaining beforehand, with commensurately lower gratuities to be expected on retirement... The tale cannot be pursued. The matter is, as the time of writing, in abeyance pending the deliberations of the Directors.

The book, I saw, had been produced in 1919, evidently late in the year.

I looked at my watch. I could not sit here all day. I collected up some of the more promising-looking papers, and put them inside the pages of the *East Indian Railway Magazine*, making a neat bundle that I thrust into my suit-coat pocket. It was time to pay a second call on Dr Ganguly at Old Court House Corner. On my way there I called in at the hotel. There was no message from Lydia.

II

On the dark staircase, the door of Miss Hatsuyo was firmly closed, and no sounds came from within. The same went for the door of Dr Ganguly, but this door was opened at my second knock by a green-eyed nurse who might have been Anglo-Indian.

She admitted me to a room that was long and thin, like a railway carriage. It was very brightly coloured because of the jumble of posters on the two long walls. At one end, a wide window looked down on to Old Court House Corner. The other end of the room was screened off by a pretty curtain of green and red stripes. The doctor must be behind there, and if he *were* behind there, then that would make three of us in the room, since no patients waited on the rows of chairs lining the two long walls.

The green-eyed nurse ushered me over to one of the chairs, and sat down next to me in a companionable way. She turned towards me with a pleasant rustling of her white cotton uniform, and in good English she asked me why I wanted to see the doctor. I said I was a policeman and would like to ask him some questions in connection with an investigation I was conducting. I showed her my warrant card. She took this in her stride, as I believe she would have taken almost anything in her stride. She walked towards the curtain, and I experienced a sad enjoyment in watching her do so. As she went behind the curtain, I thought of Miss Hatsuyo and I thought of Lydia. From behind the curtain came the sound of a door opening and closing. So these premises must be bigger than I thought. I looked at the posters. 'Chiefly for Mothers: Robinson's Patent Barley.' The stuff was bright yellow in the glass the woman was drinking from. 'Ensure a Robust Constitution: start a course of Dr Hornby's Number 9 Pills.' The man who'd done so had a very pink face, and he was contemplating a multi-coloured sunrise.

The curtain parted, and the doctor came out. He was older, taller and thinner than I had expected, with sparse and disordered grey hair. He was very well dressed though, and wore a bow tie under his white coat. I had no doubt that the colourful posters would cease once one got behind the curtain: there, all would be scientific and serious, but I would never find out for certain, because the doctor sat down next to me in the same companionable way as the nurse had. He took out a silver cigarette case and offered it to me. He had a very languid manner, and he spoke in a drawling way. He lit our cigarettes, saying, 'You are from the East Indian Railway Police, whereas the other man was from the criminal investigation department of the civil police.'

'Detective Inspector Khan,' I said, trying not to make a question of it.

'But you two are co-operating, presumably.'

'Yes,' I said, after a while.

'You don't seem very sure of that,' said Dr Ganguly.

I said, 'Did you book a ticket on the Jamalpur Night Mail of 23 April, and then cancel the booking?'

'No,' said Dr Ganguly, blowing smoke, and watching the smoke that he had blown. 'I neither booked nor cancelled. That must have been the other R. P. N. Ganguly, the fellow Khan asked me about two months ago . . . Just in case you didn't know.'

'I—'

'Khan did not seem to me the type who would share his hard-won information very readily. A good man, no doubt, but costive.'

Ganguly withdrew two newspaper cuttings from his pocket, saying, 'I had these from the offices of *The Statesman*. I didn't see them when they originally appeared.'

The cuttings were both small, and the dates were marked on them in handwriting. The first was from February of the present year, the second from March. The first was headed 'Alleged Seditious Speech.' I read:

A non-co-operation backer was arrested in Dalhousie Square on the strength of a writ of arrest issued by the Chief Presidency Magistrate. He was taken into custody on a charge of having made a seditious speech in College Square.

The second read:

On the strength of a warrant issued by the District Magistrate of North Calcutta, the Criminal Investigation Department, assisted by local police, searched the house of Ram Chandra Deep in Upper Chitpur Road. Copies of *Vanguard*, *Advance Vanguard* and other seditious publications were seized.

'Concerning the speech,' observed Dr Ganguly, as I handed back the cuttings, '. . . they had to drop the charge for insufficient evidence. As you also may or may not know. And regarding the search and seizure . . . he wasn't in the house. Khan visited me at the start of April and I managed to extract that data from him.' Dr Ganguly turned and looked kindly at me. 'Let's assume you do know everything, and that I am boring you by this repetition.'

'All right,' I said.

'Khan thinks there's more to this man who sometimes calls himself Deep than seditious speeches and papers. He's been on his tail for months. He thinks he's the brains behind the arson attacks at Howrah.'

'The burnt godowns.'

'Yes. Also two murders of police constables in the past eighteen months. Khan really has a bee in his bonnet about this man, and he thinks that, of late, he's started using my name.'

'I suppose because it's displayed in the centre of town. You'd think he would have varied the initials, at least.'

'Yes, you would think that.'

'I suppose he can't be very imaginative.'

'If anything, I'd say the fellow was over-imaginative.'

'How do you know?'

'I've met him; he consulted me. At least, I think he did. I have him down as a fellow who came to see me in February, I suppose at about the time he was making seditious speeches.'

'What did he come to see you about?'

'Oh, nerves. Nervous neuralgia. Acute toothache and pains about the jaw. I told him to drink cocoa at night and have a good long walk every day.'

'What name did he give?'

'Of course, I asked his name, and he came out with "Mr Mukerji", but he'd told the nurse it was S. T. Dutt.'

'What did he look like?'

'Pale. As Bengalis go, you understand.'

'Hair?'

'Yes. I mean, he wasn't bald.'

'Centre-parted, like mine?'

'Yes.'

'Moustache similar to mine?'

'Not dissimilar. What are you driving at?'

What I was driving at was that if his features were similar to mine, then he would have looked even more like the murdered man, John Young, being closer to Young in colour. But I kept this from Dr Ganguly.

I said, 'It seems, then, that he walked away from here with your name?'

'And a bottle of Sloan's Liniment that he bought off the nurse
. . . Didn't believe me, you see, when I told him that all he really
needed was rest.'

'It was reckless of him to take the name of a man who'd met him.'

'Yes. But then he obviously is a reckless man. I gave his description to Khan and he disclosed, in a roundabout way, that this was
very likely the fellow he was after.'

Dr Ganguly walked over to the window and looked down on
the fuming traffic of Chowringhee. He made a half turn towards
me, saying, 'And now he's in Jamalpur?'

'Not necessarily,' I said.

'You are becoming as cryptic as Detective Inspector Khan.'

'. . . But it is useful to discover it wasn't you who took the train,'
I said, hoping he wouldn't guess that I knew any more than that.

I walked up to the window, and we shook hands. We both
looked down on the traffic.

'Do you know much about women's cycles?' I asked Ganguly.

'Women's *bicycles*, you mean?'

'No.'

'Then yes, I do.'

'Well . . .'

'Yes?'

'It doesn't matter.'

'My dear sir, you have now exceeded your colleague in opacity.'

III

At eight o'clock I sat on the terrace of Willard's Hotel. Darkness
had spread over the maidan, but here the fairy lights blazed, the

caged birds chirped and the fountain played, doing its best to dispel the memory of the day's heat. There were not many on the terrace, in these evenings of the dog days. I was drinking my daily allowance of Beck's beer and smoking a cigar I had bought at Hatzopolo's on Lindsay Street. It was a Havana, a half corona. I had bought the cigar at five o'clock. At four, I had been standing in front of the massed typists of Chowringhee, and speaking to the man who had been summoned by his colleagues just in case I kept my promise of the day before, and had turned up again to seek a translation of the words on the two crumpled scraps of paper. The man had given me the translation. The language was similar to Bengali, but was not Bengali. It was called Hajong, or something like. It was a dialect spoken in the north-east of Bengal, towards Assam, a district lying a fair distance from Jamalpur; but still it was not impossible, according to the translator, that people around Jamalpur might know it, or might have relatives who knew it, or might use it for covert purposes. The first message translated roughly as follows:

Khan sahib, you asked of us a very hard thing. We had much trouble, but work is complete. Where is the payment?

The second said something to the effect of:

Khan sahib, thank you for payment. Sorry for trouble but it was not our making.

Neither was dated, but both were signed by a certain Sabir Huq, who very generously supplied an address on both occasions, or at any rate the name of a village, which translated as 'The Place of the Crossroads'. The translator had consulted one of his fellows, who, on being prised away from his typewriter, confirmed that he had heard of this spot, and it was not such a small village either. I had put it to him that it might be near the big railway colony of Jamalpur, and he had said, 'Fifty-sixty miles east', which *is* near by Indian standards.

A man had been done away with, but the wrong man, as this Sabir Huq, assassin for hire, seemed guiltily aware. I wondered which of the horsemen I'd observed fleeing the scene had been Sabir Huq.

I now had little doubt that Huq, and his fellows, had been the agents of Detective Inspector Khan. Khan had set out to dispose of the troublesome Deep or Ganguly, and he had meant to make it look like an act of banditry. He must have been overjoyed at learning through his spies that Deep/Ganguly had booked on to the Jamalpur Night Mail of 23 April. Here was his opportunity.

Why had Deep/Ganguly intended to visit Jamalpur before changing his mind? Perhaps to agitate among the young railway apprentices. A bigger question, to my mind, was whether Khan had acted under his own initiative, or whether he carried the authority of his superiors. He was very much the sort of man who *would* act alone, I believed.

A bearer came up to me.

'Telephone, sahib.'

I left the cigar smoking in the ashtray as I walked quickly to the telephone box underneath the main stairs. It was Lydia, three hundred miles away and seven thousand feet up.

'Enjoying yourself, are you?' I said. 'You and Bernadette have been riding every day, I suppose?'

'She has; not me.'

'How many cards have you had dropped on you?'

'And how many bottles of beer have you drunk?'

'One. My daily allowance.'

Silence for a space.

'We've had enough of it here,' said Lydia. 'We're coming home next week; on Tuesday.' In spite of her negative remarks, she did not seem quite as blue as she had done beforehand. 'I've had two invitations to speak.'

'Where? In Calcutta?'

'Nearby.'

'Who to?'

'Indian women.'

'Right. And what about Indian *men*?'

'*What*?'

'Khan. I saw you talking to him at the riding place when I was on the train out. You seemed to be hitting if off pretty well.'

'I was sounding him out. You idiot. I was trying to appear pleasant.'

'Well, you seemed to be managing that. Sounding him out about what?'

'About how much trouble you were in, given that you were the only man on the spot with the right sort of gun. Are there people listening on this line?'

'There probably are now.'

'I wanted to find out how much he disliked the British. I should say quite a lot, and who can blame him? But he's no Indian nationalist.'

'That's right,' I said. 'That's exactly right. It was thinking he must be a nationalist that threw me off.'

'Threw you off what?'

'I'll tell you when you get back.'

'Tell me now.'

'I think he arranged the killing, and John Young was mistaken for someone else – a revolutionary. You know, a Ghandi-ite.'

'Ghandi . . .' said the wife, after a pause. 'I mentioned the Mahatma to him and he said, "That Hindu saint" with a real sneer.'

'That might be because Khan's Moslem,' I said.

'Or just a policeman,' said Lydia.

Silence for another space.

'You've seemed a bit blue lately,' I said.

'Yes, well.'

'Are you expecting?'

A longer silence this time.

'Why would that make me blue?'

'Because you're forty-three. You're ambitious. I was thinking about our . . . thing two weeks ago, when Bernadette went to the Askwiths overnight. I was thinking that your vulcanised device might have perished in the heat.'

'Jim! There might be people listening on this line!'

She hadn't minded discussing a murder on it though.

'You were drinking the beef extract with milk,' I said, 'and you seemed annoyed with me all the time.'

'I like the way it didn't occur to you that I might seem annoyed with you because I was *annoyed* with you!'

'It did.'

She would have the child, I knew that. Those devices – of which progressive women were so in favour – were to stop children but they were also to stop abortions. I felt a great surge of excitement at the thought of this new person coming into the world, like an express train going down a line with all the signals

280

set to 'Proceed'.

'I'm bowled over, kidder,' I said. 'I'm really bowled over.'

'Well, Jim,' she said, 'Good. That's good.' And finally she laughed. 'You cottoned on. I'm amazed.'

'You shouldn't underestimate me. I've cracked the John Young case; now I'm going to see about the snakes.'

'Jim, are you sure you've only had one bottle of beer?'

'I might go on to champagne next.'

'You should have something to eat.'

'I'm having a cigar. That's a similar thing.'

'Jim.'

'What?'

'Be careful.'

Chapter Thirteen

I

The next day was Saturday. I went into the office in the morning, and spent a desultory few hours looking over Commission of Enquiry papers, and giving an occasional glance at some of the files to do with the year 1919 in the history of the East Indian Railway. Much of the time I spent considering what to do about the fact that Detective Inspector Khan had commissioned a political murder that had led to the death of an innocent man. Of course I had not much in the way of evidence, unless the two crumpled chits could be counted as such. I had considered telling the whole tale to Bennett, who might then have a word with one of Khan's superior officers, who might or might not have been in on it. Either way, that felt rather dishonourable, too much like splitting, and I was currently minded to keep that option in reserve, depending on how far Khan pushed his efforts to throw blame on me.

In the middle of the afternoon, I stepped into Fairlie Place. Having been unable to get hold of a police tonga, I hailed a motor taxi, and asked for Howrah station. The motor taxi men felt themselves a cut above the tonga-wallahs, but they all had the famous Howrah Bridge traffic block to contend with. Midway over the bridge, the driver turned his motor off. I kept the passenger window down until the first mangled beggar approached along the walkway. I had wound it up by the time he'd arrived, so that the crying of the gulls, the tooting of the horns, the blaring of the ships on the river all became muted and the air in the taxi became unbreathable. The beggar was knocking on the window with the palm of his hand, and that was because he had no fingers. The driver, a Sikh, was reading *The Statesman.* He didn't look up from his paper, still less attempt to shoo the man away.

Half an hour later, the driver pulled up at the rank in front of Howrah station. I walked a little way into the blue-black, smoky interior, and saw fewer European faces than usual, on account of the exodus to the hills. This was how it would be when the British pulled out of India. That was only a matter of time. 'The balloon', as somebody told me, had 'gone up', and it had gone up at Amritsar. It was strange that Detective Inspector Khan couldn't see that for himself; or perhaps he did, and he was merely fighting a rearguard action.

I came out of the station, and walked on to the railway lands. There was a sharp smell of white spirit in the hot air. Every so often, the pounding of my boots caused a rat to bolt into a dirty hole; but the queer thing was that I never saw the rats until the moment they did bolt. That was the one good thing you could say about snakes: they killed rats.

When I came to the end of some goods wagons I'd been shadowing, I cut diagonally across the tracks towards the passenger carriage sidings. Ahead of me lay the burnt godowns, the work of the man who had stolen the name of Dr Ganguly. Behind me the orange cloud was rising over the railway lands. The passenger carriages alongside me were dusty green, in the main. The closed venetian slats made them appear to be sleeping, and they were top-heavy with various kinds of overhanging sun canopies. Where were the armed guards? I had hardly seen a single Company employee since entering the railway lands – a couple of Anglo-Indian foremen, a couple of coolies. Fisher believed that the coolies working for the Railway should be given a different designation, something more dignified like 'charge hand'. They'd be more loyal in that case, and less likely to pilfer. He had his points, did Fisher.

I cut through a gap between two rakes of carriages, and my object was in view: a pale blue church-like building with a pretty garden surrounding, so that it looked like a kind of oasis materialising in the dusty railway lands: the Insty.

It was Saturday afternoon, and the Anglos generally stayed in town during the heat, so the place was busy. Children played a scratch game of cricket on the tennis court; one of the peacocks was on the tennis court as well, and periodically doing its display, as though practising until a more distinguished audience came along. At the burra clubs, neither incursion would have been allowed. The grass on the tennis court of the Insty was rather worn and burnt, and I imagined its upkeep did not interest the resident gardener, it affording no opportunity to grow the vivid flowers that bloomed in the remainder of the garden.

A bearer was bringing drinks out on to the terrace, where perhaps twenty men and women sat talking or reading. I passed one of the curious, half-dead bushes. Was this the manasa tree that Canon Peter Selwyn had mentioned as being supposed by the Hindus to give protection against snake bites? He had said they were common throughout Calcutta, and that you would find a statuette of the goddess Manasa beneath the trees, yet there was nothing at the base of this one but a white stone. Nodding at a couple of the terrace drinkers whom I vaguely recognised from Fairlie Place, I entered the lobby of the Insty, where a big card game was in progress. Other members sat in the basket chairs near the bookshelves, reading through the engineering journals, or the novels of the Wheeler's Indian Railway Series, and there were a couple of kids flipping through the Bumper Books.

There was a whole new crop of advertisements on the notice-boards, and their severe practicality seemed to clash with this scene of Saturday afternoon jollity. 'Goodbye Rust!' I read. 'Syronite WILL NOT rust', or 'Rupees Fifteen Thousand – save this amount yearly using Sentinel Steam Wagons'. And there were notices advertising 'homeward' sailings: 'P&O British India Companies' . . . 'Isthmian Steamship Lines' . . . 'Ellerman Line'.

I heard, 'Now with a sportsman's instinct, I was absolutely sure I had hit the beast, but I didn't see it fall. So I summoned a few of the men, and told them to take their dogs down and search the hillside . . .' The speaker was Charles Sermon, the only European in the place apart from me, as far as I could tell. He had collared some poor fellow, and was steering him into the corridor leading to the bar. I had been banking on Sermon being at the Insty; in fact, he was the main reason for my visit. I wanted a word with him about the rebellion of the Company officers in 1919. The grievances had arisen from the war, and Sermon had been in the war. Therefore I too began walking along the corridor leading to the bar. In the rooms off, the holiday mood continued. One room seemed to be hosting a table-tennis tournament; a gram played in another.

The bar was pretty crowded, and with men and women, where-as in the burra clubs the sexes were separated for drinking pur-poses. Sermon had taken his latest victim over to a corner table, where a bearer was serving them pegs, but I was looking at two middle-aged women sitting at the next-but-one table over. Before them on their table were some tasselled photograph albums, a stack of photographs, and a pot of paste. One of the two women I didn't know. The other was Sonia Young, widow of John.

Reasoning that Charles Sermon would be talking shikar for at least the next hour, I first walked across to where Mrs Young sat. She recognised me immediately. In her extremely direct way, she introduced me to her companion as 'probably the last man to see John alive, apart from whoever killed him', causing her companion to shake my hand rather gingerly. As she spoke, she was pasting a photograph into the album: it showed a European couple looking silly as they engaged in what was probably an animal dance. The woman's hair was all across her face, and the man's tongue was sticking out. The picture had been taken at the Debating Society dance, and that went for all the photographs. I knew what Sonia Young was about. She was the custodian of the albums, and it was right they be stored at the Railway Institute, since an invitation to this particular dance was one of the highest social peaks an Anglo-Indian could achieve. The next photograph to go into the book showed William Askwith being congratulated by his wife after making his speech from the stage, and the one after showed Sonia Young herself. She was in the garden, the French windows were open behind her; she held a glass of something, and she was smiling, but of course she was alone, and this must have been one of the few pictures in all the collected albums showing a sole individual rather than a couple. Mrs Young's companion was studying the photograph.

'You look absolutely lovely, my dear,' said Sonia Young's companion, as if that might make up for her being alone.

Eyeing me, Sonia Young said, 'The main thing is that I look thin,' and of course, I gave that remark the go-by, but she was now leaning towards me. 'Don't you think I look thin?' she demanded.

'You look very elegant.'

'Thin!' she said, slapping the table and laughing. She wore a single gold bangle on her wrist. An Indian woman would have worn several bangles, a European woman none at all.

'Is your son about?' I asked.

'He is right *there*,' she said, pointing through the crowd towards the bar, where Anthony Young was nursing a drink and looking like trouble. He eyed me. 'What a charming expression,' said Mrs Young, 'but you needn't worry about him coming over. He won't have anything to do with me when I'm on this job.'

I knew the score. As far as Anthony Young was concerned, the Anglo-Indians were merely being patronised by the annual inclusion of a few of their number in the Debating Society dance, and he didn't think it an event worth commemorating. Two tables over, Charles Sermon was holding forth, and I caught the sound of his rumbling tones: '. . . One of the Indian shikaris, a fine old Rajput who feared nothing this side of Nirvana . . .' The chrysanthemum in his buttonhole was as white as the one he'd been wearing last time, but his white linen suit was a shade or two grubbier. Glancing up, he saw me. He looked surprised, but then signalled a friendly greeting before resuming his lecture. Meanwhile, Anthony Young had left his post at the bar. It seemed he was coming over to us after all.

'You again,' he said, glowering over me.

Sonia Young said to me, 'He means "Hello, how are you?"'

'Have you found my dad's killer yet?' At least he'd stopped accusing *me* of being the murderer, and in answer to his question I wanted to say that yes, I had; that his dad had been killed in a bungled attempted ambush on a nationalist revolutionary. But I kept silence.

Anthony Young didn't go away. He was sipping a beer, continuing to glower.

His mother and her friend continued to paste in the photographs.

'I don't know why you bother with that rubbish,' he said to her.

She said, 'Now if you can't be polite go away.'

'How are you enjoying life as a travelling ticket inspector?' I said.

'It keeps me out of this place, anyhow.'

It didn't seem to keep him out of it very *much*.

'He won't be in that sort of job very much longer,' said Sonia Young.

Anthony Young was eyeing me. 'She's worried I'll be mixing with the bloody darkies. She wants me climbing the ladder, man. Study the loco mags! Get your special apprenticeship!'

Mrs Young and her friend had left off pasting in photographs, and they were now looking back over the pictures of earlier years at the dance. Without looking up at her son, Mrs Young said, 'With your brains, you could be a chief mechanical engineer by the time you're thirty-five.'

'Then I can join that bloody world,' he said, indicating the album, 'alongside a lot of men who keep their daughters away from me. Then, if I do get hitched, they won't dare send their kids to where I send mine in case they pick up the chi-chi way of talking.' He was eyeing me again. 'Think about it, man. That's no bloody good.'

From two tables over, Charles Sermon was saying to his Anglo-Indian friend, 'Shall we have the other half?' I had been warned that people in India would say this. It meant "Shall we have a second drink?" but this was the first time I'd actually *heard* it said.

288

Sonia Young turned one of the pages of one of the albums, and Anthony Young stabbed his finger down on a photograph of a young European woman dancing with a young European man. '*She's* a damned fine tart!'

'You bugger off!' shouted his beautiful mother, and the whole bar did fall silent for a moment.

I watched Anthony Young. It seemed to me that he was slightly *less* truculent, or slightly less drunk, than he had been the last time, but that could change, since he was now walking back to the bar. Slowly the hubbub of conversation rose again, and I wanted to give the impression to Mrs Young that I had taken this family spat smoothly in my stride, so I said: 'Do you mind if I ask . . . was your father or mother English?'

'*I* don't mind,' said Mrs Young, but her friend, addressing me for the first time, put in, 'Some people *would* do.'

'My mother was an opera singer,' said Sonia Young, 'on a tour of India. She was from Manchester. My father was an engine driver, and he was from Delhi originally, but he came here to work from the Howrah engine shed. He was a top-link man, always on the expresses. The engines called Atlantics, you know?'

'Yes,' I said. 'Big engines. The wheel arrangement is 4-4-2.'

'I daresay it is, my dear,' said Mrs Young, and she patted the back of my hand, as though I were a hopeless case.

'An engine driver and an opera singer,' I mused.

'An intriguing alliance, you are thinking.'

'It sounds almost—'

'I'll tell you what it sounded,' said Mrs Young. 'It sounded *loud*. They were forever rowing.'

She was once again looking over the photograph albums. She tapped me on the elbow, saying in a conspiratorial tone, 'Here's another intriguing alliance for you.' She was indicating a page on which had been pasted a single extra-large photograph. It showed a collection of smiling couples standing in the garden of Wright's Hotel, all taking a breather from the Debating Society dance.

'What year?' I asked, as she passed over the album.

'Nineteen-eighteen,' said Mrs Young, as a hand came over my shoulder, grabbed my tie, and pulled me backwards off my chair. Anthony Young was speaking calmly as he continued trying to strangle me on the floor of the bar. 'You get out of here, man. You talk to my dad, and the next thing we know he's bloody dead. Now you're up to some new funny business with mater, you bloody—'

It was Charles Sermon, with the assistance of a couple of others, who pulled him off me. The others took the lad away, with his mother following and shouting choice insults at him. Sermon, breathing hard and looking me up and down as I readjusted my clothes, said, 'No real harm done. Our young friend is being escorted from the premises, as they say. Now do you fancy a spot, old man? Out on the terrace, I mean?'

II

I sat on the terrace with Charles Sermon. The mali was near the low garden gate, dead-heading flowers with a pair of scissors. Beyond him, the cloud from the jute mill was conspiring with the sunset to make the whole of the railway lands orange. We had thought we were in for a display of shunting, but the tank engine in question, which had been manoeuvring promisingly some quarter of a mile off, had now stopped, remaining thoughtfully smoking in front of a rake of carriages. Sermon too was smoking, which he ought not to do since it made him wheeze. We had started with a few words about Anthony Young. Sermon was sure he could be the right sort of lad if taken in hand. He was thinking of writing to a couple of the railway colleges on the boy's behalf. I had then asked him about the rebellion among the senior officers in 1919.

'Oh yes,' he said with a chuckle. 'The supervising staff were all up in arms.'

'So you yourself had no part in it?'

He shook his head.

'But you were back with the Company by then – after your war service, I mean?'

'That's right, I came from France in late 'seventeen. The whole affair was put to rights pretty quickly. The petitioners came to terms with the Board. Pay grades and pension entitlements were redrawn in favour of the ex-army chaps, and a ten per cent war bonus was paid on top. I did pretty well out of that, I don't mind saying. You can read all about it in the Company magazine for the following year, 1920. Of course, they glossed over the original grievance, but they went to town on the story of the amicable settlement.'

He wondered why I had asked about it, and, watching him carefully, I had told him of the coincidence of dates with the first outbreak of snake attacks.

He coughed on his cigarette. 'You've found a thread to follow, have you? I mean, you think it might all arise from the grievance of a top-grade man?'

I said I didn't know.

'Well, as many crimes are committed high as low,' Sermon said, and it did occur to me that, as a man who spent half his life among the Anglo-Indians, he might not be a natural defender of the top men, even if they were British like himself.

I asked him about his coming retirement to the charming – I thought – seaside town of Scarborough. I was determined that he would like Scarborough, but he did not seem overly enthused at my mention of the funicular railway, which cost only tuppence for an all-day ticket, or the delicious Italian ices to be had at Giordano's Parlour on the front. I had thought, in view of the white chrysanthemum, that he would be galvanised by my description of the Esplanade Gardens, but he merely said, 'I suppose the air will do me good.'

I said, 'You'll be taking back a cabin-trunk full of memories.'

I was thinking of tiger skins and other souvenirs of his shikari years, but he said, 'Oh, I might just take that trunk full of memories, and pitch it into the sea.'

'A new start, then,' I said, and he didn't seem too sure about that either. He signalled to a passing bearer to bring drinks: watered whisky for himself, a lemonade for me.

I thought we'd better get off Scarborough. It was the one thing he wouldn't hold forth on. He asked if I'd been in touch with Professor Hedley Fleming. I said I had been, and I told him a little of what Fleming had said. The drinks came. Still watching Sermon carefully, I told him of my late encounter with the snake men of the Howrah railway lands, and of my proposed encounter with their infamous uncle. Sermon seemed excited by this; it set him breathing fast. I supposed this was just the sort of yarn that you wouldn't hear on the Scarborough Esplanade, and I believed he was almost on the point of asking to come along.

The mali came up, salaaming to us on his way into the Insty.

He carried flowers, no doubt to make a display in there. He paused by Sermon's chair, and they exchanged a few words, and laughed.

'Were you speaking Bengali?' I asked Sermon.

'Hindustani,' he said. 'Picked it up in my travelling days. Not much use in the traffic office, of course.'

Mention of that office prompted me to ask if he knew Harry Jebb, the fellow Dougie Poole had mentioned as suspecting corruption. Sermon nodded. 'I knew him a little. He's taken superannuation, I believe.'

'Any grievance against the Company?'

'Not that I know of. Why bring him up? He can't be responsible for the snakes. He's back in Blighty.'

'Oh, Dougie Poole just happened to mention him.'

'Poole,' said Sermon, in a thoughtful sort of way. 'Curious chap . . . deep *thinker*.'

He'd said much the same about him the last time we'd discussed Poole. I might be speaking out of turn by letting on that Poole had got the chop, but I steered the talk towards Askwith, and I did let on that he'd told me about his new system of traffic control.

Sermon frowned. 'Now I know a new scheme is being talked of – part of the drive to economical working . . . But I rather thought it was Poole himself that had cooked it up.'

It was my turn to feel an access of excitement, because I had suspected just such a thing.

'And it's not as if he was given a special duty to do it,' Sermon continued. 'He just dreamed it up on a venture, and he'd been hawking it around without much prospect of success.'

I said, 'I'll tell you another curious fact about Poole. He has an interest in venomous snakes.' I ought *not* to have said it, but I couldn't resist.

'*Does* he now? How do you *know* he has that interest?'

I was so far out on a limb, there was no going back. I said, 'When he was a boy, he wrote to one of the boys' papers asking advice on how to keep them.'

'What paper?'

'*The Captain*.'

'We have *The Captain* here. What number?'

'March 1897, page 33.'

'Hold on a moment.' Wheezing somewhat, Charles Sermon rose to his feet and walked into the Insty, as I sat in the heavy heat of late afternoon, and thought about Dougie Poole. A couple of minutes later, Charles Sermon came out holding the volume of *Captain*s that corresponded to the one I'd read in Bertram's Club, Darjeeling, but this one was bound in the maroon covers rather than blue as at Bertram's. Sermon was holding the book open.

'Rum,' he said, passing it over.

There was no 'Naturalist's Corner' on page 33; there was no page 33 at all. It – apparently alone of all the pages in the volume – had been neatly sliced out near the spine.

III

Monday dawned with a suffocating grey sky. It made the white municipal palaces of Calcutta seem whiter still, giving them a sort of gold-edged glow – and it trapped in the heat. I spent the first part of the morning in the office on Commission of Enquiry business. I then glanced again at the documents relating to

September 1919, but Charles Sermon had convinced me that the unrest among the railway top brass in 1919 was a matter of no account as far as the snake business was concerned. I had not yet unrolled the bundle of documents I'd made on the previous Friday. I'd been carrying it in my suit-coat pocket off and on, and it was there again now. At eleven o'clock I considered returning to the Insty in hopes of inspecting more closely the photograph of the Debating Society dance in 1918 – the one Mrs Sonia Young had been about to show me before I'd been pounced on by her son. I wanted to verify what – or rather who – I thought I had glimpsed in that photograph before the violent interruption. I had in fact returned to the bar of the Insty after my talk with Sermon on the Saturday afternoon, only to discover that Mrs Young had left for home and taken the albums with her. I was now frustrated again, because Jogendra Babu informed me that the Insty was closed all day Monday.

At midday, Deo Rana came into the office. He was keen to be off to the snake men's uncle, even though we'd been told he wouldn't be pitching up until the mid-afternoon. I said, 'Won't we be early?'

'Better than late,' said Deo.

I still didn't understand this assignation. Was the snake men's uncle only open for business at certain fixed times? If he were itinerant, then how could his nephews (who were apparently also his enemies) be so certain of his movements? If Deo Rana knew, he wasn't letting on. I caught up the map showing the location, and I stowed my Webley in my suit-coat pocket. We went down into Fairlie Place and, there being no police tongas available, we hailed one plying for hire, a two-horse job.

The tonga set off fast. It turned right out of Fairlie Place, and into Dalhousie Square. We then began running south along Government Place, where we came alongside trams. It seemed we were beginning to race one of them. As the tram rocked along, a spray of sparks tumbled from the pantograph collecting the power from the overhead, and it was as if the sparks had ignited the lighting that now flashed. I eyed Jogendra, waiting for the great crash of thunder. When it came there was no flicker of reaction on his face. We pressed on, now under roaring rain. Through the window slats, I saw people running in all directions, and umbrellas were sprouting at a great rate like so many black flowers.

A few minutes later we turned left off Kidderpore Road into Lower Circular Road; we then turned into Bhawanipore Road, where there were no other tongas. We were closing on the place that had been marked on the map. Bhawanipore Road had once been grand, but now some of the buildings were roofless, with palm trees sprouting inside, and most of the window shutters smashed, or sagging at odd angles. We turned again, into a nameless road, and here was further deterioration, the houses becoming so many brick or tin hutches under the worsening rain. Canvas canopies were attached to some, and all this material shuddered in the storm like rigged sails. The road ended at a stinking black canal.

Tolly's Nullah was a waterway that had been de-silted a hundred years before by a certain Colonel Tolly . . . but then it had silted up again, at least in part. It still connected the docks on the Hooghly with a couple of other rivers to the east of the city, but Colonel Tolly would have been disgusted at the state of it in 1923. In that lashing rainstorm, Tolly's Nullah resembled a black-ink *etching* of Tolly's Nullah.

We had come to rest on the black muddy south bank of it.

We climbed down, and paid off the tonga-wallah. Two white cows loitered on the black beach, one with a scrap of pink ribbon attached to a horn; there were also a number of broken carts. Immediately to the left of us stood a derelict pumping station that appeared mosque-like. In the corresponding position on the opposite bank stood a lone chimney, a mysterious vapour swirling around the top of it. A sailing ship with broken masts and spars rotted in midstream, and alongside it a smaller boat (it might once have been a lighter to the sailing ship) revolved in the swirling waters at about the speed of the second hand of a watch. We had arrived at the very spot marked on the map, but there was no sign of the snake men's uncle. Deo Rana was pointing to the right, and there – a hundred yards or so along the bank – was a parked tonga. The tonga-wallah sat up top, huddled in an oilskin cape; and two men were approaching the tonga from the direction of the water. One was a big European fellow in oilskin cape and sola topee. The other was a small Indian in loose white clothes, and with a blanket around his shoulders. These two were Charles Sermon and the gardener, or mali, of the Railway Institute. I ought to have guessed that these two were in partnership somehow. I made rapidly towards them across the black beach with Deo Rana in tow. As we walked I shouted over my shoulder, explaining to Deo Rana the identity of the two men we were approaching, because, as far as I knew, he had never clapped eyes on either before.

Charles Sermon removed his horn-rimmed glasses, fished out a handkerchief from beneath his cape, wiped his glasses and set them back on his nose. Having verified my identity, he raised a hand in greeting, before turning to say a few words to his Indian companion.

When we converged on the black beach – with the rain

repeatedly relenting with a sigh, only to then redouble its force – all was gentlemanly. Sermon, wheezing badly, shook my hand. I introduced Deo Rana to Sermon, who indicated the mali, saying 'You'll recognise Gopal from the Institute.' He added in a confidential tone, 'He's the stoutest of fellows, Jim,' although 'stout' was exactly what Gopal was not. Shouting over the rain, Sermon continued, 'I owe you an apology, Jim, for trespassing on your investigation, but when you said you were on the trail of the big snake chief of Calcutta, I spoke to Gopal, and he knew just who you meant. Gopal knows snakes, Jim. Every gardener in the city wages a constant war against them.'

'But where *is* he?' I said. 'The big snake chief?'

Sermon turned and pointed along the black waterway. Beyond the broken sailing ship, in the direction that might have been called 'upriver' if the water in Tolly's Nullah could be said to flow, there was another boat. Deo Rana was already making towards it. I had figured this craft for a bamboo hut constructed on the very edge of the water, whereas in fact the mass of thatch I had seen through the rain formed the roof of the cabin of a moored boat.

'He's in there?' I asked Sermon.

'He's in there all right, along with a lieutenant or comrade of some kind. The boat is a sort of floating reptile house. It's moored at its regular berth, Jim. According to Gopal, he sails up the Nullah every few weeks, bringing snakes from up country.'

'Why?'

'Sell to the charmers, Jim. Or anyone else who wants one, and I don't think he's too particular about his clientele. Hold on a moment,' Sermon added, and he walked over to the waiting tonga-wallah and spoke a word to him, dismissing the fellow. I began walking towards the snake boat, with Sermon and Gopal following behind. I could see that it was sharply pointed and up-raised at bow and stern, like a paper boat.

'I don't know how you want to play it, Jim,' Sermon called out, 'but I'm at your service if you want to try and run him in.'

I didn't see how we could do that, since we now had no carriage in which to convey an arrested party. Sermon was walking at my shoulder. 'I've taken the day off work especially for this, Jim.'

I had hoped to see Sermon here, but had *he* anticipated *my* arrival? Was anything to be made of the fact that he had pitched up in advance of the time I had mentioned as being that of my own rendezvous? The question went begging as two white-clad Indians emerged from the black bamboo cabin of the moored boat, and stood on the small foredeck. One of the two might have been twenty, the older might have been eighty. The younger carried an ordinary cane chair, and the elderly party now sat in it. The assistant then ducked back into the cabin, and re-emerged carrying a thick black-and-white snake – a python, I believed. He draped the snake over the shoulders of the elderly party, who now sat in state in the pounding rain, ready to receive petitions, like a mayor with his chain of office, and his assistant took up station beside him like the town clerk. But it seemed the elderly party wasn't happy with the way the snake had been draped, and he wanted it adjusted by his assistant. When this had been accomplished, the snake chief set about staring directly ahead from his chair – and I was powerfully reminded of the pet shop owner of Seven Dials, London, as depicted by Dougie Poole.

Deo Rana was the closest one of us to the boat. He stood by the half-rotted mooring post to which it was tethered. Alongside this post, and practically keeled over, was one of the half-dead-looking bushes supposed to give protection against snake bites: a manasa tree. It was the only instance of vegetation on the river-bank, and it did not look very long for this world. Half concealed beneath it, I saw a white stone.

Deo Rana called out to the two on the boat, and it was the young assistant who gave the reply. They began a conversation I could not understand. I stepped forward, so that I was by the side of Deo Rana.

'Not here,' said Deo Rana, half turning towards me.

'You mean I shouldn't be standing here, Deo?' I said. 'In that case, why are you?'

Deo Rana was indicating his own right ear, while pointing towards the old chap on the boat. He had said, 'Not *hear*.' The snake man was deaf, like his bloody snakes. I had been warned of this, and I had forgotten it. He *looked* deaf as well somehow, or at any rate appeared sunk in on himself. He looked blind too, for the matter of that, with too much white in his eyes.

Deo Rana leapt on to the foredeck of the boat. The young assistant began yelling abuse at him, while the old chap commenced a fast, low muttering, as though uttering an incantation or a curse.

'Looks like we're in for bother,' said Sermon.

'What's he saying?' I called out to Deo Rana, meaning what was the young Indian saying. It was Charles Sermon who answered: 'He says it is forbidden to board the boat.'

'That's what I thought.'

'But I'll not take orders from that gentry. We go on after your man, do we?'

I leapt aboard. Honour demanded that I follow Deo Rana. The snake man increased the speed of his cursing. The python was cir-culating about him, following a path familiar to it. His companion was screaming at Deo Rana, who had now stepped inside the bamboo cabin. I stepped in after him. There were barrels and boxes and baskets in there; an oil lamp hung from a central bamboo beam, and it smoked the place out. The rain was dripping through the roof. The boat gave a jolt, and as I put my hand up to the beam to support myself, Deo Rana called 'Huzoor!' A snake was coiled tightly around the beam; and I had touched it. I stepped back, heart racing. It was coiled like toffee; yet it had felt like oiled, rough leather, and it was green. Above all, it had *felt like leather*, like an old book, and so it was like a *moving book*. The young assistant was now inside the creaking, dripping cabin alongside us, and his rage had taken a different form. He was quite silent as he went about his business of upending boxes and kicking over baskets.

'Boat is moving, huzoor,' said Deo Rana, and the snakes were also moving, flowing all about the cabin. I had not yet touched a second snake, but there was a whole uncoiling heap of them by my boot. If I moved my boot an inch, I would touch them. And so I didn't move my boot. But the snake on the beam was also unwinding, and its head was wavering towards me, and so I needed to move. But because of the boot snakes, I could *not* move. Deo Rana had picked up a basket lid to protect himself. He was shouting, 'Huzoor, you have gun! Shoot!'

Shoot what? The snake man's assistant was no longer with us. I kicked out three times at the boot snakes. That sent some of them away, but others were coming back. Marshalling all my courage, I tried to drag the coiled snake away from its beam, but it tensed and held on, like a disembodied arm flexing its muscles. Its wandering head was looking for me again, and now its mouth was open.

Deo Rana was shouting his latest bit of bad news. 'Door is closing, huzoor.'

The door was woven bamboo like the rest of the place, but it looked pretty solid, and pressure was evidently being put on it from outside. The snake man's assistant was attempting to shut us in. I took out my pistol and fired at the door. While I was at it, I fired twice into the tangle of floor snakes, and there was now a massed hissing combined with the seething of the rain and the creaking of the bamboo. The hissing was exactly like the noise made by a human audience that disapproves of the words of a speaker's words. Heedless of snakes, with head down and eyes shut tight, I marched at the door and lunged thought it, gaining the foredeck; Deo Rana followed, and we stood there under the rain and the black sky. We were spinning forlornly in Tolly's Nullah just as the smaller boat upstream had been set spinning by the rising waters. The snake man had vacated his post, but his chair remained. Of his young companion there was no sign. My bullet would have gone through the door; therefore I might have shot him into the water. I still held the Webley. On the black riverbank, I saw Sermon and Gopal the mali. Had Sermon attempted to come on board? Who had cast the boat off from its mooring? Had that been Sermon's doing? Sermon was signing to us, indicating that we should jump for the bank, and the rotation of the boat would take us within leaping distance of the bank inside a few seconds . . . but I would not have the luxury of waiting, because with a mighty slap the python landed on the foredeck between Deo Rana and me. It was as if the weather gods had hurled down a giant snake, having concluded that the rain was not having a bad enough effect. I leapt as the beast began to flow over the deck boards, and I landed on the slimy bank, half in and halfout of Tolly's Nullah. The water was warm, and slimy like oil, and I had to claw at the bank to drag myself out of it.

Deo Rana made a better leap and he landed a few feet away. I had dropped my pistol as I landed, and Deo picked it up off the riverbank mud. I looked back at the boat. The snake man and his assistant had somehow transferred to the small *aft* deck. They must have scrambled over the roof of the cabin, and one of them must have pitched down the python from up there. But pythons were not venomous, so I supposed that was no worse than having a log pitched at you.

The snake men's boat was now spinning away, receding behind a curtain of rain. Charles Sermon and the gardener, Gopal, were now walking away along the beach, heading downriver, back in the direction from which we'd all come; and they had been joined by a third man, who wore a tightly buttoned white mackintosh. Even through the swirling rain I could see that this newcomer was Professor Hedley Fleming, and I felt pride in having lured him here. I almost had a full complement of suspects.

I rose to my feet and, half-sodden, I approached these three.

'Who cast the boat off?'

'The young fellow,' said Sermon. 'I'm sorry, but I was rather distracted.' Sermon indicated Fleming, saying, 'I was just asking the doctor if he'd be good enough to explain his business here.'

Professor Hedley Fleming's spectacles were steamed up by the storm, but that hardly mattered, since he seldom made eye contact anyway. Hedley Fleming was attempting to explain to Sermon his presence at the waterside. 'Stringer here showed me his map. As far as I could gather, he seemed to think the site was significant in terms of the dealing in snakes.'

'Did you see the boat?' I said. 'It was full of them.'

'I daresay it was.'

I said, 'You don't think there's anything queer about a boatload of bloody snakes?'

Professor Hedley Fleming removed his glasses, and wiped them with a handkerchief, but not for the purposes of looking at me. Instead, he was looking down at my mud-soaked trousers. 'Do you have any notion of how many snake charmers there are in this city?' he demanded, 'and how many snakes the average one of them gets through per mensem, never mind per annum?'

For all the success of my scheme, there was the problem of time with Fleming, as there had been with Sermon. I had told Fleming that I planned to seek out the snake man in mid-afternoon on this day. Strange though it was to speak of mere timekeeping in that apocalyptic deluge, it was not yet one o'clock. Fleming, like Sermon, had pitched up early. I put this to Fleming, and he said, 'I am not bound by *your* appointment diary, Captain Stringer.'

'Did you know of the boat beforehand?'

'What are you suggesting?'

I was suggesting that he was a regular client of the snake man, and that he had come here today in advance (as he thought) of my own visit, so as to warn him of my arrival. What I actually said was, 'We're only a short walk from the Zoological Gardens.'

Fleming got the point: he was being accused; and he turned on his heel, indignant. He was about to stalk off in a rage when his eye – and mine – fell on the figure of a man standing in the doorway of the half-wrecked pumping station. The figure retreated into the building as we looked his way. He had been a small man, overwhelmed not only by the rain, but also by his own rain cape. Charles Sermon had seen him too, and it was he who pronounced the name: 'That was Douglas Poole, wasn't it?'

'*Who?*' Fleming demanded. 'Because he's been following me around for days. Perhaps you can tell him for me, Stringer:

304

he'd better desist.'

At this, Fleming walked away, heading back towards Bhawani-pore Road, and Dougie Poole emerged from the ruined pumping station to watch him do it, eyeing Fleming in a defiant sort of way until he disappeared into the rainstorm.

Sermon, Gopal, Deo Rana and I now stood in a semicircle be-fore Dougie Poole. Behind him, in the wrecked interior of the pumping station, lay something resembling a giant riveted bath tap fallen over on its side. Poole was sipping from a flask; his rain cap was about two sizes too big.

'Well, Dougie?' I said. 'And by the way, I think you know Charles Sermon from the traffic office?'

'Yes,' said Dougie Poole, nodding. 'I saw you leaping from the boat, Jim.'

'Did you see the python?'

'I did. I thought that might account for the leap.'

Dougie Poole offered the flask to Sermon and me; we both de-clined.

'I've got some fascinating data for you about our friend Flem-ing,' said Poole.

Alongside me, Charles Sermon was breathing hard. 'Shall we step inside this waterworks?' Poole continued, indicating the pumping station. '. . . Not that it has a roof.'

We all moved through the doorway. There was *half* a roof; therefore half as much rain was falling inside as outside. I now saw that, beside the giant tap that had keeled over, another remained upright by its side, as though in mourning for its dead companion; and there was a mix of abandoned plumbing running all over the muddy floor, the pipes looking snake-like to my mind.

I said, 'What's the fascinating data about Fleming, Dougie? Is it the fact that he was walking out with the woman who became Mary Bennett?'

This *must* have been the 'intriguing alliance' – as disclosed by the photograph in the Debating Society dance album – that Mrs Young had been about to reveal to me before the intervention of her riotous son. I was sure that I had seen the glint of Hedley Fleming's glasses in that photograph. The picture had dated from 1918. Since then the relationship had soured, and Mary had transferred her affections to Superintendent Christopher Bennett.

Poole took a long time to digest this hazard of mine. 'Well, Jim,' he said at length, 'I must admit that my news isn't quite so fascinating as *that*, but it's grist to the same mill. I was only going to say that I've been tailing Professor Fleming of late, and I've twice lost him in the railway lands of Howrah. Both times he went there with a wicker basket over his shoulder. I couldn't see any motive though: why would he be stowing snakes on the trains? But now we do have the motive. The woman he loved was stolen from him by the head of the railway police. So he takes his revenge by committing a series of terrible crimes that the head of the police can't solve. What better way to do it?'

At this, Deo Rana spoke up. 'If he kill *head of police*,' he said, 'that is better way.'

'But he may have found it preferable to inflict a long humiliation,' I said, turning to Deo, and it did seem to me that Fleming himself had been subject to a long humiliation that he would want to revenge: the humiliation taking the form of Mary Bennett's incessant and very public boasting about her marriage.

Of course, Christopher Bennett knew of Hedley Fleming. It was impossible that two Cambridge graduates of about the same age in Calcutta, who attended the same social functions, would not have coincided. Bennett must also have known of the previous association of his wife and Fleming, and surely he not only suspected Fleming, but could also guess at his motive. This was what he had meant when letting slip that he found the snake crimes 'ungentlemanly'. Having identified man and motive he was, as he had said, ready to make his move. But he obviously hadn't made it yet.

It would be up to us to make it for him.

IV

Against all the odds, we found a tonga in Bhawanipore Road. There was room for only four inside, so Dougie Poole volunteered to follow on foot. Our destination was a mere half mile away: the Zoological Gardens, and the office of Hedley Fleming. Or perhaps we would overtake him on the way. I had it in mind to simply confront the professor with the facts as we knew them, and see how he reacted. I would then take those facts, and the news of that reaction, to Superintendent Christopher Bennett. I would force Bennett's hand, in other words. Later on I would likewise confront Detective Inspector Khan, and give him my theory about the killing of John Young on the Jamalpur Night Mail. I had nothing to lose; I would bail out of the Commission of Enquiry, just as Fisher had done. My wife was pregnant and I wanted to get her home as soon as possible.

But no: that train of thought was utterly illogical. I had a great deal to lose by Khan learning that I knew the truth, and not so much to gain. My knowledge of his crime was a card only to be played *in extremis.*

In the tonga, I sat next to Charles Sermon. Deo Rana and Go-pal the mali sat opposite. I unbuttoned my rain cape, so as to air my sodden trousers. Sermon had done likewise, although he could not have been as soaked through as I was. He had not, after all, gone bathing in Tolly's Nullah. In the course of arranging my clothes, I discovered in my suit-coat pocket the bundle of documents concerning the doings of the Company in 1919. I had 'borrowed' these papers from the office, and now they were no doubt ruined. Jogendra would not be pleased. I unfurled the bundle, and instantly read 'News from the Out-Stations'. That was in bold, so I didn't need my reading glasses to make it out. I had opened the bundle at a page of the Company magazine de-scribing social events, and weddings in particular. The date at the top of the page was also clear enough: September 1919, as was the sub-heading 'Burdwan Blessings'. Burdwan was on the Grand Chord, not far out. For the most part, the print of the article itself was a little more hazy, but I read, 'Mr F. De Souza, the very pop-ular engineer, married Miss Noreen Ford, late of Calcutta, and daughter of Mr P. Ford, Permanent Way Inspector.' There was a picture of the happy couple. It was a pound to a penny that they were Anglo-Indians. She was very pretty, and she carried a wreath. In a photograph without colour the flowers appeared white, and I believed that was because they *were* white.

Charles Sermon, by my side, wore glasses at all times. He could therefore read perfectly well, even in the semi-gloom of the shak-ing tonga . . . and he was breathing heavily. The flowers in the wreath held by the bride were white carnations. I turned to my left and saw the white carnation in the buttonhole of Sermon's suit coat. He wore a white carnation every day, and he had taken the trouble to obtain one this morning even though he knew the business he had in store was not of a very decorous nature. The white carnation, then, was of the greatest importance. It went to the very heart of the man. I delved into my suit coat for my reading glasses, and I put them on. Deo Rana was eyeing me carefully. Sermon was wheezing. I read the confirmatory words, 'The bride carried a beautiful bouquet made of her favourite white carnations.'

I removed my glasses, as the truth broke in upon me. The 'intriguing alliance' that Mrs Young had meant to show me at the Insty was not that of Hedley Fleming and the woman who became Mary Bennett (even though I believed I *had* glimpsed Fleming in the assembled party, and possibly standing beside that same Mary). That, I now realised, could not possibly be the liaison Mrs Young had in mind. After all, she did not *know* Christopher Bennett. When I had indicated him to her as the Debating Society dance, she had looked blankly, and on top of that, she had lowered her voice when pointing to the photograph. If she had been referring to Christopher Bennett, she would not have needed to do that: *he* was not in the bar of the Insty, but Charles Sermon had been in the bar, and sitting only a few feet away. Was it not possible that the surprising alliance was that of Charles Sermon, long-time bachelor and pukkah sahib, and a young and beautiful Anglo-Indian woman: between Charles Sermon, in fact, and the young woman smiling up at us from the page of the *East Indian Railway Magazine*: Miss Noreen Ford? Snakes had first appeared in the first class compartments of the Railway when Miss Ford, lost to Charles Sermon, had moved from Calcutta and married a fellow Anglo-Indian, an altogether less surprising alliance.

But why had the snakes made their *reappearance* in April of this year, and with far more devastating results than the first time?

I turned towards Charles Sermon. I indicated the photograph. 'What do you suppose came of *her*?'

Sermon did not answer my question, but he held a gun in his hand. At a nod from Sermon, the mali flung open the door of the tonga. We had rolled to a stop, and we were at the zoo. The giant birdcage was beyond the swinging door of the tonga, and so were two police constables. I did not know how the constables had come to be there, but the sight of them checked the flight of Gopal the mali. Sermon turned to me with gun pointed. He said, 'I will thank you not to say "she" when speaking of a lady,' and Deo Rana shot him in the head. There came a mighty screech from the giant birdcage and the giant bird inside it began circling madly at its uppermost level. The tonga had now set off again but it, like the bird, was not going anywhere, only circling. I climbed down. One of the two horses that had pulled the tonga had been killed by the continuation of the bullet that had killed Charles Sermon, and the surviving horse was endeavouring to drag the whole equipage around in a circle, which was evidently a more fascinating form of animal entertainment than offered elsewhere in the zoo, for in spite of the teeming rain, we were surrounded by quite a crowd.

Chapter Fourteen

I

It was Wednesday 16 May, and I was walking with Lydia on the Calcutta maidan. She and Bernadette had returned from Darjeeling that morning. It had been business as usual for King Sol throughout the day, and he was now winding up his operations. It was five o'clock, and we had just had tea on the terrace of Willard's Hotel. Lydia was glad to be back, beyond the range of the visiting card tyranny, and she was looking forward to giving her talk to a branch of the Women's India Association. We were fairly confident that Bernadette was at that very moment practising piano in the basement music room of the hotel.

As we walked, I said, 'What is the condition of her love life?'

'I don't know,' said Lydia, 'and I wouldn't tell you if I did.'

In fact, I believed that she did know, but I did not want to cause her undue anxiety by pressing for an answer. I had forgotten – it was becoming ever more embarrassingly evident – almost every detail of the wife's first two confinements. (I could remember little beyond the persistent smell of something called Scrubb's Cloudy Ammonia.) But I assumed that undue anxiety was the sort of thing a pregnant woman should be avoiding. Also, I myself was now less anxious about Bernadette, the wife's unexpected pregnancy having suddenly promoted her in my mind to the status of adult.

But for most of our walk, and for most of our tea, we had been discussing the shooting of John Young, and the bad business that had occurred at Tolly's Nullah two days previously. As to the first, I had explained in full Khan's actions, and I said I still didn't know to what extent he had acted alone. Lydia had not believed that Khan *could* have acted alone. He must have had the authority of his superiors. I put this down to her willingness to think anything bad of the British ruling classes, but her point was a bit more subtle. She saw the beginnings of an alliance between the imperial power and the Moslems. The British, she thought, would attempt a policy of divide and rule, buying off the Moslems with political concessions so as to get their support against the Hindus who were the mainstays of the nationalist movement. But I didn't believe Khan was anybody's stooge, and when I put that to the wife, she had nodded rather wistfully in agreement. I believed that in spite of all he'd done she rather admired Khan, found him romantic and dashing.

As for Tolly's Nullah and the bloody denouement at the zoo, I had told the wife the tale, but in a rather fragmentary way, since I had been coming and going all day between Willard's Hotel, Fairlie Place and the Alipore Jail, where Gopal, the mali of the Railway Institute was being held as yet without charge, and where Deo Rana was also being held, on a charge of murdering Charles Sermon.

Lydia said, 'When exactly did this Noreen Ford die?'

'That's not quite clear. But late March of this year, in the Railway Hospital at Burdwan.'

'And it was a cancer?'

'Yes. Sermon would have heard of it by early April one way or another, and then he started leaving the snakes on the trains.'

'In co-operation with this other fellow, the gardener at the Institute?'

'Yes.'

'What was in it for him? The gardener, I mean.'

'Money. It made sense for Sermon to have an accomplice: they could divide the duties, alternating the jobs of collecting the snakes and putting them into the carriages.'

We walked on.

It 'made sense' only insofar as any of it made sense. Charles Sermon was a nut. But then again, it appeared that he had court-ed Noreen Ford in a civilised and loving way, and it had been a genuine alliance even if a strange one. It might even have lead to marriage in spite of the age difference, but the girl had been re-jected by Sermon's fellow railway officers; rejected, that is, by first class-travelling society. Or so he thought.

Earlier that day, I had questioned the head of traffic, William Askwith, on the point. He was still in Darjeeling (although just about to return) so I had spoken to him by telephone. I had told him the story of Sermon, and he had found it 'both horrible and deeply sad', but it also seemed to me that he was relieved I was not calling on another matter.

Regarding Sermon, he said, 'We British started crooked on the Anglo-Indian question, and crooked we have remained.' For him, the Anglos were an important prop of British rule, and they were the *crucial* prop when it came to running the railways. He himself had always made efforts to bring them on. Yes, he had seen Sermon together with the girl at a couple of social events at about the time of the end of the war. He did not believe they had been ostracised. 'It was more a case of people being bemused, or even, I'm afraid, amused. Sermon was a lifelong bachelor you know... I suppose the pair of them *might* have thought they were being cold-shouldered.'

Lydia said, 'I don't quite see how the death of the girl could have triggered it all. I mean, she would presumably have died of the cancer even if she'd married him and stayed here? So how can he blame the Railway for that?'

There could be no answer, except to say that the death of the girl had put Sermon into a rage.

We continued our walk.

Lydia said, 'And tell me again . . . why were the police constables at the zoo?'

'They were accompanying Superintendent Bennett. He'd gone there either to question or arrest Hedley Fleming. He suspected there might be trouble, but at the last minute he'd asked them to hang back, and he'd gone into Fleming's office alone.'

'But Fleming was quite innocent?'

'Quite. In fact, he'd begun his own investigation of the matter, which is why he'd been going off to the railway lands . . . as observed by Dougie Poole. There's more to him than meets the eye, you know.'

'Which is probably just as well.'

'I approve of Dougie Poole. He says he hasn't much "character" but in spite of everything, he's dogged. He's what I call a "stickler".'

'That's the wrong use of the word.'

'But you know what I mean. The way he—'

'"Tenacious" is what you mean.'

'The way he agreed to come out to India because his wife wanted it . . . he tried his best for her, but then when he saw he wasn't cut out for the life, he made the decision to take his family back home. As for his difficulties at work . . . he found the system used in the office too complicated, and he put up with it for a while; then he came up with a better one. Finally, he tried to find out who the snake man was, and he'd identified his suspect and begun shadowing him. It was the *wrong* suspect, but I bet he'd

314

have got on the track of the right one before long.'

'I don't see him beating his drink addiction,' said Lydia.

'Perhaps he doesn't want to.'

'What about the snake he had when he was a boy? What kind was it after all?'

'I still don't know. He'd written in about adders, but when I think of it now, he was only asking for *advice* on them. That's no proof he actually kept one. Perhaps he knew that letter had survived in the collected volumes. Perhaps he also knew it might be a hostage to fortune given what was happening on the trains, so he tried to muddy the waters about what his true interest had been. But he didn't cut out the page of the Insty's edition of *The Captain*. Sermon did that to throw suspicion on Poole.'

'But from what you say, he went inside the building to get the book, and came out a moment later with the page cut. So that was quick work.'

'I believed he used the gardener's scissors.'

'To go back to the constables at the zoo . . .' said Lydia. 'They saw Deo Rana shoot Sermon.'

'Apparently they said they had a clear sight of it, through the open door of the tonga; and they make out that it wasn't necessary for Deo to shoot Sermon.'

'But Sermon held a gun.'

'They say he was giving the gun up.'

'Why would they say that?'

'Perhaps they really think it. I don't know *what* they really think.'

'But Deo Rana was only protecting you.'

'Yes.'

'And he could end up hanged?'

'Or in jail for a long time.'

'What are you going to do about it?'

'*Something.*'

We had come to a stand.

'How do you know all that about Sermon anyway?'

'From the confession of the mali, from diary entries and other material found in his flat.'

Whereas Lydia now wanted to return to the hotel to work on the first of the two talks she was scheduled to give to Indian women, I wanted to continue walking and revolving my thoughts. Two dusty roads, Dufferin Road and Mayo Road, intersected at this part of the maidan, and the occasional tonga would come along them. A tonga was approaching along Dufferin now. It was heading north-east, the direction of the hotel. I wouldn't have let Lydia walk back over the darkening maidan alone, but she would be all right in a tonga. So I flagged it down.

I knew the wife's talk was fixed for the coming Friday, but I had forgotten *where*, or perhaps I had never known. As she climbed up, I asked her.

'The coal place,' she said. 'Asansol.'

I'd had a vague idea it was out of town, but I hadn't realised it was quite as far out as that.

II

The tonga rattled away, and I was left alone in the velvet darkness of the maidan. The city sounded very far away. I headed due south over the blackened grass, towards the great bulk of the Victoria Memorial. After a minute I heard the fast-approaching sound of horses' hooves; I turned about to see two riders approaching at a gallop. I stepped aside, but not before the second one had shouted, 'You there – out of the bloody way!'

It was Fisher, and the rider a little way ahead of him was Detective Inspector Khan. They raced past me in the gloom, pounding on towards the reservoir called Elliot's Tank, but they slowed before reaching the Tank; they then stopped and conferred, turned about and came thundering towards me. Fisher, I realised, was very nearly as good a horseman as Khan. I was not very surprised at that – Fisher was a remarkably capable fellow all round – and I was not so very surprised to see them together either. I had sent a chit to Khan that morning, marked as being strictly for his personal attention, and hinting at everything I knew about his plot to kill the revolutionary called Deep, or sometimes Ganguly, which had resulted in the death of John Young on the Jamalpur Night Mail.

When they came up, I spoke first to Fisher, and I thought I would be rude to him before he could be rude to me.

'What are you doing here?' I asked him.

'Collecting my things, aren't I?' he said.

'Off up to Suryapore, are you?'

'That's it.'

'And you've come back here to collect your things—'

'I've just bloody said that.'

'. . . And to have one last review of the blunder you made with your co-conspirator.' I indicated Khan. I faced Khan, and I found I was shouting at him. 'Fisher here saw India as a land of opportunity. He's struck lucky with a maharajah, but a few weeks back he'd have done practically anything for cash. How much did you pay him go after Deep or Ganguly or whatever the name?'

Khan jumped down from his horse. He had a rifle attached to the saddle. The police would practise riding with rifles. He said, 'This appears to be a continuation of the absurdities you were peddling in your note.'

'They're facts, and you know it!'

'If you continue shouting at me, Stringer, I will run you in. I'm on the point of doing so anyway for the killing of Young.'

I said, 'Pull the other one, pal,' and he winced at that. I'd known he would; it was why I'd said it. 'If you were serious about pinning it on me, you'd have got Fisher to testify against me. You get credit for stopping short of that anyway. You were only questioning me to find out what I knew, and when you heard I'd been sniffing around about the reservation chart you were panicked into coming up to Darjeeling. I wonder if you two liaised up there? I doubt it. You knew you shouldn't be seen together.'

'I'm going to bloody lay you out,' said Fisher, but he remained on his horse. 'You're off your bloody nut', he said, 'if you think I shot Young.'

'You didn't shoot him. A bloke called Sabir Huq had been hired to do the job, together with some of his confederates. Your role was to supervise the thing, make sure it all went off according to plan. When you went into that compartment, and you figured out the wrong man had taken the bullet, you didn't bat an eye. You covered up brilliantly. Then you pretended to be interested in finding the culprit. For a while – until the Rajkumar came along with his business proposition. Well, I've got a proposition for the two of you: release Deo Rana from the Alipore nick, and I'll say no more about it.'

Of course, it was only Khan who could fix this for me. It was probably to be expected that Deo Rana would be run in after the shooting. But the murder charge was not to be expected. It had come from the C.I.D., and I believed it was Khan's doing in particular. I also believed he had done it because I knew I was on to him about the killing of Young, and he wanted a bargaining chip. However, he said nothing but just looked at me in a disgusted sort of way (at which he was very good), before remounting his horse and riding off with Fisher in tow, the pair of them cantering at first, then starting to gallop hard.

It was a shame. I would have liked to have told them something else they already knew, namely that Fisher's brief had also been to finish off Deep/Ganguly if Sabir Huq and his fellows should funk it. Of course, it never came to that, but Fisher would have equipped himself with a small calibre pistol, which he managed to dispose of unseen, and a silencer, which Canon Peter Selwyn had *observed* him disposing of.

I had previously concluded that the item Fisher had been seen pitching away must have been a cigar tube, but on the Friday last I had called into Hatzopolo's cigar shop on Lindsay Street. I bought myself a couple of Havanas, and I asked about 'my great pal' Major Fisher. It was Mr Hatzopolo himself that I spoke to. He knew of Fisher and was evidently amazed that anyone should speak of the man as being a 'pal'. I said I was interested in buying my pal a cigar tube, and Mr Hatzopolo regretted to inform me that Major Fisher was already in possession of such an item.

Fisher had been in the habit of coming in for Trichies, but on Wednesday 2 May (the day Fisher and I departed for Darjeeling) he had called in to buy a Havana and had also splashed out on a silver retaining tube. It had been perfectly clear that Fisher had never previously owned such a thing. Mr Hatzopolo recalled the conversation distinctly. He had attempted to persuade Fisher to buy one of the double tubes, which were only a little more expensive, and much more companionable. 'You see,' Mr Hatzopolo had explained, 'you can carry one cigar for yourself, and one for a friend,' and it was with a pained expression that Mr Hatzopolo recalled Fisher's reply: 'Sod that for a lark.'

The point was this: Fisher had not had a cigar tube in his possession when he rode on the Jamalpur Night Mail.

III

William Askwith knew something was up. Not that any expression appeared on his face as such, but when we sat down in Firpo's restaurant, he immediately asked whether I would be having wine. I replied that I would be having one Beck's beer, but that he should order away, and this he did without inhibition, going for ten rupees' worth of decent red.

I had suggested that we meet, and it was Askwith who had suggested Firpo's. Having practically ordered me to visit this famous Italian restaurant, it seemed to me that Stanley Harrington of the India Office could not begrudge the cost, and I intended to return at least once with Lydia before we sailed for Blighty. I liked Firpo's. There was an affinity between the Italians and the Indians. At any rate, I was surrounded by a special, beautiful breed, of white-coated men with highly villainous moustaches, and slender, lustrous women who flowed from one graceful pose to another with no awkward moments on the way. The small band played something that hovered between 'jass' and chamber music, and the palms, and propped-open green window shutters, and the goldenness of the sunlight made me forget the feverishness of Cal, and think instead of the Riviera.

Askwith was entitled by his wealth and standing to move in this world of beauty, even if he, with his blank, white dot of a face, could contribute nothing to it. As a rule, this knowledge would have allowed him to enjoy Firpo's, but not today. Today, on Thursday 17 May, William Askwith knew he was on the back foot.

He had returned from his house at Darjeeling just the day before, to find my chit proposing a meeting. He had agreed immediately, adding – anxiously, it seemed to me – the speculation: 'I suppose you would like further details concerning the unfortunate Mr Sermon, such as may assist you in wrapping up that case, on which successful outcome, by the way, I offer my heartfelt congratulations.'

We had spoken about Sermon at first, but only until the waiter came for our food order. I went for ravioli, and Askwith followed suit, obviously not caring at all about the food, but only about what I might have to say. He must have been cursing me inside. I didn't doubt that he thought me uncouth, barely a cut above Dougie Poole, and I had been rubbing it in by suggesting that the ravioli was 'up to scratch' and hoping that his wine – Chianti, naturally – was 'a decent drop'. But whatever he thought of me, Askwith had had the good manners to keep it pretty well hidden, and so I did not prolong his agony but got down to business directly upon the arrival of the main course.

'I received a document alleging corruption in the traffic department,' I said.

Askwith ate a mouthful of ravioli. At the moment of swallowing, his face seemed to contract, his features becoming even smaller. 'From Harold Jebb would that be?'

'The document was sent anonymously.'

'Is he not still at sea? I'm terribly sorry, Captain Stringer . . . James, if I may . . . It is imperative that I give you some important data about Harold Jebb.'

Askwith put down his knife and fork, and there was no prospect of his finishing the ravioli. His two-thousand-plus rupees per mensem, his freedom, his very life, now hung in the balance. 'Harold Jebb – some people called him Harry . . . he and I never really saw eye to eye. He was perhaps in some degree resentful not to have achieved the promotions to which he felt merited by his abilities, and it's possible he found me a hard taskmaster in a difficult and demanding job. I don't wish to appear uncharitable, but I'm afraid it's perfectly likely that this document of his would have contained numerous libels against his superior officers, and in particular against me.'

'Well, I don't know what the file said.'

'No?'

'Except that it alleged corruption. It was stolen from me on the very day I received it: 19 April.'

'But . . . who do you suppose would have stolen it?'

'I suppose you did.'

Askwith poured himself another glass of Chianti. His hand did not shake, but he drank it off fast, his face contracting with each gulp, somehow like one of those pale creatures that live on the bottom of the sea. 'I most certainly did not,' he said, setting down his glass.

'Then somebody did it on your behalf. Perhaps your friend Superintendent Bennett?'

Askwith now sat back from the table, relinquishing the whole meal.

I said, 'I have since been given some idea of the contents of the file.'

'By whom?'

'By the man who sent it.'

'You have contacted Jebb, presumably telegraphically? But surely he *is* still at sea?'

He was spot on about the telegraphic communication, but not about Jebb being at sea. He had arrived safely in Eastbourne.

I said, 'The source, when confronted, was only happy to identify himself as the author of the document, and to give the gist of its contents. He said had received intelligence that you had been given five hundred rupees by Macpherson Trading, makers of wheels for trains, in return for which you would argue the case for substantial increases in rolling stock. Of course, if that case were made successfully, the Board would sanction a big order from Macphersons.'

'I see,' said Askwith. 'And did he say how he had found that out?'

'At first, again, he was reluctant.'

'But not for long?'

'When pressed, he said the intelligence came from a senior man at the firm of Walker-Mitchell Engineering.'

'Who also make wheels,' said Askwith, nodding slowly.

'Correct.'

'But who are in a smaller way of business,' Askwith continued, 'and whom we may assume look upon the market position of Macphersons with more than a little jealousy.'

Askwith was rallying, and this wouldn't do.

'Is the allegation true?' I asked.

His small face gave another spasm, and there was suddenly a

tear in his eye. I had not bargained for this, and it quite mortified me. I asked if he would care for some water. Askwith shook his head.

'I took the money,' he said. 'It was a cheque, payable to me personally, and drawn against the Macphersons account. It was sent by a man I know a little. I am not well acquainted with him. His name is Beattie: Patrick Beattie, a director of the firm. We had had a discussion about the traffic situation on the line; about how we as a department were over-stretched, and how the fleets ought really to be supplemented, in both passenger and goods. This was, and is, genuinely the case.'

'But still you took a bribe.'

'That's how it looks, but I had discussed another matter with Beattie. The St Dunstan's Fund. I think you know of it. My wife is a patron.'

I nodded. 'She gave me a leaflet about it. Two leaflets, in fact.'

'It feeds the poor children of Calcutta. The cheque from Beattie was accompanied by a chit. It read simply, "For the cause that is dear to both our hearts."'

'But the cheque was made out to you.'

'I decided to interpret that as a slip of the pen, and it wasn't so great a sum. In any event I paid the cheque into my account, and I immediately transferred the same amount to the St Dunstan's account.'

'You have the records to prove this?'

'Of course, of course. But my action was naive. And it came to seem to me that it could prove disastrous.'

'You somehow got wind that Jebb was splitting on you. You learnt of the dossier, and you arranged for its removal from my office.'

'I did so with the assistance of a friend. I would rather not say more, except for this: what Jebb stated was true as to the facts, but wrong as to the construction put upon them.'

'You also stopped contending that new vehicles were required, and you wanted that to be a matter of record. You told me in Darjeeling that you had decided to make better use of the existing assets, and that a plan was in hand for improved diagramming of traffic.'

'There was, and there is.'

'But that is Dougie Poole's plan.'

'I did not say it wasn't. But I accept that I pooh-poohed it when it was first presented, and I was too slow to give him credit for its virtues. Poole is a clever man, but he is . . . unorthodox.'

'He rubbed you up the wrong way something rotten.'

Askwith winced at this, but I had delivered my last blow. I believed the man, or at least . . . I would give him the benefit of the doubt.

IV

This police statement requires that I recollect in accurate detail events occurring in a matter of seconds, events that went from being so much a matter of routine that I was hardly paying attention to such horror that I believe I 'blacked out', leaving only scraps of memory. But I will do my best.

I was travelling with my husband in a first class compartment of a train on the East Indian Railway. We had the compartment to ourselves, and we sat facing one another. The train was running over the main line from Calcutta, which I believe is called the 'Grand Chord'. We were heading for the town of Asansol, where I had an engagement. As we approached a station that I later found out is called Khana Junction, my husband looked about for his newspaper, *The Statesman*, which he read every day. I said, 'It's still in your bag', and he stood, and reached up to the luggage rack over the seats on his side. He got hold of his bag, and he fished about in it, saying, 'I can't see it here, did I leave it in the tonga?' for we had taken a tonga from our hotel to Howrah station, and he had been looking at the paper then. We were both looking up at the luggage rack, and all I can say is that when my husband gave up his search, and turned back around, I noticed a snake on the floor by his feet. I assumed it must have come out from under the seat on his side. It was about three foot long, and black with white stripes. My husband saw it, and I cried out 'Don't!' even as he lowered his right hand towards it. I shall never be able to account for this movement of his, but I believed he meant to grab hold of the snake behind its head as being the one sure way of eliminating the threat. Or perhaps he did not think it was venomous, but that I can't believe since my husband has, of late, had a good deal of experience with snakes.

The snake lifted its head, and it bit my husband's wrist. I screamed, and it was when I realised the snake would not let go, that it was showing the full force of its evil – that is when everything went black for me . . .

I lay aside the statement of Anne Kerry, wife of Colonel Kerry, who had been bitten at Khana Junction, on the Grand Chord, on 23 April, the day I had boarded the train to Jamalpur.

I eyed my own wife, who was sitting opposite. We too were rolling along the Grand Chord, and soon we too would be at Khana, and then Asansol, where she would be giving her talk to the women of India, or about fifty instances thereof.

The embroidered panels of our compartment were green, with a pattern of vines. The fan did not overexert itself, and yet, beyond the window slats, a mobile fire continually burned: King Sol was fighting to come in.

Lydia was sipping a soda and wearing her new reading glasses (which she would *only* wear in front of her family) as she worked on her speech. She'd got into rather a tangle with the idea of 'co-operation'. Here she was, a representative of the British Women's Co-Operative Guild (Yorkshire division), and she would be addressing a society of Indian women who would undoubtedly be keen on the Mahatma's notion of *non*-co-operation. I had suggested that her theme might be the necessity of *co*-operating in order to bring about *non*-co-operation. But this had been a joke, because pursuing any such theme would probably have got her arrested. In fact, the message she was bringing from the Yorkshire Co-Operative Guild was that socialism could help Indians – Indian women especially – to fulfil the noble Hindu idea of Vedanta, or enlightenment through oneness. (Whether her senior colleagues in Yorkshire would have approved of this message had they known about it was another matter again.)

Bernadette sat next to her mother. She also sipped a soda, while reading a magazine called *Mainly for Memsahibs*. She was looking at pictures of hats. Earlier on, she had been reading Philpott's *Hindustani Manual*, and I had watched her lips moving as she attempted to pronounce the phrase for 'I have one elephant'. Prior to that, she had been asking me how 'one' would get from York to Oxford on the train. 'There's no direct service,' I'd replied rather warily. Theoretically I should have been in a state of outright panic, since all the signs pointed to her having formed an alliance with some new young man, probably Indian, who was proposing to study at Oxford University. But the question of Lydia's pregnancy continued to override such considerations. Bernadette did not yet know that her mother was pregnant.

Bernadette put down her magazine, kicked off her shoes, and curled her legs up beneath her. She eyed me.

'Spill,' she said.

She meant that I was to tell her the full story of the killing of John Young, followed by the full story of the snakes on the trains, as I had promised to do. I gave her the two stories, with Lydia looking up and scowling at me whenever I became too graphic in describing the effects of snake bites. I would certainly not be disclosing the distressing details of Anne Kerry's statement for example, which I had brought along with me, together with all the papers I could get hold of touching on the snakes. I rather fancied there was book in it all, something in the Edgar Wallace line.

I had my future to consider, given that I would soon be resigning from the Commission of Enquiry, thereby letting down Bennett (not that he wouldn't be keen to see the back of me), but also, and more importantly, my chief in York who had recommended me in the first place.

Perhaps the R.K. would come up trumps, and push a lot of money my way for turning up some small-gauge railway kit in Blighty. Or perhaps that had been nothing more than a fleeting notion in the mind of a young man with a generous nature and far too much money. My speculations on that front were, of course, kept from Bernadette, as were those concerning the perhaps-dubious behaviour of her friend Claudine's father, William Askwith.

But as my mind ran along these lines, Bernadette was still considering the matter of Charles Sermon. Picking her magazine up again, she said, 'Well, it shows the racial question should not come into matters of romance.'

'*Yes*,' said Lydia, breaking off from her work to look with approval at her daughter.

'You feel sorry for Mr Sermon, then?' I asked Bernadette.

'No . . . No, I don't. It's the horse I feel sorry for. I think your Deo Rana jolly well *should* go to jail for shooting the horse in the head, at least for a while.'

But Deo Rana had been released from the Alipore Jail early the previous evening, the murder charge against him dropped. Then, towards midnight, a package had been left for me at the hotel reception: a single silver cigar tube with a Havana inside it, and a rolled-up note:

See how you go along with this. A better class of smoke than you're used to.

Yours,

Fisher.

Squinting through the window slats, I said, 'I don't suppose any-one's interested in seeing a superb assortment of East Indian Rail-way tank engines?'

The wife looked up at me, and smiled: 'You're right about that, Jim.'

Also by Andrew Martin

The Necropolis Railway

'A brilliant murder mystery set in Edwardian London about a
railway line that runs only to a massive cemetery.' *Mirror*

When railwayman Jim Stringer moves to the garish and tawdry
London of 1903, he finds his duties are confined to a mysterious
graveyard line. Perplexingly, the men he works alongside have
formed an instant loathing for him. And his predecessor has
disappeared under suspicious circumstances. Can Jim work out
what is going on before he too is travelling on a one-way
coffin ticket aboard the Necropolis Railway?

A gripping detective story, fabulously rich in atmosphere and
period detail, *The Necropolis Railway* steams toward an
unexpected conclusion.

'Guaranteed to make the flesh creep and the skin crawl, a masterful novel
about a mad, clanking, fog-bound world.' **Simon Winchester**

'A murderous conspiracy of a plot graced with style, wit and the sharp,
true taste of a time gone by . . . So beautifully nuanced and so effortlessly
pleasurable to read that you almost want to keep it a personal secret.'
Independent on Sunday

'A classy potboiler . . . in the best formal traditions of Dickens and
Collins (let alone Christie and Chandler).' *The Times*

ff

The Blackpool Highflyer

'Genuinely gripping . . . A brilliant evocation of Edwardian working-class life – the sort of thing DH Lawrence might have written had he been less verbose or been blessed with a sense of humour.'
Peter Parker, *Evening Standard*

The second Jim Stringer adventure, The Blackpool Highflyer is a suberbly atmospheric thriller of sabotage, suspicion and steam.

'Unique and important . . . There is no one else who is writing like Andrew Martin today.' Ian Marchant, *Guardian*

'Evokes Edwardian Yorkshire and Lancashire, their great industrial prosperity and singular ways of living, quite brilliantly in a historical whodunnit which for its fresh and stealthy approach to past times deserves the adjective Bainbridgean.'
Ian Jack, *Guardian* (Books of the Year)

'A steamy whodunnit . . . This may well be the best fiction about the railways since Dickens.' Michael Williams, *Independent on Sunday*

ff

The Lost Luggage Porter

**Edwardian detective Jim Stringer goes undercover
into the Yorkshire underworld of drifters, pickpockets
and train-robbers.**

Winter, 1906. After his adventures as an amateur sleuth, Jim Stringer
is now an official railway detective, working from York Station
for the mighty North Eastern Railway Company.
But he's not a happy man.

As the rain falls incessantly on the city's ancient, neglected streets, the
local paper carries a story highly unusual by York standards:
two brothers have been shot to death.

Meanwhile, on the station platforms, Jim Stringer meets the Lost
Luggage Porter, humblest among the employees of the North Eastern
Railway company. He tells Jim a tale which leads him to the roughest
part of town, a place where the police constables always walk in twos.
Jim is off on the trail of pickpockets, 'station loungers' and other
small fry of the York underworld.

But then in a tiny, one-room pub with a badly smoking fire
he enters the orbit of a dangerous, disturbed villain
who is playing for much higher stakes.

ff

Murder at Deviation Junction

'Andrew Martin has recreated an extraordinarily
convincing world . . . Terrific.' *Daily Telegraph*

December, 1909. A train hits a snowdrift in the frozen Cleveland
Hills. In the process of clearing the line a body is discovered, and so
begins a dangerous case for struggling railway detective Jim Stringer,
a case which will take him from the Highlands to Fleet Street to the
mighty blast furnaces of Ironopolis.

Jim's faltering career hangs on whether he can solve the murder,
but before long Jim finds himself fighting not just for his job,
but also for his life . . .

'A wonderful evocation of Edwardian Britain . . . Tough, scary
and funny, this is a novel for anyone who loves a page-turning
detective story.' *Independent on Sunday*

'Stringer is at the heart of a series of historical crime novels that
shows no sign of running out of steam.' *Sunday Times*

ff

Death on a Branch Line

It is the summer of 1911 and as Britain is gripped by paranoia about German spies and secret preparations for war, railway detective Jim Stringer decides to set out for a much-needed holiday.

But before he can leave he finds himself escorting a young aristocrat, Hugh Lambert, who is on his way to be executed for the murder of his father. When Hugh warns that a second murder is imminent in his isolated village, Jim sees a chance to kill two birds with one stone. And so, as he visits the village with his wife Lydia on the pretext of holidaying, Jim finds he has one weekend in which to stop another murder and unravel a conspiracy of international dimensions . . .

'Enough historical details and rural oddbods for a BBC serial, a baffling plot and – most importantly – good writing.'
Scotland on Sunday

'Fascinating . . . Altogether an entertaining read.' *Crimesquad*

'An eccentric and engaging novel.' *Sunday Times*

'The period detail is wonderful . . . The story builds up a good head of steam early on and rattles along nicely to a satisfying conclusion.'
Guardian

ff

The Last Train to Scarborough

It is March 1914, and Jim Stringer is uneasy
about his next assignment.

It's not so much the prospect of a Scarborough lodging house in the
gloomy off-season that bothers him, or even the fact that the last
railwayman to stay in the house has disappeared without trace. It's
more that his governor, Chief Inspector Saul Weatherhill, seems to be
deliberately holding back details of the case – and that he's been sent
to Scarborough with a trigger-happy assistant.

The lodging house is called Paradise, but, as Jim discovers, it's hardly
that in reality. It is, however, home to the seductive and beautiful
Amanda Rickerby, a woman evidently capable of derailing Jim's
marriage – and a good deal more besides.

As a storm brews in Scarborough, it becomes increasingly unlikely
that Jim will ever ride the train back to York.

'Crime dispatched with a Dickensian relish . . . Delectable stuff.'
Daily Express

'[Andrew Martin] is an original voice and the historical novels are the
best I have read this century.' Katherine A. Powers, *Boston Globe*

ff

The Somme Stations

WINNER OF THE CWA ELLIS PETERS AWARD

'A bravura picture of men in war.'
Barry Forshaw, *Independent*

The Battle of the Somme, 1916

Detective Sergeant Jim Stringer, who joined the North Eastern
Railway Battalion at the start of the war, now finds himself
at the front during the Battle of the Somme. Jim and his fellow
soldiers are responsible for operating vitally important trains
carrying munitions, a job that requires close co-operation and
trust. But his unit is still under suspicion for the unsolved
murder of own of their own. It seems that the enemy is
not only across the fields but also within. In the midst of
the carnage Jim must battle to stay alive while striving
to find the killer as the finger of accusation begin
to point towards him . . .

'As much a war book as a crime novel . . . Martin's skill at evoking
period and place takes his novels far beyond the supposed
bounds of genre fiction.' *Sunday Times*

'Superb entertainment.'
Lancashire Evening Post

ff

The Baghdad Railway Club

'Martin's novels are works of litearature, not simply puzzles.'
A. N. Wilson, *Financial Times*

1917: Invalided from the Western Front, Captain Jim Stringer
has been dispatched to Baghdad to covertly investigate what
looks like a case of treason. He arrives to find a sweltering city
on the point of insurrection, his cover apparently blown . . .
and one very dead body.

Officially Jim is working on the railways for the charming
yet enigmatic Lieutenant Colonel Shepherd – but as his
investigation proceeds, he begins to suspect that Shepherd
may be a double agent. Jim's search for the truth brings him
up against murderous violence in a heat-dazed, labyrinthine
city where an enemy waits around every corner.

'The real pleasure lies in the vision of an Englishman out of his
depth in foreign climes. Martin handles this theme with the skill
of such illustrious predecessors as Graham Greene – and there
is no higher praise than than.' Barry Forshaw, *Daily Express*